Praise for *For You and Only You*

"Joe Goldberg lives on. . . . *For You and Only You* delivers everything a fan could want. . . . Yes, it's a book about writing books, and yes it's very meta. . . . Kepnes obviously knows the world well, so the zingers land with authenticity. . . . What makes *For You and Only You* stand out is how pitch-perfect Joe's voice is when he's 'talking' to the Wonder who lives in his head. . . . [Joe's] voice is so confident that at times Kepnes puts it in all caps and it feels right. . . . Joe is an addictively charming antihero and after four books, he still feels fresh and original."

—*The Washington Post*

"Twisted . . . Delightfully creepy."

—*Rolling Stone*

"Hard to put down . . . another witty, irresistible mashup of crime fiction and romance, crafted with care and slicked with satire . . . Kepnes dissects that disturbing trope [of stalkers as romantic] with an icy scalpel. . . . Kepnes's group portrait of the workshop members and their dynamics is comedy gold. . . . The plot twists keep on coming, so fast Joe's wisecracks can hardly keep up, barreling toward a truly surprising finale. The key to *For You and Only You,* and all of this series, is Joe's unmistakable voice, seductive and sharp and, once we realize we've fallen for it, frightening."

—*Tampa Bay Times*

"Kepnes gleefully portrays the most back-stabbing seminar yet, dropping literary names with abandon as she twists the plot. Joe Goldberg might be a narcissistic, manipulative, murderous, utterly unreliable narrator, but he's damn entertaining."

—*Kirkus Review* (starred review)

"Puckish . . . Kepnes waggishly satirizes the publishing industry, and her outsized characters' egos and anxieties lay the foundations for delightfully deranged plot twists. . . . Joe's stream-of-consciousness narration engages throughout, rendering readers both confidante and accomplice. Kepnes reliably entertains."

—*Publishers Weekly*

"Within this intensity, [Joe Goldberg's] snark-laden observations about ego, love, and loyalty ring true."

—*Booklist*

Praise for Caroline Kepnes and the Joe Goldberg novels

"[A] storytelling sorcerer . . . Kepnes is brilliant."
—*The New York Times Book Review*

"My new favorite writer."

—COLLEEN HOOVER

"Fiendish, fast-paced, and very funny."

—PAULA HAWKINS

"Hypnotic and scary . . . totally original."

—STEPHEN KING

FOR YOU AND ONLY YOU

FOR YOU AND ONLY YOU

A JOE GOLDBERG NOVEL

CAROLINE KEPNES

RANDOM HOUSE
NEW YORK

2024 Random House Trade Paperback Edition

Copyright © 2023 by Caroline Kepnes

Published in the United States by Random House, an imprint and division of Penguin Random House LLC, New York.

RANDOM HOUSE and the HOUSE colophon are registered trademarks of Penguin Random House LLC.

Originally published in hardcover in the United States by Random House, an imprint and division of Penguin Random House LLC, in 2023.

LIBRARY OF CONGRESS CATALOGING-IN-PUBLICATION DATA

Names: Kepnes, Caroline, author.

Title: For you and only you / Caroline Kepnes.

Description: First Edition. | New York: Random House, [2023] | Series: You; 4

Identifiers: LCCN 2022050514 (print) | LCCN 2022050515 (ebook) | ISBN 9780593133828 (trade paperback) | ISBN 9780593597231 | ISBN 9780593133835 (Ebook)

Classification: LCC PS3611.E697 F67 2023 (print) | LCC PS3611.E697 (ebook) | DDC 813/.6—dc23

LC record available at https://lccn.loc.gov/2022050514

LC ebook record available at https://lccn.loc.gov/2022050515ISBN 978-0-593-13382-8

Printed in the United States of America on acid-free paper

randomhousebooks.com

1 2 3 4 5 6 7 8 9

Book design by Susan Turner

The eyes of others our prisons; their thoughts our cages. Air above, air below. And the moon and immortality . . . Oh, but I drop to the turf! Are you down too, you in the corner, what's your name—woman—Minnie Marsh; some such name as that?

—Virginia Woolf, "An Unwritten Novel"

FOR YOU AND ONLY YOU

I

You think you're special and you are, to a degree. You go to Harvard. A grad student if I had to guess. You wear a vintage T-shirt that probably belonged to your father, who no doubt went here as well, carried you on his shoulders at his reunions when you were too young to wonder if you were good enough to get here. There was no need to worry. You were always going to wind up perched on the steps of the Barker Center in your flowery *midi* skirt. Little Miss Muffet with your Faulkner in your hands, open and your phone face-down, as if to prove that you prefer novels over nuisance. The world is your tuffet, the steps too, and you arch your back and aah. You're not *really* lost in that book. You're a little outside of yourself, yearning for someone new in September. I'm on the move. You tap your toes and lift your eyes—blue and horny—and you go there.

"Hi."

"Hey."

I know it hurts. You took a leap of faith, and I said *thanks, but no*

4   CAROLINE KEPNES

thanks with a *hey* and walked into the Barker Center. I had to leave you. You women disappoint or disappear—or sometimes both—and none of you can bear to look at me once I know who you really are. You run, you try so hard to kill your feelings for me that you wind up dead in real life, dead inside. I'm not built like you. I never get over you, any of you. Something had to change, so I put all my feelings about my tragic, no-good love stories into a blender and wrote a novel. That's the reason I'm here. Not you. *Me.* I walk up to Barker 222 ready to join the ranks of the good and the terrible—Harvard monsters are a special breed—but a piece of paper is taped to the door: *Too nice to be inside. See you fellows on the south side of the lawn! Yours, G.S.*

I don't want to go outside and sit in a room that isn't a room— I want the Algonquin fucking round table—and I expect better from Glenn "G.S." Shoddy. He's running this fiction writing fellowship because he's the author of *Scabies for Breakfast.* He knows what makes people tick—*Scabies* earned him a Pulitzer—and he's the anti-Franzen—over two million copies sold, almost no one ticked off about his success. He's my teacher, my mentor, the kind of guy who assured me that he too comes from a "humble" background . . . as in he grew up in the Mid-fucking-west with married teacher parents who *raised* him to be a writer. I liked him for trying, and I (mostly) meant what I said when I sent him twenty pages of my soul.

Whether or not you offer me a spot, I want to thank you, Mr. Shoddy. I wouldn't have started writing if I had never read your book. You're exceptionally gifted, Glenn. Yours, Joe

Glenn did the right thing. He offered me a spot in the fellowship via a warm, chummy email, and Harvard *is* paying me to be here, so I follow the orders and hustle back outside like I'm late for a job interview—*No, Joe, you* got *the job*—and I didn't leave Florida to prowl around in the sun like a dirty old man playing Duck, Duck, Fucking Goose, but off I go.

I can do this. All I fucking *do* is survive. I made it through the first few decades of my life and back in Orlando, when the world shut down, the first real snow days of my life, I took the break as a gift from my beloved, my would-have-been wife, Mary Kay DiMarco. She was gone, dead, and I had been wasting my time, slinging drinks and sulking, *hooking up* with girls who came into the bar, licked their lips, asked me about the last great book I read.

Predators, all of them, and that's what I look like now, like I'm on the hunt for girls and no. No! "Sorry," I say to a group of fucking teenagers. "I'm just trying to find my people."

They look right through me—the truth is always a bad share—and I need to Taylor Swift it, I *need to calm down*. I will find my fellows. I made RIP Mary Kay's dream come true—I opened the Empathy Bordello Bar & Books—and I killed myself writing my book, finding a reader since it's not *really* a book unless someone else consumes it. I killed myself *again* kissing up to the gatekeeper—*You're exceptionally gifted, Glenn*—and when I sold the bar and hightailed it up I-95 with the jukebox of RIP Mary Kay's dreams in the back of a U-Haul, well, that's when multiple incompetent motorists almost killed *me*. No one knows how to drive anymore, or how to run a fucking fellowship, but I made it. The skeletons in my closet aren't so menacing anymore—the best writers all take risks—and I live here now, in a one-bedroom two-bath right by campus, and I "go" here, but where the fucking *fuck* are my fellows?

A guy in an MIT T-shirt shouts, "Hey! Are you looking for the Shoddies?"

So that's what we're calling ourselves. *Shoddies.* Glenn's not here yet and the guy tells me to *pop a squat* and jumps right back into conversation with a woman who doesn't bother to turn around and check me out—weird—and the other three Shoddies are buried in a huddle and oh. I see. There was a plan to meet up before class and not one of my "fellows" gave me a heads-up, and the ice is broken, the ice in their drinks is melted. It's not like I expected to fall in love, but the possibility would be nice—I am human, I am single—and all three of my female fellows are Little *Mrs.* Tuffets. Visibly married. That's a *Duck,*

Duck, Never-a-ducking-gain for this guy—and wait. That woman talking to the MIT guy. Is that? No. Yes. That's Sarah Elizabeth Swallows. I know her, but I don't. She's a thriller queen—*How to Kill Your Husband by The Wife*—and I saw her face every day in the Bordello, beaming on the backs of her books and now here she is in real life, eating Wheat Thins out of a little plastic bag. Just . . . no.

But the other clique isn't any better. The girl doing all the talking has a whiny Connecticut kind of voice and she's in a one-up war with some douchebag in a Pringles T-shirt. She *met her hubby at Dartmouth* and Pringles turned Dartmouth *down* to go to Tulane.

"My lady is magic," he says. "Last night, she rescued a sparrow."

The Dartmouth girl claps back. "Aw, Lou. My guy and I saved this parrot last year . . ."

Of course his name is *Lou* and the older woman, the one who they're performing for, she says her daughter is a freshman here and then she takes off her sunglasses and wait . . . Is that? No. I will not play another round of I Know Her, But I Don't in my fucking head. I got a fellowship, same as them, and I drop my messenger bag on the grass.

"Sorry," I say. "Are you Ani Platt?"

The one-uppers eyeball me, and I was right. It *is* Ani Platt. "Oh no," she says. "You must have seen that puff piece in the *Globe* . . ."

"Well, yeah," I say. "But also . . . congrats on the Obie."

The Dartmouth girl giggles. "Ani, I bet you didn't expect to be signing autographs . . ."

I did *not* ask for an autograph and the Dartmouth girl ignores me, resumes telling the "story" of her honeymoon, *so low-key, just a few days at my dad's place in Chilmark.* I *pop a squat* in the dead zone. I got in, but I didn't, and I knock over my own bag—fuck you, bag, fuck you, foot—and it takes a half-empty cup of coffee-water down with it. Great.

I grab the cup—servants gonna servant—and the Dartmouth girl makes obligatory eye contact with my forehead. "It's okay," she says.

"I am, too." I don't know what's so funny—the *Shoddies* are all chuckling—and she looks at me like I'm ringing up her groceries, like she has *diamonds on the soles of her clogs*. "Literally," she says. "That's my name. I'm O.K."

A normal person would ask about me now, but she'd rather listen to Lou wax on about *his* honeymoon. They went off the grid—how original!—and Ani Platt eats people like this up in her plays, and maybe that's why she's encouraging them? For material? I could pry my way into the conversation—*I killed a girl from Nantucket!*—but there's no fucking point. You can make one person love you, but you can't make a group of people like you, not when they already have each other, when they are a "them" in a way that makes you a "you." I take my phone out of my bag and I go to the fellowship website and there it is, The Big Lie:

> *I want to discover undiscovered writers. I don't care where or if you went to college. I don't care if you have an MFA. I don't care about your publications. Just send me your guts.*
>
> *Yours,*
>
> *Glenn Shoddy*

I'm a pigeon. I know how to get by on crumbs and I *know* that all my fellows went to college. They've already been *discovered*, which is no doubt how they knew to show up so fucking early. Lou brought galleys of his novel—*O'er Under*, oh fuck off—and his galleys become a book in December. I check the time on my phone—it's only September—and O.K. takes a picture of Lou's dick, his book, same difference. I can't relate to these people, and the one guy who seems kinda normal, kinda nice? Mr. Pop-a-Squat?

He went to MIT before he got an MFA, and he has a "day job" designing videogames.

I'm in a corner of the circle—geometry is a lie—flicking ants off my pants. Nobody *else* is under attack, and I guess this is why you don't go around killing people, because then it's not so easy to spin yay-me stories about your life to a bunch of strangers.

"Aw," O.K. simpers, quoting Lou's fucking book. "'For my lady and my ma.'"

"I know," he says. "And right now, they're out finding me a sofa."

I bought my couch online, alone, and these people have something in common. Never mind their careers. They were loved. Protected. Lou's *Ma* was on his side, so he knew how to find a *lady*, how to stay with her. My fellows had love then and they have it now and my spine is on fire—I prefer chairs—and finally there's some action. Glenn is here, storming the lawn, all wrapped up in spandex— Michael Cunningham would *never*—and he says hi to Lou first— I thought I'd be the Charlie in this Chocolate Factory—and then he gives us all a big round of applause and a smile and ah. So that's what he did with his Pulitzer money. He got veneers.

"Before we get into it," he says. "I have to tell you about my ride."

This is a *writing* fellowship, but he waterboards us with details about his *ride* and the other Shoddies feed his ego, literally. O.K. brought *brownies* and that's cheating, that's brownie points scored. I wanted us to be misfits together. *Undiscovered.* I passed up my chance with that grad student because I believed something better was waiting for me here. True friends. Connection. There will be no absinthe-soaked nights of debauchery, no marathon conversations about Faulkner. They have families to get home to, real jobs, real lives.

I was early today, but in the end, in life, I'm still too late.

"Sorry I'm late but the T was a shit show."

You came out of nowhere—Duck, duck, *you*—and the nerve of you, walking us through your *shit show* of a day as if we can't see that you had time to stop at Dunkin' for a Coolatta, that you had time to grab a straw. *Tsk, tsk.* You plunk your ass in the grass in a good spot, right across from me, and thank God I didn't fall prey to Little Miss Muffet on the steps. She's not you. She's not my *Shoddy* fellow in too-short shorts that make me adjust *my* shorts. What you and I have is real and intimate by design. *Harvard* is playing matchmaker and I will know you, read you and you will know me, read me. No escape for either fucking one of us—fair—and the room that isn't a room becomes a room because of you, your smirking smile as you pull your sweater up and off and turn all of us men into fat boys in *Caddyshack*. I wish Lou's *lady* could see him now—theirs probably isn't the first honeymoon you accidentally ended with your charisma—and your T-shirt is a tell: THEY HATE US 'CAUSE THEY AIN'T US.

"Well," Glenn says. "Try not to let it happen again, Wonder."

Wonder and Ani pumps a fist—"Go Sox!"—and you say you liked it better when they were the underdogs and O.K. lets her hair down. "My aunt has a box at Fenway, but the noise is a lot."

"Wow," you say. "That's freaking cool. My cousin is always claiming he can get us into a box, but the dude is full of it."

Lou leans in. "Are you local?"

It's a fake question—you have an accent—and you adjust your *Swatch*. "Yeah," you say. "Born and raised. And I really *am* sorry I'm late. The T . . . my dad's wound vac, ugh I swear, I love the man, but once a teen dad, *always* a teen dad . . . Plus, my sister, Cherish, she's pissed at me. Tuesdays are *my* day to pick up my niece at school, but obviously . . . not today."

I want to hear more but Glenn takes the reins. "This is good," he says, as if you weren't just getting started. "Let's run with it. Lou, you're up. Tell us your story."

Because of you, Lou wants to seem "real." He claims that he used to work at Arby's—I bet it was one summer, if that—and he scratches the back of his neck. "I did eventually make it to grad school, where I met my main mensch, Mr. George Saunders."

O.K. has to one-up *him* now. "Ooh, I love that man. I worked on his last book."

You widen your eyes. "Sorry," you say, as if you owe us an apology. "George who? I didn't go to college, so I missed some stuff along the way."

That was a terrible thing to say and now they're all vying to sum up George Fucking Saunders—Help me, I'm *Bored*—and Glenn cuts 'em off with a clap of his hands—good—but then he looks at me. "Actually," he says. "Joe didn't go to college either."

My lack of a degree is the opposite of an Obie and Lou might come in his pants. "No shit."

"Wow," O.K. says. "I love that we have *two* autodidacts in our midst. My second cousin is an autodidact, and she is *amazing*. So creative, you know? She's an artist. Pottery."

Nothing from Sarah Elizabeth—she will stick you and me in one of her books and take away half our teeth—and the *sharing* continues. It's a bullshit word, this is class, this is war. I see you, Wonder. You gulp when they move on to *their* life stories, when they announce their MFAs and their time abroad, their *previous publications,* their *sabbaticals.* You're not one of them but neither am I, and I'm here, right across from you—look at me, please, just once—but you're the *owner of a lonely heart* and then it hits me.

You're a writer. A *true* writer. Mercurial and solitary. You're not a flirt like RIP Guinevere Beck—she would have been eye-fucking me by now—but at the same time, you're too closed off for your own good. You're letting them get to you, same way I did when I first arrived, but it doesn't have to be this way. Yes, we're the outliers, but Glenn was casting a season of *Survivor* and he did right by us—we have each other—and we need to form an alliance, same way we have to clap our hands every time someone finishes "humble" bragging. I try to make eye contact with you, but you avoid me, too busy shooting yourself in the foot. *This grass is so freaking green, I think my sister's ex does landscaping here.* I lift us out of the muck—*I audited a few classes at Columbia*—but I fuck up the details and that's because of you. Duck, duck, *you,* sitting there like a bowl of eye candy. My brain is rotting from all the sugar—I called your skin *porcelain* in my head just now—and Glenn brings it back to me, by way of you.

"See," he says. "This is why I was so adamant about socioeconomic diversity . . ."

I tune out his rambling about some article he half-read in *The Atlantic*—we are people, not props—and where is a thunderstorm when you need one?

"Well," he says. "How about we tell each other the last great thing we read? I'll go first. The screenplay for *Scabies for Breakfast* is blowing my mind . . ." Oh, Glenn, *no*. "Those Coen brothers, they really know what they're doing. Ani, what about you?"

You get a notepad out of your backpack, and you are earnest, noting all the books. You tell Lou that you already read *his* book—you won a galley in a Goodreads giveaway—and ah. You're *a Goodreads girl*. You "love to read"—good—and you're "all about freebies"—bad—and it's my turn, and you look at me, but it doesn't really count because everyone else does, too.

"Well," I say. "The last book I read was *Conching* by Ethel Rose-Baker and—"

"That's all right," Glenn says. "We can google it if we so desire."

I wanted to tell *you* about it, Goddammit, and he calls for a break—*clap, clap, clap*—and I want to pull you aside and give you a ticket for dragging us both down but you're on your phone, on the move. I can't talk to you, and I have nothing to say about kayaks, cleaning ladies, or fried clams, so I can't talk to my fellows, and don't you get it, Wonder?

They *do* hate us 'cause they ain't us. And that's why we have to stick together.

Glenn waves—it's time—and "class" resumes—it's just fucking small talk—and all of it goes over my head because of you. You're a doozy. You're above us, you're below us, a wonder wheel spinning, but when you do open up, you are mesmerizing, raving about Pat Conroy and Dorothy Allison—What *did* your parents do to you?—but then you dump ketchup on the steak—*Don't listen to me. I'll shut up.* Everyone knows the rules. If you repeatedly tell people to shit on you, they will eventually heed the call. I'm sure you're talented, but talent isn't everything. Like it or not, if we want to get published, we need Glenn to like us.

We need our fellow *Shoddies* to blurb us, to *tweet* with us.

And you're doing it all wrong. You talk about the *25K* stipend like that's the reason we're here, like that's real money. When Sarah Elizabeth piggybacks on Ani's story about her play to talk about her Hulu series, you stir your Coolatta—we need to do something about your resting sarcasm face—and yes, O.K.'s analysis of her experience as a *freelance sensitivity reader* for *the big houses* is long-winded but come on! You can't check the time on your *Swatch*. Not now.

I can't fucking take it anymore, so I fix my eyes on you and clear my throat. I give you and your Swatch a playful little smile and you light up. You touch your hair and scratch your leg and then you clear *your* throat. "Hey, Lou." Your voice is suddenly full of sex. "Can you say that again? I spaced out."

Lou is happy to repeat himself—shocker—and you're focused on him, but the way you run your hand over your forearm and touch your other hand again, that's what really matters, and all that is for me.

Finally, class ends—*clap, clap, clap*—and we had a moment, but you glance around the room that isn't a room, not anymore, and now you're hightailing it across the lawn like a fifth grader.

I chase you down because I have to chase you down. I sense something new with you. Something fresh. You're my equal, Wonder. You're not my married boss and you're not impossibly, unreachably wealthy. You're not a sociopath flirt or a social fucking climber. You're gonna read the books that everyone read and that's good, that's part of it, but I want you to *write*. I see the future. You and me with RIP Spalding Gray reincarnated, laughing about how we met in a fellowship, the only two autodidacts in the room. I'm not saying we have to get married, but when everyone was *my-husbanding* and *my-wifing* you were quiet. You didn't have an inborn support system—your parents were teenagers when they made you—and you need me. Who else is gonna push you to show up on time?

You duck into a corner store, and I hang back. No. Not just yet.

This is the opportunity of a lifetime, and you have an attitude problem. You put on your armor—*They hate us 'cause they ain't us*—and you are *Stubborn* Will Hunting. You grew up in the gutter and you are long past looking at the stars, content to make small talk with the guy working the register. *Take something for that cough, Eddie!*

You emerge from the store with *scratchers* and what are you doing, Wonder? We got into *Harvard*. We got our Golden Tickets, and they're not fucking *scratchers*. I want you to want it all, and if there's one thing I learned from my Floridian pandemic, it's that sometimes people need a push. RIP Ethel Rose-Baker gave *me* a push, and I can do it for you. Glenn compared me to J. D. Fucking *Salinger* and in twenty years, you'll be famous in your own right, rhapsodizing in *The Atlantic* about sex with a legend, sex with *me,* and the best part of all . . . Your essays about our wild lusty days at Harvard won't be tinged with regret because unlike *some* men, I'm not a fucking pig when it comes to women.

I'm one step ahead of you, twenty feet behind you—and *this* is what I wanted from Harvard because what is class without a crush? It's *Good Will Hunting* without the girl, and that's what you are: the girl. I'm about to touch your shoulder and this is it. 3 . . . 2 . . .

No. I can't go in cold. It's like the fellowship. I read about Glenn before I wrote my personal essay. I learned about his background. I studied his voice. I wasn't trying to manipulate him. I was just showing my respect. Why should starting up with you be any different?

I find that email that he sent, the one with our contact information, the one I didn't open because I wanted to go in blind, because I expected exciting war stories from our fellows, and there it is.

Your home address.

2

As of three days ago, Ethel Rose-Baker's one and only book had 242 reviews on Goodreads. But two days ago, she got another, a review she would have read out loud to me at the bar, a review that makes me wish I could go back to Orlando and pull her out of the swamp. A review by *you*, Wonder Parish. You read her book because I told you about it and you gave Ethel five golden stars. You were kind. Generous.

I wanna hug Ethel, right? I see a lot of you saying that she seems a little full of herself, as if she's the narrator. The narrator was "unlikable" because of how she poisoned Brian's wife, but you guys, the wife was terrible! She was lying to her husband about everything and I just . . . there are things worse than murder. When someone hurts someone you love . . . Let's just say that my sister's estranged husband is not unlike Brian and we say it to him a lot, how if he got run over by a bus, well, sometimes we all joke that we're gonna become bus drivers. Reading is so personal. It's insane that we even try to be

objective. See, this is again why I always give five stars. Let's get some nu-
ance up in here because no two people read the same book because no two
people are the same person. If you knew my brother-in-law . . . well, any-
way. Five stars!

Yes, you're a Goodreads girl and I put my phone away. It's day
three of my *author tour* and I love walking in your neighborhood. This
is the world you know, the only world, the one that is always *ready to fall
on your little shoulders.* Here is the playground where you learned to flirt,
empty at this early hour, and here is the church where your niece,
Caridad, was christened, and here is the bar where your best friend,
Tara, slings boilermakers.

Goodreads is your world away from this one. You talk to strangers about books because you still live at home, in a *two-family* house
on Sesame Street—seriously, there are silver trash cans on the
sidewalk—and you grew up here. You've outgrown it. Your sister's
not a reader—her Facebook is Vanderpump this and *Below Deck*
that—and your dad's not a reader. He's a housebound widower
plagued with health issues and you leave every morning at 5:30 A.M.
to go to the corner store and buy him *scratchers.* He never *hits 25K,*
and he blames you for "picking losers," and you always promise to
"do better tomorrow," and don't you get it, Wonder? Harvard picked
a winner. *You.*

I pull the tarp—the house across the street is under renovation—
and I sit on my crate.

I haven't read all your reviews on Goodreads—there are too fucking many—but you use that phrase a lot, *my tendency is to love.* It's the
understatement of the year, Wonder, and you deserve a life worthy of
your love. But you can't do that, meaning you *won't* do that. You take
care of your old man in one house while your sister's on the phone
screaming at her husband's lawyer in the other house, which is a part
of your house, only not, and here we go again.

Caridad is playing in the street and you're back from your *scratcher* run. You shout at the house—"Cherish!"—and your sister opens the door. Tube top. Hair extensions. "What?"

"Caridad needs a coat."

"Bullshit she does."

Your neighbor across the street opens *her* door and stands by her secure heavy-duty plastic trash cans, one of which is for fucking *composting* and yes, gentrification is a slow process, no different from a psychological breakthrough. She purses her lips and navigates her high-end stroller, wondering why you people don't cash out on your teardown and move away.

Cherish rolls her eyes in that way that girls in movies about Boston do and the neighbor grips the handlebars of her stroller. "Wonder," she says, loud enough for Cherish to hear, too. "It might be a good idea to put some rocks on the lids of your trash cans."

Cherish folds her arms and you want to stand by your sister, but you know the neighbor has made a good point and gentrification is also like falling in love, bumpy. You thank the neighbor for the tip and Cherish mutters, "I'll tell that bitch what she can do with her rocks."

You are not your mouthy sister, and you are not *that bitch*. You rub Caridad's bare cold shoulders with the same tenderness you bring to every book you caress on Goodreads. "Seriously, C. This kid needs a jacket."

Caridad bobs her head—you are always right—and Cherish grabs a windbreaker for the kid, and it's the same every day. She's bringing Caridad to school and then she's off to the salon—she does nails, she has a *skill*—and you're on Dad patrol, except when you're at work—you manage a Dunkin', you really do—and you are slow on your way up the seven stairs of your stoop, like me, climbing the stairs of the Barker Center. Your grandparents moved into this house in the forties—I did my homework, your reviews are peppered with details of your life—and your father grew up in this house. Then you, and now Caridad, and when does it end? I know how you *think* it ends. You take care of your *pops* until he passes away and then you stay because your sister doesn't want some fucking stranger living next door. You can't abandon Caridad—her mother named her after a criminal in a *Law & Order* episode—and you can't leave the block—your people have to stand their ground—and this is why you won't embrace your new identity as a Shoddy.

There is a way out, but it's like Cherish is constantly screaming on Facebook.

Family is everything. Loyalty is love.

You're not on Facebook, you're not on any social sites except for Goodreads. You don't *want* to find a life off the block. You babysit Caridad when your sister goes to the casino and you have a "best friend"—that's Tara, Tara's getting married—and you go to her bar and laugh with her about the *customahs* and I bet the two of you used to run around.

Sometimes, the way you greet certain guys, I can tell you've been with them.

But they know they're not good enough, they're the Blake Livelys to your Ben Affleck, and when they go back to virtual duck hunting, Tara looks at you like *maybe?* and you shake your head like *definitely not.* It's clockwork in the worst possible way and I go home, I fall asleep reading your reviews online, and in the morning, I walk back to my spot, and you return from the corner store and find Caridad is in the street, with jelly-stained hands.

"Cherish!"

She emerges from her half of the house, and it will never sit right with me, two front doors so close together. "What?"

"Caridad needs a Wet-Nap or something."

"Covid's freaking over, Wonder. Calm yourself."

"I don't mean germs," you say, lowering your voice, trying to get your sister to lower *her* voice, as if that's ever worked, as if it ever will. "They're all sticky with jelly."

Your sister grabs Caridad's wrist and licks the jelly and little Caridad laughs and that's *the mother and child reunion.* That's not your child, this isn't your life. Cherish wipes something off your cheek with her saliva-stained finger and tells you to put on some makeup. She takes Caridad away from you and your dad rings his bell—he has an actual fucking bell—and you run inside for another day of being a daughter instead of being a woman.

Nine minutes later, your father steps onto the porch with his oxygen and his wound vac and his Parliaments and oh, the way your neighbors must talk about the real estate agent who failed to tell them about you. You join him outside. You move his chair for him, and it's amazing, how easily even the weakest of men turn women into handmaids. You sit on the stoop because there is no other chair and your father looks up the street, down the street. "You got a quarter?"

You hand the old man a quarter. "Good luck."

"With my luck, I'll get some newfangled mess where the state says I owe *them*."

Your dad is scratching and you're on your phone, back to Goodreads. Someone started a fight with you—*This review is not helpful*—and you're defending yourself—*It's not a "review," it's my inherently subjective response to the book*—and it kills me to see you waste your fucking time like this, serving egg wraps made with zero love, extra efficiency, going home every night to wilt away with your family, ignoring all the chatter in your *new* family, the Shoddy group text.

RIP Ethel was the same way, Wonder.

Ethel would show up at my bar every morning at 11:45 and sit there on her phone, raging at the machines, damn Goodreads, damn headlines on *Publishers Weekly*, damn *Crawdads*. Why that book? Why not hers? I told her to stay off Goodreads—it's for readers, and writers should be writing—but she didn't listen. She had a reason to be crushed. Demented. She was out of print, literally, in permanent PTSD from failing to sell a second book, self-medicating with alcohol and Bejeweled Fucking Blitz.

I got a rare gem, Joe!

I got a green gem, Joe!

That was me—*Gem Joe*—and Ethel lost at the game of life, which is why she celebrated every win in a game that didn't matter. It's easy to stop writing, to whittle away the hours weaponizing rare fucking gems instead of self-isolating, killing your darlings in the privacy of your room. You're not Ethel—she's out of print, she's dead—but you're not even *in* print yet. All time is borrowed, and we need to use it wisely. You need to get off Goodreads—it's your Bejeweled Fucking Blitz—and I need to get off this crate—the construction workers are starting to show up.

Your dad lost again—*Those crooks!*—and you help him back inside. That's it for us today, and again I leave you to your devices, to your *Sesame Street* and your star giving, and I really do wish I could tell you about Ethel.

I wouldn't be here if not for her. It started a couple years ago, just after Christmas. She was reading *Scabies for Breakfast* and for the first time since I'd known her, she was alive. Hopeful. She even looked different, like she got a face-lift.

Now this is a book, Joe. This book deserves all the love.

I will never feel sorry for myself ever again. This man deserves it all.

Mark my words. No one on this planet will ever top Glenn Shoddy. He's a genius.

And then Covid hit, and the CD Fucking C said what I've known for years: People are toxic, they can kill you, so keep your distance. I wanted to show Ethel that I was just as smart as Glenn Shoddy. I started writing. I was in flow. I needed my time, my space, but Ethel wouldn't play by the rules. Every day there she was, knocking on my door.

Can I please come in? Ralph is driving me nuts.

I let her in, but Out of Print Ethel was turning back to the dark side. She didn't gush about *Scabies* anymore. She was bitter again. She had a new enemy: the CD Fucking C.

Masks are bad for you, you know. That's a fact.

You can't legally make me cover my face. This is America. I have rights!

I finished a draft of my book and Ethel's husband, Ralph, got Covid—gee, I wonder how *that* happened—and she didn't even have the decency to tell me. (I found out on her *Facebook*.) He went fast and I thought Ethel would fall into a pit of guilt. She killed him, she exposed *me* to the virus, but she went the other way.

They can't prove he died from Covid. It's all a big lie.

The CDC killed Ralph. He wasn't the same after he had to work from home.

Someone had to do something, so I "invited" her down to the basement—You're welcome, citizens of Orlando—and she whined about her *rights* as if I wasn't doing a public fucking service. Everyone on this planet needs purpose, so I gave Ethel my pages.

Since when are you writing a book?

You expect me to sit down here and read?

I was honest with Ethel. I promised I would dedicate my book to her. But she was cruel.

You're no Glenn Shoddy and this is kidnapping.

You have no idea how to write. I went to Vassar. I got an MFA.

But any cage is an ideal space for getting lost in a good book. Ethel was reading and Ethel was impressed. I caught her laughing, crying, shaking. And she denied all of it.

You're a hack, Joe. Glenn Shoddy is a writer. You're a copycat.

You can't call it impostor syndrome when you are the impostor.

Ethel died of Covid-related issues—she never would have been in my basement were it not for that pandemic—but her death was not in vain. She gave me some great notes before she passed away, and I took her notes. I honored her wishes. She said she would never step foot in a hospital for the rest of her life, so I lugged her body upstairs, into my car. I drove her out to the swamp and gave her to the gators.

She's gone, she's with the angels, but she can still help from afar.

The next morning, I go to Sesame Street and open Goodreads and sign on to her account.

Dear Wonder,

Thank you so much for taking the time to read my book. I can tell by the way you write that you're a writer, too. I admit I googled you, and I read a short story you published at Necessary Fiction. Wonder, I was blown away. No need to get back to me, I hope you're busy writing.

Best,

Ethel

Send.

My leg is shaking—come on, come on—and here you come, back from your scratcher run, same as yesterday and the day before that. Caridad needs a Kleenex and Cherish calls you a drama queen—come on, come on—and finally they go and here comes your dad. He's got his scratchers and you've got your phone and you're doing it, Wonder. You're reading the note from Ethel.

Your body opens like a flower *petal by petal* and it's just the push you needed. You're not slouching, you're glowing. Your father tears up his scratcher. "Damn Monopoly. Don't you have to get to the store?"

Your *tendency is to love* but today, your tendency is to accept love. "I think I'm gonna call in sick."

Your dad shakes his head. "And do what? Sit on that damn computer making up stories?"

You are gentle with him because of me, because of RIP Ethel's vote of confidence. Finally, you participate in the group text with our fellows—*My favorite death is the suicide in* Flesh and Blood—and you go upstairs to your room. You close a window—that's a first—and you sit at your desk in the window and you're doing it, Wonder. You're writing. You won't be able to be with me until you're able to take care of you, to be the whole you, the full you, the writer you, and I lift my body off my crate, but something stops me.

A BMW with tinted windows pulls onto your street—too fast, too much bass—and it brakes in front of your houses. I've never seen that car—dealer plates—and I've never seen him. The driver. Silk pants. Loafers without socks. He carries a small bag from Macy's and he walks up the steps to your house—maybe he's a Postmate—but he doesn't ring a bell. He has a *key* and he's inside and you disappear from your desk, from your window. You're not writing, and the minutes are passing—this is your sick day, your *writing* day—and here he is again, minus the bag from *Macy's*. I give you an hour. I give you another hour.

But you don't go back to your desk.

3

I'm not going to lie, Wonder. I have flaws. Sometimes I talk about my "Tesla" when I could just as easily call it a car. I fall too hard too fast. I don't always see the "best" in people, especially when they show me their worst—Mr. Macy's *was* driving too fast—but I'm not at my best right now either. And it's not easy being in a new city, trying to keep up with the group fucking text and liking our fellows' fake-self-deprecating, self-aggrandizing *tweets* while everything good in my life is out of my reach, and I'm sure as hell not gonna let some asshole in silk pants get the best of me.

I slept on it, and this morning it all looks different to me.

I had nothing to worry about because think about it, Wonder. He has a key. I should be happy about that. He's not your boyfriend—Cherish worries about you being "an old maid" on her fucking Facebook at least twice a week—and what do I care if he's a third cousin, twice estranged, or a home health aide with a generous streak?

It's like Ethel said in the cage: *Make the book your own. Embrace your power.*

I don't want to sit around staring at you from afar. I want to see you, and it's a free country, and your Dunkin' *is* within walking distance of my place, so fuck it, Wonder.

It's 7:32 A.M. and I'm in your line. It might be a mistake. You noticed me when I walked in, and you didn't exactly look happy to see me. You're in uniform, and it is *kind of* weird that you would choose to work in a Dunkin' when you could make better tips as a waitress, but then, you're a manager. I imagine that you like to be in charge of this crew and it's clear to me that your co-workers respect you and finally it's my turn and I smile but you don't.

"This is crazy. I didn't know you work here!"

"Hi," you say. "What can I get for you?"

I was too over-the-top—I really *don't* know how to lie to you—and I order the easiest thing on the menu—an *Extra-large, regular*—and you grab a cup and pour. "Anything else?"

"Do you have a break coming up?"

You groan a little, and who can blame you, this guy from your class showing up at your work and asking you about your *break*. You couldn't know that I have been where you are, against the world, the line, living a life behind the counter with no control over who comes in. I have to set myself apart, let you know that we're the same, but no stories of laugh-out-loud asshole customers from my days at Mooney's Rare & New are gonna cut it, because facts are facts. I don't work there anymore and as someone who *did* deal with the awful public all day, I know from firsthand experience that there is nothing more annoying than someone trying to relate by whining about a job they *used* to have.

"No, I actually don't. Anything else?"

I ask you for a cruller and you grab a bag and snap it open, and I ask you how you are—so original—and you dump my cruller in the bag. It's a short one, the runt of the litter, and you huff. "Busy," you say. "Anything else?"

The woman behind me clears her throat. "Miss, could you possibly get started on mine? Almond milk iced latte with sugar. Medium."

You apologize to her as if you did anything wrong—you didn't—and I want you to know who I am, how I am. I catch your eye—*watch this*—and I turn around and look the Peloton bitch right in the eye. "Sorry about the holdup," I say. "Your order's on me."

The Peloton bitch grins—*Well, that's the spirit*—and she won't harass you anymore. It's like I made your colicky baby stop crying and you smile. My presence is a surprise, not a disruption. "So," you say. "The coolest thing happened to me."

Ethel Rose-Baker sent you fan mail. "Oh?"

"O.K. came in this morning, right?" Wrong. "And she brought her mom and her mom is . . . I'm still in shock . . . Her mom is Diane Janz."

You're in shock but as far as I'm concerned, Diane Janz's real name is Not Joan Didion. She's an NPR yammerer. Name-dropper of obscure flowers. "Uh-huh."

"Joe, that legend is her freaking her *mom*. Can you imagine?"

I gave you access to the machine on Goodreads and you're supposed to be telling me about Out of Print Ethel and I shrug. "I didn't know O.K. had a mom." Dumb. Everyone has a mother.

You raise your eyebrows and you want me to be interested, and this is the worst part of being a fucking man, when I have to pretend to care about people like Diane Fucking Janz. "So, how was Diane Janz in real life? Was she cool?" *Cool.*

"'Cool.'" You laugh. "She doesn't have to be cool. She's a rock star. I'm still in shock." You hand off the latte to the lady behind me. And then you look at me. "Anything else, *sir*?"

You. To go. "An egg wrap. And a Coolatta."

You laugh and lighten up and my timing is good—Boston wakes

up early, the line isn't what it was two minutes ago—and you ask me if I even *freaking* like Coolattas and I shrug. "You do."

"Well, that's me," you say. "I have a sweet tooth." And then you nibble on your lip. Sweetness. "So I read that book you told me about. *Conching.*"

We're back on track and I have two beverages, one hot, one cold. I sip the hot one. "And?"

"How did you find it? It seems so random."

"Well, I lived in Orlando, and Ethel was a local writer."

You frown at me, and my veins go on strike. That quizzical turn of your head. "'Was'? Is she dead or something?"

No, she's not *dead*, not to you or the world, and I sip from my Coolatta but it's too cold and you smile. "I told you it would be too sweet. Give it."

I *give it* and you wrap your lips around the straw that was just in my mouth, and see that, Wonder? I bought you a drink. Your co-workers step in to give you time with *me* and you expound on your mixed feelings about the book. I like the way you talk—your voice with me is your voice on the page in the story you don't know I read—and then you sigh. "She sent me a message, you know."

Yes, I know. "No way?"

I was too *too* and you laugh. "I know. It was probably just her assistant, but it was a kind thing to do. Do you know her?"

She edited my book and died in my hands and I shrug. "A little. She only came in from time to time."

"Came in where?"

It's happening. We're not on our first date but we *are* on our first date. I'm telling you about the Empathy Bordello, the bookstore slash bar that I had down in Orlando, and you're starting to see me clearly now. I tell you what you need to know, that it was a one-man operation, that I emptied the trash and cleaned the toilets, that I'm not *Mr. Fancy Pants*, and you ask me if Ethel was a regular and I want to tell you everything but I shrug. "Semiregular . . ." It's *Florida* and there is no trace of her—gators are thorough—and the strip mall that was home to my bar was bulldozed. So, I go there. A little bit. "She was a . . . character."

"I'm not saying I'm perfect . . ." Yes, you are. And you are, maybe. "But working here, I know the big dirty secret about people." You motion for me to come closer. And then you whisper. "Everyone is an asshole. *Everyone.*"

I tell you that's too easy but you hold the line. "It's why *my* tendency is to love everyone, even the assholes, because who am I?"

It's your Goodreads in real life and now I lean in. "So do you think *I'm* an asshole?"

You blush. I turned your cheeks red before noon. "Well, that remains to be seen, doesn't it?"

You want to jump over the counter and mount me right here in front of all the upstanding *asshole* citizens. It's a moment. The noise around us turns white and irrelevant. I won't be greedy, I won't *push*. I drop a twenty in the tip jar. "Does an asshole do this?"

You size up the bill. Folded. Crisp. "Sometimes," you sass. "But I'll give you the benefit of the doubt . . . I mean a twenty's not a Benjamin, it's not like you're trying to buy your way into my pants or anything . . . But then again, the stipend *is* only 25K, so twenty's a lot for people like us, in which case . . . Hmmm."

You went there, you made things sexual, and that makes *you* the best kind of asshole, horny on the job. Assuming that all men want the same thing, happy to score off that assumption. Smitten. I raise my *extra-large regular.* "See you next Tuesday."

And you grin. Not a drop of cunt blood in your blue-collared, hard, taut body. "You bet."

We're doing it the right way, Wonder. Bantering on our phones, but not so much that we're both cringing like *What did this loser do before I came into the picture?* This is the part of our life where everything we do, everything we say is loaded with intention, two fucking peacocks that haven't fucked, that might fuck, that want to be seen as worth fucking.

You are spunky. Bristling about our fellow Lou. You went to his website, where he claims that George Saunders described him as "the love child of Faulkner and Franzen," and you want us to drive to New York and hunt down Mr. Saunders and find out the truth.

A.k.a. you want to go on a road trip with me.

According to you, I know "a lot more about Boston" than most new people. I tell you I learn a lot from *Chronicle* and you think I have a crush on one of the hosts, Shayna—I do, kind of—and you wax poetic about the '04 Red Sox and I tell you I think you have a crush on Kevin Youkilis—and you do, kind of.

A.k.a. our crushes are semifamous and married, therefore nonthreatening to our future.

You're a Bruce Springsteen girl—you love "New York City Serenade"—and you've never been to Manhattan or Jersey or anywhere, really.

A.k.a. that's the song you play when you think about *me*.

I'm on a J. D. Souther kick—"When You're Only Lonely" is my favorite—and you never heard of him until now.

A.k.a. that's the song I play when I think about you.

We are language buffs. You would say that the world's most misunderstood, overused word is *iconic*, and I think the world's most misunderstood, overused word is *love*.

A.k.a. our love is going to be iconic.

You don't play favorites when it comes to books, but if you had to, you would choose the popular southern man's saga that is Pat Conroy's *The Prince of Tides* for the language and the family at the center of the story, all the secrets that weigh them down. I don't lie to you. My favorite book is mine, *Me*.

A.k.a. I inspire honesty in you because nobody loves all books equally, and you make me feel safe enough to tell you the truth.

Our fellowship meets once a week, every Tuesday, and every Tuesday we are tasked with dissecting someone's pages. Next week it's O.K.'s and you are *not* impressed. You're right, her pages *are* "mommy fan fiction." It made you sad, that she's clearly in the program because of where she comes from, not because of her writing, and I lifted you up, I told you to have faith, and you were brusque: *I'm a Red Sox fan, Joe. Faith is my middle freaking name.*

A.k.a. you wanted me to know your middle name because I am the only person in the world you can really talk to about your new life at Harvard.

And then yesterday morning I woke up to a little present. My first drunk text from you!

> *So I'm with my best friend Tara cuz she's getting married and this is like one of the last nights we get to go crrrrazy and she's freaking hysterical she says you're hot and real hahaha right? Anyway hiiii! I'm gonna say some shit. Ready? Ready. They hate us 'cause they ain't us. US. You and me. So even if Lou ever drives us nuts, I can't bail on you and you can't bail on me everrrrr. And I know I should delete this because obviously you can do what you want but at the same time . . . Like fuck you can. This is war. We're in a foxhole and there is no freaking WAY we can ever ditch and now I'm gonna hit send before I realize I have no freaking business saying any of this haha SEND MOTHERFUCKER SEND.*

And what great timing, Wonder! It's Tuesday, the one day of the week that our fellowship convenes, and I get to walk into the room knowing that I am the guy you write to when you had *one too many* with Tara.

I'm here, in Barker 222, and it's a relief to be inside instead of on that stupid lawn, even if the room is hardly the Algonquin stuff of dreams.

You catch my eye—*Sorry for the drunk text*—and I hold your eyes with mine—*I loved it*—and you take a deep breath, relieved that you didn't blow it with me. Class starts but it doesn't—Glenn is telling us about the new tires on his bike—and you blush when our eyes meet again—I am real, this is real—and finally Glenn gets down to business.

"So, let's do this," he says, as if he wasn't the one holding us back. "I was in my sitting room last night . . ." Just call it a living room. "Ruminating on O.K.'s story, a family visits their summer home in the off season for the first time, and this is them without the sun, without the tennis . . ." You *hate* this kind of a review, one that's more of a summary, and Glenn plays with the zipper on his stupid fucking shirt. "And there's potential here . . ." Such bullshit because any setup, by definition, has "potential" and he opens the floor. "Tell me, what do we love about this?"

I know what you're thinking—nothing—but our fellows are supportive. Ani could "literally smell the orchids" and Sarah Beth is "intrigued" by the family dynamics—"It feels like the mother wants to kill her husband"—and Lou says his mother would eat this book *up*.

O.K. grunts. "It's not women's fiction."

You light up like we're watching a boxing match, because we are, and Glenn wants to avoid bloodshed, so he cuts off Lou's weak defense of his oopsy-daisy misogyny by asking what *you* think.

You gulp. "Well, first off, I can't imagine having a whole freaking extra house!"

That's not you. You're smarter than that, and most books are about rich people with too many houses and you're doing it again, occupying your territory as an autodidact. In our texts, you were eloquent about poor O.K.'s *botany overload* and bemoaning the reality of her life, reduced to cherry-picking flowers from her mother's oeuvre.

Glenn scratches his arm and this is Harvard. He should be wearing a long-sleeved shirt. "Wonder, what did you make of all the flowers?"

Good job, Glenn! Say it, Wonder. Say it! "The flowers . . . I mean I was on my couch . . ." Please say *sofa*. "I'm reading and going to the dictionary app on my phone because like . . . I have a lot to learn about flowers!"

That's a lie. You didn't need to look up any words in the fucking *dictionary* and you're not the girl from our texts. You fawn over O.K.'s useless fucking mums and you told me Tara says I'm "real" but what about you? You pull your hands into the pilled sleeves of your simple black sweater. "Fun fact. I've never even been to Connecticut."

That's not true! You saw some fucking band at some fucking club in New Haven.

"Wow," O.K. says. "It's so easy to forget that travel, even local travel, isn't sort of the norm for everyone. Mom would say this is why it's so important that we write."

Now our fellows rub their chins like what O.K. said was profound—NOPE—and you pucker up to her Connecticunt ass again—"I feel like you did so much research"—and O.K. is in full-on NPR mode, as if her book is good, as if it's done. "Regarding all things botanical, I have to give credit to Mom."

It's not "Mom." It's *my* mom and you clap your hands like a trained fucking seal. "You guys, I met O.K.'s mom at my store and she was the coolest, so real, so down-to-earth. Black coffee, two sugars, for the record."

NO SHE WAS NOT THE COOLEST and O.K. claims that "Mom" *adores* her stupid summerhouse story and even if that's true—doubtful—moms don't count! Not when it comes to *literary criticism*. Glenn claps his hands—"Let's take five"—and you turn to O.K., as if I didn't come here for you, and you pull one of her mother's meh books out of your bag. "How weird is it if I ask you to ask your mom to sign?"

I can't look at you right now, so I go to the bathroom and before the door closes it swings open. *Glenn.* "Greetings, my fellow."

I have nothing to say to that, so I salute him like I'm a soldier—wrong, I was meant to be in the foxhole with *you*—and this is why teachers shouldn't wear spandex. The snapping snarl of him trying to jam his limp dick out of his shorts is enough to make me quit right now.

"So?" he says. "What do you think so far?"

I think O.K. wouldn't be here if her mom wasn't Diane Janz. "Well, it's the longest conversation I've ever had about flowers and summerhouses."

"Ha," he says, which is to be expected. Anyone at the top of their game isn't going to laugh when they can *ha* to convey that your intention to make them laugh was a failure. "But be careful with that attitude, my friend."

"Attitude."

"Look, I know it stinks in there today. All our emails, our talks . . . You know I'm not *actually* into what O.K's doing . . ."

"Well, it's not *Scabies*. I mean in *Scabies*, you're doing an autopsy on the modern brain, there's *purpose*."

He takes the compliment with a grunt, and you gotta like the guy, in spite of his spandex, the way he doesn't raise his bowl for more pudding. "Thing is, Joe, there's more to being a writer than writing. A little story . . ." He doesn't have to take a leak. He came in here to save me. "Never mind the story . . . I don't do the gossip thing, but the moral of the story is simple. You don't win when you knock down a woman. It's not 'political,' it's not about 'trends,' it's deeper than that. And it's something I wish somebody told me on *my* second day at Iowa."

It's like getting a key to the corporate washroom and Glenn chose me, and of course he did. He's a good writer, I thank him for the advice, and his stream hits the porcelain. Potent. Both of us are silent as if his toxic cleanse is a fucking opera. And then he flushes. "One more tidbit," he says. "O.K. wasn't supposed to be first up, but she asked if she could go first because her mom's in town."

BREAKING: ELITIST MIDDLING WOMAN RIDES HER

MOTHER'S COATTAILS TO THE FRONT OF THE LINE. "I didn't know."

"O.K. emails me, she ccs her mom, who wants to 'pop in,' so of course I say yes, because who doesn't want a guest lecturer, but you know how it is . . . Or rather, I'm trying to tell you how it is so that you'll be wiser when you're in my place . . ." He runs his dirty hands through his hair. "An hour before class, I get the blow off. Diane Janz couldn't make it into the room. Point is, authors are flaky. You want a guest lecturer, set it up through her agent."

There's something medical about the way he washes his hands, lathering up like he's about to do surgery, and I have a mentor, Wonder. You will never be in my shoes, in the men's room with our leader. This is Harvard. This is life. It's beyond you, it's before you, and past you and it has nothing to do with you. You and I are in the foxhole together, but we can't utilize the same strategies. We can't fight the same way. You'll never know the Glenn that I know, the guy who nearly breaks his phone with his damp fingers because he just can't *wait* to see all the nice things Roxane Gay said about him while he was "teaching." You weren't being phony in the room. You're a strategist. And if we're going to be in this together, we're both gonna have to be double agents.

Glenn crumples up his paper towel and he shoots and he scores and he pulls the door. "Protégés first."

You see us come into the room together. You see us in conversation and feel what I felt before. Betrayed. Stung. But you *persevere*, you make nice with O.K. and the second half of class is breezier. Faster, like the last leg of a road trip when the destination appears on the signs. It's different because I'm different. It doesn't bother me when O.K. references "Auntie Joan," and you gasp like an awestruck little autodidact—*As in Didion?*—because I get it now. Being "real" for you looks different than being "real" for me. You're a woman, so you're supposed to use your voice, and I'm a white guy so it's *o.k.* for me to be quiet, to show everyone that unlike Lou, I know where we are in history. I know it's my job to shut the fuck up.

"And what about you, Joe?" It's a needle scratch on the record and it's her, it's O.K. She smiles. "You're clearly thinking about *something* over there."

Glenn manspreads his hands across the back of his head and you raise your eyebrows at me and it's not fair. The pseudo-anthropological gaze, they're all so curious about how we handle ourselves as second-class citizens. *Auntie Joan?* I know what Glenn wants from me—support for women's fiction—and I know what you want from me—the real me—and I can't gush about O.K.'s pages—I'll sound condescending—but I can't mince words—I'll sound like I think her work doesn't warrant my critical thinking skills. My palms sweat. The clock ticks. "There's so much potential, my only concern is that the botany . . . it's a bit distracting. Maybe less is more?"

I served up a classic shit sandwich—good bad good—and O.K. squeezes the bun on the top of her head. "Funny," she says. "Joan thought the exact opposite . . ."

YOU CAN'T PUT WORDS IN JOAN DIDION'S MOUTH. SHE'S DEAD. "Well, it's been a while . . ." *Gently, Joseph.* "Did she read an earlier draft?"

O.K. insists that she spent "the better part of the past four years on these pages"—what a waste of time—and you're looking down at the table, same as everyone.

"Well, that's amazing," I say. "But I guess I think of flowers as your mother's thing."

"Oh, so because Mom wrote about flowers, I *can't* write about flowers?"

You look like you're going to die right here, right now, and Sarah Beth zips up her Wheat Thins and Ani glances at the clock and Mats doodles on his notepad and Lou grins because he's not the asshole and wait. I'm not the asshole either. This is a workshop. We're supposed to eat our shit sandwiches and tip the fucking server, but apparently a Harvard classroom is a bougie bistro where the customer is always right.

"Look," I begin. "Let me start over. If I were you, if my mom was *the* Diane Janz, if my 'aunt' was Joan Fucking Didion, may she rest in peace . . . I don't think I'd even dare to write a fucking book. Hell, I'd probably become a dentist!"

That gets a laugh, a few riffs on dentistry, and your cheeks are rosy. You were the one who cracked that dentist joke first, and I *told* you it was funny.

O.K. pulls her knees to her chest. "So, my flowers might not be fire. Hmm . . ."

Glenn's eyeing me—*down, boy*—but this is the room. We are all the server and we are all the customer and truth is necessary. I tell O.K. what you thought she needed to hear, that every time she gives a shout-out to an obscure fucking flower, she's suggesting that the most interesting thing about her is the fact that her mother is Diane Janz. I finish on a positive note. All Angelou. "I just think it would be wild to read your stuff and think, Wow, I can't believe this is Diane Janz's daughter. You'd never know because O.K. DeLuca is so singular . . . I have no idea what it's like to be in your family, but also, I know it's not your job to water your mother's flowers."

O.K. *does* know—she says I sound like her shrink—and Sarah Elizabeth digs *my* flower metaphor—*I have this pressure to feed my readers, to water them like flowers*—and Glenn says I made an "interesting" point. The fellowship isn't a theory anymore. Our room is alive with debate about metaphorical flowers, the need to nip them in the bud. I am good in the room, I am real, but then I look at you and your hair is frizzing up, and your roots are darker now than they were four hours ago, bleaker than they were in the sun on day one, at Dunkin'. You won't look at me even though you damn well *know* I'm looking at you, and wait.

Are you . . . are you *mad* at me?

4

Y ou're not "mad" at me. You're worried. It's been twenty-three
minutes since class ended and you didn't break our date. We're
walking to God (you) only knows where, but you're edgy. I ask
you what's wrong and you tell me I "fucked up big-time."

"You mean with O.K.? Were we in the same room? Because I
thought that went great. It was everything we talked about on the
phone."

"But that was between us. I had no desire to hurt the girl's feelings.
I mean why did you do that? Are you *trying* to get kicked out?"

You make no sense—I saved the class!—and you rub your forehead. "Let's get the T."

"Good idea. I miss the train."

You don't like the way I called it a train, but I don't like the way
your people call it the T and we're belowground, in the bowels of the
station with the hardworking folks on their way home from normal
jobs. It's impossible to be optimistic in the dank, stank air and are you

right? Did I fuck up? I have no cell phone service and who am I to tell anyone how to write a book? I did the undoable. I scolded the daughter of a *famous* woman and we elbow our way into the grungy car of the *T* and is this what we are? Autodidacts for life? The train grinds and sparks and I want us to be special. I never should have said anything to O.K. and the more I think about it, that look on Glenn's face, that word he chose—"interesting"—it's one of the vaguest worst fucking words there is. It doesn't mean *good*.

You sigh. "I'm sorry."

"You're right. Her mom could kill me with one phone call. That's how these people roll."

We ride in silence and you're nervous for me. Biting your nails. You try to make light of it. You say that if they do kick me out, you will quit to protest the injustice, but we both know you won't do that. You need the money, the 25K. The light shifts and I see our reflections and we're not special. They hate us because we *are* us, you with your sycophant autograph hunting and me with my patriarchal know-it-all misogyny. It was a mistake for us to think we could win in that room and the conductor shouts, "Charles/MGH!"

You nudge me and we're slow to exit, as if we both know this might be the end. We take out our phones, and then we're fools in the good way.

Sixteen new messages in the group text, all of them raves about the *best workshop ever.* You turn red and smile. "Okay, I guess I was kinda wrong."

Kinda wrong? I laugh and you smile and it's our first time in Boston proper. "So where are you taking me?"

You nod at the hospital, the Mass Fucking General. "I haven't been here since my mom died and I felt like I was ready. Is that weird?"

Yes. "Not at all."

I assume we're headed to Harvard Gardens, a restaurant, but you wince. "I kinda don't want us to get wasted, you know?"

I didn't say that *I* wanted us to get wasted and you lead the way into a Finagle a Bagel that's practically attached to the hospital. This isn't datey. It's a chain! This is where people sit and wait to see if their loved ones make it out of surgery and you settle into your chair like we're in a real restaurant, like some cheery waitress is going to approach with menus. You stare at me. Not datey. Shrinky. "What would you be like if your mom was Diane Janz?"

"I'd know my flowers, and I'd probably have written a book by now, maybe even two."

You shake your head. "Not what I meant."

I stare at you. Not datey. Shrinky. "It's literally what you asked."

"It's not, though. I asked about you. Not your résumé. You the person."

"But it's absurd. I'm . . . me. And thank God for that because I can't think of anything worse than being born a card-carrying member of the Diane Janz fan club."

You don't laugh at my joke and you don't say that we should order our bagels. *Bagels.* Anti-romance! "Forget about books. I'm talking about who we are. Me, for instance. I mom out hardcore because my mom's gone, and when she *was* here, she was too much of a shit show to mom out on me . . . I'm guessing that your mom . . . Is she alive?"

RIPCandaceBeckLoveMaryKay but nope, Alma's still kicking, I think. "She is."

"So, are you guys close? She must be so proud of you!"

You're not supposed to ask me about my mother and I nod. "Yep."

My *yep* landed like the slam of a door and you suck air through your teeth like *okay then* and no! I don't want you to go home and talk about my "mommy issues" with Tara or your fucking sister and you're staring at me, studying me as if you're waiting for me to unload all my "issues" and I laugh. "You really do love *The Prince of Tides.*"

"What's that supposed to mean?"

"Well, I know the book. You chose your mother's deathbed for our second date."

"First," you say. "*First* date."

"Wonder, I don't know how to say this but I'm not Tom Wingo. I'm not full of demons and it doesn't eat me alive that my mother isn't Diane Janz. We all have a mother."

You exhale and we need menus. Distraction. Normalcy. "So, they don't have Coolattas, but do you want a coffee?"

"I know it's weird, taking you here, but it's like . . . It's like my book."

This is more like it, and I lean in. Close. "Tell me everything."

You reach under the table and pull your sock and show me a tattoo on your left ankle: *Faithful*. "I got this two years ago when I started writing it. That's my title, because that's what it is, you know? In my family, in my city, it's about faith. You're told to be faithful, so you think you are. But then my mom got sick. I lost *all* my faith and my book . . . it's the girl's journey. Everyone she knows and loves, they think she's gone faith*less*. But if I ever finish, well, by the end of it all, losing that cheap 'faith' is how she becomes . . ."

I say it the way I will when I'm interviewing you one day in one of those obnoxious writer-on-writer pieces in a fucking lit mag. "Faithful."

"Bingo," you say. "Classic first novel, all about me and my family. I break it up with these scenes where Alice, the narrator, she has these adventures . . ." You gulp. You are Alice. "With guys . . ." You're cute and bashful, but I'm not the type to slut-shame. "Her one-night-stand scenes are kinda like raunchy lampposts . . ." *Raunchy*. "Anyway, it's the most New England thing ever. It spans thirty-plus years, which is probably what it will take me to finish."

Wrong. You don't need more *lampposts*. "Maybe you'll be inspired and finish it this year. You never know."

"Anyway . . . what's your book about?"

That's even *more* like it. "Well, *Me* is about a couple. Joy and Dane . . . like Joy and *Pain*. They're in a vacuum."

"Like an actual vacuum? Is it surreal? I love surreal."

"No, it's just . . . It's intense. This is obnoxious, but Glenn said it does for the love story what Salinger did for the coming-of-age story, that it's about the phoniness in every human relationship, even when people are being honest, *especially* when they're being honest."

You whistle and "wow" and I am exposed. Naked. Self-Salingered. Do I get up and get the coffee? Do I stay? You tuck your frizzies behind your ears. "So did your mom read it?"

Oh, come on, Wonder. Leave our mothers alone. "Not yet," I say.

And now it's awkward because I can't ask *you* if your mom read *Faithful*—the dead can't read—and we don't have food to distract us. You sigh at the hospital. "I think about it a lot," you say. "What my mom would think of my book . . ."

I'm the same way about *RIPCandaceBeckLoveMaryKay* and I take a deep breath. "And?"

"Well, my mom was bad, Stage Four breast cancer, but if you get the chemo, you get time. My delusional sister would get in my mom's head. 'Fuck chemo, let's go on a road trip!' Cherish said this like we even had a car that could make it across the country. She said *she* was the positive one. 'Go out with a bang! *Thelma and Louise!*' And I'm like no, *I'm* the positive one. You buy time, you fight for it . . . Anyway, you know how it is. You start writing about your life and you're not so sure you were right about anything. Maybe we could have hit the road in some jalopy and my mom could have died at a rest stop in California. It's a mindfuck, writing a novel, questioning your whole past. Do you go through the same thing?"

No, I do not. "Absolutely."

You gulp, and we're talking road trips—you've never done one—and I tell you about growing up in a bookstore, about my crappy apartment in L.A., and your stories are different. They all take place here.

Your phone pings and you pick it up. "Okay, wow. Glenn's having a potluck at his house, and we are invited."

I pick up my phone. "Where do you think he keeps his Pulitzer?"

You smile. "In his bathroom. But he will have copies of *Scabies* on his coffee table."

"No," I say. "I bet the prize is right there on the mantel, unless he hides it to seem cool, and there's no *way* he's gonna have *Scabies* out front and center. He's cooler than that."

You shrug. "Ten bucks says I'm right."

It's on—our next date is a dinner party—and you're overanalyzing the responses in the group text invite. "Jesus," you say. "Ani is like . . . I mean everything she says is so Ani. 'Fully expect a workshop on my garlic-infused flounder cakes and at the same time not open to any of your notes.' I'm so happy I didn't just go 'See ya there!'"

"This is why I despise group texts."

You roll your eyes with a smile—I amuse you—and I want to tell you that confidence begins with you, that you're not on call to deliver well-crafted texts to your Shoddy "family." So I double down with my response to our fucking fellows: *See ya there!*

You tell me that was *good* but you're busy in your notepad, *composing* a response, as if you have to be witty because Ani was witty. "Wonder, you don't have to put on a show."

"I know," you say. "It probably seems so gross but every time I'm gonna pop into the group text, I try out all my replies in the notepad first. Pathetic, right?"

This is who you are, underneath the feathers. You think you owe everyone, that your wants and needs come second. You're allowed to have a life, to go on a date with a great guy from school, and you Eminemed it in the room on day one—*They hate us 'cause they ain't us*—but you're not that woman right now. Less bravado, more duty. Our second first date, and you had to double-book it as a tribute to your dead mother. But that's why you're drawn to me, isn't it? You sense it too, that I'm your golden ticket to paradise.

You toss your phone in your purse. "So, what do we bring to a freaking potluck?"

"Coffee and cigarettes?"

You nudge me. "Let's have fun with it. Autodidact delights."

I like you. "I like it."

"I'm gonna do my Tony Tuna Casserole. Mom's secret recipe . . . Frosted Freaking *Flakes*."

"Well, then I have to top that."

"Don't even try . . ."

"Pigs in a blanket . . ." You wave your hand like *eh*. But I'm not done yet. "With two cans of squeeze cheese for garnish."

You whistle—you are *impressed*—and I want to walk into Glenn's house with you. "So should we cook at your place or mine?"

"Oh," you say. "I wish but I gotta be home to help out with my niece and it would be crazy for you to come all the way over and turn around when you live so close to Glenn's."

Crazy is what people do when Harvard University plays matchmaker, but I can't fight you, you're being too fucking logical—I hate logic—and you pick up your buzzing phone. "Ugh," you say. "See this is why it will be so fun to fuck with Glenn. He just informed us that there's no parking at 'his house' like duh. There's no parking *anywhere*."

He's my mentor and you're my girlfriend (almost). "Ha."

"First of all it's not 'his' house. The school like freaking *gave* it to him, and it's his whole vibe. He is *such* an Ivy League Douchebag."

I am an Ivy League *man* but what if your type is Mr. Macy's? I forgot about that man with a key to your house and you elbow me. "One more thing. You know he's only having this party so he can brag about the freaking Coen brothers."

"Well, one day that might be us . . ."

You laugh, as if that's absurd, as if we're not Harvard. "Sure, Joe. Sure. *Anyway!* I'm pumped for you to meet my family."

Whoa. "You're gonna bring them?"

"Jesus, Joe, turn your notifications on and keep up with the group freaking text! He said to bring our families. And the invitation says six, and you know by six he means six-thirty."

"So, let's say six thirty-four."

"Six thirty-four. And no bailing on me. No going to Whole Foods for a plate of canapés so you can fit in with the didacts. We're auto to the didact all the way and we're in this together, right?"

There's nothing like wanting something in the form of someone and knowing that you're going to get it. You said it—*we're in this together*—and you gulp. "I didn't mean to be talking shit just now."

"You weren't."

"Glenn brings out the 'How do ya like *them* apples?' in me. But also like . . . I don't want our thing to be talking shit about everyone. It's like I tell the girls at work . . . That's the road to hell."

"Right there with you, Good Wonder Hunting."

You bite your lip and shrug—I won't call you that again—and something catches your eye, a mother fighting with her sons, both of whom can't be more than sixteen, both of whom want a cigarette. The mother tells them to share and they don't want to fucking share and she bursts into tears and the boys look at each other and they can't fix that, so they do what they can do. They stop fighting and light the cigarette. They share.

When I turn back, you're smiling. "Thanks for coming here with me."

You say that like I knew where we were going and you need to leave but you don't *want* to leave. You're bursting with stories, you talk like someone who just got out of prison, like someone who was on mute for most of her life. You want to know if I think it's weird that you've never left home—yes, I do—and you want to know if I think it's weird that you'd rather keep your job at Dunkin' than get a *freaking* book deal—yes, I do—and I ask you if you think it's weird that we sat in this chain for almost two fucking hours without bagels, let alone coffee, and you smile.

"Yes, I do."

That's the hallmark of a good second first date, that moment where three little words become code. *Yes, I do.* We're not going to have some secret language and *Yes, I do* each other to death, but it's real with you and it's time for us to seal the deal in a dark booth in a dark bar.

You sigh. "I feel so bad we sat here and didn't get anything. I'm gonna throw a ten in the tip jar before we leave."

I love you, but it's too soon to say it. "Wanna grab a bite somewhere?"

You cringe like Cinderella and say you have to get home to your family and it stings a little. You denied us the right to share a meal and yes, you *are* weird. A thirty-five-year-old sixteen-year-old with a curfew. But I like being in this metal chair, inside of this soulless fast-food joint with you. I like it because it makes me know who I am, the only man who can help you bust out of your cage.

5

I show up at Casa de Shoddy right on time, just as we planned. I knock on the half-open door at 6:34 P.M. and it's loud in there—the party is in full swing—and I take a deep breath—I hope you wore a dress—and I walk into Glenn's house, directly into his wife, Sly Caron, in real life, taller in person, wearing an *apron* as if her guests didn't do all the cooking. She's an author, too. She wrote a book called *Flour Girls*. RIP Ethel Rose-Baker shrugged it off—*They'll publish anyone with an MFA*—and I didn't think it was *that* bad. But what do I know? I don't have an MF Fucking A. Or a fucking date.

"Oh," Sly says, looking down at my plate. "I adore kitsch. You must be Joe!"

I search the room for you because it's a full room, packed with people and children, *books*, but you're not here. Sly rolls up her sleeves like an Anthropologie mannequin. "Sorry," she says. "I'm Sly, honey."

"Nice to meet you, Sly. Big fan."

She laughs and why shouldn't she? *Flour Girls* tanked and her own husband's probably not a "big fan" and I wouldn't be fucking up if you were here. Where are you? She points to a side table where I can *drop my kitsch* and if you were here, you would elbow me right now and whisper, "'Kitsch.'" Our mini rebellion doesn't work without you. No one with an MFA would bring mini hot dogs with a squeeze cheese garnish to a potluck, so I'm the butt of a joke, standing here with my plastic fucking tray. You should be here with your Tony Tuna Casserole, but you're *not* here. I'm in the foxhole alone with no backup and the novelty of my little fucking hot dogs wears off fast. Sly's already gone to mingle with other people, people who are already here, half-baked, semi-stuffed—if I'm late you're *really* late—and I deliver my blanketed pigs to the lowly side table. There's no real food anymore. It's tarts and cupcakes, and what the fuck *is* it with these people and their early starts? I check the group text and the plan for a 5:30 kickoff was made hours ago—kiddos, etc.—and you *knew* about the plan—*Sounds good!*—and you know I avoid the group fucking text and you didn't give me a heads-up, and we're supposed to be in this *together*. All the boats left the dock a while ago and I'm far behind and I missed the meat of the party—literally, it's all gone, no more burgers—and I missed the appetizer time, when it's easier to mingle and it hurts more tonight than it did on that lawn, because I thought it would be us on that sofa, holding court center stage, but instead it's Lou and his *lady* and I can't catch up to them, Wonder, not without you.

And where are you? I check my watch. 6:48.

I would be a hypocrite if I didn't *try* so I make the rounds, I say my hellos and I pretend to be *so excited* to meet the *significant others*—not significant to me, thank you!—and time is passing—it's 7:03 and there is nowhere for me to be, because I am supposed to be here with you.

Earlier today, you were a woman of *your* word. You texted me at 1:06 and again at 2:05—*Very excited about Tony's Tuna Casserole*—and now it's 7:09—the party is dying, *I* am a human bottle of untouchable squeeze cheese—and my mind goes to the bad place.

Is it him? Are you with Mr. Fucking Macy's?

Does his key to your house double as a key to your heart? To your body?

I go into the kitchen to stare at Glenn's fridge because that's me, *The Man Who Stares at Pictures of Life Instead of Living It.* Glenn slaps me on the back.

"Hey, Joe. Did you try Ani's flounder cakes?"

"Yeah," I say. "It's terrific . . ." A beat. And I guess I have to do all the talking. "Hey, I didn't know you guys had kids."

"We don't," he says. And he should say more, but he does this in class, too. One fucking silence after another and WHERE ARE YOU, WONDER?

"Oh," I say. "Well, they're cute kids." The most common lie in the world. "Niece and nephew?"

Glenn laughs. "Yes and no," he says, and he loves a *yes and no* and you *hate* his double-talk and seriously, Wonder, WHERE THE FUCK ARE YOU?

"See," he says. "Sly and I, we met in workshop, back in Iowa, and the first time we went out, she took me to this place where you make pottery . . ."

Another silence, as if I'm supposed to ask to see the amateur ash-trays. "Cool."

"Remember, Joe, we can't fulfill our potential as writers if we don't go to that page with all the gusto of a kid running into the water. You *have* to stay young. Spry. That's why I ride."

I want to google him right now and show him a picture of himself when he was at Iowa, before he became the lean, boring biking machine that he is now and I don't want to be this way. Tense and marooned. He's gone already—he's the host, he *has* to spread the love—and I need you, Wonder. Ani and her husband are blocking my escape, so I am stuck by the open fridge, still staring at the picture of kids I don't know on a beach on some island in paradise.

Where are you, Wonder? Where?

My parents didn't take me to the fucking beach and if yours did, I bet the sea was part sewage, and if you were here, this moment would be fun, instead of painfully awkward. Finally, Ani's husband finds the *mochi* and the path is clear but where am I supposed to fucking go? I can't go into the living room. The people on the love seats are too together. I cut through a bathroom—his guest bathroom has two doors—and I duck into the library and now I *really* wish you were here.

We would size up their stacks together and I would smile at his Wolitzer—he has every single one of her books—and you would tell me they're probably Sly's. I would tell you not to be so cynical and you would open his *Corrections* and show me how he makes his notes in pencil, as opposed to his wife, who uses a pen.

I put the book back on the shelf. It's no use, Wonder.

Last night was real. It was you and me at a table alone, so consumed with each other that we didn't eat or drink. You're not my fantasy anymore. You're real and the reality is you are *late* and I wish you were behind me, placing your hands on my back as I step into the garage. You would gasp—*the horror*—and we would be counting all the bicycles together, nine-fucking-teen of them, vintage and new. You would laugh when I said that his cycling hobby is a disease that he picked up during the pandemic, that money is a chalice because look at all these bikes! No *wonder* he still hasn't finished his second book. Every wheel represents an hour of online bike surfing, an hour that he wasn't fucking writing.

And then we would realize we are trespassing in the dark. You would start with a kiss and you would fuck me like you mean it. Like you were trying to get at the soul inside my body.

I check my phone—I don't have a watch or a *Swatch*—and it's 7:23. I looked online, Wonder. They *do* sell Swatches at Macy's and you have six of them at least—I've studied your wrists on Cherish's Facebook—and is this how you treat me? You're the one who made me promise I wouldn't betray you with a trip to Whole Foods and now you leave me stranded alone, in a garage full of bikes? I count Glenn's bikes the way I've counted your Swatches and they say this about people, that we criticize in others what we like least about ourselves. Are you a collector? A hoarder? Are you with Cherish right now, comparing me to Mr. Macy's? Glenn can't ride all his bicycles at once and you can't wear all your Swatches at once and you didn't answer my text. I check the *shit show* that is your sister's Facebook again and it's a hard part-time job, so many memes, two new pictures of Caridad, and here's something new, a two-thousand-word rant but it's not about you. It's just one of her YOU KNOW WHAT YOU DID rage notes about some woman who stole her parking spot.

I'm getting scared and it's getting dark, *too dark to see,* and what's the holdup? Did you literally get held up? Is the *pregaming* so fucking fun that you decided to bail on me? On *your* fellows?

I head back into the house and Mats slaps a hand on my back. "Sup, Goldberg?"

I shove my phone in my pocket. Maybe you're a pot and you will boil through the front fucking door if I stop waiting for you. "Hey, Mats, I didn't realize you were here."

He says he was in *the crapper* and advises me to skip the oysters if any are left—nope—and he tells me more than I need to know about his day job while I watch Sly run around, manically adding images to her story, pictures of everyone but me and Mats. Glenn stubs his toe on a Lego—Ani and her husband adopted a toddler when the children they made started high school—and all the kids are still out back—there's a yard, we know—and the couples hold court in the living room, and none of it bothers Mats—he is building a robot—and he picks up a pig in a blanket.

"Classic," he says. "Especially if you dip 'em in O.K.'s *guac.*"

I spare Mats my feelings about *guac,* especially the kind that's been exposed to the air for almost two fucking hours. A love seat opens up in the living room—Mrs. and Mr. Sarah Elizabeth Swallows are going outside to see the *kiddos*—and this room is like the world, it's built for couples. We belong on that couch but you're not here and when you *do* get here you might be on that fucking sofa with *him*, with Mr. Macy's, the reason I can't send you a text.

Mats burps. As if he *wants* the couples to see all single guys, even the Harvard ones, as socially inept. "Hey, how long do you think we have to stay?"

"We can't leave before everyone gets here."

"Yeah, but you can tell it's winding down."

"Did you know they were all gonna get here so early?

He shrugs. "My sister has kids. She's the same way." He shoves his pointer finger into the guac. "Fuck it," he says. "I'm still starving."

I feel eyes on us—Lou's *lady* saw the faux pas—and he rubs his hand on her leg and whispers in her ear and she throws her hair over her *little shoulder* and beams at Glenn's wife.

"Sly," she says. "You *must* tell me where you found that wallpaper in the bathroom."

Sly is talking about the *liberating fun of removable wallpaper* and if you were here, you'd be squeezing my knee—*It's not their freaking house*—and Glenn is deep in conversation with Ani's husband and Mats elbows me. "There's still pizza in the kitchen."

I don't want pizza, so I'm alone with the couples and the tiny pies and you said you were coming with your autodidact delight and Lou is feeling up his lady and for all I know, Mr. Fucking Macy's is doing the same thing to you. I go into the kitchen and gorge on pizza with Mats and maybe he has the right idea. Maybe *I* should give up on you and get a sex robot.

My phone pings—you are psychic—but no you aren't. It's Glenn: *Side yard in 5.*

I pop a slice of pepperoni in my mouth: *Sounds good.*

It's a plot twist out of one of Sarah Elizabeth's books, a reminder of who I was before you, a guy with a manuscript, a guy who came to Harvard for one reason and one reason only: to get Glenn Shoddy on my side.

I slip out to the side yard and in the cold, in the dark, I remember what I told myself before I got here, before I met you, that the great love of my life was here all along, as is the way of so many classic love stories, that it was fucking *me*. I'm supposed to be looking out for myself right now and maybe I got ahead of myself. Maybe I was fixated on you because I too suffer from a *tendency to love*. Yes, you can write, but I read you *after* I saw you. I was honored when you lured me to your mother's tomb. I barely know you and then a car comes along, a BMW like Mr. Macy's, and it kills me. You said we were in this together, *autodidacts all the way,* and I let myself *believe* like a fucking Sox fan in April. Are you gonna do this to me? Breeze into this house late with a date? No. The windows aren't tinted and the Beamer is gone. But it doesn't make me feel any better.

Glenn opens the screen door, stoned and smiling. "If anyone asks, you left when everyone left. C'mon. Sly saved you a burger."

6

You want to know why you're evil, Wonder? Because you've ruined the best night of my life, my career. It's official. I am Charlie and Glenn is Willy Wonka and I fucking *won*. Sly says that Glenn has been raving about me for months, that I am his "favorite of his favorites," and if I were a ten-year-old boy, this would be enough. I am it. I won. The other Shoddies are all home, but I am in the glass elevator and because of you, it's not enough.

I'm not a ten-year-old boy. I'm a *man*. I wish I was more of a prick. I wish I could forget about you. I wish I could be here, eating my burger, relishing every bite, soaking up praise. But the burger I'm eating is only here because Sly put it aside for you. She saved it, in case you showed up late, in case you were hungry.

But you didn't show up. You didn't even text me and I ate your burger and it's me and Glenn and Sly in the living room. It's a *salon*.

I compliment their living room and Glenn puffs up. "Yes," he says.

"The sitting room is the best spot in the house, except of course for my office."

He's a little annoying, but what teacher isn't? What author isn't? You said it yourself. *Everyone is an asshole* but at least these assholes didn't bail on me. This special time with Glenn is my reward for running the room and I'm going to enjoy it, Wonder. Sly's legs are draped over Glenn's lap and he is petting her like she's a cat and I want it to be the four of us. I want you to be Charlie too, but I don't even know where you are.

"You make a point," Glenn says. "But the poor girl *means* well."

No, we're not talking about you, we're talking about O.K. We've been talking about *all* the fellows—not you, though, you didn't show up—and Sly sweeps her legs off Glenn's lap. She lights another long, hand-rolled joint and you would *loathe* this woman in that way that only a woman can loathe another, the way she reeks of self-care and casual jaunts to the *market*—you call it a "grocery store"—and then you would have come around, the way that only a woman can when it comes to another woman because you would like the way she *slyly* gave it to Glenn all night to his face, behind his back.

Hey, genius, the grill is on fire.

Oh, we're the opposite. If twenty million people liked my book, I think I'd jump off a cliff.

My guy means well with the "Read Her Too" hashtag, but yes, it is somewhat grotesque.

He knows when I'm mad at him. All I have to do is leave David Foster Wallace in the bathroom.

And now, she's doing it again. "Face it, Glenn. You wouldn't say that if she were a man."

"But she isn't," he says and he growls at me—me!—and even you would have to admit that this whole fucking thing is pretty cool. And if I'd never met you, I would be complete in this moment, yet I don't know where you are, if you're with *him*, Mr. Macy's. Are you?

Sly sits up and claps her hands at me. "Listen up, boys." She does that a lot because I keep spacing out. Because of *you*. And this is how it works in the world. I'm half-here and Glenn senses my distraction, which means he *too* is half-here and Sly elbows him, and that's more wine on the rug. "Boys," she says. "This is my problem with O.K."

I let Glenn be the dumb one and he delivers. "Okay, Sly."

She ignores her silly husband—Glenn Shoddy, just another drunken bore!—and says that O.K. shouldn't be in the fellowship—and why can't you be here? You would get to expound on the life O.K. could be living as a dentist! "It's an Electra complex. She's only playing writer because she wants to be a critic. She can't 'kill' her mother, so she'll settle for picking apart other writers. But what a waste of an ambition because those jobs barely exist and criticism is all but dead."

"Um," Glenn says. "It's called Twitter."

"Exactly," Sly says. And she smiles at me and waves her phone. "I've been doing my homework." She goes to O.K.'s page and she scrolls and Glenn yawns—no, Glenn, not yet, there's still a chance you'll show up—and she smiles. "Boom," she says. "And I quote, 'Joyce Carol Oates has it all wrong.'"

"Has what all wrong?"

"Glenn, focus. That's irrelevant. My point is that O.K.is sharing an opinion, which is by nature subjective. But she is framing it as a statement of fact, omitting the crucial disclaimer."

I only speak when spoken to in this room and I get the feeling it's my turn so I go for it. "It should be 'I *think* Joyce Carol Oates has it all wrong.'"

Glenn rolls his eyes and Sly raises her glass to me and says that O.K. is too opinionated and biased and mommy-obsessed to be a true fiction writer and where are you, Wonder? Glenn grabs his hair—Glenn Shoddy! Glenn *Fucking Shoddy*—and he claps his hands, and I know what that means.

"Lay it down, Joe."

He keeps Faulkner on the coffee table—I told you his books would not be on display—and I lay my hand on the bible that is the Faulkner. "I swear that what is said in this room stays in this room."

And then I make the unspoken disclaimer that's just for us: *Unless, of course, we wind up together, in which case I will tell you everything.*

Glenn takes a big swig of his drink. I knew he was that way. I've seen his interviews, all the *I-can-be-a-little-too-Hemingway-for-my-own-good* crap that's code for borderline alcoholic. But it's a whole other thing to see him in action, veering into blackout territory. "What my lovely wife fails to understand is that a fellowship is a puzzle. I *know* that O.K.'s not a writer."

Sly puffs on her joint. "*Thank* you."

"But most writers aren't writers," he says. "You pick most to serve a few . . . okay . . . to serve *one*."

I am different on this love seat, I am born again *again,* religious, baptized. Chosen. "Geez Louise," I say, like that guy from *Girls* in Noah Baumbach's world. "Glenn, that's outta hand."

Sly is eyeing me, no doubt *wondering* if her husband picked the wrong horse. "Watch out, Joe," she says. "My husband is about to come all over your face . . ."

"No," Glenn says. "Don't be crass."

"Oh, please," Sly says. Instead of telling him to fuck off, she scoops his bike helmet off the end table and tosses it on another love seat. "I'm with you. I loved Joe's short story."

"Actually," I say. "It's a novel."

Sly nods, unconvinced, but she's not an expert—her book tanked—and *Me is* a novel—I finished it!—and Glenn rejoices—"Hell yes, it is"—and I don't blame Sly for cooling off. A woman can only take so much from men like us. Especially a woman who got robbed— her book deserved better—but did you hear that, Wonder? I'm right up there with Glenn. Me!

"It's like this," Glenn says. "Think of tennis camp."

You would die. You would grab my thigh and die. "Okay."

"I'm the coach. I want you to get better . . ." I'm fine, Glenn, my book is *done*. "You can't get better unless you play with people who are better than you, but you won't *keep* playing unless you give yourself a chance to have those ego-boosting wins."

Sly groans. "And this, Joe, this right here is why you will *never* see me in a workshop ever again, let alone teaching one. The performance of it all, the plotting and the showboating!"

Glenn concedes that he doesn't exactly *mind* the sound of his own voice and then he lays it down. Ani and Lou and Sarah Elizabeth and Mats aren't "better" than me, but they're more advanced. They've done the work, "their strokes have been stroked." And O.K. is here because I can *beat her with my serve*, because I have to get over my envy of her lineage, her privilege. Glenn's cooking now—he skipped you, but he'll get there—and he rubs his hands together.

"And here's the thing about Sarah Elizabeth."

Sly fixes her eyes on his helmet. "Watch it, Genius. Moms need beach reads. Dads, too."

"Hear me out," he says. "I'm saying that Joe needs to learn about *twists*."

Well, now I'm glad you're not here because my book doesn't need any fucking twists and you're lucky you don't have to watch Sly second-grade slobber all over him—*I love you even now, Schwinny*—and Schwinny is because of his favorite bike and is this how you are with Mr. Macy's? Are you in the back of his fucking Beamer?

Sly is holding the helmet again, staring into it like it's a Magic Fucking 8 Ball—*Will my husband ever shut the hell up?*—and Glenn rolls on. He's not a tennis coach anymore. Now he's Cameron Crowe on the last page of *Fast Times*. "Let me tell you how it's all gonna go . . ."

His predictions are predictable.

O.K. and "Mom" will start an imprint, so it would behoove all of us to be nice to her.

Ani will thrive in that small press literary way because she's already an established playwright, but mostly because she's not driven by ego.

Lou will flounder in noir mixed with horror because he's *all* ego. No heart.

Sarah Elizabeth will write one *offbeat book* and go back to the airport and write the best book of *her fucking life* when she decides she doesn't have that book in her.

And Mats? He's "all imagination." He'll "*Ready Player One* us all into the multiplex within three years."

Me? I will *set the world on fire* and now it's your turn—come on, Glenn, do Wonder—but Sly yawns in that way wives do, and Glenn takes the hint.

"All right," he says. "I guess I am blowing a little hard."

"No, you're not, honey," Sly says. "I just have to be up so early. I mean someone's gotta deal with your Facebook page and all the various little labors that keep the air in your tires."

They're acting like we're through here but we're not through. What about *you*? Sly is folding a blanket—another hint—but I won't let him erase you, not on my *Swatch*.

"Hey, Glenn," I say. "What about Wonder?"

Sly pecks the top of Glenn's head and looks at me. "Wonder is a genius, and if you'll excuse me, boys, this hostess has to be at a certain bike shop at seven-thirty in the morning. Night, Schwinny. Night, Joe."

She said the g-word—wish you were here yet?—and now he needs to say it, too. The stairs creak under the weight of her feet and she closes a door and a faucet runs and Glenn rubs his eyes. "My new gig has been a *lot* for both of us. I don't know what I'd do without Sly, my literal angel who makes it possible for me to be me."

He's deflecting, but he's my fucking teacher. "It's got to be a lot."

"See, I *need* to ride or I can't write and I can't go to the bike shop . . . The department heads, they keep calling these *meetings* and poor Sly's clearly a little overtasked and—"

"I can do it. I can stop by the bike shop."

He lights up. "Seriously? Joe, I can't ask you to do that."

"You didn't," I say, because I'm not doing it for him. It's for *you*. "It's no sweat."

He scratches the back of his neck the way he did when Oprah asked him about his teacher parents. "That would actually be . . . That would be good for me *and* my marriage . . ."

He moseys into the kitchen, more mumbling about Sly, and how can someone this smart be so stupid? Obviously, I can't talk about his wife while we're in *her house*. His eyes are bloodshot and he's whiny, he's tired—probably up late reading the snide tweets about his delayed second book and the backlash about the adaptation of his *first* book and then taking refuge in the evergreen gold, those first, gooey blue check tweets about *Scabies*—and yes. His wife is put-upon, but you have a future, too.

He grabs a bag of trash and winces. "Oof. My back."

I take the damn bag off his hands and that's rich people for you, too sore to take the trash out, but not too sore to ride a bike. He downs a leftover glass of water. "Thanks for that, too," he says.

I am holding the trash. His wife is washing her face. All signs point to *GO HOME* but I'm not leaving without his take on you. "Hey," I say. "Real quick, the whole future thing . . . What do you see happening for Wonder?"

His smile is one I haven't seen. The one he'd never show to Oprah. "I have to know," he says. "Are you two . . ."

"Glenn, no."

He shakes his head. "Back in the day . . ." As in what, seven years ago? "Sly wanted to be the next Meg Wolitzer."

I tell him I loved Sly's book. It's like a baby on a fridge. You just fucking have to love it.

"Nice," he says. "And I reiterate what I said in the loo . . ." *Loo.* "It's wise of you to read wide, women's fiction . . ."

I should know better than to have heroes, let alone to meet them, and I want to smack him, but I nod. "Agree."

He opens a bottle of Fiji water and shrugs. "As for Wonder . . . She didn't show up."

FUCK THIS FUCK. "Well, her voice, though. She definitely has a voice."

He snickers—"Among other assets"—and I want to report all his *#ReadHerToo* tweets. "Oh, come on," he says. "I know she has a 'voice.' So does Sly. So do we all. A lot of people can sing . . . Look at all those women on the street, on the Internet . . . It takes more than talent to make a mark." I hate that he's right and I hate that you're not here and he leans in, glowering. "I'm just bummed for you, though . . ."

"For me?"

"I thought you'd be going home with her tonight. But hey, there's always next week."

I can't stand up for you because you gave him a leg to stand on— You didn't show up tonight—and he promises to send me *deets* about the bike shop and it's over. I'm outta there, dumping his *trash* in his side fucking yard and damn it, Wonder. If you'd showed up, I wouldn't have been stuck in that kitchen with him and now I really do have to keep it all a secret. I can't revel in all the good things he said about me because of what he said about *you*.

You saw this coming, didn't you? You said it was dangerous for two people to bond by talking shit about other people and that's what I just did with Glenn. We're in the danger zone. *I'm* in the danger zone. I almost punched my mentor in the aquiline nose, which means I almost lost my spot in the circle, and why? Because of you, you who didn't even bother to show up. I don't want you to be a notch in my belt and I know. You're smart and you're sexy and it's what they say about geniuses. We're *all* a little "off." We're inconsistent. We Bukowski and we bumble and you probably think I'll like you *more* because you bailed on me tonight, because you stranded me with my pigs in a blanket and showed me your "crazy" streak, which in your mind probably proves that you're an artist, an unpredictable sexy beast, *just* the kind of woman that a controlling male artist seeks to tame because he *just* can't seem to figure her out.

Well, that *just* ain't me, Wonder.

You should have been here tonight and Cambridge is like Bainbridge, its tendency is to *sleep* and I want to go to your house. I want to knock down your door and tell you what Glenn said, that you're on the verge of throwing it all away, but you live with a *child* and you don't know that I know where you live and it's 2:00 A.M.—how long have I been walking?—and I open Goddamn motherfucking *Facebook*—you are turning me into something I am not—and I stop cold in front of the Goddamn Gap.

It's you. You're with him—it's Mr. Macy's—and he has a name—it's Bobby Skelly—and there's a knife in my heart, in the form of a fork in his hand, dipping into your Tony Tuna Casserole, the one you made for us, for tonight. Cherish's hyperbole is a curse disguised as a blessing.

#TrueLove #TheseTwo #BobbyandWonder #WondersMan

I am in the glass elevator—Glenn loves me, he picked me—and I could stay where I am. I could fly away and leave you in a sea of mayonnaise and meaningless likes. You betrayed me. You froze me out and there is mayonnaise on your dress, the one you put on for me, and you don't deserve my help, not right now.

But you got a Golden Ticket, same as me. And this is the curse of being a *Charlie* in this world. I can't let you do this, Wonder. I can't let you waste your life on his soft, silky lap.

7

Two days later, and you think it's over between us, don't you? You downgraded me from a new man in your life to a fellow you see in a classroom once a fucking week. You haven't called or texted and you killed all the momentum we built at Finagle a Bagel. But I won't let our story become a book we don't finish. After I left the stiff, upper-crust life with Sly and Glenn, I stayed up all night gorging on the dark, day-old bread of your sister's retooled Facebook memories. I've been bingeing for twenty-four minutes and thirty-six hours, minus two pleasureless breaks to run errands for Glenn— you're not the only one with a job—and everything makes sense now. You're shying away from me because that wasn't you at the bagel place, not really. As it turns out, you didn't tell me your "life story." You sold me a fantasy reboot about a woman who's tied to her close- knit family, no serious boyfriends in the past, and you cut the most important part: Bobby Fucking Skelly. He's Mr. Macy's and his family *owns* the Dunkin' where you work—he thinks he owns you—and he doesn't own his fancy car the way I own my Tesla—it's a lease—and your families were *neighbors*. Worse still, when you were in high school, his family sold out to compost people. They left Sesame Street, but Your Bobby wanted to stay, and your parents let him squat in your fucking *basement*.

Yeah, it's not a *cellar*, much as Cherish loves to use that word, and you're in the worst kind of danger. The silk pants stalker still has a key.

You're a writer. You should know better. The first rule of storytelling: Lay it all down in that first draft. Every gross, humiliating idea in your fucked-up little head. Stories are messy. Our job is to make the mess so unbiased *editors* can help us shape it. You can't edit your own book or your life story and you can't edit the truth just because you think I *can't handle the truth*. I'm coping, whiplashed and knocked back onto my crate in the alley across the street from your houses like a stranger while I dig through your past, as presented by Your Bobby.

I knew you had a rough childhood. It's all over your writing, Pat Conroy via the T, that line about *the serial monogamist who puts all serial killers to shame*. That wasn't your imagination. You were born in a booby trap, a Bobby trap. Before you had language, you had this *thing* in the crib with you, this baby named Bobby. The day you were born, your mother fixed you up with him. She wanted you to be the pink to his blue, and, thirty-five years later, your sister wants to make your mother's living, dying wish come true.

She wants you to marry Bobby Skelly.

The little reunion at your house wasn't *fun*. Your dictator/documentarian sister spent the night posting pictures in real time, mixing up the past with the present. I saw you in a stroller with Bobby and I saw you do *shots* with him—*GET MARRIED ALREADY*—but you're not meant to be Bobby Skelly's final girl. The guy has a pattern. He gets "serious" with a girl—this time around, a twenty-four-year-old influencer named *Kelli*—and he fades away from your inner circle. Your sister *defriends* him, but eventually—as in last night—Bobby gets dumped. Cherish hears the news and she *refriends* Bobby—nice job again, Zuckerberg—and soon enough, he's crying *on your little shoulder* as you miss out on your life, on me.

But this isn't about me, Wonder. I'm worried about *you*. You won't grow as a writer if you're with Bobby Fucking Skelly. Have you seen his Facebook page? He's the kind of douchebag who submits a flattering photo of himself to some database designed for narcissists. The algorithm concludes that he's a 95 percent dead ringer for a young Al Pacino—he wishes—and every one of his "friends" hits the idiot button to reinforce the lie. You're above all that shit, but you're stuck because Bobby isn't just a friend, he's your motherfucking *boss*.

The local papers call him and his siblings "the Skelly kids," but that's a misnomer—they're all over thirty-five—and Bobby's brother and sister are both married, hunkered down with kids. What were you thinking? Bailing on me to be with that perma-bachelor Nordstrom Rack skirt-chaser. He's just using you, Wonder. That's his MO.

Fact: Bobby's aunt Ro loved him like he was her own kid. Eight months ago, Ro died, and you were Bobby's "date" at Ro's funeral. You were "there" for him, and how did he thank you? He dumped you for *Kelli*. Bobby's a sham. "Honoring" his dead aunt by sharing "memories" of her old posts praising him, the "prince," for doing the most menial things, fixing her old refrigerator or replacing the lint filter in her ancient dryer. You know what I mean, the kind of shit a decent guy just fucking *does* for his family. I did that shit for Mr. Mooney, Wonder, but I didn't brag about it on *Facebook*.

Real love is quiet. A whisper between two people.

Bobby doesn't "love" you and he didn't "love" his aunt Fucking Ro. He changed her light bulbs so she'd testify to all the Kellis that he's "a catch." And then there's the money. The rich always want to get richer, and Your Bobby knew that if he did Ro's bidding she would give him her three-bedroom raised ranch in Braintree. That's exactly what she did in her will, and he never lets anyone forget that the house is just sitting there, waiting to be filled with mini Bobbies. The horror.

You don't see through him because you can't see through him. You never got the distance required to adjust your eyes. You turned down the great escape of college to help care for your mother, and here come the goose bumps because how did you do it, Wonder? How did you sleep at night with that lecherous horny tween in your basement, jerking off to pictures of you?

I know. You could have a certain kind of comfort with Bobby, the "Vice President of Employee Relations," whose "job" is cruising around harassing the women who *work* at the stores. He "works" nights too, moonlighting for *finishers* who bail on donut frosting duties. But again, he has an agenda, milking the Nicolas Cage in *Moonstruck* martyrdom with 4:00 A.M. selfies, alone in the back of a dreary Dunkin', wearing a wifebeater and an invisible crown.

Four hundred donuts done. This boy is tired. I'd rather be up taking care of a baby!

Gimme a fucking break. Bobby isn't a hardworking commoner sweating his ass off in the central bakery to make the rent. His family owns the business. His life is *want*-to, not *have*-to.

A video. Grainy but clear. You and Bobby romp on a cruddy swath of sand, Quincy, maybe. You're a toddler in a Wonder Woman bathing suit—the irony—and your mother hovers off-camera, pointing at a little boy, little Bobby. *Wonder*man. She squawks, "Who's that, Wonder?"

You are a trained seal, cute and blinking. Smart. "That's my Bobby!"

His mother hovers, eighties glamour gal, big black sunglasses, long pink nails. "Whose Bobby?"

The pressure is on, and you deliver: "My Bobby!"

Your mother claps—*Yes, Wonder! That's your Bobby!*—and your sister hands you a Fudgsicle and that's it. You're a goner. The neural pathways in your impressionable, exceptional little brain learn that it's biologically rewarding for you to label Bobby Skelly *your* Bobby and imagine the level of a mind that looks at an *infant* and thinks about who that baby will be *banging* one day! Your own *mother* fantasizing about your sexual future.

He's not *Your Bobby*, Wonder. It's like his hard-bodied ex-fiancée Kelli said in her Instagram story at 3:00 A.M:

Ladies, you can't turn a boy into a man. Take it from me, don't waste your time trying.

I'll probably never say this again, but man, that influencer is smart!

You are too, and it can't be easy being surrounded by people who aren't on your level, the kind of people who call you *wicked freaking smart* to your face, cornering you into proving you're one of them. Tara plied you with Jäger shots and karaoke last night and she liked the picture of you and Bobby—*Can they just get married already?*—and she's not alone. There are more compliments pouring in now.

lol took them long enough!

Tell that kid to fix the Coolatta machine on Broadway already. We're dying over here!

Wooh just watched American Hustle last night GO BOBBY GO.

That's a bump and I go to IMDb and oh. It gets worse.

In 2012, Your Bobby got it in his head that he should be an actor. That's the real Boston curse, the yearning to be a Wahlberg or an Affleck, and according to the *Herald,* Your Bobby was "discovered" by David O. Russell. That hothead director gave Bobby four lines and a SAG card, but even *auteurs* know when they're wrong (sometimes), and lucky for us, Russell cut Your Bobby's scene from the movie *and* the DVD extras.

You can cut him too, Wonder, and I know you want out of the Bobby trap. At 11:43 P.M. you sent an SOS text to our Shoddy family: *Sorry I missed out! I got stuck with family stuff. Hope you guys had FUN!*

You chose your words well—yes, you are *stuck*—and it's killing you. Last night at 12:36 A.M., you turned to Goodreads. You were too shy to reach out to me directly, so you edited your review of Sarah

Elizabeth's latest picket fence thriller, a book we talked about in our texts:

> *I've been thinking about it lately, and I did have one problem with this book. Spoiler Alert. I didn't want Claire to end up with Roger. You ever think about that phrase? "End up together"? It's dark. What should be the beginning feels more like the walls closing in. It would be one thing if Sarah Elizabeth meant for it to play that way, the relationship depicted as doom, the security nullified by the barbed wire fence. I know they've known each other forever. I get that the world was always bringing them back to each other, but I wanted to see Claire happy, not just settled in this way that reeked of settling for less, ya know?*

Yes, I do know. And as you Goodreads girls like to say, here's a spoiler alert: I am going to get you out of that fucking Bobby trap.

Action on your porch and *snap back to reality*, it's you. You're up and out the door and I adjust my crate—*Gently, Joseph*—and so far, so normal. Caridad runs into the street with her bright pink ball and you yawn. You have bedhead—that hurts—but I bet he was too wasted to please you. You blow a kiss to Caridad and head to the store to get your dad's scratchers and I could chase you down right now, except I can't because again the door opens and this time it's *him*. It's Your Bobby in one of his fucking *wifebeaters* and he plays the gentleman, holding the door for your father, who obsequiously thanks him, as if holding the door for an old fucking man isn't the kind of decency that's to be expected, not rewarded. Your old man sits on his chair and fusses with his Parliaments and Your Bobby is quick with his lighter. "Here ya go, Jerry."

I'm surprised that I can hear everything so clearly, but the acoustics are on my side, and Masshole men like Your Bobby and your father want the whole fucking *world* to hear everything they say, as if they're hosting some morning radio show for dickheads.

Your father smiles. "Thanks, son."

The two of them shoot the early morning shit about the Sox—Bobby thinks they're going all the way—and your old man shrugs. "I stopped caring a long time ago."

It's your fiction come to life and Your Bobby nods—could he try any harder?—and your dad almost growls. "For Chrissake, Bobby, do you know *why* I don't give a rat's ass about the Sox? Because they did it. They won. They broke the choke and they Goddamn *did* it."

Your Bobby scratches the back of head. "I know, Jerry. I'm working on it."

"She's not getting any younger, Bobby. Every year it's the same. You go for these girls and you show up here and then . . . nothing."

"I know," Bobby says. "But it feels different this time, Uncle Jerry."

"Don't give me that *different* shit, Goddammit. Give me a grandson! You kids and your 'timing' and before you know it, you're my age, and that ship's sailed." Your Bobby says he's trying and your father spits on his deck. "Don't try," he says. "Just do. Knock her up."

Your Bobby balks—he has *some* fucking sense—but your father won't back down. He wants Your Bobby to poke a hole in a condom and he says women don't know what they want—*especially the book-smart ones*—until they get what they want and my palms are sweaty and Your Bobby is watching Caridad and your father shakes his old, sexist head. "Why do you think it's on us to propose? Because if it was up to a *woman* to take action . . . Well, just do something already." He taps his wound vac against the leg of his chair and goes for the jugular, whistling at Caridad, asking if she wants a little cousin and she's a *child*. It's not her fucking decision—it's your body, not hers, not his—and Bobby laughs as if this is funny—it isn't—and your father sighs. "The other night, before you came by, Wonder was in the kitchen baking a casserole for *strangers,* this fellowship nonsense. She's thirty-five years old. She should be baking a casserole for her *family*. Do it tonight. Just put a ring on it or poke a hole in it."

Your Bobby promises to act—what fucking year is it?—and here you come, rounding the corner with your daily booty, your father's fucking scratch tickets. You see them together and you smile—no—and Caridad calls your name and Bobby high-fives your father.

"See you tonight," he says. "Should I bring donuts or bear claws?"

You're too busy playing auntie to Caridad to hear your father grumbling—*Just gimme a grandson already*—and this is *The Handmaid's Tale* and you send Caridad inside to her hungover mother and you aren't a Stepford wife on a shelf waiting for this Neanderthal to buy you and you don't want a baby with him. You always walk to work—you're a writer, you need that time to think—but Your Bobby opens the passenger door for you, as if it's chivalrous, as if he isn't trying to trap you, and your dad wants his scratchers and Bobby wants you in his Beamer and both of those fucking fucks get what they want and finally, your old man goes back inside—I can't help but hope his heart decides enough is enough—and I make a break for it.

By the time I get to Dunkin', your Dunkin' that is *Bobby's* Dunkin', you have turned into someone I don't recognize. There you are, twenty feet away, screaming and screeching. "Bobby, *stop* it!"

I make a fist—I will *stop* it—but no can do. You're not *really* in danger. He's pelting you with Munchkins while you sweep the patio. It's the part of your life you didn't want me to know about, the very worst part. I take advantage of the flirty fucking "fun" you're having and step behind a truck—*all the better to hear you*—and so help me God if the driver blows my cover, but this is who I am—I take risks—and this is who you are—you eat *shit*. You side with him because your life is heavy on the have-to. It's capitalism on crack, your obligation to tell him that you never trusted Kelli, even as he throws a fucking Munchkin at your head and grunts. "Nice of you to say it now, Won."

You are good to him, *too* good, apologizing for giving him space, as if whatever the fuck happened with *Kelli* is anyone's fault but his, and then you pick up your broom. "Life's a bitch," you say. "The fellowship thing I bailed on this week . . . There's this guy . . ."

Me! I'm the guy, but Your Bobby shakes his head like he's the boss of you, which he is, technically. "Don't even. Don't even talk to me about some Ivy League Douchebag. You know better. Those guys always think they're better than you, so fuck 'em, as in *don't* fuck 'em."

He's allowed to leave you for every Nordstrom Rack influencer who comes his way, but you are never allowed to leave him. You tell him he's right, but you speak in that high-pitched tenor we all get when we're telling someone what they want to hear, and then you lower your voice to a whisper, and I crane my neck. *All the better to see you.*

Your Bobby calls you a *nasty girl* and that is wrong—I don't slut-shame, ever—and he's *American* fucking *Hustling* you, lumping me in with *Ivy League Douchebags* as if anything even *happened* between us. He puts his foot down, mashing a perfectly good Munchkin on the patio. "Seriously," he says. "No more influencers for me, no more Ivy League pricks for *you.*"

You laugh—that's a symptom of Stockholm syndrome—and he pokes you with a *cruller* and you take a bite of his cruller, a chunk of my heart, and he pops the rest of it into his mouth and this is the dark side of your people, you Massholes. You are smart. You know that origin stories are prologue, at best. Hell, you're writing a book about becoming your own person, yet here you are being *his* person and why? Because you were born in the same fucking hospital? Because you'd be "faithless" if you went to work at a local place like Black Sheep, where you might acquire skills that would enable you to, gasp, *leave*? Black sheep are brave, but the world is stacked against us, always. It's legal for your family to hold you hostage in a Bobby trap but it would be *illegal* for me to walk across the street and wrap my hand around his neck. Because of him, you *want* to lose faith in me, in you, in us. You want outsiders to be the enemy and look at you, picking up his Munchkins while he's on his phone, ordering groceries for the family feast at your house tonight, ditching Instacart to read new reviews of your "relationship," quoting all the people from your past who think you belong together, the same people who thought Tom Brady was God, the same people who think Bobby is a dead ringer for Al Pacino—nope!—and I want to choke him out right now, in broad daylight, but my phone pings. Glenn.

How's it going at the bike shop?

8

I should be driving Your Bobby's body out to some *Mystic River–*esque swamp, but instead I'm idling in Broadway Bicycle, waiting for a bike that isn't mine.

How do I do it, Wonder?

How do I kill Your Bobby?

The clock is ticking. I remember the day Ethel downloaded Bejeweled Blitz—*I heard games can help you get over writer's block*—and five months later, she wasn't planning an anniversary party for her first book or trying to write another book. She was living for Bejeweled Fucking Blitz—*I got a gem, Joe!*—and that's where you are right now. Bobby is your Bejeweled Blitz and I have to delete him like the soul-killing, time-wasting app that he is and I have to do it now, today. As I stand in this bike shop, your sister is up early, making Jell-O shots for the *shindig* at your place tonight. He's going to propose to you or *poke a hole in it* and I can't spike the Jell-O shots with antifreeze—*you'll be* drinking them—and I can't catch him on your front porch—your dad *lives* on that front porch—and the composting *Ivy League Douchebags* in this place are tapping their feet, hostile and impatient, which only makes me realize why you feel safer with Your Bobby on *your* side of Sesame Street.

Think, Joe, think. I could go the route of the grand gesture, barge into Dunkin' and get down on one knee and remind you that we're in this together. But I can't do that. We haven't even kissed, let alone fucked, and it's not about me. It's about men, the way you think about men. It's all over your fiction, that half-baked, premise-over-prose short story you wrote three years ago, where all men have the same name and play the same game, no matter how different they appear. You think that deep down we're all greedy bastards who don't *really* care about you, the way a Red Sox first baseman becomes a Yankee without a second fucking thought. That's why you haven't texted me. You're telling yourself a story instead of telling yourself the truth, the same way you told *me* a story. You're telling yourself that I'm probably not as wonderful as I seem because who the fuck is? *Everyone's an asshole.*

"Shoddy!"

I answer to the name of another man—bad, bad, bad—and I lug Glenn's *Fuji* past the campus gates, the lawn where we're not sitting together. Undergrads look at me like something's wrong with me, pushing a bike instead of riding it and something *is* wrong with me. I am failing you, Wonder. I turn down Glenn's precious street—I still have no plan—and his electronic doorbell is out of order—of course it is, of course—so I pound my fist on the mahogany as if it's Your Bobby's excessively moisturized face, and here's Glenn, a sausage in spandex, sizing me up like *I'm* the problem. "Oh, drat," he says. "Did you sleep at all? You look like feline vomit."

It's bad writing—I'm not vomit—and he starts apologizing for his "behavior" on "the dark night post-potluck." The omniscient, naïve narcissism of this man, assuming that *the dark night* ended at his house.

My dark night never *ended*. It turned into an all-nighter that turned into another all-nighter that morphed into this morning, into the unbreakable Bobby trap. It's exhausting, dealing with someone dumb enough to think he's smarter than me, and I laugh. "No," I say. "You were fine. I've had a rough week. I'm just tired."

Tired of men getting in my way, treating women like property, and how do I do it, Wonder? How do I fucking kill Your Bobby? "Come on," Glenn says. "Get in here."

It's easy to walk into someone's house when you're invited, but you're not going to invite me to your big family blowout and I can't set the place on fire and Glenn pops open a Powerade. "Thirsty?"

Yes, for Bobby's blood. "No thanks," I say. "And I should get going . . ."

He orders me to have a seat and I clock his Pulitzer on the mantel, and you were right, Wonder. He *does* keep his trophies on display. He hid them during the potluck to seem like someone stronger. "Okay," he says. "Let me guess. I blew smoke up your ass and cast aspersions on your comrades and you felt good. Wired. You sauntered home, fired up to tickle the Apple ivories, and then you hit the wall . . . writer's block."

The phrase is *killer's* block and I nod because a block is a block is a block and the man probably hit a few snags with *Scabies*. "Well, I am a little stuck. Any advice?"

He scratches his head. I want him to stay on topic—me, me, me—but people are people, they want to talk about themselves, so he leans back and sighs. "See," he says. "I don't know if you know how we met . . ." He knows that I know and the Jell-O shots are setting, and you are *nothing* like Sly. "See, the wife and I were in workshop together. It was day one of our first year at Iowa, and we go around the room, and our professor tells Sly that *she's* the genius, the North Star in our galaxy and in the moment, of course, she loves it. Hell, *I* love it because it gives me an excuse to go up to her after class. But for a solid year, the woman can't write, you know? She can *write* but she can't write like she did, because it's like she says now . . . Praise is poison."

He wants me to repeat Sly's alliterative little motto, so I do. "Wow," I say. "That's deep. Praise is poison."

He's lecturing me now. *Praise is poison.* It's true. You're a Goodreads girl and the reviews are in. Everyone wants you to be with Bobby. The easiest trap would be a good old-fashioned Facebook catfish, but even I can't seduce Bobby under *these* circumstances. There's no time.

Glenn picks up his prize. "You wanna hold it?"

Imagine being so desperate for trophies that you want to hold one you didn't earn, and I smile—"I'm good"—but he hands it to me anyway, and I hate that it feels good in my hand, that Glenn knows it, and is this what it's been like for you? Constantly being forced to do what you don't want to do, then hating yourself for almost *liking* it? "Wow," I say. "It's heavy."

I could crack his skull, old school, *Murder, She Wrote* style but then there would be an investigation. *Who killed Bobby? Who had motivation to take him out at this particular moment in his life?* I get a flash of you in some small, gray room, admitting that you spent a little time with someone new recently, someone from school, someone you stood up to be with Your motherfucking Bobby.

"Look," Glenn says, reclaiming his coin. "I don't want you to end up like Sly. Sure, she's published, but she's the first one to say that her book isn't what she wanted it to be. And to this day . . . she blames Reardon, our professor. The genius label was a scarlet G. The pressure killed her spirit, her imagination . . ." That's me, Wonder. *Where is my mind?* Why don't I know how to kill him? "But never mind that," he says. "Point is, now is now. I fucked up and I owe you one, so here."

He throws me a helmet—no—and now I'm holding a helmet—no—and he rubs his hands together. "You need to get out of your head, do something else, challenge yourself in a way that makes you forget all about writing."

I hold on to my helmet. It's a hard object, dense enough to knock Your Bobby out cold, but how would I even get to him? He's probably out buying you a ring. Glenn blinks in that way where I remember what I am, what we are, *autofuckingdidacts*. "Wait," he says. "Do you know how to ride a bike?"

FUCK YOU GLENN and I laugh. "It's like they say . . . You never forget."

"No," he says. "You know it's not that simple. Riding is like writing. You think you know how to do it . . ." I have killed *how* many shitheads like Bobby? "But it's not an inborn skill. You always need to be learning from scratch . . ." This is a new world, Wonder. Your Bobby doesn't have a history of addiction—RIP Phil, RIP Benji—and I have more to lose right now than ever. "See," Glenn says. "Writing is a sport . . . *Life* is a sport . . ." No wonder he won a Pulitzer. The man is right. Of *course* I don't know how to eliminate Your Bobby from the equation. We're not in Kansas and we're not in anonymous New York or sprawling Los Angeles or sleepy Bainbridge or hush-hush Mexico and Your Bobby isn't a runner. I'm not gonna surprise him on a private beach in Little, Isolated Compton.

Glenn flings a pair of *spandex fucking shorts* at me. "Try these."

I say no and he shrugs. "Suit yourself. But nobody ever stole a KOM in jeans."

"What's a KOM?"

He tosses me a spandex shirt. CYCOPATH. That rare moment in life, the right pun at the right time. "Humor me," he says. "Let me help you kill writer's block once and for all, right now, *today*."

An hour later, I am on a bicycle, trailing Glenn, waiting for inspiration to strike. I don't know how to ride a bike, not in the way that Glenn does, but he wants to be my friend and he's trying so hard to care about me, looking over his shoulder—*You alive? You okay?*—and I'm alive, I'm okay, and Glenn says that riding is Zen. It's meditation. It lets the back of your head solve all the problems in your writing, but we've gone six miles and ten feet—fuck you, metric system, no thanks—and I *still* don't know how to do it, Wonder. I don't know how to kill Your Fucking Bobby, the prince to your princess-in-waiting.

Glenn is used to this, he can breathe, so he does all the talking while I bear down and give audience to my "superior," who informs me that KOM is shorthand for King of the Mountain. It's a *Strava* thing, a badge you earn when you set a record. If I wasn't so worried about how to kill Bobby, I could almost enjoy riding with Glenn as he spins the tale of how he became a *cyclist*. He didn't even own a bike in Iowa. That's when he was at his creative best, transcribing Denis Johnson stories by hand while typing the fuck out of *Scabies*. "I *was* Denis Johnson and Denis was *me* and the writing and reading were as one . . . That's how it's done. You read your heroes, and then you write 'em. But then along came the spider that is the business of writing. Pro tip: Reading time is *infinitely* more important than writing time." He spits at the sky like a mourner at his own funeral. "Anyway, Sly says they call it 'skinny fat.'"

I'm too fucking tired for this, but a wingman has no choice. "You're not fat, Glenn."

He sighs like we're above our bodies. "*Scabies* took off and it was champagne and pastries, the book tour, the small talk, 'doing' me instead of *being* me . . . You catch that?"

I'm riding hard to keep up and so help me God if I have a fucking heart attack before I kill Your Bobby. "Doing me, got it!"

"Swell," he says, gliding without sweating. "So Harvard invites me to be here, and I'm hesitant . . . After all, I'm *not* Denis Johnson . . ."

It hurts to lie, but that's the theme of today, all pain, no gain. "Oh, sure you are, Glenn."

"But the wife thought the fellowship would be good for me, grounding . . . And when your feet haven't hit the ground in ages after flying so high, well, here we are stuck in Cambridge . . ." *Stuck.* "I was *too* grounded. I forgot how to write because I talked so much about writing, and I needed to fly . . ." I know, Wonder. This is *just* the sort of thing he should have told us in class to come off like more of a human, but Glenn and I aren't charming fuckwads like Your Bobby— we're better one-on-one—and this is Glenn's life now.

He rides because he can't write. He laughs about that *New York Times* profile on his authorial daily grind, and admits the real deal is hardly *fit for print*. He doesn't wake up every day and *read*. He checks his Strava app, mostly to keep tabs on his "enemy," a man named Kilroy. Kilroy designs a course. The app honors him with a *KOM* and our professor dons his spandex suit to *steal* that fucking KOM. It's Tom and Jerry for wealthy white men with too much time on their hands, wives they need to avoid in order to preserve what's left of the marriage. The saddest part is that Glenn doesn't even fucking *know* this Kilroy guy and I can't take it anymore. I won't die in these woods.

I call a time-out and Glenn's enjoying this, Wonder, the sight of me, the lesser man, panting, knees wobbling, hoping like hell that I don't puke on my shoes.

"It's not about Kilroy as a person," he says, as if my ailments are unworthy of discourse. "I'm just *using* Kilroy to bring out the best in myself. Just another Denis Johnson, see."

He shows me his phone, his latest KOM, and it's flashbacks to Ethel—*I got a gem, Joe!*—and now I really do puke, and you'd think I would have a flash of inspiration, but nope. I'm still stuck. Still no clue how to kill Your Bobby. He grabs his helmet. "You good, Joe?"

No, I'm not *good*. "You bet."

So now we're riding again and I'm getting nowhere—*How do I get Your Bobby alone?*—and Glenn turns his head to check on me. "You okay back there?"

My legs are going to fall off but I give him a thumbs-up and he brakes. "Well, I'm not. Snack time."

Thank fucking *God* and he offers me a *Quest* bar and we are two men in the woods. The bar is chewy and warm, and I don't want this to be my fucking *life*. I want to be with you. But if Bobby disappears tonight, on the heels of his proposal, people will ask questions. They will wonder about the king of your mountain. Where's Bobby? Is he okay?

"You okay, Joe?"

I swallow a lump of gas-inducing protein powder. "Well, this is helping a *lot* . . ." You have to give an apple to the teacher, especially when he's stuck on his second book and his wife has no use for him.

Glenn drinks water from the straw attached to the pouch on his back. "Stealing a KOM is the same as writing, Joe. It's a battle for control."

I don't want to control you and I like it when the words flow on their own, but I nod. "I get it."

"Do you know much about Roald Dahl?"

I'm a writer, you asshole. I know all about Roald Fucking Dahl. "Probably not as much as you."

"Well, he's a good example of the interplay between control and process. We're men . . ." No shit, Glenn. "We're writers. We want to be in control all the time . . ."

I have never tried to control anyone in my entire life. I have only tried to help people make good decisions. "Absofuckinglutely."

"Roald Dahl wanted to write about that chocolate factory. He only *climbed* that mountain when he confronted issues in his life that were beyond his control. His kids were sick. Science was failing them. The book was in him all along, but the book never would have made it to the page if his kids hadn't gotten sick. One of them even died, poor guy."

I know what's going on in his head. He's comparing himself to Roald Dahl, wishing his wife would get sick, wishing they had some child who would fall ill, knowing deep down that all this KOM hunting is an act of procrastination. I feel bad for Glenn, Wonder. I really do. He peels a twig. "I don't really remember what 'inspired' me to write *Scabies*. Inspiration is blurry, and we live in this time where everyone wants excruciating high-def clarity but then you remember that *all* writers look around at the world and think . . . 'I have to make something out of this mess, out of my pain, my life, out of the Denis Johnson that made me who I am.' That's the great tradition, the writer's burden, the writer's *gift*."

Something in his little lecture set off a spark in the Walden Woods of my mind and the clouds of self-doubt parted. I got it, Wonder. I know how to kill Your Bobby, and it must be all over my face because Glenn is staring at me.

"What's with you?" he says.

"I think I figured out how to fix the scene in my manuscript."

Something like a teardrop forms in his eye and yes, praise is poison. I have *one* minor theoretical victory—my brainstorm for killing Bobby is only in my head, there's no body yet, no book—but already Glenn is sick with envy. More stuck than his wife, so paralyzed by success that he's out here on a fucking bicycle envying his unpublished "protégé." I feel for the guy, bound to go down as a one-hit *wonder*, and he doesn't care about Sly the way that I care about you. He's like most people, he doesn't have that kind of love in him.

But I do.

9

*C*harlie and the Chocolate Factory was published in 1964 and we're still talking about it today because Roald Fucking Dahl cracked the code of people. He knew how to kill off *children*! He turned them into caricatures and killed them softly, off the page, and it's a magic trick. Millions of readers climb into that book and identify with Charlie—ha—and they go and encourage their *children* to be like Charlie—double ha—when the reality is both ugly and undeniable.

Most people are flawed. They're not *Charlie*. They're Mr. Dahl or Veruca Fucking Salt.

And how did he do it, Wonder? How did he kill off those terrible, irredeemable children? Easy-peasy. He used his fucking *factory*, his house. Houses kill people in a myriad of ways because all houses are booby traps. I know from personal, harrowing experience that houses can fucking kill. Hell, the woman I mistook for the love of my life met her end when she fell down the stairs in *our* house. RIP Mary Kay

DiMarco was stubborn. Making like Tom Cruise in *Risky Business* and wearing socks on hardwood floors. There was no investigation into her death because the proof was in the pudding—socks meet floors, floors meet stairs, skull meets concrete—but Mary Kay DiMarco did not die in vain.

She is an angel *on our shoulders*. Because of her, I figured out how to kill Your Bobby—he's gonna fall down the stairs—but don't fret, my jealous darling Wonder. You helped, too.

You wrote a short story called "Lost Marbles." I found it online after we first met, and the story is set in Bobby's aunt Ro's house, the one where he now lives. You offered me vivid, useful descriptions of the house:

> She hoarded everything, long-expired tin cans of coffee in the cabinet "just in case," and she collected end tables, end tables topped with bowls of marbles. It was the chicken and the egg in real life. Did she buy the tables so that she would have a place to put the marbles or did she buy the marbles so that she would need all those rickety folding tables?

Even in your early writing, you were coming to terms with being raised in a trap. Ro left the house to her "favorite nephew" and Your Bobby *uses* the house as fodder for Instagram—*big-box TV, God bless ya, Ro*—and you and countless other women see Bobby as a sentimental fool because he hasn't changed a *thing* about the house since Ro passed away. He gripes about *the dryer from hell* and the *world's worst wallpaper* and fact-check, Wonder! He isn't "sentimental." He's a sexist bastard who expects *you* to renovate when he gets tired of stringing you along and invites you to move in with him.

And here's another fact-check: Bobby's brother and sister don't think of him as a sentimental fool. To Mick and Ginnie Your Bobby is a greedy stubborn prick.

For a long time now Mick and Ginnie have wanted Bobby to sell Ro's house. Yes, once upon a time, the Skellys were a donut fucking dynasty, your heroes across the street who sponsored Little League teams, opening one store after another. But times change. It's like Mick screamed a couple years ago on Facebook: FUCKING AVO-CADO TOAST?! WHAT NEXT? The Skelly family business has been sliding ever since Dunkin' dropped the Donuts. They've closed stores, openly yearned for the times when it was *Here's your coffee, here's your cruller, now go fuck your mother and come back tomorrow!*

Bobby's sister, Ginnie, projects positivity to the *Globe* when asked about rising costs at their central bakery, but the real estate records tell the story of a dynasty crumbling. Mick sold his lake house in New Hampshire and Ginnie's family downsized, but what has Prince Bobby done to help the family?

Nothing.

Aunt Ro's house is a cash cow, but Bobby won't fucking milk it. Mick posts the Zillow link to Ro's three-bedroom raised ranch in Braintree three, sometimes four times a week—*Ideal teardown for a family!*—and Ginnie is in all caps realtor mode—*PRICE REDUC-TION! BE THE LUCKIEST FAMILY AND BUY THIS LAND! IT'S A STEAL!*—but Your Bobby has the keys to that castle, and He. Won't. Sell.

It's like writing, isn't it? You obsess and you brainstorm and you turn to your "mentor" for advice, and in the end, the solution is sim-ple: Use his family to drag him away from you.

So I did it. I channeled my inner Casey Affleck and I called Mick and told him that his brother is *pissing me off* because I want to buy that house in Braintree but I haven't even gotten to *see it* because Bobby's giving me the runaround and *I'm leaving town tomorrow*. I was good—David O. Russell wouldn't cut me out of his fucking movie—and Mick called his *flaky* brother and demanded that Your Bobby leave your house to come to Ro's house as in his house as in *this* house.

Yes, I get here first, and I pick up the fake rock on the side lawn and here's the key and I'm in—mothballs and marbles—and it's a PTSD-inducing doozy, the way this house even *smells* like the Bainbridge Public Library. I pick up a bowl of marbles and I am in your fiction, the words on the page inspired by the first and worst part of your life. I open the door to the basement and POW—kitty litter and Pine-Sol and man sweat, *Bobby* sweat—and you should have called your story "The Damp," but I know, titles are hard. I set up marbles on the steps that lead to the concrete floor, and this is a writer's life. We take the terrible things that happened to us, and we pour them into our art.

Your Bobby could arrive any minute—assholes in foreign cars drive like assholes in foreign cars—so I cross the basement and open the barrel of the old dryer, the one Bobby waxes nostalgic about on his fucking Instagram. He's got a load in there and I toss some marbles *in* the dryer. I push the button and I leap backward because holy fucking shit, Wonder.

That beast is roaring and will I be collateral damage in my selfless quest to set you free?

I crouch behind old cardboard boxes—another fucking fire hazard, this house is a death trap—and no. The dryer won't explode, not now. Things are going my way because I put in the work. Cherish already defriended Bobby on Facebook—that was fast—and I'm in charge of this house. I've pulled the strings and laid down the marbles and this is how Roald Dahl felt when he was executing those children off the page, in the recesses of the factory. The house will kill Your Bobby, not me. It's like that nurse said when I was sitting by Mary Kay's coma bed.

People relax when they're at home. People fall down the stairs. It's not your fault.

Bless all nurses, and the ceiling above me that is the floor below Bobby's feet is rattling and this is it. He's here.

The future is so close I can taste it. Your Bobby will hear the dryer acting up—nobody runs a janky old appliance to impress a fucking buyer—and he'll rush to the stairs, oblivious to the marbles that wait for him like snakes in the grass. *Crunk.* Blood spills and his phone flies across the floor and it's like reading a book, when you're so sucked into the story that the future is speeding and before you know it you are *in* the fucking future because we made it, Wonder. Your Bobby heard the call of the dryer, and he is slipping on the marbles on the stairs and he is tumbling and there it is.

Crunk.

For a beat I don't move. The dryer is so loud that I can't hear him—Is he gasping? Is he gurgling?—and I can't shut the dryer *off* because Mary Kay survived the fall—it's very hard to kill someone, even when you're a house with a concrete fist—but I can't stay here forever, and it's just like Stephen King says in *On Writing.* If you wait for inspiration to strike, for everything to be perfect, you'll never get anywhere.

Gently, Joseph, and I stand, still squatting, really half-standing. I see him now, still as Mary Kay but oh that's right. She didn't die right away. Houses sometimes kill slowly, sinister motherfuckers.

I walk through the basement—so not a *cellar*—sidestepping giant topless storage boxes of broken coffee machines and I *can see clearly now, the rain is gone.* He's out cold and one of his legs is going in the wrong direction as blood trickles from his head onto his hair, onto the floor.

He was probably holding his phone when he pounded down those stairs—so *not* a Charlie thing to do—and the phone is about a foot away from him. Cracked.

I give it a little *push* with my right foot in case he wakes up and reaches.

It's a tragic world for people who live alone, and when the cops find him and he's on Channel 5 news, the newsies will remind people who live alone to be careful. I'm breathing again—I did it—and what a relief. A tiny naysaying part of me was worried that I was wrong about you, that you loved him and would come here with him tonight.

But you didn't—take *that,* inner self-doubting fucking critic—and I feel his wrist for a pulse—still ticking, just like Mary Kay—but she only hung on because I loved her, because her daughter loved her (sort of). Love can't save Bobby. He never loved you or anyone. Bobby was a player and Stevie Nicks was dreaming—"players" don't love *anyone* when they're playing—and he only played Ro's favorite so that she would cut his brother and sister out of her will.

Real estate, Wonder. It turns people into monsters.

Outside of the house, all quiet on the crabgrass front and I remember the end of "Lost Marbles": *Lo thought about leaving, about having a garage sale and selling off all the old TVs, the 1987 calendars, and the broken coffeepots. But every day, there were more reasons to hold on to the past than there were to let go. Maybe someday she would see that the past was holding on to her, but not today.*

I gave your story the epilogue you wanted. You'll never know I was here, your most *faithful* reader, the one who gave you the ending you never thought you'd have, the kind that feels like a beginning. And that's perfect. I don't live for compliments. All I want to do with my work, with my writing, is touch you, my faithful reader, and I have done that. I changed your life with my imagination, with my hands, with my heart.

Your city is growing on me, Wonder. The second I slid the key back into that rock, something clicked. Without Your Bobby in the way, it feels different here. Compact. Charming. Maybe when your dad sees you with me, maybe when it's *me* on that porch, maybe he'll evolve. I hit a backup on Mass Ave and spot that billboard in the rearview mirror—*If you lived here, you'd be home now*—and I could do that, Wonder. I could live here with you, not in your fucking *two-family*, but in my place.

I send a text to Glenn—*You really helped me today, thanks G*—and he gets right back to me—*Good. Ride again tomorrow? You mind picking up coffee?*—and I don't mind. It's really hitting me now. I did it, Wonder. Cherish is vague screaming on Facebook—*When people show you who they are, believe them*—and I don't mind getting coffee for Glenn. Your

Bobby is gone and I'm a writer, I really am, and I made it. I live here. I am a Harvard fucking *fellow* and I don't have a shitty job to worry about. I'm free for the first time in my life, and it was hard. I was in a bad way when I lost Mary Kay, but there she was today, in the ether, guiding me like an angel.

What a thing. Life. I wouldn't have thought to set a booby trap on the stairs if I never lost Mary Kay. It's like Glenn said. Inspiration is blurry. The best you can do is learn from your hard knocks and keep writing, keep living. I know how to be with you, Wonder. I don't want to rush things. I don't even want to see you until workshop on Tuesday. It's better for us both if we nurture our fellowship before we jump into a relationship.

I take the long way home, smiling at people when they smile at me, and when is the last time I was so relaxed? He's gone, Wonder. He's really gone.

Miracles beget miracles—I find a spot on a side street—and I'm walking and wait . . . am I whistling? Yes, I'm fucking *whistling.* I turn a corner and I love Cambridge, the way the average Joe *might* just be smarter than me, but are any of these confident, ID-card-carrying fuckers intellectually self-sufficient enough to pull off what I just did in Braintree? Doubtful.

My toe catches the pavement. That's you. You're on my street and you're on my stoop and no—I just *killed* your fucking Bobby—and you see me, and you know I see you, you and a *Box O' Joe.*

My fresh new confidence drips through the soles of my sneakers— tell me I didn't step in Bobby's blood—and I know nothing about life, about writing, about women. All I know is that you don't fucking belong here, not right now.

"Hi," you say. "Is this weird?"

I t's not weird. It's *Wonder*ful in theory. You're here. On a Friday, just in time for the weekend, hoping that you can have me back, wanting me to know that I am more than your *fellow*. But you're here by default. You're here because I trapped Your Bobby in Ro's basement and it's too much, too soon. Your impish smile, as if you enjoyed having me on the back burner and we're not in the clear just yet. He's only been "away from his phone" for eighty minutes or so and it takes a long time to die from a head injury but there's no way you could know what I did.

Could you?

You throw your arms around me. "I missed you."

I was being paranoid—you don't know—but I don't like you like this, talking for two, sputtering words because of my awkward silence, as if you alone can get us where we need to be. You're forthcoming but you're not, rolling your eyes that it's been a *total freaking shit show* with your family, and you can't use the f-word when it's not about family.

You fucked another man. You chose Your Bobby over me. "Can we go inside?"

It's all I want, but you iced me out, you bailed on me and, you fed your Tony casserole to *him,* to Bobby. You put the onus on me—*I kinda thought I'd hear from you*—and it's a miracle I don't explode—I dealt with Your Bobby and you're not even my girlfriend—and I remind you that you blew me off, but you shrug—*it was just a stupid party*—and you know that's not true—*we're in this together*—and you wave the white flag. "I'm sorry, okay? I had family stuff and . . ."

You nod at my door and I guess we're doing this. I lead the way in—this is wrong, you weren't supposed to be here, not yet, not now— and the key jams in the door—I'm still shaking, he's dying in a basement—and you put a hand on my shoulder. You squeeze.

"I really am sorry."

The lock gives and I follow you up the stairs and if I was done with Your Bobby, if I knew for a fact that he was dead, I could enjoy this, the way you slide your phone into your back pocket, guiding my eyes to your ass.

You step aside and I unlock the next door and you groan. "Okay," you say. "I can't take it anymore."

You don't have to. He's dead. Almost. "Take what?"

"Joe, come on . . ." You look around. "Wait, do you have a roommate?"

It's an insult. I'm a man, a *Harvard* man. I snarl. "No, I don't have a *roommate.*"

You fold your arms. "You're still mad at me."

You sit on my couch like you own the place, like it's your right to put your flip-flops on my coffee table, and I'm not mad at you. I'm mad for you. Things have changed, Wonder. I've seen the pages of your life that you hid because you lacked the courage to burn them. I know that you chose Bobby over me, over your *career.* I can't show you *my* secret pages or let you know that I read yours. You'd be so embarrassed about what you wrote that you would cover your shame and cast aspersions at me. But you made a good choice today and Bobby is (almost) a part of the past, and I do love your eyes roaming over my walls. "I can't imagine living alone."

I can't imagine living with my dad and you size up my jukebox—you clearly don't approve—and I check my shoes for blood—clean—and I pick out two mugs—did I leave a mug of piss at Your Bobby's?—and I open the fridge. No, I didn't take a piss in his house, and I grab the cream and head back to the small excuse of a *sitting room*. You take the cream and you whistle. "Whole Foods," you say. "In my house it's just freaking Hood."

"It's a misconception."

Okay, so that was a little snooty of me, and I offer you a cup from the Box O' Joe.

You take it, and you thank me. And then you speak. "Okay, so what's a misconception?"

"Whole Foods cream isn't that expensive. It's not that Omega stuff with the cow on the label and it's not some kind of indulgence."

You put the cream down. Silence. "I'm sorry, okay?"

I can't stay mad at you, and I pick up the cream. "Me, too."

You cozy up on my couch, laughing at my Ben Affleck mug, amused when I tell you that it was a gift from old friends, Blythe the writer and Ethan the kickball coach, and you ask about them like you care, like you are starved for new humans, for a new life. I did the right thing and I'm happy but then I remember you on the patio with Your Bobby.

Ivy League pricks.

You kick off your flip-flops and put your feet back on my table. "Is this okay?"

"It's okay."

"Do you wish I would go away?"

I wish you would have come here last night. "You know I don't want you to go away."

You study all the Bens on your mug, and you look around my

apartment like a writer, like there's this secretary in your mind making notes. I have to tread lightly. We've talked about your family, but as far as you know, I don't know anyone by the name of Bobby Fucking Skelly.

"Did you paint that?"

I follow your eyeline to an abstract portrait of RIP Mary Kay. It's just the sort of thing I would have taken down if I'd had time to prepare, a piece of art by my almost ex-wife's fucking daughter, whom I barely speak to anymore. "My friend's daughter."

"Your 'friend' . . ."

You're projecting. You assume that because you have Your Bobby, I have some equivalent, but I'm not like you, Wonder. I cut cords. I shed my past by giving the people I used to know new names, same way you do when you write a fucking book. "Natalie is like a niece."

"But she's not your actual niece?"

"She's my friend's daughter."

"And we're back to the friend . . ."

Sometimes I wish I didn't perpetually fall for smart, intuitive women, but such is life. I tell you about "Monica," about my last "big relationship."

"You were *married*?"

"Well, we had the reception, but we never made it official."

"Ah," you say. "Kevin Youkilis went through something like that."

I bet his "wife" didn't fall down the stairs and *die* and I carry on with my sob story, I tell you that Mary Kay was married when we met, that her sad sack husband died, and then I get to the end. "We'd only been married for a minute and she and Natalie had a fight and things got out of hand. Monica slipped and fell and . . ."

You plant your hand on your chest. "No."

It's the first time I've said it all out loud—Ethel didn't want to hear about my past—and I don't mean to cry. I don't *want* to cry, but the tears don't care. You beg me to let it out, and this has to be a mistake—I am crying in front of you, on you—and you stroke my head and rock me.

"It's okay," you say. "All families are the same."

It's that word again. *Family*. The real fucking *f-word*. It shouldn't be like this with you. Mary Kay *made* a family, but you're not her. Your family is the least interesting part of your life, the part you didn't ask for, the people who got here before you. I pull away from you. I want to fuck you. I want to go so deep that you forget about your f-word on Sesame Street and I want to be your f-word, the one who comes first. I'm not myself. Adrenaline crashing from Your Bobby, rising because of your body.

"Look," you say. "You know that I wanted to be at that party, but some stuff went down at my house and . . . No. I'm not gonna freaking bullshit you."

You hang your head and hide your face in your hair. This is it. You're gonna tell me that you fucked him. That you love Your Bobby best. Cradle to the grave. "What is it, Wonder?"

"You know how there's a difference between an excuse and the truth? Just now, I was gonna give you the excuse. Yes, some stuff went down with my family. That's 'true' but the *truth* is . . . I'm not used to this."

"Harvard's strange for me, too."

"No," you say. "I'm talking about *you*. I'm not used to wanting to be with someone. I freaked out when I realized how excited I was to see you, how I probably sounded crazy to you with all my 'we're in this together' stuff."

"You were fine."

"'Fine'? I dragged you to a freaking *hospital* and I don't know . . . I got scared. I like you and that's hard for me, so I wimped out."

You're too shy to look at me and who could blame you? Your Bobby dumps you when you get too close, so you make him jealous by giving yourself over to *Ivy League Douchebags*. You met me at Harvard.

You think I'm one of them, and I can't win you over by telling you I'm not like that. I have to show you. "Okay," I say. "Well, here's my deal. I 'freaked out' a little when you didn't show up at Glenn's, but the *truth* is that it only made me realize how much I wanted you to be there because I . . . I like you, too."

You get up and sit on the table and you are facing me. You emanate strength, as if every fiber of your being is closer to ideal because of me and you ask me what's so funny and I tell you that you remind me of Jennifer Beals in *Flashdance,* part welder, part dancer, all muscle, and you call me crazy. You're not "pretty like that."

I run my hands over your legs. Hard. Thick. Perfect. "This is also true."

You raise your eyebrows at me. "This is how you woo me? You tell me I'm not pretty?"

"Pretty is everywhere. What you are is rare. You aren't just beautiful. You're full of beauty and even if I couldn't see you, I would feel it."

You don't need to tell me Bobby never said anything like that to you, that the Ivy League bastards and the townie keno players went with *sexy* or *smokin'*. You're on top of the world, on top of me, and I slip a hand under your shirt, but you flinch, so I stop. *Push, pull.* You latch onto my hair and you tug, but you don't want my hands on your skin, not yet. *Push, pull.* I obey the boundaries as you set them—we are in this together—and your hands find my torso—push—and I yank my shirt over my head and you grab your shirt to cover up—pull—and you can reach into my pants, but I can't reach into yours. It's eighth-grade basement hot and I feel the wheels turning in your head as if they're inside of me—you want to be my Madonna and you're afraid to be a whore and one minute you know I'm different—those are your fingers under my jeans—but the next minute you're not so sure—those are your fingers retreating—and you bite my ear and stroke the side of my head. You purr. "Can we go in the bedroom?"

If I say yes, you might *freak* out on me again, treat me like shit to beat me to the punch. If I say no, I don't get to be with you, and you might *freak* out on me because you feel rejected, because what hot-blooded man says no to you?

"Wonder, I want to do what *you* want to do."

You bang your head against my bare chest and feel the beads of sweat that you drew with your push, your pull. You tell me that you want me, but you worry because we are fellows.

I tickle your chin. "So what?"

"So, if it doesn't work out, we're stuck in that room and then what?"

Not possible. "Well, it's like you said. We're fellows. We'll be adults."

You climb off my lap and okay. You want to take it slow. I can do that. I put on my shirt and pick up the remote. "Do you wanna watch a movie?"

"You're not mad?"

"Wonder, I'm in no rush. I mean it. I'm just happy you're here."

It's the *truth*—the sex will be even hotter after Bobby's burial—and I turn on the TV and picture you clinging to me in a cemetery, celebrating his exodus by mauling me in the back of a limousine on the way home. Slow is good and Bobby has the home field advantage—you probably lost your virginity to him in the eighth fucking grade—and you only recently had sex with him. The more I think about that asshole stringing you along, having you whenever he wants, having the nerve to call *me* the douchebag, the more I know it really is for the best that we take it slow, that we stay in middle school for now.

And then you grasp my thigh. "Joe."

II

I could have lasted longer—push, pull takes a lot out of a guy— but our first time was good. Feral and free. You're satisfied and slaphappy, and you murmur that you didn't know it could be like this, *so special,* and it feels like a line, like the kind of thing you think men want to hear, but it's okay. We all grab on to clichés as we fall in love with someone new. Falling is drowning. It's scary to be so certain of what we want, devoid of "wonder," and it's gonna be a good long life. I'm hardly a great wordsmith after I come, so I keep it short—*Same to you, Won*—and it's over. I'm better than Bobby. I could feel it in your fingernails, in your voice. You love me even though it's too soon and you graze my nipple with your fingers. "Can I overexplain myself to you so you fully get why I didn't show up at the potluck?"

No. Bobby's dead (probably). We're in this together and it doesn't matter. "Of course."

You turn sideways and oh God, you really are full of beauty. "You ever know someone where you wish you could grab them and just freaking *make* them do the right thing?"

Yes, I told you about Mary Kay, but that was before you and I had sex. You can't expect me to listen to you pout about Your Fucking Bobby right *now*. "I know the type."

"Well, my brother is kind of like that."

"I thought you had a sister."

You shrug. "Bobby . . . he's like my brother."

That's a certain kind of asshole, the guy who claims he can't commit to you because you're more like a sister, and I nod. "But he's not your actual brother."

"*Anyway*," you say. "He's Bobby, Bobby Skelly, and he grew up across the street from me and his family actually owns the Dunkin' where I work . . ."

You're building a defense and I nod. "Okay."

"He's my best friend in the whole freaking world, seriously, best friends since birth."

Infants aren't capable of friendship and you can't be best friends with someone who fucks with your head for your entire adolescent "adult" life, but I tell you he sounds great, that I can't *wait* to meet him. Ha!

"So, we're getting ready for the potluck and he barges in and he's a wreck. His girlfriend dumped him . . ." You say that like it's the first time he's done this to you. "The backstory is that everyone has always wanted us to end up together . . ." Tough luck, fuckers. "And nobody understands why we haven't settled down. He's the best guy, never comes over without a gift for Caridad . . ." How brave, buying affection with an AmEx. "He's got the biggest heart, and he will sacrifice *anything* for family . . ." ANYTHING EXCEPT RO'S FUCKING HOUSE. "In a parallel universe, we'd be married with two kids by now . . ." I obliterated the parallel universe. It's gone. Poof! "But that's never gonna happen because between you and me . . ." He's dead. "He's gay."

Gay? No. Your Bobby's not *gay*. "Gay?"

You blink at me like I'm some kind of homophobe and I tell you I'm just confused—"You said everyone wants you guys to get married"—and you are snippy with me—"That's why they call it the closet"—and I saw Your Bobby. You sat on his lap on Facebook and I watched your father put the pressure on him and oh God . . . oh no. How could I be so stupid? Facebook is fake news, and I killed him for *nothing* and it's the worst fucking plot twist of all time. You squirm. "Do you have an issue with people who put off their own happiness to keep their family ties in order? Because he's my best freaking friend and you don't even know him."

I HAVE AN ISSUE WITH KILLING THE WRONG MAN. "Wonder, sorry. I'm just . . . Are you sure? . . . Is he maybe . . . Is he bi?"

"First of all, no. Bobby likes dudes. Second of all, if you ever tell anyone what I'm telling you—"

I KILLED HIM FOR NOTHING. "You don't have to worry about that."

"Okay," you say. "So my dad and my sister aren't the sharpest tools in the shed, they see what they want to see. They are clueless. Bobby's family on the other hand . . . Oof, his brother and his sister are total homophobes. But—"

"There is no *but*. That alone is reason enough for him to cut them out of his life."

"Joe, between the two of 'em, they have five kids. Bobby loves those kids and those kids love Bobby and if Bobby comes out . . ."

"Bye bye, kids."

Bye bye, me if you find out what I did and it's not fair. Let his hate-mongering *family* go to prison. I'm not a homophobe and I'm a *Harvard* man—I should be the sharpest tool in town—and you're a Harvard woman—you should have been honest with me about Your Bobby.

I have to save him, assuming he's not dead—is he dead?—and you touch my arm. "Hello?"

"Sorry. I was just thinking how sad it is, your best friend trapped in hell." In a basement in Braintree, dying. His marbles of blood pooling on the hard, cold floor.

"Right," you say. And you flop down, flat on your back, and sigh. "And it's all my fault."

Yes, it is. "No, it isn't."

"Let me say this. He uses me to assure his family that he's not Priding out on them anytime soon. And I use him to make every guy I meet jealous. It's embarrassing and terrible and I can't believe I'm telling you this."

YOU SHOULD HAVE TOLD ME BEFORE! "Well, what's it like when you get involved with someone? I mean in the past . . . when you got serious with someone."

You sit up straight and pull your knees into your chest. "I don't. I've never . . . I mean you know my situation. I never left home, never had my own place, so that makes it easy to stay single. My sister says I'm a bad picker. Hell, *Bobby* says I'm a bad picker. And they're right . . ."

Until now.

You wanted to wait until we hooked up to show me what makes you you, and your story is like most stories. You change *one* thing about one character and it alters the whole landscape and you finally did it, Wonder. You picked me, and I'm yours but we have a Skelly in the closet in the basement and I don't know how to fix it. Is he dead?

You shake your head. "I can't believe I'm telling you all this . . ."

I tell you it's just the kind of stuff I want to know—WHY DIDN'T YOU TELL ME ABOUT HIM BEFORE?—and you're feeling up the books on my nightstand—oh God, oh yes, and oh, oh *Braintree*. You belong here. But because of your senseless omission, your best friend might be dead and we don't have the luxury to segue into a big fucking talk about *Faulkner*.

I am panicking and you are talking to me about things I already know—Ro's house, the pressure on Your Bobby to sell—and I have to get out of here. I have to think positive—he was alive when I left—but he took a bad fall and if you lose him, you won't come back from it. I don't want that for you, Wonder. You're not sick and strong and young like Nomi. You won't bounce back by painting abstract fucking portraits of him and is this some pseudo-Christmas parable where we're fucked because we fucked? Is he already dead?

Unacceptable. All of it. I have to save you, which means I have to save him. And maybe on some level I *did* sense the good in him because I didn't pick up his head and bash it into the cement floor.

"So, did you hear from him yet?"

"Nah," you say. "My sister's pissed that he walked out on the party to go see some guy who wants to buy his aunt's house . . . but it's like I said to you, it's just a party . . . Cherish flips her lid on Bobby, but he always comes back."

Not this time he doesn't—does he?—and *I'm* the one who lost my fucking marbles. I can't leave you in this bed and waltz back into Ro's *house*. I set a booby trap. I need a Good Samaritan to step in and help. I need you to get the fuck away from me, even if only for three minutes.

"Hey," I say. "Wanna take a shower?"

You blush and you're on your feet, but first you want to call Bobby and you say that like it's a thing you can do, like his cell phone isn't cracked and out of his reach and if you call him and it rings, if he crawls across the floor, if he noticed me before he passed out, I'm a dead man. *Gently, Joseph.* I wrap you in my arms. "Bobby can wait"— can he?—"I *really* want to get in the shower with you . . ."

I win and we walk into my bathroom and you turn on the water and you strip and arch your back and the water hits your face and your breasts and my bathroom is *Flashdance* and life is cruel.

"Hang on," I say. "I'm gonna grab some bodywash."

I make a run for the kitchen and dig up the just-in-case-shit-goes-south burner phone I bought. You're calling me—*Joe! Come on!*—and I'm calling 9-1-1—*My nosy kid looked in a storm window and swears he saw a guy out cold in a basement*—and they're sending an ambulance and am I too late? Is he dead?

"Joe! Forget the freaking bodywash and get in here!"

I don't *have* any fucking bodywash so I snag a can of whipped cream and hightail it to the shower. "Oh," you say. "So that's what you meant by 'bodywash.'"

The floor of the tub is *Slippery When Wet* and the whipped cream is going sour and I've never gone down on you and I'm not doing it right because I *can't* do it right—Is he dead? Did I kill him?—and again you turned me into something I am not, the murderer of an innocent man. You pat my head and tell me that you don't always enjoy oral—nice try, honey—and we're out of the shower and we're toweling off, we're throwing on clothes and you're doing what any girl would do when her new boyfriend fails to get her off in the fucking shower.

You're reaching for your phone. One new voicemail.

My hands shake so much that I can't zip my fly. "Who is it?"

You hurl your phone at your purse and fight with your flip-flops and I ask if everything's okay and you snap. "Where are your keys?"

"Wonder, what happened?"

"Just tell me where they are!"

I point at the coffee table and you grab the keys and tell me that you're driving and I ask you again—"What's wrong?"—and you tell me you had a voicemail from South Shore Hospital.

"Bobby's in the emergency room."

"Is he okay?"

"Joe, obviously I don't know anything. Where's your freaking car?"

When we get to my Tesla you take the wheel—this is *your* town, not mine—and you drive like a Masshole. No turn signals, no regard for life, and we are in this *together*. I almost hope that we do die in a wreck because if Bobby is dead, I murdered a man who didn't deserve to die, and yet if Bobby is alive . . . if he saw me . . .

"Okay," you say. "Fuck it. I'm leaving the car here."

That's not allowed—it's a drop-off for the ER—but there's no point in reasoning with you and your love is fierce, potent. You want to see Your Bobby and you want to see him *now* and no *freaking* gatekeeper is going to stop you and we're here. We're in the trauma wing and it's a quiet night and you pull one curtain—old lady asleep—and you pull another—a woman and her expectant wife—and all I can do is think of us, that we might not get to grow old together and then you pull a third sheet and this is it.

"Bobby."

He blinks. He coughs. He lives.

Your hands are all over him, as if your touch can heal his elevated leg, clear the dried blood from his scalp. And it's a good thing that your *tendency is to love*. It gives me time to breathe. I did it. The EMTs got there in time, and this isn't Mary Kay Revisited. Mr. Macy's survived. His marbles are intact and broken legs heal and we're in the clear, but then he glances at me. Our first eye contact. His pupils are dilated—painkillers—or is it something worse? Does he know it was me? Are those the eyes of a man faced with his assailant?

"Wonder," he says. "I know who did this to me."

12

"Okay," you say. "Tell me who did this to you. I'm calling the cops."

I am nervous. Ghostly and ghastly. He knows who did this—I did this—and he pushes the gadget for morphine and you are patient. "Take your time."

But time isn't the issue. There are three of us in this room. Your Bobby pushes the button on another gadget and is he calling a nurse? Will he wait until the nurse arrives to point his finger at me? I was there. I did it. And I didn't commit a hate crime. I did a *stupid* crime like some idiot on *Cops*. Your Bobby smacks his lips, and you hold his hand and there is no world in which you would ever forgive me.

"My fucking bookie," he says. "I owe him, and I knew this was coming."

I am off the hook—yay!—and you blast him—*You told me you stopped gambling*—and he blasts you right back—*I got screwed by a guy who hit a flush on the river*—and it is quite a thing to witness, you and Your Bobby sparring like Greek fucking gods armed with lightning bolts, words. You want him to sic the police on Griff and you call it his "civic duty." Bobby is gruff—*Here we go again, Wonder living in a fantasy*—and what a blessing for me at this early stage in our relationship, a front-row ticket to the show, a chance for a close read of your love language. You make your demands—*You are pressing charges*—and I close the curtain. I keep quiet. Bobby pushes back—*Who's gonna give me a seat at the table if I rat out Griff? Find me a game. You can't! I fucked up. I got beat up so now I pay up. That's it.*

You know I am listening, and you liked it better when the story was yours to edit, when Bobby was all victim, and this is where you have a lot to learn about people, about character. Until now, you stayed in the shallow end, you never let anyone get close enough to wrap your heart up in clover.

I pull the curtain and put my hand on your shoulder. I speak in my voice, the non-Affleck voice I was born with, the one Bobby doesn't know. "I know I have no business saying anything, but Bobby makes a good point, Wonder . . ."

Bobby doesn't recognize my voice, I'm sure of it, the way he nods. "Yes, I do."

"You don't want to piss off a bookie."

"Thank you," he says. "A voice of reason!"

Bobby knows what he has in me, a comrade, a realist, a friend. Before we leave, he shakes my hand. "I like this kid," he says. "Joe's different."

We're in a good place, Wonder. We're at my place—you stayed over Friday, and then again last night—and Your Bobby is on the mend, out of the hospital and back home at RIP Aunt Ro's. His misfortune was our Krazy Glue, and we are in this together now more than ever, more than we would be if he'd never fallen down those stairs. It's a big day for you, your first workshop, and you slip on your J.Lo hoops and smile. "My superpower accessories."

"Your writing is your superpower, Won. It's gonna be great."

You huff and tell me that it's easy for me to say and you check yourself in the mirror, your brand-new black turtleneck, the one you told me you bought at *TakeMeSeriously.com*. I wrap my arms around you like a boyfriend. "Wonder, I'm gonna say it again. Your pages are outstanding." For a first draft.

"I'm no Pat Conroy."

"No, you're not. And that's a good thing. You're you."

You furrow your brow and tug at the hem of your sweater. "I look like I'm trying too hard. Maybe the turtleneck is too much?"

"It doesn't matter what you wear. It's about your work, and I will say it over and over again until you believe me."

Our eyes meet in the mirror. "Glenn really didn't say anything on your ride?"

"No."

"I mean you gotta see it from my perspective. You ride with him all the time and you expect me to believe he *never* freaking says a word about my stuff?"

Irrelevant. I'm not his secretary. "No. Not a word."

You go back to messing with your hair and another good thing about Bobby's "accident": You have to spend time with Bobby, help him recover, which means we can't do the dumb fucking thing where we spend twenty-four hours a day together. You've been busy with Bobby, and I've been busy helping Glenn. You're a little wary of my "bro-ternship"—I don't like that word—and you find it hard to believe that in spite of all the time we spend together—it's not that much fucking time—we have yet to discuss your pages.

"I swear to God, Wonder. We don't talk about your work. We don't talk about anyone's work. Ever." Hey, you didn't go to the pot-luck, and the potluck was before we had sex.

"But I don't get it. You don't talk about us . . . You don't talk about writing . . . There's no freaking *way* you spend all the time talking about *bikes*."

"Remember, this is good for both of us. If I help him out, he's gonna help me out, and eventually, he's gonna help you, too."

You pat my hand and tell me it doesn't matter. You don't need anyone's approval and you don't *really* care what anyone says. You just need the 25K. It's one of the most attractive things about you. At a time when most people are in a rush to get famous, you are the opposite. "Okay," you say. "I am ready for my execution."

It's officially off to a bad start. A nonstarting start. It's 2:14 P.M. and we've yet to talk about your pages because Glenn isn't here. He's "running late." You're nervous. You're biting your nails and you backslid—you claimed that you were cold and pulled a toxic rabbit out of your hat, a sweatshirt that screams YANKEES SUCK—as if you're prompting our fellows to say that *you* suck. The room is sizzling with awkward small talk, as if power lines are down, swinging from the rafters. We all know why we're here—we read your fucking pages—but Ani is dissecting an episode of *Bosch* with Lou and Sarah Elizabeth is mining Mats for tips on how to hack a fucking videogame and O.K. is worst of all, standing in a corner FaceTiming with Mom, who's at lunch with *Anne Tyler*.

You and I sit across from each other like autodidacts who think "school" means shut up and sit up straight until the teacher arrives.

I look at you. *It's gonna be fine.*

Your eyebrows bend. *Is it?*

I am shaking for you, Wonder. Raging for you. Where the fuck *is* he? The clock on the wall is loud, tallying up the minutes that belong to you, to your work, and I know this is a thing that happens in these "workshops." We only gather for four hours once a fucking week, so you'd *think* everyone would always be on time because every session belongs to one of us, but life is messy, even for the cream of the crop, and sometimes people are late. All that aside, it's starting to feel like a power play and I hope I'm wrong. I hope he fell off his bike into a ditch because I *see* you taking it personally, longing for the peace and ease you feel at Dunkin' and then I hear him, Glenn.

Finally.

I nod toward the stairwell, and you hear him too and you smile in the good way, nervous. You didn't think he was gonna show and yes, he's late, but he's here.

I play footsie with you under the table, and you blush. I don't condone flimsy rah-rah speak like *You got this,* but you do.

Glenn is close, within earshot, and he is late for the most important date, but we all hear him in the hallway, dillydallying, talking about *nothing* with a colleague and again, you are turning to the dark side. It's your day, and your teacher is ensuring that it's a short day—come *on,* Glenn—and finally he enters the room. It's 2:32 P.M. and he's wearing my shirt—CYCOPATH, it looked better on me—and he makes no apology about being late. He drops his bike crap on the floor, and he looks at me.

"Heads up, Joe."

He tosses me a New England fucking *trail* guide and tells me it's a must-read before our next ride and your bones all squeeze together—you don't want me on a bike—and I look at you, but you stare at the floor, wishing you didn't let me so deep into your world, and that's not fair, Wonder. It's not that simple.

Instead of starting class, Glenn is stretching. "So, did anyone else read that Hari Kunzru op-ed this weekend? Utter genius."

It's *your* day to be a genius and everyone is hailing Kunzru and you are breathing through your nostrils and stroking your fucking *Swatch,* a security blanket, a reminder that you can leave these people—including me—for those people, those people who are beneath you, and Glenn rummages through his bag. "Aw shucks," he says. "I forgot the pages."

It's a direct fucking shot and you flip your hair. "I brought extra copies."

Fuck yes, that's you owning your J.Lo hoops and Glenn laughs in a shithead way, but you need to remember something, Wonder. The man invited you to his house and you didn't show up. Rich, insecure people are sensitive. The more accolades a man like him receives in this world, the more he wants a woman like you to show up at his house with your tits out, fawning.

"So," Glenn says. "Before we get started . . . I should let you guys know. We have to cut things short today. I gotta jet at three-thirty."

Your eyes pop out of your head and what the fuck, Glenn?

"I know," he says. "But I have a call about my adaptation and well, they're the Coen brothers and I'm the lowly author. They won't arrange their schedule around *me*."

Ani picks up your pages. "So, let's just get right down to it," she says. "Wonder . . . I don't write sex scenes because who wants to be on that list of the most ridiculous sex scenes of the year, but the sex in these pages . . . This is how you do it. Literally."

You gulp and I told you so. I fucking *told* you.

"I know," Lou says, and who knew Lou had it in him? "I read that part to my lady, and we tried to put our finger on it . . . pun intended . . . but it's hard to say why it doesn't feel the slightest bit extraneous or exploitative. Alice is hot."

He meant that *you're* hot, and you are, and you do write good sex—you tweaked those pages after our first fuck—and Sarah Elizabeth says your sex is *on fire* because you mastered the art of *placement*. She is such a *fan* that she cut your fucking pages into pieces, like a puzzle, and she is laying them on the table, showing us why you are a genius, why you knew what goes where, and Mats concurs—*It's a master class in world building*—and Lou is reading the passage where the father belts his daughter Alice on Yawkey Way. He was so moved, he had to call his shithead father after he read your pages, and do you feel it, Wonder?

They love you.

O.K. could've been a problem. Your pages hit home in a way that hers didn't when it was *her* time in the room, but even she "has to admit" that Mom was impressed. "We both feel like literary fiction by women is sex at its best. Not to make it about me . . ." Ha! "But I read your pages and realized that so many of my flowers were sort of my unconscious way of touching on sexuality without going there."

Last week, because of her, we were in the doldrums of botany, but today it's an outright praise party—there should be a cake—and Sly was wrong. Praise isn't poison. Not when it's a two-way street, when your writing is inspiring the others to think about their writing and Glenn is taking it all in, peering.

"Wonder," he says. "You capitalized *peloton* on the second page, but you're not using it as a proper noun . . ." Okay, so he's on the defense and he's butt hurt. Yes, Alice vents about *pelotons of sad, lonely men ruining it for the real people on the roads of this crowded town,* but you started writing this book long before you even knew fucking Glenn, when Glenn didn't even own one bicycle, let alone a whole fucking flock of them. He takes off his glasses and pinches the bridge of his nose. "Wow," he says. "It's quite a sun storm in this room today." And then he slips his glasses back on and rests his chin on his hand and smiles. "Wonder," he says. "I have a question for you."

Ha! You see that, Wonder? Even our *teacher* wants you to tell us how it's done.

"Is this a short story or do you mean for this to go on?"

"It's a book," you say. "I have about a hundred and fifty pages."

Ani lowers her voice like Cookie Monster. "Give them to me now."

I tell you that I want them too, and Lou says he doesn't want them, he *needs* them and Mats says we have Wi-Fi, you can print them, he can make that happen, and Sarah Elizabeth leaps off her fucking chair. "I will go get them! I need the steps anyway!"

Glenn laughs. "Put the phone away, Mats. Nobody's printing anything."

He does that thing again, that silence. It's on him to sign the bill and turn it into a law, but he picks up his phone and does the undoable. He reads a fucking text. "Sorry," he says. "Joel and Ethan sent another draft . . ."

I know how it feels, Wonder, but you don't get it. Glenn actually believes that *praise is poison* and he's trying to save you, same way he tried to save me. You are right to fidget, but can't you give him the benefit of the fucking doubt? You give it to your family but you can't be even a little bit empathetic for the man who gave you a Golden Ticket?

He turns his phone to silent, but he puts it down face*up* and he looks at Lou, not you. "Did you miss the typo on page seventeen? *Fellatio* is misspelled."

You're turning your pages like a secretary and that's it, Glenn? That's all you're gonna give her?

"Ironic," he says. "Given the subject matter . . ." Pig. "In any case, this isn't a novel."

Your heart breaks. "What did you say?"

"Wonder, the bones aren't there. You're all over the place. Distracted. The writing itself . . . it's distracted. There's a whiff of snake oil, and you're a snake charmer with all these references and these *musical* references. What is Bruce Springsteen doing in a Boston book?"

You eke out a "well" but he just keeps punching. "Never mind. But a novel is meant to be the work of a writer, a writer as in someone with something to say about this world. You, you're just telling us about your family, as if everyone doesn't have a family, your sex life, as if everyone doesn't have a sex life. But the most disappointing thing of all . . . Well, see, think of a peloton . . ." Oh no, not cycling. "You ride in a pack because life is more productive in a pack. The others are looking out for you and you're looking out for them, and this room . . . Are we here? Because I expect honesty in a room. What I see in these pages . . . there's another typo on page sixteen . . . This is a slipshod, antifeminist beauty product. An infomercial for Dunkin', a generic family 'drama' and the real disappointment isn't the work. It's you people, and the only thing I can fathom is that your lack of intention hasn't inspired your fellows to dig, because you didn't dig, you're bonking, riding backward, and does no one in this room have the courage to put the peloton first? To be *honest*?"

I am shaking. You are shaking. I want to bash him in the back of the head and Lou is first to defect. He found another typo on page twenty-seven and Sarah Beth Swallows is "concerned" about the Springsteen references—"Wonder, you'd have to pay for these lyrics. Are you prepared to do that?" and *Shoddies, leave them kids alone.* Ani tilts her head. "I don't see the antifeminism, but structurally, it does feel like a short story. A 'Where Are You Going, Where Have You Been?', because at the end of that story, we are left with guilt and relief that we know what comes next, that we don't have to live through it, and in *Faithful* we're like 'Who's Alice gonna hook up with next?' And I do feel a little . . . dirty."

"Yeah," Mats says. "I sort of feel like I'm reading a diary. Not entering a world."

I'm your hero and I will rally the troops. "But we *are* entering a world. Alice's one-night stands are literally lighting the path as she charts her course and strives to learn how to be loyal to her family without forsaking her own needs."

You blush—I got that from your pitch on our second first date—and Sarah Beth scratches the side of her head, which is Glenn's nervous tic, not hers. "No, I think Glenn's onto something. When I think about spending three hundred pages with Alice . . . I don't like her enough."

Five minutes ago, you were writing the novel of the year and Alice was literary gold but now O.K. is walking back *her* praise and "admitting" that Mom "wasn't so sure that sex is the best way to define a female character. It's like this part on page four . . . The guy at the corner store cuts up Alice's credit card, and we want to see Alice get crafty and solve her problems, confront her issues head-on but instead . . . Well, it's right here, she 'gives head to get out of her head' . . ." You blush and she shudders. "As women . . . I can only speak for me and Mom, but I don't know that I want a female protagonist who's so . . . avoidant."

Glenn kicks back like he won, and it's not dodgeball. He didn't *win* anything. They're all just afraid to disagree with him and Sarah Beth pets your pages like they're a dying fucking puppy. "Yes. God, Glenn, you nailed it. You really did. It is such a short story."

But Glenn scratches the back of *his* fucking head. "No," he says, and this should be more like a fucking improv class, where the only word is *yes.* "It's not even a short story. The lead character . . ." Your heroine, you. "She's a caricature. A simpleton. This is the work of someone shooting for the stars before learning how to load the gun." Fuck you, Glenn. I know *praise is poison* but so is actual fucking *poison* and he looks at the clock. "Speaking of which," and oh no, there's more. "We all know the rule. When you put a gun in a story, the gun has to go off. Alice is sleeping around a lot and there's not even one mention of STDs or even . . . just *one* psycho girlfriend character who corners Alice like, 'Back off my man, bitch.'"

Everyone laughs except for you and me and I furrow my brow. We are in this *together.* "I sort of thought that was the point, reversing that trope, emphasizing the *burden* of a loaded gun that never goes off . . ." I don't even know what I'm saying but does anyone? "We're waiting to see if Alice gets someone in her crosshairs. It's *about* the suspense, the lack of relief."

What I said was good, and like you said, *it's a novel,* and this is when we should get started but Glenn pops his phone into his fucking backpack and calls me a *voyeur* and our fellows laugh like you're not dead inside, like I'm a pervert in the bushes. "There's no shame in failing, Wonder. You're not here to win the five K . . ."

That's a cycling metaphor and you clap the fuck back. "Actually," you say. "We get *twenty-five* K for being here so if you think about it, we all kinda win if we show up."

The room is dead silent because that's not what we do in here, Wonder. You can say that kind of thing to me, but you can't say it to *the room.* We don't talk about money. We're purists leaning into our "art" as if there is no financial incentive to tell stories. Our fellows squirm the way people do when you draw attention to the dollar signs in your eyes, dollar signs and tears.

"Just do better," he says. "Nothing wrong with quitting one course to chart another." And then he straps that helmet on his fucking head, as if he knows I'm about to bash his head into the table. "Time's up. The Coen brothers are calling."

13

After class. Outside. Light rain. Charmless clouds. You clutch your J.Lo hoops and you do not hold my hand and everything I say is wrong. We are walking toward the store and the store is open and I reach for the door, but you bark at me. "Not now. Fuck it."

"Wonder, come on. Think about all the *good* stuff people said. And me . . . I loved it."

You fold your arms over your chest. "Until your little bike buddy told them I suck."

"He's not my *buddy.* I'm helping him with errands and yeah, sometimes we ride."

You close your eyes and shove your hoops in your bag. "The worst part is, I fucking *knew* this would happen. I grew up getting hit on by Ivy League Douchebags and I know better. I never should have done this."

"You don't get it, though."

"Oh really?"

"The night of the potluck, you weren't there . . ." You roll your eyes. "There's a lot you don't know, there's context. Sly got the genius treatment in grad school, and the way he sees it, the way *she* sees it, writers are better off when we *don't* get the genius treatment, especially women who are constantly taught that praise from authority figures is the goal."

"Oh, so you guys *do* talk about me. Freaking bro-ternship. I knew it! Same way I told you this was gonna be a bloodbath. I saw this coming. I freaking felt it."

"Wonder, I'm talking about the night of the potluck. And *you* weren't there. Glenn and his wife . . . they think 'praise is poison.'"

"Ah, and O.K. skipped the potluck to chill with her mom, but that's fine because she's one of *them*? Perfect. Praise ain't poison if you're a freaking princess. Makes sense."

"He was just trying to light a fire in you so in a way . . . this is *good*."

"That's the sickest thing I ever heard." You smack your lips. "Look, I don't want to be around you right now because I'm obviously pissed at *him* and the whole spineless fucking herd, the way they were so quick to turn on me."

"It's a *workshop*."

"There's nothing you can say to change the way I feel, and I don't want to take it out on you."

I take your hand. You let me hold it like a dead fish. "I'm sorry."

"The fucker called me a simpleton."

"He wasn't talking about you. He was talking about your character."

You wipe away a tear. "Did he call *you* a simpleton?"

I don't tell you the truth. It wouldn't make you feel better to know that Glenn isn't harsh like that with me. "I really *am* sorry."

"I think I should quit."

"Don't be crazy."

"Oh, it's crazy for me to want to remove myself from a situation that is toxic for me? Sorry, Joe, but I would never jump on a band-wagon to pad that bastard's ego. I know guys in a way that you don't, and I know he's gonna help you, and I don't begrudge you that, but that man is never going to help me. I mean right now . . . right now I don't even *want* to write. I just want to see my niece and check my dad's wound vac and make sure Bobby changed his bandage and . . . Just go. Go ride with your mentor."

"I see how upset you are. You think I wanna so much as look at him right now?"

You put your hands on my shoulders. "Go. Please. I am begging you. You did nothing wrong back there. And this . . . us . . . this has nothing to do with that, okay? It's not your fault that you don't know what it's like to be a girl dealing with a guy like that."

True, but I know some things. I know you reverted to YANKEES SUCK mode. I know that you want to be superhuman, invincible. You've never been in a serious relationship and you're a novice. You aren't carrying the baggage that most of us lug around at this age. You don't know what it's like to be *faithful* to the wrong person. I let Ivy League girls get the best of me, I nearly died in the war to find a companion. But you've pushed every man away, and like it or not, your lack of experience *is* reflected in your writing. I love you for that—you were saving yourself for one true love—and we are in this *together*.

You kiss me like you're in the mood for a kiss—you are not—and you're gonna go back to *Sesame Street*, maybe go see Tara. I can't let you crawl back into your comfort zone, and I can't let Glenn drive you back down to that dingy bar, to fucking *keno*.

He's not a bad guy, not at heart. For fuck's sake, Glenn Shoddy is an ally. He wrote a book about what it's like to *be* a woman and he will make this right with you. His #1 bestseller is set in a world without the concept of God, and at the center of *Scabies for Breakfast* there is a put-upon single mother named Éclair, who finds her voice and becomes God when her children get run over by a bus. Everyone in her orbit acts like it's her fault, implying that the mites that descended on her body when she was in third grade did something to her brain, which of course they did, but they didn't. You read *Scabies*. You're exploring the same themes in *your* novel, and I know there's a way for the two of you to co-fucking-exist.

As for our fellows . . . Well, come on, Wonder. They were jammed up. Glenn runs that room, and writers *live* to be criticized, so of course when he implied that they were all sucking your dick, well, of course they all assumed they were at fault, but it works both ways, and if he sends a missive to the *group fucking text* explaining that he was in a mood, that he crossed a line and led us astray, everyone will revert to loving you.

I know what you'd say if you were here. *That's all nice but Glenn did wrong by me.* You're not wrong. He's a cycling man baby, sun poisoned from so much time in the spotlight, who's stuck on his second book, but you have rights, too. What he did to you was abhorrent. You are an *excellent* writer and I will not go home. I will not collect two hundred dollars. I'm no better than our fellows. I got jammed up, I failed you, but we're not in that room anymore and I will find Willy Wonka right fucking now and I will make him see your lampposts.

I take out my phone and open Twitter and check his feed.

And then I die.

14

Glenn's a liar. He didn't have a call with the fucking *Coen* brothers. He walked his needy ass over to the Coop, where he signed copies of *Scabies*. He wanted us to know—he posed for photographs with the "fans" and the helpless booksellers—and he capped it off with a *#ReadHerToo* tweet: Driving in Cars with Home-less Men *by Kate Wisel. This woman shines a light on the dark side of Boston families. Short stories, tremendous depth. Best woman writing about Boston. #ReadHerToo*

And to think of you gnashing your teeth, knowing that he did it all for *you*, that he was only able to say something nice about Wisel because he doesn't have to see her in the room. I don't get it, Wonder. The man is married. Okay, he's stuck on his second book, but he has a *Pulitzer*. Why does he have it out for you? He *invited* you into the fellowship and even someone like Glenn Shoddy has to answer to his overlords. The heads of the English department read your work, concurred that you are worthy, so why is he hell-bent on killing your confidence?

It's a free world, so I head into the Coop. I'm too late—he's in the wind—and I hide the *Scabies* he marked with his Sharpie behind books by women—I am an ally, a true ally—and I am his "bro-tern" and you know what?

Fuck it. He tried to kill you today and I can't let him get away with that.

I march out of the bookstore and beeline past the students and the service workers and I storm his front yard. I am Jesse Eisenberg in *The End of the Tour* and this is my peek into the lair of the genius. Glenn is home, blasting the work of another successful writer who works in a different medium—*Ice Cube, Baby*—and Mr. Peloton is just *full* of surprises. I ring the bell and the music dies and I'm not gonna pussyfoot around. I'm gonna confront him right off the bat: *Why were you so rude to Wonder?*

But the door opens and it's . . . Sly. High-waisted leggings and a half shirt. No bra. Nipples. Not fit for company, let alone *male* company. She licks Flamin' Hot Cheeto dust off her fingertips. "Joe," she says. "What a surprise!"

"Sorry to bother you."

"Oh, honey, please. You know how it is. I get the place to myself, and I sit down to write and, well . . . I'm hardly killing it today. Come on in!"

She struts into her kitchen like *Flour Girls* is the reason they live here. She offers to make tea and she's a married woman, she's *Home Alone*. Marriage is a contract and part of that contract means your wife doesn't bring an attractive man into the house. I should leave. Now. But I can't do that to you, can I?

"Tea sounds good."

She apologizes for the mess the way sloppy rich people so often do, praising Glenn for giving her space to write. He's not good to *all* women and I cut her off right fucking there. "Speaking of which . . . Is he on his way home?"

"Likely," she says. "He'll be here any second now."

She peruses her tea bags and yaps about her "goat yoga" and I know about goat yoga from an episode of *9-1-1* and we laugh like Harvard assholes, giddy over our "guilty pleasures," as if all people don't watch TV. But it's better this way, talking small. There's nothing less sexual than goats, yoga, tea, and procedural network television.

I glance at her *shit show* of a workspace, the Flamin' Hot Cheetos and *People* magazines. Her computer, where Anthropologie.com is a paper covering the rock of her "work in progress." She hits the Mute button on the TV.

"I know," she says. "Glenn's office is all Colson Whitehead and grammar books . . . But I like the noise. And I only watch Laura Ingraham because I like to get both sides. Please don't mention it to Glenn. He's sort of off politics. He can't take it anymore. He's just too sensitive."

Too *privileged* is what I'd say and I swear on *People* to keep my mouth shut.

She lifts the Breville kettle. "Glenn *loathes* tea. Are you sure?"

Stay polite. Trite. "Sure!"

Her phone rings and she exhales, and her nipples are right there. I really do wish she'd put on a sweater. "Sorry," she says. "It's my *agent.*"

I tell her not to worry about me and I raise my Elizabeth Warren mug and her call is quick—could've been a telemarketer—and then she puts down her phone and grins. "So now it's your turn," she says. "How was it today? Gimme all the *tea.*"

I may be an auto-fucking-didact but I came here to talk to Glenn, not her. "I don't have any tea."

"Wonder was up today, right?"

"Yes, she was, and it was great. Everyone loved it."

She sniffs an avocado and tosses it into a compost bin. "God, it is just impossible for him to throw anything *away.*"

It's a lose-lose situation and I won't fall into *that* fucking trap and let her vent about my buddy. "So, what did your agent want?"

"Oh, you know . . . Here are your lousy numbers . . . They're burning hardcovers if you want to buy them in bulk."

"I'm sorry, Sly. That's terrible." And that will never be us, Wonder.

"Thanks," she says, and she fiddles with her diamond. "But it's actually a compliment. Not all of us have that overweening ego where we need every book club in America to be talking about us. My work isn't so accessible. It's not supposed to be. My husband was gunning for twenty-eight seconds on the *Today* show since the day we met, before that even. It's why we're sort of so . . . compatible. We don't want the same things out of our careers, you know?"

Nope! "Absolutely," I say. "I relate."

She fusses with the compost bin and I hope failure's not contagious, because that's what she is, sadly. A *sort of* high-end Ethel Rose-Baker. I read Sly's book, the story of one woman helping another woman through a bout with cancer, the crying and the baking, and there's no fucking *way* Sly didn't want to be on the *Today* show. But she didn't get there, and that's what a good writer does, she tells herself a story to make it all better, to lift herself up so she can try again.

"So," I ask. "What are you working on now?"

She grabs a cardigan—it's about time—and lets her hair down— uh-oh. "One of the benefits of having a best *sellout* husband is that I don't have to rush myself with my art."

At the party, she poked him here and there, but at the party, it was teasing. This is different. But maybe we can use her, Wonder. Glenn doesn't want you to have a seat at the table—you probably remind him of some girl who rejected him in high school—but Sly could be the ideal ambassador. She's bitter, self-therapizing with gossip rags and overpriced coats. What woman in her position wouldn't want to stand up for a woman like you?

There is something lonely about her, like a goat in a yoga class wondering what the hell went wrong, and I follow her into her *sitting room*, vowing not to pick up her bad-book cooties and bring them back to you. We sit on her sofa. Nice and far apart.

"Honey," she says. "Let me ask you something. Do you even *like* riding a bike?"

Honey. "I'm not opposed . . . It feels good to exercise and of course, it's great to spend so much time with Glenn. I feel like I'm learning a lot. Nothing like a new hobby, right?"

But she is pensive. "Just so you know, there are rules at Harvard, at any institution . . . sending you out to run his errands . . . it's not right. So, if you want me to say something to Schwinny . . ."

Doesn't she fucking get it? She can't use me as a pawn in her Cheeveresque cold war with her husband. "Silence noted," she says. "I'm just glad it went well for Wonder today. I was bummed when she didn't show up for the potluck. She's just *so* talented and so . . . local. I am dying to meet her. I mean, her pages . . ."

"You read them?"

"Oops," she says. "Cone of silence?"

"Cone of silence."

As it turns out, Sly "devoured" your pages back when she was helping Glenn deal with submissions. After what we went through today, it's nice to listen to her rave about you. I know. Her blurb won't carry the weight of Glenn's, but she calls your writing *fresh and real*—yes and yes—and she can't wait for *Faithful* to be on shelves—I wish I was taping this—and then I choke on my tea because if she read you and loved you . . . did she also read *Me*?

She laughs. "Relax, honey. I liked your stuff, too."

She called my book *stuff* and I don't like having my mind read. "Thanks."

"Glenn adored you, but I had to beg him to give Wonder a chance. So obviously, I'm relieved to know that her workshop went off without a hitch. You know Schwinny . . . He can be a little contrarian, but he's evolving, seeing Wonder for who she is. I'm tickled, truly."

You are probably at home crying and reading Kate Wisel and I can't hold out much longer. She has to know what he's done to you and she puts down her mug. "What?"

It's my turn to ask for the *cone of silence* and she nods—"Absolutely"—and I take a deep breath. It goes against my grain, Wonder. It doesn't feel right to walk Sly through your workshop. I don't *want* to echo Glenn's abusive words, but fellowship requires honesty. Sly deserves to know the truth about her husband and she *is* on your side. They're a couple. She can talk to him in a way that I can't, and she is livid. On her feet and pacing. She can't *believe* he pointed out a *typo* in your "unforgettably raw pages" and there will be trouble in this house tonight, but it will be *good* trouble.

But I don't want *bad* trouble, so I walk it back, and tell her that it wasn't *a total disaster* and she puts her hands on her hips. "You're not a tattletale, honey. You're a whistleblower. And I know. You're worried Glenn will think you're a rat if I bring it up, but you don't have to worry. I know how to talk to him without, you know, talking *to* him."

"Of course you do." She fucking *better* know.

"I just can't believe he did this. Wonder deserves better, and I have every reason to call that department and tell them he's too exhausted to run that room."

He can't do that to you but she can't do that to *me*. Every time we ride, he says he can't wait to scream about my book from the rooftops, and in this loud, crowded world I need him.

I tell her that you would *never* want her to do that and she assures me that she never actually would do it and then she picks up his Pulitzer. "Tell me, Joe. Why do you think you're so well adjusted when it comes to women? Is it your mother?"

It's that rare occasion when I'm happy to field a question about my mother. I laugh a little because we *have* to lighten the fucking mood. "I don't know that I'd say I'm 'well adjusted' when it comes to women . . ." The phrase is *perfectly* well adjusted. "But if it seems that way to you, it's because I've always read women . . . Paula Fox and Ann Petry, Lucinda Rosenfeld and the Brontë sisters . . . *Flour Girls,* that scene in the bakery when they might *both* just Sylvia Fucking

Plath it . . . If I ran the world, every man would have to read a book written by a woman at least once a month."

"A typo," she says, squeezing her husband's gold-plated prize. "He started Wonder's workshop by pointing out a *typo*."

"For all we know, he was just having a bad day . . ."

She looks at me the way that Ice Cube looks at the camera. Like he knows it all. "Honey," she says. "Glenn wasn't having a bad day. He's having a bad life."

This is how it works with people who have it all. They want you to feel sorry for them *because* they have it all. And because I'm someone who doesn't have it all (yet), it's my job to make her go back to feeling sorry for the real victim here: you. "Well," I say. "It can't be easy to be Glenn, to write a book that takes over the world . . . He's a genius. And that's a burden . . . Maybe he doesn't even know what he did today. Maybe he was cracking the nut of his book and mad that he had to deal with us, Wonder would get that. We're all here because of him. And being in his shoes, in this house, with the whole world waiting to see what he does next . . ." Barf. "Nobody would be quicker to forgive him than Wonder. She admires the living *hell* out of him. I really don't think it has to be a big deal. He calls her, they talk it out, that's it."

She is unmoved by my improv purple prose, but she's a failed writer touching her husband's Pulitzer. And then she looks at me. "Cone of silence?"

I nod. "Cone of silence."

"I'm serious, Joe. This does not, cannot, will not leave this room."

Ah, so the cone of silence wasn't real until now, and she places the Pulitzer on the mantel and returns to our sofa. She's facing me, staring into my eyes in this way where . . . No. She isn't going to fucking *kiss* me, is she?

"Honey, I wrote the book."

"I know. You wrote *Flour Girls*."

"Yes," she says. "That's a good place to start. This whole mess did start with *Flour Girls*. A paint-by-numbers 'page-turner' . . ." It's not *not* true. "There I was. I had two chapters of this book and my professor sent the pages to the woman who would become my agent, and she then sent those pages to Grove and Grove said, 'Yes! We want this!'"

It will be so fucking easy to keep this in the cone of silence. "How cool."

"At first, but then I was young. It was so new. I didn't know what 'this' was. I had all these existential ideas about why I was even *thinking* that I was meant to write about these likable, plain women. Why did Grove even *like* these pages?"

Because some fucker at Iowa told some other fuckers to like them and it's *really* not that complicated. "You had impostor syndrome."

"No," she says. "I knew I was good, but when I sat down to keep going, I realized I was at war with myself. The intellectual Iowa darling in me believed a book was only truly good if the author was only a household name in a few elitist homes. But this other part of me, the public-school kid who worshipped Jennifer Weiner . . . I wanted to feed *her* readers, the ones who crave authentic, actual, you know . . . *story*. I couldn't decide what to do, which is why *Flour Girls* is the unsure work of an indecisive woman. I disappointed all the Mrs. Smiths as well as Zadie Smith. I knew it, honey. I was choking, so as I was blowing it with *Flour Girls*, I distracted myself by writing another book . . . *Scabies*."

That's . . . not true and she closes her eyes like she's back in goat yoga. I'm a little scared, Wonder. She's deluded. Crazy. Possibly dangerous. I've met enough authors to know that they will say *anything* to make their failure into something grand, eso-fucking-teric. She's lying to save face and it serves me right for going behind my mentor's back and talking to his *wife*. If I stay here another minute, who knows? She might claim she wrote *my* fucking book. I stand up and smile. "Cone of silence. I'll let you get back to work."

"Ah," she says. "So, you don't believe me . . ."

No one would believe her and where is her fucking husband? Oh right. He's not here yet. She lied about that, too. "Sly, I don't think we should get into this."

"Well, it's too late, Joe. We're in it. I told you what I've never told anyone. *Scabies* was my own sort of Hedonism II, this oasis where I owed nothing to no one, where I wasn't a woman, where I didn't *have* to 'find' my voice, where my only job was the work."

This is so much worse than a kiss and she pats the sofa. I sit.

"Look, honey, I'm sorry I crossed a line. But so did you. You marched into this house to confront Wonder's abuser—"

"I didn't call him an abuser."

"I'm telling you what I never told anyone *because* you came here, because it broke my heart, to think of Glenn hurting Wonder, to see you so upset over her being hurt . . . This is why they say not to meet your heroes, and as the one who *pushed* him to take on a fellowship and enabled him to *become* her hero I just . . . I feel responsible for all of it."

I say nothing. You can't reason with crazy and now would be a nice time for Glenn to get home. She pulls up the sleeve of her sweater and points at a tiny scar. "Scabies at summer camp . . ." It could be chicken pox. "Okay, I know. That's insulting. Physical. So let me ask you a question. Were you not even a *little* surprised that Glenn was running a fellowship?"

"He won a Pulitzer."

"True, but he's not Gore Vidal. He's not Wallace Stegner. His name doesn't have *that* level of gravitas . . . Don't you think it's strange that *Harvard* gave him all this power?"

"I got into Harvard, and I don't have any power."

She laughs. "Don't put the place on a pedestal. You're not in an MFA program. You're not walking away with a degree. Which is great, honestly. But you're here because of Glenn. And Glenn is here because of me. Nothing just 'happens.' I campaigned for him to get this job. I made this fellowship 'happen' for Schwinny because he needed a way out of his own future. We didn't move here so he can write another *book*. We moved here because he *can't* write another book, because he never wrote *one* book. And we both thought teaching would be good for him, to make peace and sort of transition in plain sight so that in a year or two he can say that he prefers teaching. I *wanted* him to feel good about himself, to be in a position to help writers like you, but what he's doing to Wonder, that is not part of my plan. And it's very disconcerting."

So its's the truth, Wonder. Sly Caron wrote *Scabies for Breakfast*. I can't explain why I know. I just do. I hang my head. "A *parking ticket* is disconcerting. This is . . . you're serious."

"You said it yourself. You love women writers. You love *Scabies*."

"But it's all a lie."

"Oh, come on. You love someone and you do things for them . . . Isn't that why you rang my doorbell today?"

My doorbell not *our* doorbell and that's it, in a nutshell. She's more possessive of the doorbell than she is of her own fucking words—she wrote *Scabies*, she really did—and I don't know what that means for us. Secrets destroy relationships and I have to fucking tell you, but secrets destroy careers and I *can't* fucking tell you. She's pontificating about *identity* and I'm skimming *Scabies* in my mind. We all fell for it. Not just me. The whole world. The *Atlantic* sucker who remarked that Glenn was "writing a woman as a woman, not a woman as written by a man" and Jesus Fucking Christ. Sly Caron wrote *Scabies for Breakfast*. But Glenn is *still* the one with all the power, power he's using to hurt you. And what is *she* doing right now?

She's defending him. Trying to sell their sham as an act of "love."

"Sly, wait . . . There's doing things for someone you love and then there's plagiarism. Fraud, *lying*." I shake my head in pious fucking disgust. "And obviously, the cone of silence is impossible. I have to tell Wonder."

She picks lint off her cardigan. "You know you can't do that. And you shouldn't judge. You've never been where we were. You don't know what it's like to be in a house with the person you love, to watch your *partner* dying of writer's block . . . You weren't there. We were under pressure to teach and participate at a level that you don't have as a 'Shoddy fellow' . . ." This is true. "I was 'the one,' the darling who got the most love in the room, and Glenn *wanted* to support me, and he came out of the shower with this title, with *Scabies for Breakfast*. He couldn't do it. He was drinking himself to death, driving every waitress at our diner nuts with his big talk about his big, sprawling book . . ." We are lucky to be us, but we are unlucky to need them, him, her. "And you know what else?"

Did she write every Philip Roth book, too? "What else?"

"Scrap what I said about my 'angst' over *Flour Girls*. It was simpler. An act of love. Same way he'd scrape ice off the windshield for me because that sound always bothered me."

THAT'S CALLED BEING A BOYFRIEND and why do women reward men for being fucked-up? "Well, I guess you made it up to him."

"Don't be sarcastic, honey. Glenn had enough talent to get in, but he didn't have enough confidence to get *through*. I like writing. Schwinny likes having written. He didn't know that about himself. Do you know what it was like for him to realize that he couldn't do it? So I did it for him. I'm not playing the martyr. I rescued *Scabies* because that's what you do when you love someone. You save them. Like you, coming to see Glenn . . . me."

Our emperor has no spandex and what does this mean for us? "His whole life is a lie."

"Honey, life is a lie, which is why I was always so obsessed with religion . . ."

More truth right there—Glenn *never* talks about religion—and everything is upside down. The genius doesn't ride bicycles. The genius doesn't transcribe Denis Johnson with a ballpoint fucking pen. The genius blasts Ice Cube and loves hot tubs and bends her body around *goats*. And if Sly is the genius—she is—then Glenn is *not* a genius, and if he's not a genius, then what the fuck does he know about recognizing the fucking genius in others? In *me*.

"Oh, come on," she says. "A big lie isn't so bad if it keeps you together. And you should know that the guilt is killing him. Once a week or so he says he's gonna turn himself in for fraud and I'm like 'Okay. Let's play it out. You tell the truth, and we go on tour and I'm onstage talking about *Scabies* while you're in the hot tub with a Klonopin.' He *despises* hot tubs. And 'drugs.' He's so midwestern and I can say that because I *am* the Midwest . . . Either way, never mind all that. *Scabies* is all grown up, bigger than us. We wouldn't dare taint the sanctity of that book. It means too much to people, to Mrs. Smith and Zadie Smith and people like you . . . they all love it."

People like you, and I gulp.

She pats my leg and I'm tired of her reading my mind. "Don't be that way," she says. "You know him. You spend time with him. It's very pleasurable to please him because he loves to feel good about himself. Some flowers need the sun, and some don't. But I know . . . here you are, your favorite author is your new best friend, which is why you came here today, because friends do that, they call each other out when they're misbehaving and now you feel lost, but it's good that you came here and I really can get him to do better with Wonder."

My skin crawls like I'm the one with scabies. "I didn't say he's my 'favorite.'"

She laughs. "I'm not trying to pat myself on the back . . . But it's the way of the world. The industry loves a darling new boy genius, the man who will be king."

"There are plenty of queens, too."

"But I don't want to be a queen. Should I give up writing because I don't like having written? Because I loathe nothing more than being perched on a dais *talking* about my *process*? *Scabies* is better as a book by a man. It wouldn't read the same way if it was my face out there."

"Well, you can't know that."

"But, honey, we *do* know it. Every ten years, an 'aw-shucks' white guy comes around to 'blow' everyone's minds. I wanted that for Glenn, and I . . ." Her voice trails off. Real geniuses don't need the world to know that they're geniuses and my fan mail to him was for her. She reaches for her phone and I don't need *proof*. I go with my gut, same way I do in writing. But it's like a car crash. We all want to see the body parts that belong inside the body lying there on the blacktop. Here is Glenn in August, worrying that a roomful of writers will be a dangerous place, that one of us will see through him. Sly's advice is on point—*GO RIDE A BIKE!*—and his response is both endearing and pathetic: *Stop being smarter than me!!*

We are what they can never be—we're *equally* fucking smart— and she mews at her phone. "He can be good, you know? And I have a plan to coax him into doing right by Wonder. This typo thing . . . he did that to me too, still does. I'll ask him to read my pages and I'll say it's *my* turn to let loose. I'll open a bottle of wine and pretend to be in a mood. A little *Who's Afraid of Virginia Woolf?* I'll tear into him about the way he was back in Iowa, pointing out *my* typos when *he* was drunk, railing on about how I'm the smarter one, how he loved me for it, *hated* me for it, much as he didn't *want* to hate me for it. And then he'll open up to *me* about Wonder because he *will* feel bad. Trust me. It's like I wrote in *Scabies*. Love and hate are two Twix bars and the only way to separate them is to tear that sucker open."

The book *was* a bit pretentious, and I nod. "Why didn't you just leave him?"

She rolls her eyes like I'm an idiot. "Because I love him. And I was wrong, I know. *Cycling* is no substitute for therapy . . ." No shit, genius. "But how can he go to therapy? Who could he trust?"

More like who can *I* trust? "I don't know what to say."

"You don't have to say anything. All you do is let Wonder know that she's a diamond in the rough, an absolute genius and you . . ." *You're not a genius.* "You're a good egg. Wonder is lucky to have you, honey. You can read her. Love her. Support her. And be happy that you're not that guy who unravels when a woman is talented, beautiful, and productive."

With that, she stands up and walks me to the door and she is not the woman I met when I got here. She doesn't wait for me to leave the property. The second she closes the door, Ice Cube picks up where he left off—*check yo' self before you wreck yo' self*—and it's too little, too late, Mr. Cube. You're a genius, Wonder. And I'm a *good egg*.

On the way home, I try to be optimistic. Maybe Glenn's brilliant wife really can make it all better. But I feel heavy. Flat-footed. Their secret is worse than my secrets. Knowing where a body is buried is earthly—books are eternal, bodies disintegrate—but knowing how a *novel* was born is a cosmic eternal mindfuck. I almost wish that you *weren't* so smart. You might feel me holding out on you, hoarding a secret in a *cone of silence*. And then what?

I stop at the Coop to stare at the new display: *Signed Scabies!* Did I even like *Scabies for Breakfast*? The novel won me over before I read it because I watched that book give Ethel Rose-Baker a face-lift, a soul-lift, and I wanted that for myself. I went into the book *wanting* to love it, hoping it would restore my faith in this fucking world, and then I wrote to Glenn *wanting* him to like me so I could be here and it's one thing for him to fool the whole fucking world.

But the motherfucker fooled me—I'm his *bro-tern*—and as of now he's still out to destroy you. Some helmetless fuckwad on a scooter almost kills me and I snarl—"Take it to the street, asshole"—and I can't do this. I can't lose my cool. Glenn Shoddy is a spandex-clad phony, but he can still help me get a book deal.

It's harder for you, Wonder. You kept your distance from Glenn Shoddy. But evil, bitter liars find a way to get under your skin. I need to see you. I need to shake his poison out of your system before it sinks in.

I send you a little text: *You busy?*

You send me a blurry drunk selfie from Tara's bar: *lol yes!*

15

It's a bad *blur* of a week and I'm not the one who hurt you, Wonder, but you've blown me off four nights in a row. You're not writing and all you wanna do is "live your life," as in take care of your broken-legged Bobby, help out at home, pour sugar at Dunkin', and hang out in Tara's fucking bar. It's a sinking ship—Tara is pregnant, she's moving to the North Fucking Shore—and I hate it there, Wonder. The floors are sticky and keno is suicide and you're smarter than this, you're *better* than this, but when I tell you I think you should be writing, you get all sarcastic and glib—*Your buddy Glenn said it's not a book, remember lol*—and when I make it about me, about us, when I say that I miss you, you push even harder—*My family comes first, I can't spend every night at your house*—and when I push back and tell you I'll take anything, a cup of coffee on your fucking stoop, you treat me like a traitor—*Do your thing, bro-tern. Tell your friend Glenn I said hi.*

I'm stuck with him now, carrying his *Sharpies* through another day of hunting KOMs and hitting up a stupid fucking farmers' market. He's inspecting an *apple* like it's his last fucking supper because that's the level of tedium with this guy and it's amazing, Wonder. When I thought he cracked the code of the book-buying masses, when I thought he was the kind of "genius" who knows what people want, I would have seen this as a teachable moment. *Great writers analyze apples.* But I know the truth. Hot tubs, frilly cardigans, *Ice Cube, Baby*.

Glenn shows me an apple and I stare at it like it matters. "Looks all right to me."

"No," he says, as if he knows anything about books, about fruit. "This little fella spent too much time on the ground. We can do better. *Always* demand better."

The farmer says he has a good eye—ugh—and he says it's the "pain of being" a writer, and she perks up—"Would I have read any of your work?"—and here we go again. Glenn hasn't *changed*. Yeah, Sly tried. He told me about their "minor dispute," but he blamed it on "self-medicating wifey." He hasn't reached out to you to apologize and he's the same old Glenn, playing the bashful humble fucker, asking the farmer if she's ever heard of *Scabies for Breakfast* and she yelps, she grabs her partner and the partner hands me the phone—"Will you take our picture?"—and Glenn beams with his *fans* as if he wrote the fucking book, as if it's his.

I hold the iPhone steady and wish it was a gun. "Say apples!"

Do you think this is what I want out of life, Wonder? Do you think I *like* strangling my nuts in spandex? Riding into the suburbs with Glenn so he can commune with his readers who don't know what he is, a fucking fraud? In *Faithful* you bemoan farmers' markets, the affluent people with time to relax while the people who actually *need* fresh fruit are stuck at some awful, minimum-wage job. I look across the street at a Dunkin' and I wonder if you would even *want* to be with me if you saw me right now. I'm that asshole in those click-clack shoes. *I* don't want to be with me.

Never mind me. You're checking out of all of it, ignoring the group text and calling me a "bro-tern" as if I'm not in this for you, for us. I'm trying to build our future and it's the reason we're here, to make inroads, to make *connections,* and it's not even a shock that Glenn's a misogynist fraud. That's just life. The people in power are corrupt, and the only way to change the system is from within.

I pick up a pear. "I always forget about pears."

"Ha," Glenn says. "That's a good line. Write it down."

Bullshit. "Yep."

"Another tip for you, Joe. Don't be the guy who writes about apples. Be the guy who owns pears."

Oh, how you'd die if you saw me take out my little notepad—I am now that asshole with a notepad in my spandex side pocket—and I scribble—*GLENN SHODDY IS OUR USEFUL IDIOT*—and one day, when I'm published, when we're published, when we're bigger than him, and Sly has filed for divorce and sent him to the list of canceled men, I will tell him what he can do with his patronizing *pears*.

I point at a perfectly good picnic table and he points at another like the contrarian that he is. "Another piece of advice," he says. "Don't be such a writer all the time, you know? When you take a picture, just say 'cheese.' Be confident. Clichés exist for a reason."

It's a prompt so I'm back in my notepad—*THIS FRAUDDY FUCKER DOESN'T HAVE A QUARTER OF YOUR TALENT*—and my pear is mushy. Gross. Nothing like my first and only taste of you, a day that feels like ten thousand years ago, back when Glenn was a genius, when I was on my knees in the shower licking whipped cream off your—

"So, I saw our friend Lou last night."

That's not right. Glenn and I were supposed to grab a burger, but he canceled on me to "write" and I want to shove my pear down his throat, but I play the game. "And how's Lou?"

"His *lady,* she was the main attraction . . . a Farrah Fawcett type, an absolute ten."

Do you see how I suffer? I have to listen to Glenn size up women and walk me through their double fucking date—it should have been the four of *us*—and sit here as he does the play-by-play, every scene the same, Lou's lady openly flirting with her husband's fucking teacher. It's strange, Wonder. I almost feel bad for him sometimes. Praise *is* poison. I think at this point he believes that he really *did* write that stupid fucking book.

He picks an apple seed out of his chompers, as if winning a Pulitzer means you're beyond manners. "True story," he says, as if I'm his fucking biographer. "One that I didn't tell Oprah . . ." Oh, fuck off. "After I wrote the last three chapters of *Scabies,* I went blind."

LIAR. "Wow."

"The physicians . . ." Just say *doctors*. "They blamed my screen time, the lack of sleep, malnutrition, but they were wrong."

Ha. "How so?"

"A novel is supposed to eat your heart out, your loins. I lost my vision because my eyes physically inverted, they pulled a 180 and pointed inward, all the way to that drag-down knock-out last scene with Ray and Marnie. Lou's *lady* was drawn to me because I died for *Scabies.* Lou is learning the hard way that he didn't die for his work. *O'er Under* is a fine piece of crime fiction, but he didn't go blind for that book."

I start to say something about *my* book, so he takes out his phone and goes into starfucker mode, claiming that he got a text from "Fran"—it's Frances McDormand, you fuckwad—and then it's back to Lou. "I did Lou a solid and sent Fran his book. Who knows? Maybe she'll wanna do something with it."

WHAT ABOUT MY BOOK and don't you get it, Wonder? *This* is why we have to play the game, because we'll need him to do nice things for us. He hops off the table. "Another tip for you, Joe . . ."

"Ready, Freddy."

"I spent three months in an attic in Iowa with *Scabies* . . ." Not true. He was at bars and diners. "I put every sentence on trial . . ." Sly did that. "Writing the *fuck* out of a book is a lonely, miserable, self-doubt-inducing hell. If you're smiling and sober, if you're living the life with your lady, then you're doing it wrong. Always."

I scribble in my notepad: GLENN SHODDY LIVES IN A LONELY, MISERABLE, LYING HELL OF HIS OWN MAKING— and he snaps his helmet onto his helium-infused head.

"All right," he says. "Real talk?"

He's gonna do it. He's gonna tell me he didn't write his own book. He made a big mistake and he's not deaf to the sound of his own boorish voice and he picks at his helmet. Humbled. No doubt nervous about letting me down. I put down my pear. "Okay."

He grins, and that is not the face of a man about to confess his sins. "Gimme the notepad."

It's my notepad and he's my fucking boss and if he sees what I wrote I'm worse than dead, I'm *blacklisted* and fired. But that won't happen, Wonder. Even as a bro-tern, I have rights. "I can't do that, Glenn."

"Sure, you can. See, I'm sharing with you, but honestly . . ." He lost the right to use that word. "I'm talking to you like I know what I'm doing, but this second book . . ." There is no second book. "I'm stuck in the shadow of my own *Scabies* and maybe if I looked at all the advice I'm giving to you . . ."

"But this is my only copy, Glenn. And your notes are . . ." He reaches for the notepad but I know what he *really* fucking wants. "Glenn, come on. You don't 'need' these notes. You're Glenn Fucking Shoddy. You're the best living writer on the planet."

He shakes his head in an obligatory display of false modesty, but then he gives up the battle for the notepad—*phew*—and his ego is something out of a horror movie, seeping out of his pores, through the spandex. "So tonight, my writer buddy Mike's in town . . . He wants to have beer, sort of a boys' night. You're welcome to join . . ."

Mike as in Michael who? "Is it Mike as in Michael Chabon?"

He hands me his Ray-Bans and laughs. "We're meeting at the Spee at six."

"Glenn, I can't take your sunglasses."

"Sure you can," he says, as he jumps on his bike. "And if you're hard up for cash, you can put 'em on eBay."

The Pulitzer putz speeds off and it's Michael Chabon, Wonder. It's the Spee, one of those private clubs and I know. Final clubs are vile and exclusive, just the sort of thing that drove Mark Jesse Eisen-Zuck to rabid psychosis in *The Social Network*. But I'm not a sociopath or an undergrad and the Spee was good enough for JFK. They were also the first club to admit Black people and they even allow *women*—so appalling, what counts as progress when it comes to white privileged elites—and their mascot is a bear. A giant taxidermy brown bear. Or black. Who fucking cares? It's the Spee! It's Michael Chabon! It's my reward for all the apples, all the *Strava*, all the hand-me-a-*Sharpie* shit.

I'm calling you with good news and it's ringing—will you pick up?—and you do. "Joe, omigod! I was just thinking how much I freaking miss you."

Your voice is the opening chords of "At Last" and I smile. "I miss you too and—"

"Okay good! So tonight, here's the plan . . ." Uh-oh. "There's karaoke at Tara's bar and I do *not* expect you to sing but she reserved seats for us and I know I've been MIA . . . The Coolatta machine crapped out again and Bobby's having a hard time and I was in a mood cuz of . . . Forget it. I just freaking miss you. So, I'll see you at six?"

Gently, Joseph. "It sounds great . . ." It sounds like hell. "But I might be a little late." You grumble about my *bro-ternship* but you'll change your tune soon enough. "Wonder," I say. "Glenn invited me to drinks . . . with Michael Chabon."

"His wife is more my style, but whatever. Just tell them you'll be late."

"Well, we're meeting at a final club, so . . ."

"I was over final clubs in high school when Tara dragged me to parties, but it's fine. Go. Have fun. Tell Chabon his wife is awesome and while you're at it, tell him he has shitty taste in friends, and I'll tell my best friend something better came along."

Tara's not your "best" friend, she's your old friend, and this is *our* future. "Won, come on. It's not like I have Michael Chabon's phone number. I can't text him to reschedule."

"It's funny. When you called, I thought, Oh good, he misses me, too."

"And I do miss you, but—"

"I gotta go pick up Caridad. I'll just see you tomorrow!" *Click.*

I was stupid. I chased "I miss you" with a *but*, but what about you? It's been cold getting colder all week with you. Maybe I've been fooling myself. Maybe you got over *me* in the room when I didn't do what a macho Masshole would have done, when I didn't punch Glenn Shoddy in the face.

There's no going back, and there might be no going forward, but I can't dwell. I have to pick up my suit at the dry cleaners.

It's Michael Fucking *Chabon*, Wonder. I mean come on!

16

Glenn can't stop laughing at me—he's in a Fudgie the Whale T-shirt and a stupid leather jacket—and I'm in a fucking suit. Is there anything worse than being dressed for the prom when everyone else looks like they just rolled out of bed?

"A suit!" he says, for the fifth time, such a nonwriter that he can't even form a joke as he pours more vodka into his highball glass and *good*. Drink up, Frauddy. I hope he's wasted by the time "Mike" gets here because it'll only make me seem more together and you see, Wonder? This is what I mean about *strength*. I don't cave in to my insecurities. I don't *punch* our teacher in the face. I give myself a break from Glenn. I take time to stop and smell the taxidermy—disgusting—and I steal a monogrammed hand towel from a closet—I think you'll like it—and I study the portraits. Generations of monstrous men have sat in this room and refused to apologize for their shortcomings, so why should I beat myself up for wearing a suit? Finally, I look at my phone, at the text you sent before you went to Tara's bar: *Sorry I was snippy. I'm very ready for Tara to move already and if Ayelet Waldman shows up you HAVE to tell her she RULES. Also, hug the bear for me* ☺

It takes so little to restore love, and we're back, and of course we are. It's my night.

I maneuver my way around people in T-shirts, people who need to brush their hair, and when I reclaim my spot on the couch, Glenn asks if I got lost. *Fucker.*

"Yes," I say. "So is Mike here yet?"

Glenn avoids the question and starts pontificating about *Star Trek* and I let him ramble. Soon enough, Mike will be here and we'll bond over our disgust with Glenn—that's *two* vodka-vodkas and it's not even 6:14—and the next time Mikey comes back into town, he'll email me, not Glenn. I can already see the four of us, you and me and Mike and Ayelet. They'll be our mentors, and you will forget all about the pigs who did wrong by you and—

"Ah, cripes."

"What's wrong?"

"Mike's running late."

That's okay by me, Wonder. I like it in the *Spee* with the velveteen sofas and the dank red curtains that scream *We are the cream of the cream of the crop.* You're right. These clubs are historically vile, but I've worked hard in the *bro-ship* and finally, I'm getting something out of it. Something real.

People recognize him, Wonder. They shake his hand, they ask him how the movie's going, and he plays the bashful dufus, insisting that the writer they *really* need to meet is me. *Me.* I'm smart by association—it's a start—and Glenn was a dickhead, but your *tendency is to love.* If he apologizes to you, you'll accept it, and I have to move fast—Mike could be here any minute—so when Glenn finishes showing his album of *bicycles* to a visibly bored guy who regrets approaching the table, I *carpe* the *diem.* "Hey, Glenn," I say. "You know what this reminds me of?"

He looks around the room, fixating on the young women. "*Porky*'s?"

"It reminds me of that scene in Wonder's book, when Alice goes to the country club."

He shrugs and makes like a politician—"I don't recall"—and that is bullshit. And then he grins. Evil. Predictable. "So, I take it that my wife was right. You *are* hitting that?"

I'm not *hitting* anything. "Glenn, I think you owe her an apology."

He chomps on ice cubes and looks around the room. "*Good Wonder Hunting*. She's beneath you . . ." That grin again. So lascivious that I wish the bear would come back to life and bite. "Or *is* she?"

I won't do it, Wonder. I won't tell him about our sex life. But he won't do it either. He won't take you seriously and own up to his crimes, so I laugh like a *bro* and tell him I'm just worried about him.

"Me?"

"Well, someone in your position, a white male authority figure coming down so hard on a woman, in the presence of other women . . ."

He's not even done with his third vodka-vodka but he's signaling for his fourth, snapping his fingers like it's 1957, and people notice. They see him drinking to get drunk. "Pro tip," he says, and I'm so happy I didn't bring my fucking notepad. "You should be thinking about your career right now. Did you even start another novel yet?"

One nice thing about drunk people is that you can repeat yourself whenever you want. "I think you should call Wonder."

"You sound like my wife."

Good. I'm happy Sly has your back. "So, she agrees with me?"

"Enough about *Wonder*. You're a genius. Do you hear me? A *genius*."

I know he's not a genius, but none of the people in this room know what I know, and they heard what he said and they're whispering like they just got a hot literary stock tip. "Thanks, Glenn."

"Don't thank me," he says, lowering his voice. "Thank the gods of this fine institution who put me in a position to choose you. If they went another way . . . if they followed the wave of liberal equity and chose someone else to run the room . . ." He eyes a Black man talking to an Asian woman and the bear really *does* need to come back to life. "My wife's novel fizzled. She didn't go blind for it, so she's on the Wonder train. Wonder doesn't have it, I knew it when I read her, but it's a hell of a lot cheaper to let your wife have a win when she's down on her luck than it is to get divorced. Plus, this way . . . I still get laid. And, we have something to look at."

He's officially drunk now, and it's not fair. The real genius believes in you, not me, and you don't know it, you *can't* know it, and I hate this little part of me that wishes Sly believed in me *and* you, not *just* you, and I want to be strong and tell Glenn that I know he's chock-full of shit but I can't do that—I need his agent, I need him to scream when my book is out in the world—and where the fuck is Mike?

"All right," Glenn says. "So, I guess she told you . . ."

It's a vague pronoun. Is he talking about you? About Sly? Is he on the verge of a blackout drunk confession of his fraud in the worst possible place . . . a *final* club? There's a guy three feet away and he's craning his neck . . . Is he that fucking Kennedy kid? The people at the next table laugh hard in that way that privileged people do, like they're all activating their cores, not actually, you know, laughing.

I sip my vodka-vodka. "She might have told me something."

"Yep, the hardest part about all this . . . sometimes the women, the Wonders of the world, they throw themselves at me so hard I feel bad for saying no."

I choke. You, he was talking about you. Him. You. No.

He motions for me to lean in, and we're huddled and the Speople probably think we're in the middle of some lofty intellectual debate about modern fucking literature. "Her headshot, the blow job lips. You saw her on the lawn . . . the daddy issues and the tight shirt . . . chewing on that straw, making eyes at me . . ." No, you did not, and he stabs his little ice cubes with his little straw. "Sadly, the 'spank me Daddy' genre is not for me. I like my women a little more . . . nuanced."

I have so many fucking questions but we have company in the form of a pompous Brooks Brothers prick who looks like he wishes he got into the Porcellian. He holds up his copy of *Scabies*. "Sorry I'm late."

Glenn claps his hands. "Mike! Good to see you, kid!"

Okay, so Michael Chabon was never on the docket and *Mike* is just a kid with connections—his mother is friends with Glenn's attorney—and Glenn elbows me for a Sharpie like I'm his assistant.

Did you make a pass at him? Did you?

I hand Glenn his fucking Sharpie—no *Thank you, Joe*—and he signs the book like the phony that he is, and he's ready for more, but Mike only set this up as a favor to his mother. He saunters away, and Glenn drops his Sharpie on the table.

"It's a shame," he says to me. "You failed the Bechdel test."

Him and his wife and that played-out stupid test. "Huh?"

"I had thoughts about your novel. Big ones. But we spent all our time talking about Wonder and now I have to go."

I don't need his thoughts any more than I'd need his prayers if I was going into surgery, but the game's not over yet—Without Mike *Chabon* in my life I need Glenn now more than ever—so I nod. "Lesson learned."

He leers at two undergrad women who pass by and laugh *at*, not with, his Fudgie the Whale shirt and he zips up his jacket. He's in a mood. He only signed *one* fucking book tonight. "Look," he says. "Wonder's not a writer, Joe. She's a storyteller and you're a writer and there is a difference. There is a *difference*. And the difference is huge!"

It's time to go and Mike and his peeps are scoffing at him like the stumbling drunk literary "it boy" that he is, probably vowing to go into investment fucking banking. I slap him on the back—"Your Uber's here"—and it's a relief to leave the *club* and shove him into the backseat of a shiny black car. He's fighting with the seatbelt, mumbling that you "wanted him."

I buckle him up—no, Glenn, the seatbelt is not fucking broken—and he bursts out laughing and I ask him what's so funny—he better not make another libelous dig at you—and he spits through a laugh in my face. "A suit!"

17

I wake up on my sofa in my suit. I have six texts and two missed calls from Glenn—he wants to go for a ride—and I have three texts and one missed call from you—you want to meet for brunch. I am your *Prince of Tides* and no man can live two lives, but I come pretty damn close. You're amenable when I tell you I'm in a jam—*All good and lol The Spee and the bicycle, a whole new you, truly*—and soon, I'm in the woods with Glenn, and it's wonderful to see him like this, gassy and bloated, fuzzy on the details about last night. "Look," he says. "It's part of my process, I'm at my most creative when I'm drinking, it's a way to cleanse the spirit, to wipe the slate . . . It's a part of my process. Ugly but real."

Oh, for fuck's sake. "So, Wonder didn't put the moves on you?"

He grabs his leg and farts. "Nope."

It's all I needed to hear—you're an angel!—and I'm so relieved that I let him babble about "leading with his id" and "confess" that he wrote half of *Scabies* while he was blackout drunk—nope—and that's it for me. I'm up. "I know we said we'd do another trail, but my calves are feeling it today."

"No worries," he says. "You'll get stronger in time. It really is *just like writing.*"

Fuck you, Glenn, and I ride hard back to Boston, crossing bridges and overpasses. I can't get to you fast enough. You didn't make a pass at him—he's just jealous that you love me, not him—and I can do this. I can bring you back into the fold.

You're on the patio at Sonsie, covering my coffee with a napkin to keep it hot, and you are Brahmin in a good way, like one of those earthy girls in a nineties movie who finds out her blue blood runs royal—*I was there when you were a queen*—and I'm the luckiest man on the planet, the way you jump out of your seat to hug me, to kiss me, to tease me about my *spandex*.

I sit in my chair and smile. "What did we decide about you mocking me?"

"We decided that I will do it every time you show up in your bike shorts because you look fucking ridiculous."

"The word is *cycling*, my dear."

"What's up with your sunglasses? I don't think of you as a Ray-Bans guy."

Glenn gave them to me. "Then I guess I'll have to get new ones."

We open our menus and the conversation flows. You took your niece to the playground and then you went to Tara's—she's finally gone, yay!—and you want to know what's new with me and I shrug. "I stole my first KOM a couple days ago."

"Oh God," you say. "Quick, let's order before you start thinking that your freaking bike rides can pass for conversation."

I love your wit and your sparkle and the way you say *eggs benny* and pooh-pooh the coffee—*Sorry but ours is better*—and the sun is shining in that way where it's impossible to be at this table with you and think that we can't have it all. I don't want to live in a world where my girlfriend and my mentor can't be in the same room together. I want you to know that Glenn's a fraud, I want to let you in on the secret history of *Scabies*, because the truth really would set you free. But that's the problem, Wonder. You would be free to confront him, and if he told Sly, she would know that I violated the cone of silence, and then *he* would know and where would that leave us? Agentless. Fellowshipless. Hopeless. No. We deserve better. We deserve everything that Glenn and Sly have, and we can't have any of it if those fucked-up elites are against us.

You peer at me. "What's on your mind?"

It's tempting. We're in this together, at this tiny table for two, and I could make you swear on *Chronicle* and Fenway that it doesn't leave this table, but then I'd be like that guy who tells his wife that he cheated on her because he's too weak to carry his own dirty fucking laundry.

"Nothing," I say. "I was just thinking about Alice in that country club."

You chew your lip—you don't want to talk about your book—and you are giving up on the fellowship, leaning into your life as a Goodreads girl. "Did I tell you I started that book Glenn tweeted . . . *Driving in Cars with Homeless Men*. It's freaking amazing. CVS and Advil PMs and the *prose* . . . I'm obsessed."

"Well, I'm sure the author would feel the same way about your book . . ."

"Nah, I stuck it in a drawer, maybe I'll go back to it after the fellowship. And maybe not. Anyway, the stories are connected and—"

"Wonder, you can't just give up because you hate Glenn."

"I don't 'hate' Glenn. And you were there. Everyone in the room agreed with him, and fifty million Englishmen can't be wrong. If I go back to it . . . I mean who knows if I will. I'll tell you this, I'm not Kate Freaking Wisel. Anyway, should we get dessert?"

We order a slice of carrot cake and if only I were a pig. If only I didn't care about your career. I pick up the tab and you wave bye to our table—your *tendency to love* is profound, it even applies to furniture—and I want to restore your faith in *Faithful*, and you squeeze my arm and smile. "Should we go in?"

We're outside of Trident Books and yes! Yes, we should go in. When everything is impossible, when you can't have your golden ticket and your pot of gold, that's when you go to the bookstore. Every novel is a triumph. Author versus herself, versus the system, versus the call of the Internet, the naysayers. We're in fiction and my fingers are crossed and it's here, Sly's *Flour Girls*. Her dedication is a knife in the back—*For my dear and loving husband*—and you peer at the cover. "What's this?"

"Glenn's wife's book."

"Oh, right," you say. "Lovely."

You're better than that. *Gently, Joseph.* "I think you'd actually like it."

You shrug. You're hung up on *Driving in Cars with Homeless Men*, the book Glenn passive-aggressively recommended, but we're here for a reason. We have to get your mojo back, make you remember why you applied to the fellowship, not because of Glenn, not because of the 25K, but because you love books. This is my turf, where I shine, and I am Elliot in *Hannah and Her Sisters*. "Let me get this for you. You'll see."

You are as wary as Lee in *Hannah*, hesitant. "Joe, what are you freaking doing? With all the books in this world, you think I wanna read one that reminds me of *him*?"

"I'm just trying to buy you a present."

"Just let it go already, okay? I told you. I'm done. Done. I know he's your friend, and if you ask me, it's pretty freaking cool that I put up with it. But if you think you can humanize him by getting me to read his wife's freaking book . . ."

"I'm not trying to 'humanize' him. He's . . ." A fraud. "Fuck him. Sly's a great writer and I know you like that short story collection, but maybe a novel is the right thing for you to read right now since you're writing a novel."

You bang your teeth together and snarl. "I am not writing *anything*."

I *push* and tell you that reading a novel might make you *want* to write your own, and you roll your eyes, but I see you clock *Flour Girls*.

But then you regress. "Can we go? I don't know what I was thinking, I can't blow any more money on books."

"Look," I say. "The other day, I saw Sly and she raved about you."

"Oh, so now you're hanging out with his *wife*."

"Wonder, she thinks you're a fucking genius. Seriously."

"Can we just go?"

"Don't you get it? You trigger Glenn because he knows his wife is better, but her book flopped. That's why he was so hard on you. It wasn't about you. He's a stereotypical fake feminist. He didn't *mean* any of it. He's just jealous, trying to get a rise out of you."

You pinch your nose and rub your forehead, and this is good. You're hearing me. You reach for Sly's *Flour Girls*. You turn the pages and sense what you can't possibly know—*She sounds like him . . . They both like their cicadas, don't they?*—and the answer is yes. Yes, they do. They are one. Sly saved her best stuff for her husband's book because she knew he could never love her if she put her best into *her* work. You close *Flour Girls* and you see the light, you see Glenn for what he is, another *Ivy League Douchebag* who wants to smack you down. But then you plop the half-baked bakery novel on the shelf.

"If I leave now, I can get home before Cherish takes Caridad to my cousin's."

It's a bump—this is our day—and I stammer. "I thought we were going to my place?"

"Where I come from, people give it to you straight."

"That's what I'm trying to do." BUT I CAN'T TELL YOU ABOUT GLENN FRAUDDY.

"No, Joe. You're just selling me on these people. As if I'm supposed to forgive Glenn because you're all buddy-buddy with his *wife*."

"That's not what I said."

"All the school yard nonsense—'He was a dick to you because he likes you'—It's not for me. I don't want all this the way you do and I'm tired of fighting about it."

"Wonder, wait."

You turn to me and this is a bookstore, a place of hope where a guy like me can find a girl like you. But then your eyes land on my bike shorts, on the Ray-Bans resting on my head.

"Sorry," you say. "But I just . . . I can't do it anymore. You're great and I know you mean well but . . ."

"You're not ending this right here. Wonder, it's me."

But you shake your head no, as if it's not "me." And the truth is . . . you're right. Never mind the spandex or the *cycling* or the broternship. I'm keeping a secret from you, something major, and though you're struggling for words, shaking, unable to pinpoint what's "missing" between us, you do know that something is missing. And you are confident about your instincts.

"I feel it in my bones, okay? I just . . . We can't do this anymore. We're different or you're different . . ."

"Wonder, wait."

But this is really happening to me. You're breaking up with me in a bookstore. You wave. "I'll just . . . I'll see you in class."

18

We're two workshops into our terrible, no-good life as the couple that almost was, polite fellows who check our personal history at the door. I think about you all the time, when I see you on Goodreads, raving that you "could never write anything as on point as *Driving in Cars with Homeless Men*." It hurts, Wonder. It hurts when I see you in the room, when I see your panties next to my boxers in my chest of drawers, when I sit on my velveteen chair, when I go to Cherish's Facebook and see you leaning into your roots, as if you like Canobie Lake Park, as if you had any business skipping Lou's reading at the Coop to go to Tara's fucking *housewarming* party.

I'm still here. Still reading between your lines. I overheard you whining about pulling a double to Sarah Beth. You're doing everything in your power to remind our fellows that you work at Dunkin', that you're not one of them, not *really*, and you told her you feel like Goldie Hawn in *Private Benjamin:* "I wanna go out to lunch."

I rented the movie, Wonder. Goldie Hawn plays a spoiled princess and for some hackneyed, plotty reason, she's in boot camp, fatigued in fatigues. It's raining and it's dismal and her mascara is running down her face. She whimpers for all the women watching, all the women who know the feeling of wanting to give up the fight once and for all: "I wanna go out to lunch."

But that's not how it ends. At her lowest, Private Princess Benjamin is weary—*Women do get weary*—but she bucks up and finds that she *does* want more than lunch. It's the lesson of countless stories. Obstacles are our friends. Heroes despair, we think the mountain is insurmountable, we could never steal that fucking KOM, but we recover. Nobody wants stories about people who let the obstacles win, and that's what Glenn Shoddy is: an obstacle.

You're *real* and you're weary. You don't have it in you to fight another *Ivy League Douchebag*, especially one in charge of our room. I see you fading. You don't wear your J.Lo hoops and you slouch, you say as little as possible like some delinquent coasting through math class. It was Mats's turn in the room, and at first I was happy for you. O.K. was hardly sold on his work—*Mom says videogame references will alienate tastemakers*—and Sarah Beth "didn't care about the characters" and Lou, who is himself a genre writer, said he "can't get it up for genre." I was hopeful that you would realize that it's why they call it a workshop, that the whole point is for us to *push* each other. But then Glenn slammed his phone on the table. "Stop it," he said. "While it saddens me to say this, none of you are smart enough to see what Mats is doing. He's brilliant."

And then it was your workshop in reverse. Our fellows played follow-the-leader, walking back their criticism, reversing their position, and the worst part of all was you. You were happy for our fellow Mats, which proves that you don't have a bitchy, self-obsessed bone in your body. You're the most talented and gracious living woman writer and I can't let you go on like this, wandering down the stairs of the Barker Center onto campus and then into your world alone. You have someone who loves you, someone you love, and people don't throw that kind of love away, at least, not on my watch they don't.

All that resolve and I have nothing to show for it. Another drastically horrible week without you. I stopped by Dunkin' the day after workshop—bad idea—and you gave me a free extra-large regular— the pity and the pain—and then a couple days later, I texted you, nothing too needy, just a simple *thinking of you* but you blew me off with a *busy but hope you're good*. I'm not *good*. How the fuck could I be good? You're still not writing. In our last workshop, you told the room that some of your favorite authors didn't publish until they were in their sixties, that you're "a late bloomer" in every possible way. Message received—you think it's not time for you to write your book, to let me into your heart—but that's where you're wrong, Wonder.

I pull my bike shorts up, the ones I was wearing the day you dumped me.

I loved it when you were mine, when you worried about me and warned me that bicycles bring out the worst in people, especially people behind the wheel of a car. "Some guy who's late for work is gonna run you over—*smash*—and what a waste!" I know why you said that. If I died, you'd be stuck with your family, and that was an unbearable thought for you.

You inspire great things in me, Wonder. And I ride smart because of you.

Well, most of the time.

Today, I have to be a daredevil. If you knew about the mountain I'm climbing you would tell me I'm crazy to do it, and honestly . . . you would be right. But that's life. It's the line in that god-awful Mass-hole movie you made me watch, Jessica Biel licking an ice cream cone and taunting Sarah Michelle Gellar's husband. *You want big rewards, you gotta take big risks.*

I've tried to do things the nice way. I've been coping with our split by riding with Glenn, challenging *him* to climb a mountain that matters, pushing him to make things right with you. Every time I go there, it's the same.

My wife likes Wonder's stuff too, but I stand by what I said, Joe. She's a hack. A hot hack, but a hack.

That's your dick talking. You just miss fucking her.

Given what Sly told me, there is no doubt in my mind that he is projecting all his self-loathing onto you. It's not lost on me that every time I bring you up in conversation, it takes him about two nanoseconds to go into name-dropping mode.

Joel and Ethan called last night. They want me to fly out and visit the set.

I have to say . . . I am surprised by how well I got on with Clooney. But I guess that's why people like him so much. Of course, it doesn't hurt that he called me a genius all night.

Two weeks is a long time. I remember back in Florida, when Ethel was two weeks into her stay in my basement, that's when she started to come around, that's when she admitted that my book *had potential.* Anyone who remains as pigheaded as Glenn after two fucking *weeks* of communing with someone like me is beyond hope, and the logic is simple. You can't take down the king of the mountain unless you dethrone him.

He's the one who reminded me of the happenstance of all Ivy League order. He's here because someone gave him a golden ticket and I'm here because he gave me a golden ticket. It's a fucking pyramid scheme but at the same time, Glenn Shoddy believes in me. He wants to use his power to give me *another* golden ticket—entrée to the literary elite—and it's crazy that I'm here, about to eliminate the man hell-bent on being my champion and any aspiring writer would be flabbergasted, they would ask how I could shoot myself in the foot, why would I take down my own mentor?

And the answer is simple. Because he doesn't believe in you.

Yes, I was lucky when the overlords chose Glenn to run the room, and when he's gone, they'll choose somebody else and fresh blood in the room means a fresh start for us. This time around, you'll be my champion and I will be yours and we will climb the mountain together.

I strap on my helmet and I'm not ready for this trail. I think of a *9-1-1* episode—I binge to purge thoughts of you but it doesn't work—but this one episode, it was helpful. There's a woman married to a cyclist. His dying wish is that she learn to ride. Months pass before she's at ease on a bike and even then, she falls, she comes dangerously close to death, and the wind is against me—fuck you too, Mother Nature—and this boulder wasn't here when I hiked this trail last week—fuck you, boulder—and my thighs aren't there yet—I can only push so much—and I am fighting gravity—I didn't have a bike when I was a kid—and the pine trees smack me in the face—*Go back to the city*—and I am dying—my lungs are a vital organ, same as anyone's—and the clearing isn't where it was last time—and who the fuck invented the bicycle in the first place?

But then I'm here.

I throw my bike at a tree and kiss the moss and the grass—I will brush my teeth before I kiss you—and I hug the earth and thank *God* for Mother Nature.

I did it, Wonder. I built a mountain. I am king.

It's been a dance, competing with Glenn, who likes it better when he's at war with Kilroy, a man who means nothing to him.

But last week I stole a KOM from Glenn. I was smart about it. I texted him immediately and called it a fluke. And he fell into the trap—he stole it back from me the next day—and I waited four days to do it again—*Lol the wind was very much on my side*—but Glenn wouldn't let me reign—he bailed on dinner with his wife to ride at night—and that's why I know he won't let me reign today.

I pull the fishing wire out of my pack, and I set the trap low, but not too low. It's that point in the trail where you can't look anywhere but up, which is why Glenn won't see it coming.

And then I text him. *Shit! Okay this IS pretty cool, laying out a trail. Might have to do it again tomorrow. You said it buddy. This is addictive in the best possible way.*

He doesn't write back to me—I knew he wouldn't—and I build a little fort out of branches and leaves. I like it up here, Wonder. I still have cell phone service—it's not *that* fucking high—but it's like treading water in the middle of the ocean. The chirping birds and the soaring hawks, the bunnies and the foxes, the reminder of what death is, the most integral part of life. No matter what you believe about how it all got started, whether it was a big fucking bang or a bored fucking God, there is no doubt that we live in a world that calls for some to die so others may live.

I walk over to the edge, to the cliff, and I look down, and it's an old Sacriphil lyric, the deathly drop of it, *a gun in a barrel, a barrel in a gun.* I'm excited for Glenn to soar, to fall. If you think about it, this is what he wants. He rides so he doesn't have to write, because he *can't* write, because the world thinks he *can* write and he drowns his sorrows in vodka and Twitter and honestly, this is a more dignified way to go.

It's the snap of a branch I've been waiting for—it's him—and he's better than me—he's close—and I run like hell back to my fort and cross my fingers—I want him to fly—and he's pumping his heart out on his Fuji, as if stealing a KOM from me will make him what he is not—talented, productive—and part of the reason he's not a good writer is that he suffers from a lack of patience.

See, Glenn isn't a *Ride or Die* guy, not really. He's in this for the steal. I noticed it the second time I rode with him for real, when he was hunting one of Kilroy's KOMs. He knew he'd beaten Kilroy's time, and while some people would pump harder in that moment, Glenn threw his hands up in a V and tore his helmet off his head.

Afterward, I asked him what that was about, and he laughed. "I won."

"But why not wait until it's over to celebrate?"

"I've done enough waiting in my life. You'll see what I mean when you're in the game, in publishing I mean."

It sounded crazy to me then and it sounds even crazier to me now. Everyone knows that waiting is hard—we all know Tom Fucking

Petty—but we also know that waiting is part of life, not just the writing business. Lucky for us, Glenn is an impatient man.

He is ten feet away from the wire and his eyes are on the prize and he lifts his arms up in a V—ten feet turns into two feet—and he unclips the helmet—two feet turns into ten inches—and *that* is why Glenn is flying. It's almost beautiful and I wish you could see him. The man obsessed with control has none whatsoever and I swear to you, he is smiling while he swims in the air, screaming into the abyss.

And then his bones meet the rocks. *Crunch.*

Life goes on around us. The squirrel that was eating a nut is eating another nut and I peer over the edge. He's dead, like so many other creatures in these parts.

I was taking a risk today, Wonder. Glenn does that helmet removal schtick when he's riding with me, but that's mano a mano, that's *dude* crap. I had no way of knowing if he would do it today, on his own. And I was prepared for the alternative ending. I knew that he might survive the crash, that he might not actually die. I was at peace with the reality that come tomorrow, you and I might be visiting him in some hospital for rich people, watching him on *Good Morning America* turning his accident into some kind of hero's fucking journey.

But deep down, maybe he knew what I know, what Sly knows, that his oft-lauded brain isn't anything special, that it can't even begin to compete with that larger organ inside of him, the one no surgeon can remove . . . the male fucking ego. I didn't kill Glenn.

He died because he took off his helmet. He's gone for the same reason Ethel couldn't produce a second book. Some people want to be king so badly that they can't get out of their own way and finish that damn draft, and then finish it again, and live for the act of writing a scene or riding a bike. The royal moments are supposed to be the fortune cookies that come after the meal, the cherries on the top of the sundaes. They're rare for a reason, Wonder. It's external validation of the work you did, the big meal you fed the world, the meal you devoured. But Glenn wanted to live on Maraschino cherries and boxes of fucking fortune cookies, *KOMs*. He wanted to win a battle every fucking day, as if all the KOMs in the world would make it easier for him to trudge through this life knowing that his literary KOM, the one he cared about, wasn't his. It's sad that he went ahead with *Scabies*, so desperate to raise his arms in a V that he couldn't learn the most important lesson in life, in cycling, in writing, in love.

It's better to be in flow than it is to be validated for evidence that you were once in flow. And poor Glenn, with his do-gooder, well-intentioned parents who taped his report cards to the fridge and read him *Charlie and the Chocolate Factory,* he just couldn't do it. First he thought he was Charlie and his parents emboldened him, they made him feel like he *deserved* to be Charlie, to graduate to Willy Fucking Wonka and control the words on the page, the access to the kingdom, the factory, the future.

But he wasn't Charlie and he sure as fuck wasn't Willy Wonka. We don't need him, Wonder. The glass elevator is ours now.

19

I wasn't gonna tell you about our dead mentor in a *text* so I called you and you gasped—*No, no this is impossible*—and then you made it all about me, ☺—*That could have been you*—and my voice wasn't good enough.

You needed to see me in person. You had to hug me, hold me, and scold me—*Strava is a pissing contest death cult*—and I promised you that I learned my lesson. "I'm done riding, Wonder. There's no way I'm gonna fly into my demise in a Cycopath shirt."

And now we are what we were before, we are *in this together.*

My bike is locked to a radiator by my front door, and look at you, on my sofa. When it comes to getting back together with your ex, there is nothing like death. It does wonders for the living. You won't leave my side because you get it now. Time is precious, just like love. And it's fucking *fun,* analyzing the ongoing eulogy group text with you, wading into the betting pool about our next professor. Ani's money is on Edwidge Danticat and Lou's set on Lou Berney—Oh,

Lou—and Mats is crossing his fingers for Chuck Wendig and Sarah Beth is team Lauren Groff. O.K. wants Mom—duh—and I still feel like I got the short end of the stick at the Spee, so I'm pro Michael Chabon. We all swear not to tell *anyone* that we've turned this into a game, because how awful of us, how callous. Glenn *just* fucking died. But it's only natural. It's Robin Williams in *Dead Poets Society*. Jump up on the desk and seize the fucking day!

"Hey, Won," I say. "Who are you gonna put your money on?"

"No one," you say. "I just hope they let us keep the stipend."

That's you these days, stunned and bruised by Glenn's verbal whip, as if he can ever hurt you again. There's your computer, on the other side of the room. It's not even plugged in. I eliminated the gate-keeper from the Chocolate Factory. I sacrificed my Wonka for you, but you won't join me in the glass elevator and you're on a campaign to make it all go away, our big bright future as fellows.

You lurk in the group text, but you don't participate, and you groan. "Can you believe these people? The man is dead, and Lou's saying how Glenn was gonna host his freaking *book launch party* and O.K.'s like *Oh, we traded* Paris Review *tweets constantly*. They're *still* trying to one-up about who knew him best, as if we don't know it was you." You put down your phone. "I'm so done with all of it. I mean it's cursed."

I sigh. "It's not 'cursed.' He was a ride-or-die kinda guy and he died."

Your shoulders drop. Your head and your heart are on the wonder wheel, spinning. One minute you're mad at him. The next minute you're mad at me. He was terrible to you and his behavior didn't stop me from riding with him and I can't tell you the one thing that would make it all go away—THAT'S WHY I ASSISTED HIS CLICK-BAIT MURDER BY EGO—and you lean into me, and maybe you're right. Maybe the fellowship *is* cursed.

"Wonder, we don't have to go."

"Yes, we do. Let's go say goodbye to your friend."

Your friend. "Wait. Is that what this is about?"

"Tara and I used to have this friend Vicky, right? Vicky was freaking *terrible* to me, but she was good to Tara, and Tara was like *If you want me to hate her I will.* That's not how I roll, Joe, okay? The man was *your friend* and I'm sad for you, so that's it."

You say that like you're like my plus one, like we're not in this fellowship *together* and it's a funeral party for dead Glenn, for your dead spirit, and so help me God, if killing Glenn killed your spirit, *no*.

"You're gonna bite my head off, but I really think you'd feel better if you wrote some of this down, not for the book, just because that's what writers do. We process things on paper."

You detach your little body from mine and pick up the remote. "Nope," you say. "I have no desire to write. I'm not a freaking writer and I know that now. I'm gonna go through the motions and finish the fellowship and get my stipend and then I'm out."

You turn up the volume on the ladies of *The View.* You taped it because you can't get enough of the coverage, all the wallowing about the "untimely and unnecessary" death of a rising star, the hyperbolic segments about the dangers of the Strava app. I want to jump into the screen and tell them that he didn't die because of "the burden of success." He died because he was an asshole, and his death was timely and necessary, and speaking of which . . . it's time to go to his death party. I'm dressed and ready but you're still on the sofa, glued to Joy Behar.

"Okay," I say. "You don't have to go. Everyone will understand."

"I don't care about those people. We're going."

You pull yourself off the sofa and gather your hair into a topknot and throw on a "Devil in a Blue Dress" kind of frock and all the while you're talking, but not so much to me as to you, your conscience. "See, I know who I am. When someone passes, I pay respect. I'm not going because I care what our freaking *fellows* think. I'm going because it's the right thing to do." You pause in front of the mirror in my hallway. "I need my hoops. Have you seen them?"

You're not J.Lo. You don't "need" your oversized gold fucking hoops. She wouldn't wear them to a memorial and you're a writer and the clock is ticking—I don't want to miss the Coen brothers—and you're pulling the cushions off the sofa and I'm opening the cabinets and you tell me the earrings aren't in a cabinet and then you squeal. "Boom," you say. "Got 'em. You ready?"

I sink onto the cushionless sofa and you come to me, gentle. "Look," you say. "Don't worry about me, okay? I'm . . . I'm happy. I mean in some weird way, it's like this monkey off my back. I don't wanna finish my book. I'm happy I got a fellowship because I got to meet you and your 'fellows' and it's a *good* thing. It's kinda like . . . My whole life I wanted to go to the sausage factory and see how the sausage gets made . . ." It's a *chocolate* factory. "And now I've been there, you know? I saw it. And it's not for me. I don't like how much I cared what he thought of me, what they thought of me, and in my heart, I'm just happier as a reader, okay?"

Glenn's death can't fix all problems—you are meant to be a writer and you need to get back on the horse—but we'll get there, Wonder, and I kiss the back of your hand. "Of course."

On the way to the death party, you link your arm through mine and we are #BrahminStrong, all dressed up on a Tuesday in that way that makes sleep-deprived undergrads gawk at us, you in your J.Lo hoops, me in my Hugo Boss suit.

I try to see things your way. I imagine us in the future, I'm famous and you're a writer slash critic, one of those Twitter tastemakers who helps people who don't trust their instincts know what book they should be talking about, but you get a text from Tara and no, Wonder. She's a part of your past and you're *too* happy for her, the same way you're too easily satisfied with your day job, mastering the art of small talk at Dunkin', knocking back Jell-O shots with Your Bobby in his outdoor man cave and I know you.

If you give up on writing, you won't become an editor or a critic or a book Twitter person. Your *tendency is to love* and you will think it's your job to take care of me, same way you take care of your dad, Your Bobby, your Tara, who has a fucking husband as well as in-laws.

We make it to RIP Glenn's street, same way we made it to Harvard, but you see all the ritzy mourners milling around in his front yard. You grab my arm. "So do I look all right?"

I say yes, that *you look wonderful tonight* even though we're back to square one, day one, and your J.Lo hoops are your THEY HATE US 'CAUSE THEY AIN'T US T-shirt. You are nervous, and you correct me— "You mean wonderful *today*"—and I feel it too, Wonder. The Shoddy home is intimidating even under normal circumstances, but this is a scene, with the property itself all dressed up for the death party, adorned by caterers beelining from trucks, while luxury mourners emerge from luxury sedans. We cross the lawn, moving like service workers who couldn't find the back entrance, and we're in the house, in the *Vanity Fucking Fair* spread of all the swanky people on all the swanky sofas. I see power players who could *discover* me, help me, and I feel your heart pounding in your hand. I tell you it's okay and you gulp. "I don't know."

I don't either, and I've never felt more autofuckingdidact in my life. Lou knows people and Sarah Beth is a name and Ani got in with O.K. and Mom and Mats's blood runs naturally cool, which means even when he's standing alone by a makeshift bar, he seems self-sustained, content. RIP Glenn's not around to sing my praises—I miss being the special one—and the widow Sly excuses herself from a Coen brother. She weaves her way to us, and we let go of our hands—I'll hug her, but not too hard—except no, I won't. She throws her arms around *you* and she tells you that she's been worried about you, that Glenn was *going through some soul chaos* and was projecting his frustrations about his own work onto you.

"Sly," you say. "I don't want you to worry for one second about me. How are *you*?"

Sly says all the widow things, the shock, the horror, the empty other half of the bed, etc., and she seizes your hand. "But really, Wonder. It means so much to me that you're here. You have to know that he thought the world of you. He just wasn't in a place where he could handle it."

Women fascinate me, Wonder. You were against Sly, you wouldn't even consider reading her novel in the bookstore. But this is the magic of murder. He's gone, she's here, and you don't open *slowly, petal by petal*. You blossom into something entirely new to me, to you. You tell her she's too kind—you never say things like that—and you tell her you just read *Flour Girls* on Kindle—I offered to buy you the paperback!—and the widow Sly could be talking to anyone right now, but she's putting you first, and you know it. You feel it. Redemption.

You praise her *cicadas* and she is giddy for your "Fenway frankness." *You're* the talented one, and you tell her that you know Glenn "made some good points" and I thought it would be hate at first sight—she doesn't even have her ears pierced—but death is an X factor. Because I killed the bastard, you skipped the part where you size each other up on the surface. You bring it back to her now. "Everything aside, my dad lost my mom early on, and it was brutal. You're with someone and they're gone and I just . . . I feel for you, Sly."

I keep waiting for one of you to realize I'm here and Sly rubs her nose. "Thank you, honey. I love your hoops, by the way."

Your smile isn't for me, but it is. This is why I did it and I can be invisible, for now. The rust is falling off the wonder wheel of defensive anti–Ivy League resentment that's been spinning in your head for your whole adult life. Sly is shaking, she's going to cry, and you put your arm around her—you'll be a great mother one day—and you shepherd the widow off to a half bathroom and now it's a new game.

It's *my* time to shine. I rode with the king. I was the chosen one. I start small, with our fellows, joining Lou and Ani to remind them that Glenn chose *me* to be his bro-tern.

"The last time I saw him, the night we went to the Spee, he was so revved up about your book, Lou. He told me the two of you had dinner, with the ladies."

Ya hear that, Lou? You were just *fodder* for me and Glenn! The play works, and Mr. *O'er Under* makes a big fucking deal of introducing me to his *lady* and Ani and Mats vie for my attention—*Were you always a cyclist? Are you gonna make a speech today?*—and you come back alone, having helped Sly hold it together, and you soak up all the love for you, for me. I see it in your shoulders, in your hoops. You're blossoming at warp speed, a peony in a time-lapse video, and the other mourners are whispering about us as a whole—*Those are Glenn's writers*—and it's a baptism of gossipy, powerful gazes. I'm not the kind of asshole to say I told you so, but I fucking did, same way I just told REDACTED OUT OF RESPECT FOR RIP GLENN'S PRIVACY where he could find the bottle opener, same way I asked REDACTED LITERARY GOD about his favorite part of *Scabies*.

We're *Almost Famous* and "it's all happening" and REDACTED OSCAR WINNER elbows me at the buffet. "Rabbits don't eat baby carrots."

I let her go—I am not a starfucker—and Sly nudges me. "Okay," she says. "I should not be about business right now, but it's Klonopin and wine and a widow's prerogative. Come on. You *have* to meet Glenn's agent."

I want you there with me but you're in the backyard with a Coen brother and Lou and his *lady* and we lock eyes like Kate and Leo in the first five minutes of *Revolutionary Road* and it's *good* that you're busy. You're not ready for an agent just yet, but I am, and Sly links her arm through mine. "Also, I am in love with Wonder."

"She's pretty great."

"Yes," she says. "And I told her how much it means to me that she's here, not even for Glenn, but for her, you know? I don't know if I could have come to this if . . . Well, I just can't wait for Tuesday."

"What happens Tuesday?"

"Wonder didn't tell you? Of course she didn't. I only just told her. I'm taking over the workshop."

No one wins the betting pool and nepotism is real—the author of *Flour Girls* is teaching at *Harvard*—but what's good for you is good for me. "I love it. Congratulations."

She smiles. "We'll see. I haven't run a room since grad school . . ."

We are in a roomful of overqualified REDACTEDs and I assumed one of *them* would assume the position. But I'm happy for Sly. She's coming out of her shell because of what I did, and she adores you—*the girl is a genius*—and *the doggone girl is mine*, the doggone girl is you. At the buffet table, REDACTED PRETTY BOY refers to Glenn as *the only man in the history of the universe who made* Scabies *a beautiful thing* and Sly heard it too and good for her. She deserves a death party favor in the form of a little boost, and I'm the keeper of her secret, the only one on the planet who knows that she *does* deserve her job. "We're really lucky, Sly, and it's amazing you're up for it, considering the circumstances . . ."

She knows what I mean—the pricks in the room think her *husband* was the genius, that she is the lesser widow—and she feels seen, which is good. The more she likes me, the more likely she is to keep the pedal to the metal and deliver me to her dead husband's agent. It's hitting me now. Sly is our new Willa Wonka. I need her to love me, to trust me, to *owe* me. "It's nice to feel all the love for Glenn, but how are *you* holding up?"

She looks around the room. Wild-eyed. "I'm a widow," she says, waving at REDACTED LITERARY BASEBALL FANATIC—he's here!—and rubbing her upturned nose. "I'm *Emily, Alone* at thirty-five and I forgot to put out the good hand towels and do I throw out Glenn's coconut water or do I save it because other people like coconut water? His parents didn't invite me to stay in their house when I was out there for the funeral, and I left my favorite sweater in the shitty hotel, and I called the hotel, but I hung up when they answered because it's a sweater, right? It's meaningless and I'm a widow and shouldn't I be sobbing about my dead husband?"

I don't know what to say to that and I don't have to know what to say because *ta-da*. Glenn's agent is upon us. I recognize her face from the Internet, shiny as a businessman's shoes after a sit-down in a train station. "Oh honey," she says, pulling Sly into a soulless embrace. "If you want me to start a small but just big enough house fire to clear the joint, I am here for you."

A little laughter. A little small talk. And finally, Bernie—short for Bernice—takes charge. "Darling, let me give you a Xanax."

Sly tops off her Klonopin with a Xanax. Yikes. "Bernie," she says, already calmer. "I am so rude. So, this is *that* Joe. Glenn's Joe."

I open my mouth to charm Bernie into an on-the-spot signing but O.K. and "Mom" interrupt to say goodbye, and it's goodbye in a big way—O.K. is dropping out of the fellowship to go to NPR—*I just can't be in that room without Glenn*—and I'm a good writer because I can read Mom's mind—*Thank God my daughter finally knows her place*—and it's hugs and kisses and get the fuck out of here and where were we?

We were about to talk about *Me*. I reach for Bernie's hand. "So good to meet you."

Sly hard-sells me and my writing, my *moving raw tone*, and Bernie is stone-cold sober—she will *remember* this fucking moment—and Bernie can't cut her off—widows have rights, especially writer widows—but she seizes Sly's arm in a cold, agenty kind of way. "Well, then you have to let me read this book."

No one on this planet has read the whole book except RIP Glenn and RIP Ethel Rose-Baker and I'm shaking like Diane Keaton in *Baby Boom*. This is it. The Food Chain wants me. I play it cool as a working single mom CEO. "Well," I say. "I'm happy to share it with you, but I have to warn you, Sly hasn't read the whole draft, so it might need a little work . . ."

I want Bernie to sign me right here, right now, but Lou and his *lady* and Sarah Beth and her *hubby* break into our circle. We can't do business now and I need a boost from you, but you're deep in it with the REDACTEDs, and what kind of a boyfriend would I be if I were mad about that? I hold my tongue while everyone shares their *quar stories*—shouldn't we be talking about the death-day boy?—and it's needling me, Wonder. Bernie was in Hawaii and Lou and his *lady* got "stranded" in the Maldives—she was doing research and she's a scientist, and Lou is a sexist asshole for painting her as a swanky sofa-hunting housewife—and Sarah Beth and her *hubby* took the whole brood up north to her family's place in Maine and THIS IS SUPPOSED TO BE MY MOMENT and Bernie looks right at me.

"What about you, Joe? Where were you?"

"Orlando," I say, and okay, Wonder. You're a *little* bit right. The open elitism at my mention of the F-word is offensive, but I owe it to RIP Glenn to focus on my career. "Well," I say. "Before that, home was Bainbridge Island . . ."

"Ooh," Bernie coos. "It's divine there."

I have placated the liberal elite and Lou's *lady* has to pee and Sarah Beth needs to get home to the *kiddos*—bye, bye, GO—and at long last, this is it. My turn.

"So," I say to Bernie. "Should I send you my manuscript?"

She smiles the way rich ladies do. "We'll see what Sly thinks. Anyhow, did you do much boating in Bainbridge?"

20

I feel like a kid again. Fifth-grade itchy. Trapped on a big yellow bus and ready for the field trip to the New York Public Library, but nope! Gotta wait for the driver to get on the fucking bus, for the teacher to do the fucking head count. This is the same thing, Wonder. We're all on the same bus—the fellowship is on hiatus for two weeks—but I'm the only one itching. You're busy writing, and our fellows are overgrown kids. Instead of occupying themselves with spitballs and hijinks, they're on antisocial media eulogizing the fuck out of Glenn.

Everything's in front of me—Bernie wants my book—but everything's on hold, out of my control. Bernie won't read *Me* until Sly deems the book worthy—gatekeepers can't think for themselves—and I couldn't exactly bug Sly to read *Me* at her husband's fucking memorial. We haven't even seen our new widow Willa Wonka—she needed time to "heal"—and it's been exhausting, waiting for my bus to hit the road, focusing on the "positive," which I should do because things *are* good. We both know the room will be different without Glenn—you're welcome, my love—and it was wonderful to see you get back on your computer, tapping slowly, dipping a toe in the water of *Faithful,* encouraging me to do the same. It wasn't gonna happen, Won. I couldn't start a new *novel* right now. It's my own "Bohemian Rhapsody"—*Mamaaaa, . . . Just killed a man*—and I too needed time to "heal."

But Maria Semple was right—*Today Will Be Different*—because at long last, it's Tuesday. *Heigh-ho, heigh-ho, back to workshop we go!* I send you a text—*lunch?*—and you hit me back, literally—*Sorry, I lost track of time jotting down ideas and I gotta deal with my dad but see you at school!*—and it's a letdown, but I won't get in the way of you and your words.

How could I when you're the one and only wonder in my world? You've flourished in Glenn's absence. You're invested in the fellowship, just as I hoped, and when I arrive on campus the department smells like apple pie and something else. Is that . . . Do I smell *paint?* I charge up the stairs, and you wave at me with purple fingertips. "Hi, Joe!"

This isn't the fucking *room.* It's not even vaguely Algonquin, an assault to my sensibilities as a writer, as a man, as an adult. There's a balloon tied to every chair. A drawing pad and a palette of *finger paints* laid out for each fellow. Sly nods to my spot and it's a bad spot, it's not my spot, it's not directly across from you. "Have a seat," she says. "Welcome to the reset!"

I can't play footsies with you or make eye contact with you and RIP Glenn would die all over again if he saw this display. "So, what's a reset?"

"Well, honey, I used to think that praise is poison . . ." I know, Glenn told me before he died. "I loved my husband the man and I loved my husband the writer . . ." Nope! "But I think he took what I said too literally . . ." She closes the door—I was last to show up—and she sighs. "Happy first day of school, kids!"

It really is the fifth fucking grade and we *clap, clap, clap clap, clap.*

"I know it probably seems strange that I'm here. Let's just address the elephant in the room. I'm not my husband."

Laugh, laugh, laugh, laugh, laugh.

"But here's who I am. I'm an Iowa Workshop grad, I just got a cat . . ." They all do this, pair the achievements with the common personal tidbits. I prefer blunt bragging. "My debut novel *Flour Girls* got a Kirkus star and was longlisted for a Women's Prize for Fiction in the UK . . ." Drumroll for the part where she normalizes herself by circling back to her fucking pet. "Ooh, and I named my cat after my favorite writer, Donna Tartt. What else?" I WROTE *SCABIES FOR BREAKFAST.* "Well, I believe that we are here to support each other. The balloons, the finger paints . . . our room is a place where we reconnect with our inner, unselfconscious children."

Lou Instagrams his finger-painting "art," which he dubs an "alternate cover" for *O'er Under.* That should be enough to end this sham right now, but everyone claps and this is "free time," so I dip my finger in the black. I didn't like being a kid when I was a kid and Sarah Beth Swallows is directly across from me, staring at my single black dot. That's . . . kind of weird.

She tilts her head. "I was surprised you didn't chime in on the group text."

"Yeah," I say. "I was rereading *Scabies* and kind of in my own world, too sad to text."

"No," she says. "Look at the whiteboard."

I look up at the whiteboard and in all caps: THE BODY ON BAINBRIDGE. Names abound, names I never wanted to see again . . . *Mary Kay and Phil, the daughter Nomi.* I can't breathe, can't speak, can't stay. *Reset* my fucking ass.

"Well," she says. "Do you know *The Body on Bainbridge*? We've all been bingeing."

Sarah Beth Swallows eyes my black dot, Rorshaching me with her writer eyes and I dip my thumb in yellow paint. Yellow, the color of peace. "I don't think so."

Ani holds up a finger with red paint, red blood. "Oh, Joe, it's so good. One episode and you will be hooked!"

This *is* a reset—this is hell—and you lean over the table and smile. "See, babe, *this* is why you gotta keep up with the group text! It's the best freaking podcast ever."

Last night, while I was reading Dostoyevsky like the Harvard fellow that I am, all of you were devouring *The Body on Bainbridge,* a new whodunit podcast about the remains of a local teacher named Melanda Ruby Schmid. I don't *follow* the gory headlines, so I didn't know that someone found her bones in the Grand Fucking Forest and now it's a trendy *whodunit*—she done it—and you're all *obsessed*—Who did it? Who killed Melanda?—and I knew it in *my* bones. I knew Melanda Ruby Schmid would come back to haunt me. My past is pulling a sucker punch on my present, and you. *You.* I told you about my past. I was smart—I used fake names—and you don't know Bainbridge from Bozeman so you haven't put two and two together, but the whiteboard is a nightmare. I should have fucking *known* that something was amiss. Last week Nomi called me and I sent her to voicemail because I *just* killed Glenn—I needed some downtime—and Nomi is a sociopath in college. I figured she was drunk.

Sarah Beth looks at me. "Speaking of which . . . this is so random, but you lived there, right?"

Insidious oohs and aahs from our lookie-loo fellows and fuck, fuck, *Goose.* Am I cooked? "Just for a little while."

Sly gasps. "Oh that's *right.* You did live there. Did you know her?"

I wish my aorta would relax and I can do this. I can pass. "Know who?"

"Melanda Schmid," Ani says. "That's the story. They found her body on the island."

I shrug and say I "heard she moved" and Lou says it's *noir as fuck* and Mats *can't wait* for the next episode and Sarah Beth brings it back to the body, to the death. "Well," she says. "They found the remains of it anyway . . . There wasn't much left of her because she was found in the woods."

I know. I *left* her body in the woods, but I didn't kill her and I won't panic. Murder podcasts are driven by the collective lust of the public to solve cold cases. This is kindergarten. This is Harvard. There's a balloon on my chair and no one in this room knows what I did.

"Oh, God," I say. "Who found it?"

"Hikers with a dog," Sly says. "Who else? But the story is absolutely wild."

Sarah Elizabeth is not quite as subtle as she'd like to think she is. I'm well aware that she's deliberately resting her eyes on Sly so that I won't feel like I'm in the spotlight. But all animals know when the predator is nearby. We sense it.

Lou grins. "*Wild* is the word. And my money's on Seamus. My lady is right. The man killed innocent animals. The next step is people."

But Ani's not convinced—*He seems more bark than bite*—and Mats observes that guys like Seamus are more likely to be keyboard warriors than *real-life psychos* and your *tendency is to love* so you say you can't imagine anyone killing that *sweet public servant* and Sarah Beth keeps tabs on me, noting the yellow clouds above my big black dot. Is that what a psycho would paint? No. I'm not a *psycho*. Mary Kay's incestuous family, *they* were the psychos.

Sly studies the whiteboard. "All I know is that bless you, Sarah Beth, for sending us the link . . ." More like fuck you. The *nerve*. "And I stand by my theory. Mr. Sacriphil dude did it."

I'm going to faint and they're doing it, Wonder. *You're* doing it, dredging up all the people from my old life, the one that isn't mine, not anymore. Sarah Beth is so *obsessed* that she wants to make a pilgrimage to the island and Sly's eyes bulge with excitement.

"Yes," she says. "Field trip! So on theme with our kindergarten ethos. I love it."

I HATE IT and Sarah Beth says she'd have to run it by the *hubs* and I see the wheels turning in Sarah Beth's head. There isn't a mouse in my house. There are *mice in my hice* and fucking murder-obsessed women and Mats is on my side. He thinks it was a suicide, but Sarah Beth throws down the gauntlet.

"No," she says. "If Melanda were to kill herself, she would have done it in her condo with the candles and the Carly Simon . . ." That detail kills me, but that's from Melanda's Instagram, not *me*. "See," she says, and she's practicing for *Dateline*. "Women commit suicide at home, where they're comfortable."

You are impressed with Sarah Beth's *expertise*, and this is a fucking fiction workshop. Why are we even talking about a podcast? What about Lou's pages?

But this is America, where people love podcasts. Sly doesn't believe that RIP Melanda ever went to Minnesota—Spoiler Alert: Melanda killed herself with a flat-screen TV in my basement—but what if they find out? I was reception-married to her best fucking frenemy and I should have returned Nomi's call—kids her age text, they don't call unless it's bad—and *The Body on Bainbridge* is only just getting started— there are more episodes to come, courtesy of two teachers in the Kitsap County school system—and I use my one paint-free thumb to shoot a text to Nomi.

Sorry I missed you. You okay?

Nomi responds with a link to *The Body on Bainbridge* followed by an emoji, the shrugging brunette woman, and Sarah Beth isn't a writer. Not wholly. She's got the soul of a detective. She saw me send that text.

"Okay, sorry," Sly says. "If we don't stop now, we'll never get to work."

Finally. Talk shifts to books and books always make me feel better, even Lou's new writing, in which he, a straight white man, will "end racism and sexism." I'm okay. Sarah Beth won't figure me out and you're not that girl who likes to talk about my exes because you don't have exes of your own. Sarah Beth Swallows is a pantser, not a plotter.

I covered my tracks, and there's a new fucking *murder podcast* every day. People move on. True, Sarah Beth wouldn't have a career without real-life murder. She's a professional obsessive. The kind of woman who snorts podcasts to get high on unsolved mysteries and then recreates the action on her MacBook Fucking Air in her *murder shed*. But I'm her *writing* fellow. I'm not a suspect. Even Dr. Nicky gave up trying to turn people against me and Sarah Beth knows that in real life, you're never *actually* sitting across from the killer. Life is not a book. It's boring.

"Okay," Sly begins. "We're almost out of time, but before we go, I need to set the record straight about one of our fellows." She looks at you. "Wonder," she says. "You're a ridiculously talented writer, and next week, it's reset part two. You're up again."

You gulp. "I already had my workshop."

"I know," Sly says. "But Glenn was recovering from a rejection, this short story no one wanted, and he brought that negativity into the room. He took his frustrations out on you, and that was wrong. Human error. But like I said, it's a reset. So, you're going again."

"Well, I feel bad so can I . . . I mean is it okay if I send more pages?"

More pages mean you're officially *back* and I needed some good news. I'm the world's best boyfriend, the first one to clap—See that, Sarah Beth? I don't kill women, I love them!—and she *did* see it— she's leaving—and you have to run, you're "dying to write" and Sly asks me to stick around and help her with the mess. See that, everyone? I'm not a *murderer*. I'm the kind of guy who helps the teacher clean up the fucking finger paints! "Happily!"

"Wait," she says. "I don't really need your help. I just have to say something."

Did you murder Melanda Ruby Schmid? "I'm all ears."

"I saw your face light up as if I'd said nice things about Wonder and that's . . . You're a good man, Joe."

Take *that*, whiteboard, and I nod. "I'm just me."

"Cone of silence?"

"Always."

"It's sort of untoward of me to be focused on your work when it's not time just yet, but I feel the need to say that I just can't wait to read the rest of your book. It was triggering, seeing you do for Wonder what Glenn never did for me. So will you go ahead and send it to me?"

I'm happy I killed him. "I'm sorry to hear that. And I can send it right now."

I forward her my final draft of *Me* and it's a thrill to hear her phone buzz with one new email. "Got it," she says. "The thing is, I think I get it now, why Glenn was so in awe of you. Schwinny couldn't write women . . . He didn't want women to be interesting. But you . . . I can't wait to read this. I will print it when I get home and put it on top of my *TBR*."

"That means the world to me, Sly, and it's funny . . ." *Gently, Joseph.* "Well, at the memorial, Bernie seemed like she sort of wanted to have a look at it, too. At *Me*. That's the title."

She smiles. "Well, that's my job, honey. The more I talk you up, the more she'll want to read it, and I have a hunch that I'll be talking you up *big*-time, both you and Wonder."

Did you hear that, Won? It's official. There can be two Charlies in the chocolate factory. Sly loves your work, and she says she wouldn't even be here without me, that I'm the only one who knows her secret. I am a trustworthy feminist and a keeper of secrets and I'm going to be big, bigger than Glenn. Sly takes an eraser to the whiteboard, to my past, and it's on the nose in the good way. "Thank you, Sly. Seriously."

"And, please," she says. "Cone of silence. No need for anyone to know I'm making your book a priority!"

I wish I knew how to slide down a banister, but at the same time it's good that I don't because it's not time to celebrate, not *yet* anyway. I didn't like the way Sarah Beth Swallows was sizing me up. We have so much to lose, we have a new teacher who loves us and it's like you've been telling me. I do need a new project: Operation Stop Sarah

Beth Swallows from bringing me down. The deadline is two fucking days ago and I'm happy that you ran away to write because I need to start right now, tonight. I can turn Sarah Beth on to a better murder mystery or play the *poor widower card* or—

My phone pings. You.

Sooooo I might have been gushing about you so much that my family wants to meet you tonight? Can you do supper at 6? And it wouldn't be the worst thing in the world if you brought éclairs!

21

S arah Beth started the fire with a single text an hour after you
invited me to dinner—*Can I pick your brain about Bainbridge?*—and
six hours later, the fire is spreading. I'm in your house. I should
be in your living room charming the shorts off your father—the man
put on *swim trunks* to show his disrespect for me—and I should be popping Fireball nips with your sister—they're her "candy"—and I should
be playing *Candy Land* with your niece—she took a shine to me right
away—but instead, I'm in your guest bathroom for the second time in
the last ten minutes because Sarah Beth Swallows will not.

Leave.

Me.

Alone.

And no, Wonder. You asked me to shut off my phone, but I can't
do that. It's Machiavellian law: Keep your enemies closer. If Sarah
Beth is gonna abuse the privileges of fellowship and hammer me with
nosy questions—*Your ex-wife was married to that guy from Sacriphil? And*

wait, he's dead, TOO?—I'm gonna *Whac-A-Mole* her right back in real time—*Yeah, Phil overdosed, he had issues.* It's all so unseemly and Nomi is right. Before I left to come here, I called to ask her about *The Body on Bainbridge,* and she grunted: "Don't mention that stupid podcast to me. It won't bring back Melanda or my mom *or* my dad."

Ah, to be young and carefree. Sarah Beth wouldn't harass Nomi because she's a young, orphaned woman struggling through Psych 101, but this is what it means to be me. Male. Inherently suspicious. Last year, Sarah Beth told *Chronicle* about her dream. She doesn't want to win a Pulitzer. She wants to solve a *real-life crime.* She's not a *fiction* writer. She's a True Crime writer in disguise and her questions are getting scary: *Did you know Seamus? Did Seamus and Melanda have a history? I still can't believe Nomi is your stepdaughter. Are you guys in touch?*

I put out the fires—*Barely, just to say hello . . . I have no idea, I didn't know Melanda that well either . . . Nomi and I don't talk much since we never really knew each other that well, but I'm sad for her, this invasion of her privacy*—and I want to go make a good first impression on your family, but she's typing. You knock on the door and I open it.

Your face is an Arnold Palmer, half-rage, half-worry. "What's going on? Are you sick?"

I should have put my phone in my pocket, and you hiss. "Just hurry up, okay?"

You stomp off to the kitchen and in your world, I'm being weird and Caridad is shouting—"Where's Joe?"—and your dad bellows for my benefit—"He's in the can . . . again." I could put out this fire right now. Sarah Beth lives on a farm in Foster, Rhode Island, and she spends the bulk of her nights in her "Dead Shed," a tiny house on her property where she comes up with all her sordid ideas. I could be at her house in eighty-three minutes, but how can I kill her when RIP Glenn *just* fucking died, when she's been *tweeting* about her "obsession" with *The Body on Bainbridge?*

Your house is too quiet—you and your family are whispering

about me—and then you raise your voice and groan. "Dad, he's not on *pills*. He's on the toilet, okay?"

You lied for me, because of me, and this isn't fair to you. You finally meet someone great, you meet *me*. And what do I do? I hide out in the fucking *toilet*. This is the system failing us both. I only told Sarah Beth about Bainbridge because I was insecure, in a roomful of people who know Franzen, and *that's* how the fire got started, how you came to be defending me to your own father—"Dad, he doesn't need a Tums, let him be"—and Sarah Beth is texting—*How long did you live there?*—and this is not fair.

I followed your advice. I brought éclairs and I told all the right lies. I said Cherish looks younger than you—like a young Lisa Rinna—and I complimented your dad's mounted dead marlin. I was batting a thousand but my average is slipping and my phone pings—*I promise I'll leave you alone now!*—but she's a liar. She's not leaving me alone. She's typing and erasing and typing and erasing and I open the medicine cabinet—more fucking nips—and I get another text—*It's just that I'm starstruck and on deadline so this is all I can think about! Terrible, I know, but did you ever go to Melanda's house?*—and she *is* terrible, hiding from her own children pretending to write while she's texting with another man, forcing me to hide from *you*. Her children deserve better. *We* deserve better. I didn't kill Melanda—she committed *suicide*—and Sarah Beth blasts me again—*Wait, they just talked to Nomi. She sounds very cold to me. Is there any way she did it?*

Wow. So, Nomi's a liar, too. She *participated* in the podcast, and nobody wants to throw a kid under the bus, but Nomi stoked this fucking fire and I need to get Sarah Beth into another rabbit hole, so I can get back to you. I type: *I don't think so, but Nomi was obsessed with Columbine. It gave me the creeps.*

Sarah Beth is excited—sick—and she tells me to have a good night, so I flush the toilet and run the faucet and I open the door and BAM. It's your dad. He sniffs. "Everything come out okay?"

He was spying on me—disgusting—and he fans his half-scratched scratcher, and my bowels are none of his business, but he's your father, so I laugh along with his "dad" humor, but my phone buzzes—not *now*, Sarah Beth—and your old man grunts—"You're popular!"—and when I leave, he's gonna tell you that I'm a cokehead or a pill popper or a cheater and I am *none* of those things.

"Surprise!"

You greet me with a box of On-Cor chicken parmesan. "Your favorite home-cooked meal!"

I was so worried about Sarah Beth that I almost forgot about you, the way you love me, the way you listen. I kiss you on the cheek. "Looks just like I remember."

Your father mad-dogs me—it was just a peck—and Cherish rolls her eyes—it was just a peck—and you laugh. Shy. "Nothing to see here folks . . . move on!"

My phone is blowing up again—*buzz buzz buzz*—and your father says the radiation is bad for my loins—oh for fuck's sake—and your sister presents me with a bag of Brussels sprouts—"So we have something fancy on the table"—and she found a recipe on Facebook—God help us—and you're glaring at me—this *could* bode poorly for my loins—and Caridad is crying—"What about Candy Land?"—and your sister groans. "Caridad, he'll play when he wants to play. He's too busy for us!"

My past is on fire and my future is on fire and Sarah Beth texts *again*. I am dead if I check my messages, but I am also dead if it's BREAKING NEWS about the death of Melanda Ruby Schmid. Your dad's eyes are moving from my head to my pocket, *back, back, forth and forth*—and Cherish smacks his wound vac—"Help me out and find the garlic"—and he's on the hunt and your sister is chopping sprouts and you shoot me a look. Your eyes flash red—*Enough*—so I ignore the fire alarm in my pocket and roll up my sleeves. "How can I help?"

And then Cherish shrieks. "Fuck! My fucking hand!"

There is blood on the counter, on her hands, and you're on her with a dirty dishrag—why don't you guys have paper towels?—and your father blames Cherish—*You don't know how to hold a knife*—and Cherish blames your father—*These knives are too dull, where are the ones I got off Instagram?*—and you know how to put out the fire. "Hey C," you say. "This reminds me of that part in Sarah Beth's last book where the wife stabs her husband's eye out with a butter knife."

I don't want to talk about Sarah Fucking *Beth* rhymes with *Death* and Cherish pulls a nip of Fireball off the counter. Swoosh. "That wasn't in the movie," she says. "But thanks."

Your dad tears his scratcher in half. "Bastards," he says. "If only I had an L."

"You're in luck," I say. "I have a spare L in my pocket."

You watch your father reject my dad humor and the back door swings open. "Yo!"

It's Your Bobby—you should have told me he was coming—and he's Santa Claus. He's got scratchers for your dad—*These feel like winners, Bobby*—and he brought another fucking *Swatch* that doubles as candy for Caridad—*I love you Bobby*—and a handle of Tito's for Cherish—*Speaking my language, Bobby*—and it's all code for *You're a loser, Joe! We don't love you, Joe! You don't speak my language, asshole!*

Bobby elbows me, conspiratorial. "How's it going?"

I have no reason to be jealous but they like him more than they like me. "Good," I say, and my phone pings again, and your dad says what you said, that he *hates* cell phones and he wants a vodka root beer—gross—and I offer to make the drink but he shakes me off—*Bobby knows how I like it*—and I check Sarah Beth's latest missive—*I'm so curious about the other guys in Sacriphil*—and your dad grunts. "Look at that, Bobby. I was worried he'd be handsy with my daughter, but the man can't keep his hands off his phone."

"Yeah," Cherish says. "You're worse than me, Joe."

Your Bobby says his sister has a no phones policy at dinner, and your dad says that's a *great* idea and you're on a fool's errand, wiping blood off Brussels sprouts, and I know what you want. You want me to stop looking at my fucking phone and participate in the small talk about Cherish's fucking *Housewives*, but the fire is like Glenn Close in *Fatal Attraction*. I can't ignore it. Not now.

"I'm sorry about this," I say. "Last one, I swear."

Cherish grunts and your dad asks Your Bobby about his new *sauna* and I pick up my phone and you put down your pot holder. Under your breath, for my ears only: "You're not making this easy for either one of us."

I grip my phone, my lifeline to the outside, civilized world. "Wonder, I sold this guy a signed *Heart of Darkness* and he thinks the signature is invalid. I'm sorry but I have a life, too."

My words don't cut it. We're supposed to be *in this together*, so I make another promise I can't keep—"Last text, I swear"—and I tell the queen of butter knife suspense that I simply *can't talk right now*. She is responding—I see those telltale dots—but then those dots disappear, like I'm a reader hanging on the cliff at the end of one of her fucking chapters. I know what you see. Your boyfriend is choosing his phone over your family, your *people*. You're a writer. You notice everything. And still your *tendency is to love*.

"Babe, I'm just worried. You're never like this. Maybe you turn it off and tell him it died or something."

ARGHGHGHGH. No, I can't turn it off because if Sarah Beth can't turn to me, she might turn to *you*. "I can't ignore this guy, Won. He's threatening to sue me."

Another text comes through—Fuck you, Sarah Beth—and I know what you're thinking. *He's not a brain surgeon, he's a bookseller. Why is he sabotaging this freaking night?* Your Bobby is fully engaged with Caridad in Candy Land, and at this rate, who knows? Maybe you'd rather have a sexless moneyed marriage with him than be with an asshole like me. I shove my phone in my pocket. "Wonder," I say. "Can I help?"

"Yes," you say. "You can turn off your phone."

You need a win, so I put my phone on vibrate and you chew your upper lip. "You know the dad in *Faithful* is my dad, so you know that he *freaking hates* phones. He is *not* happy right now."

Your dad is a sexist pig with a boatload of issues and it's never gonna be me and him camped out on the porch with his *scratchers*. "I'm sorry," I say. "I'll do better, I promise."

But then my phone vibrates and it's a terrible confirmation of what we all fucking know: Vibrate isn't *off*. It's passive-aggressive, it's worse than the no-holds-barred fuck you of a *ping* and the buzzer on the oven sounds—*bing*—and you pull the bubbling On-Cor chicken parmesan out of the oven. I breathe it in, my childhood, my mother, and this could be my last supper. The police could break down this door at any moment—Sarah Beth knows where I am—but this is do-or-die. You wanted me to feel at home, so you're surprising me with a piece of my home. I ignore my buzzing phone and take the tray out of your hands and you're happy to see my hands occupied. Actions speak louder than words, especially to someone like you, a writer.

I follow you into the dining room and your dad tells me to grab a seat and he's king of this house, he sits at the end of the table, and I am the guest of honor, so I pull out the chair opposite him, but he clears his throat. Cherish interprets for me—"He means anywhere but *there*"—that's Your Bobby's throne—of course it is—so I sit by Caridad. My phone vibrates again—Is it her? Is it over?—and your dad asks if I own or rent—the nerve—and my phone vibrates again—Does Sarah Beth know what I did on that uptight little island?—and I choke on Brussels sprouts. *Bloody* Sprouts.

Cherish smacks her gums. "You don't have to eat 'em if you don't like 'em."

My phone is officially blowing up and you groan about the vibrations—bad, very bad—and I cough again and I know your sister—I am dead to her—and your father raises a forkful of Bloody Sprouts and sets his eyes on Your Bobby, who raises *his* fucking forkful—they think the blood adds a "kick"—and they're the good guys and I'm the bad guy and my phone is *ringing* now. You put down your fork. Worse. Very worse. And Caridad picks a Bloody Sprout off my plate. "Mmmm."

The sadness in your eyes and my untouched On-Cor chicken

parm and the telltale vibration—I have voicemail—and I wipe a hand over my forehead, because what else can I do? The fire is encroaching and if I don't evacuate now, I die.

"I'm so sorry," I say. "I think I'm coming down with something."

"Huh," your dad says. "I never get sick."

The man has a fucking WOUND VAC attached to his body. He is permanently sick, but never mind him. Before I told you I was distracted because of a customer, and now, I'm playing sick and your sister tells Caridad to go to her room—I have germs—and your dad asks Your Bobby about the last time *he* got sick and Your Bobby can't remember—he is Wonderman, I am weak man—and you slide out of your chair, onto your feet.

"Come on," you say. "We'll do this another night."

I can't give proper hugs—I'm an excuse-blubbering contagion— and you walk me to the door and I say the pathetic thing. "I'm sorry."

"No," you say. "Don't apologize for being sick . . . or busy."

"It came out of nowhere. The stuff with the customer . . . the cold, too. My stomach is off."

I used the word *customer* to remind you that we're alike, we deal in customer service, but your dad sneezes—or he fakes it—and you take the hint and open the door so it's just us, outside, alone. "Do you wanna maybe tell me the truth? Because I know you, okay? You were in the bathroom for half the freaking night and you're not 'sick' and your 'customers' aren't a thing, so what is it? Is it someone else? Are you like . . . disgusted by my family?"

I want to tell you the truth. I want you to know that Sarah Beth Swallows is harassing me, threatening to destroy our future. "I'm too embarrassed to say it."

"All right, fine," you say. "Thanks for the éclairs."

"Wonder, wait."

The fire is ice now, thin and cracking. You could so easily write me off, never speak to me again, file me away with all the other jerks. "I freaked out."

"Right, because my family is *soooo* intimidating . . ."

"Your family is everything to you and what can I say? I choked."

You're quiet. Ruminating. And my phone is loud. Buzzing.

"You've lived all over, hobnobbing with fancy people, and you expect me to believe that you were nervous about my freaking *family*?"

"What you have is what I *don't* have, Candy Land and old stories and home-cooked meals."

It's the best thing in the world, the way you blush, the way you smile. "I hate to say it, babe, but the only 'home-cooked' thing on that table was covered in *blood*."

We're laughing now and we made it through the fire. You tell me that you were nervous, too. It was such a good *reset* in the room, the first time you ever felt at home in the fellowship. "But then I get to my 'real' home, and I'm embarrassed to say it, but I worried you would look down on us, because this new little voice in my head was kind of looking down on us."

We're having a moment. We needed a moment. But your dad is calling for you and my phone is buzzing so we pull apart. I give you a tight-lipped smile, the kind that puts out a good fire, the campfire that is two people falling in love. "I really am sorry."

You swear that we're okay, but actions really do speak louder than words. You close the door on me, and I walk away from Sesame Street. We're going backward. We should be in your living room by now, devouring my éclairs and watching NESN, while I quietly figure out how to avoid this place in the future. The point is, we would be in your living room if Sarah Beth Swallows had never found *The Body on Bainbridge*.

But she did.

I pull up that old email from RIP Glenn, the one I turned to the day we met, the one with all of our home addresses. It's déjà vu except this time, I'm not looking for you.

I'm looking for *her*.

22

S arah Beth Swallows lives on twelve acres in Foster, Rhode Island. It's eighty-three minutes according to Google, but what can I say? She lit a fire under my ass and I made it in seventy-two minutes. It's another rule of war, of writing: Know thine enemy.

She left me a conciliatory voicemail, apologizing *from the bottom of her heart* about "badgering" me. Her voice was high. "And I know I've said it all day, but this time I really will leave you alone because I'm going for a night ride with the fam!" Psychos have something in common: They're never fucking sorry. I dump my car in the woods—so many woods—and I move through the dark on foot, guided by a lamp strapped to my head—thanks, RIP Glenn!—and I spot the clearing, her house, and her "Dead Shed."

She didn't lie to me. The lights are out and the family trucksters are gone. I replay her *Chronicle* segment, the last part, when she allowed strangers (Shayna and her crew) into the "Dead Shed."

Shayna is confounded by the space, so small, so sparsely decorated and she gasps at the lock on the door, the lock that only opens from the *outside*.

"And this is how you write? You feel safe locked up in here?"

"Oddly, yes," Sarah Beth says. "I write a book a year, and that requires discipline."

"But what if you have to pee?"

"I write my best when I have to pee." She laughs.

"But what if there's a fire?"

Sarah Beth says they've only had one "fire" in twelve years of marriage. Her daughter's appendix burst when she was playing volleyball, and her husband knew his wife's phone was off, so he called a neighbor.

I fast-forward through the next part, boring history of the repurposed barn-wood desk, and here's what I need.

"Now it's forty degrees and you have no heat in here, but the window is open."

Smug Sarah Beth nods. "Yes, it is."

"Don't you freeze?"

"Well, that's kind of like having to pee . . . I like being physically tested when I'm under the gun, plus which . . ." She taps a button on her computer. "No spoilers, but I just killed someone today . . ." Giggles, as if murder is so funny. "And whenever I do that, I open a window. My characters are real to me, same as friends, and when someone dies . . . It's the Scandinavian tradition. You open a window so the soul can detach and pass through."

Shayna takes over via voice-over, raving about how readers all over the world are grateful for this *murderous mom*—thanks for nothing, ladies—and I scope out the shed and there it is.

The window. Open.

I make my way through the tall grass and the air is clean in Foster. Clear. It's yet another unseasonably warm, calm night—thank you, climate deniers!—and I find the window and my phone buzzes—you—and I push. Rich people take things like this for granted, high-end windows that slide *with the greatest of ease* and the window is low, just above her desk. I push her computer aside and give myself a boost and I did it, Wonder.

I'm in.

There's a hissing sound, maybe a space heater she left on—*tsk tsk*—and I check your text—*Home safe?*—and I hit you back—*Home thinking about you*—and you throw a heart on my text and this is it. This is the Dead Shed in real life and it's funny. When *Chronicle* was here, she had a glass of water on her desk but now there's a plastic bottle—tsk tsk—and in lieu of bananas there's an open bag of Cool Ranch Doritos—ha!—and this is how the other half *really* fucking lives.

I sit in her chair. It's a high-tech contraption, the type that goes for a thousand bucks, but she reupholstered the cushions with buttery soft leather. I can see us in this house, taking turns in this shed, and I'm not going to "kill her," Wonder. And she's not going to kill herself. She has the kids, the *hubby*, the career.

Three months ago, she did an event on Zoom where she said even *more* about her Dead Shed, that the other reason she locks it down so thoroughly is because she stashes all kinds of poisons in here. They inspire her. Much like mint tea. And because this is a *No Kiddos* zone, the bottles of toxins are all lined up on a bookshelf and I have to laugh again because when *Chronicle* came to town, she had some of her "favorite" books on display, but those books are in a mess on the floor in the corner, and *her* books are on the shelf, on display.

I open a jar of cyanide, and this is a thing she does, watching chemicals dissipate in liquid so that she can make it real for the reader, who would never do such a thing in real life. I close the jar and return it to its little home above her copies of *Our Family Isn't Your Family* and I can't poison her tea, she's too smart. I remember that scene in *The Firm* where the ex-con, good-guy P.I. has a gun attached to the underside of his desk—people who deal with the worst in the world prepare for the worst—so I crawl under her gigantic desk and whaddya know?

No gun, but she's a liar, Wonder! Her desk isn't *found barn wood* from her dad's old house. The Restoration Fucking Hardware logo is right above my head—ha!—and my phone rings—fuck!—and it's you. You're still worried about me. You care.

"Wonder, hi."

"Where are you?"

Under Sarah Beth's mass-produced, environmentally unfriendly desk. "I'm half-asleep."

"I felt bad you didn't finish your dinner and you did seem like you were getting a cold so I sent you soup and the Postmate couldn't get in. Do you want me to come by?"

No no no no *no* but I fucked up big-time tonight—I hear Your Bobby and your dad talking in the background—and I told you I'm *sick* and you told me to rest and why the hell did you have to send me soup? It's the first rule of writing—Show, don't tell—so I think of those blood-soaked Brussels sprouts and burp.

"No," I say. "I think it's a twenty-four-hour bug. You should stay home."

"I can wear a mask. We can catch up on *The White Lotus*."

FUCK YOU COVID. FUCK YOU FOR NORMALIZING MASKS. "Thanks," I say. "But I don't think your family would want you coming over to my place right now, not until I make things right with them. I just need to sleep it off."

A beat. Another beat. You know damn *well* that I'm right about your family. "Well, okay. But seriously, they're over it and next time everything will be fine . . ." That hissing sound again, an omen. "Just grab the soup when you're up for it, okay?"

"I will," I say. "Thank you for that and . . . I love you."

Your dad is within earshot and your voice drops to a whisper. "You, too. Feel better, babe."

You didn't say *I love you too* and I *am* sick, sick in the head. It's getting hard to breathe, it's getting dark, *too dark to see,* and I need air. I need to move. But I'm dizzy. My legs are useless bags of sand and I push Sarah Beth's customized fucking chair out of my way and I'm on the floor, on my back, and my lungs are shutting down and it's not a fucking panic attack and it's not in my head and the hiss I detected wasn't coming from a fucking space heater.

When I opened the window, I set off a booby trap. There's a spray can lodged on the wall above the window and it's hissing—I overlooked the sound because you called—and my eyes are closing against my will and my first instincts were right. People who dabble in the dark arts anticipate the darkness in others, but instincts are of no use to me now, and that's it for me.

Lights out.

23

Sarah Beth is in a Cycopath shirt and she's drinking *tea* and taking a red pen to her pages—fucking *psychopath*—and I'm in her chair, all tied up. I remember her talking about a "research" trip.

I can't break out of these ropes, and she flashes a *Hello, my dear readers* big white smile—"Good morning, sleepyhead!"—and she drops her pages on the desk. "Do you want a sip of tea? Don't worry. It's clean . . ."

It's still dark out—I wasn't out for that long—and my phone is on my lap and I have *six* notifications—you've been calling, you've been texting—and Sarah Beth has twelve acres of private land and a healthy relationship with the local police and a gun.

A *gun*.

"So," she says. "Tell me how you did it. How did you kill Melanda?"

"This is insane."

"Joe, with all due respect, I've visited dozens of men and women in dozens of prisons all over the world, and I'm not going to judge you. I'm just *really* addicted to that podcast."

"I didn't kill her, Sarah Beth, and this is . . . You're my *fellow*."

"I know," she says. "And that's what's so impressive. I hear you in class . . . I know that you look down on my little 'murder' books and I saw you fawning over Franzen at the memorial but it's funny, right? If you had a modicum of respect for me, if you really thought about my books . . . I mean I can't believe it was this easy. You really fell *hard* for that voicemail." She's laughing like this is funny and she's not a *writer*. She's a criminal. I bet she dominates up in the bedroom. I bet the *hubby* has been where I am, trapped, and she smiles. "So come on," she says. "Tell me what happened to Melanda Ruby Schmid."

"I didn't kill her, Sarah Beth Swallows."

"Ah," she says. "I can be down with mirroring, Joe Goldberg." I'm not *mirroring* her and she guzzles her tea. "So, what was the impetus? Were you having an affair with her?"

"God no."

She grunts. "Right," she says. "I guess she's not as doe-eyed as your ex-wife . . . or Wonder . . . or . . ." She licks her finger and flips through the pages of a wrinkled, full yellow notepad. "Ah yes," she says. "Love Quinn and Guinevere Beck."

"This is crazy. Love died of *cancer* . . ." Of the soul. "And if you read about Beck, then you know her hack 'psychologist' is the reason she's gone."

"So many dead girls," she says, and then she writes it down, as if it's a good title.

"Sarah Beth, look at me. I never hurt *anyone* and I came here to talk to you, and this is what you do to me? You want to go down like this? Tying me up in your shed because you got carried away over some fucking podcast? Think about your family inside."

"Okay," she says. "So Melanda was in the way of your 'family' . . ."

"I'm not a bad guy."

"I know that. Nobody said anyone's bad. Nobody said anyone's good. I mean I found some of Beck's short fiction and I went down the Peach Salinger rabbit hole and Forty Quinn . . . He was no better than Henderson . . ."

She knows it all and her notepad is *Homeland* from hell. "I've never killed anyone. I swear."

"Joe, did you read *The Husband's Wife*?"

Half of it. *Enough* of it. "Yes."

"Well, then you should know where I come from in terms of people. I don't do 'good guys' and 'bad guys.' Most people who commit crimes of passion aren't 'bad.' They're cornered. And it seems like you were cornered in Bainbridge, no?"

"Look," I say. "You can hook me up to a lie detector."

She scoffs and rolls her eyes and lectures me about the unreliable nature of all lie detectors and I cut her the fuck off. "I was *happy* in Bainbridge and I didn't . . . I would never have killed my wife's best friend. I mean come on. This is insane. I barely knew Melanda, and Nomi, the poor kid, she's out there, trying to move on with her life, and she goes online and all these people are speculating that she killed her own *mother* . . ."—she did—"And just . . . this is wrong. Melanda's gone, and I have no idea what happened."

"Yes," she says. "As opposed to Phil . . . I mean he overdosed at home. No mystery there . . ."

She glances at her tea as if I'm the sicko, as if I wasn't merely responding to her fucking witch hunt. "Joe," she says. "I read your pages."

No, she didn't. "I haven't sent them out yet."

"Oh, I know," she says. "But you made an impression on me during O.K.'s workshop . . ." It's awful the way some limbic part of my writer brain just lit up with dopamine. "So, I texted Glenn . . ." She looks at me. "You know, our teacher, the one who died on a bike ride, which is crazy because you two rode together a lot, no?"

"I wasn't with him that day."

"Right," she says. "The one time he goes it alone without his new little buddy, he flies off a cliff. It's funny, no?"

"It's not 'funny.' I was nowhere *near* good enough to be on that trail."

"In my business we call that 'convenient,'" she says, glancing at her stacks of murder books. "Anyway, I asked him for your pages, and he said no, as he should, as that's against the rules, but then I worked him over, you know, sent him a couple of glowing reviews of *Scabies* that I found and . . . Well, that's the thing about you guys. You are just *so* easily won over."

RIP Glenn is dead and he's still fucking with me and my phone rings—you—and Sarah Beth grabs it. She sends you to voicemail and shivers—"Not now, Wonder"—and then she picks up her yellow notepad again. Her *legal* pad. The law. The end.

"So let's get into it! *The Body on Bainbridge.*"

"I don't do podcasts."

"Joe, don't be that way. You think it makes you sound smart, like you're at the Odeon in the eighties telling everyone that you don't watch TV, but it only makes you sound ignorant."

"Well, I *am* ignorant, Sarah Beth. I never 'killed' anyone and I don't know anything about Melanda."

I didn't sell the lie—I'm tied up, I'm hazy—and she grins. "But you were close with her best friend, so you must know that Melanda claimed to be involved with a married man from Minnesota by the name of Carl?"

Yes. "No."

"Joe, come on. Of *course* you do. You kidnapped Melanda."

Yes, in an act of self-defense. She attacked *me* and accused me of being a fucking pedophile. "No."

"You stole her phone and texted with Mary Kay."

Yes, because those women *needed* to end their toxic friendship once and for all. "No."

But it's the worst episode of *Murder, She Wrote*, and Sarah Beth is twisting things, as if I didn't do it all for the right reasons. I was trying to *help* Melanda. I wanted her to go to Minnesota, and it's not my fault that she went and *killed* herself. *My* part of the plan was a good fucking plan. It *worked*. Mary Kay believed Melanda's story about "Carl" because Sly is right about me, Wonder.

I do know how to write women. "Sarah Beth, I'm telling you, I know you mean well, but you're barking up the wrong tree."

She looks right through me. "You thought you were being clever when you invented 'Carl from Bumble' . . ." Yes, it *was* fucking clever, me playing Melanda and texting Mary Kay about this new guy. I was good, I sounded just like Melanda, and Mary Kay *believed* that her best friend was running off to Minnesota to be with Carl, and again Sarah Beth tilts her head. "But clever isn't always *wise* . . ." That's projection. That's what critics say about *her* books. "Do you know the women who started the podcast?"

"Probably not."

"Well, they were Melanda's interns at the time, Eileen and DeAnn."

I know all about Eileen and DeAnn. They loathed Melanda because she wouldn't let them take credit for all their hard work and this is what they do? They start a *podcast* trying to find out what happened to her? "I don't know them."

She rolls her eyes as if it's a foregone conclusion that everything I say is a lie—not true—and she begins preaching about podcasts. "DeAnn and Eileen didn't have much to go on, but that's the beauty of our world. A whistleblower at Bumble listened to the first episode and hacked Melanda's account. The whistleblower told Eileen and DeAnn what they suspected, what we both already know . . . There *is* no Carl from Minnesota. You made him up when you hacked Melanda's phone."

It's the worst kind of enemy, a smart, accomplished woman with a *clever* mind, but I'm smart, too. *Clever.* "Look, I know you're all in this for the right reasons, and I understand. It's a sad scene. The women doing this podcast, they missed the signs, and it's hard to accept that their friend made up a story about some guy named Carl. All I know is what Mary Kay told me in passing, that Melanda really did want to meet someone. Maybe that's why she killed herself."

"Oh, please. Melanda didn't go into the woods and lie down to die . . ." No, she didn't, I carried her into the woods. "She was literally spearheading an incubator to help young women called *The Future Is Female*. Does that sound like someone who commits suicide?"

"We think we know people, but does anyone ever really know anyone?"

She cackles as if what I said was funny. "Yes," she says. "I know you. I know what you did."

"You're wrong."

"DeAnn and Eileen knew Melanda. She had her flaws, but she didn't go around making up fake boyfriends and she wasn't at all self-conscious about her marital status . . ." BULL-FUCKING-SHIT SHE WASN'T. "She didn't lie about Carl. That was you, Joe."

Finally, I get a little break because Sarah Beth has to "deal with her life," some nonsense with a middle-of-the-night notification about an overdue cable bill, and I am trapped. Her confidence is toxic, worse than the gas that knocked me out but maybe that's how I get out of here, by weaponizing her confidence, by making this about her imagination instead of my fucking past.

She drops her phone into her purse and grits her teeth. "You'd think my husband could deal with the bills, but anyway, where were we?"

"You were dazzling me with your creative prowess. It's no surprise you sell so many books."

"Aw," she says, and I fucked up. I made it about sales. "Well, isn't that sweet."

"It's the truth. I've been in awe of your ability as a world builder, the way you pull off these twists . . ." Nope, wrong angle. "What I mean is . . . You're a literary genius. Seriously. Other people listen to a podcast, but you take what's there and blow it up into so much more."

She gulps and I'm getting there. I am fucking *getting* there.

"Look, Sarah Beth, everything you're saying about me, the theory about me stealing her phone . . . I'm in awe right now. Seriously. I would read this book, and if I get to know that I was a part of your process, well, I swear on all your books . . ." No, no, no. She doesn't want praise for the books, she wants the better blurb, the one that's about the *author*. "You're a genius, okay? And I know how it looks. I've made some mistakes because I'm not a genius. I've been accused of some serious things. But I didn't do any of it, and when you make this all into a book . . . You're the only one to tell this story you came up with, the murderer who made it to Harvard, the paranoid autodidact with impostor syndrome. I mean I'm guilty. I am. I got your voice-mail, and I panicked and I broke the law. I snuck onto your property. I broke into your shed. There's no excuse. But I respect the hell out of you, and if you can forgive me for what I did . . . I think you need to get back to your book."

"Is that all?"

I did it, Wonder. I'm the number one hitter on the Sox and I'm at home plate and the count is full and it's the bottom of the ninth and I gave it my all. I sent the ball flying over the Green Monster because of you. You warned me the day we met. *They hate us 'cause they ain't us.* And then you taught me that anything is possible in this world when a person embraces their *tendency to love* and that's why I'm gonna get out of this mess, because of you, and I wish she would stop staring at me and let me go already and this is it. She crosses her legs. She sets her notepad on the floor. She . . .

24

. . . claps. Three times. Slowly. It's a crushing defeat and my walk-off homer was a lousy fly ball and she's gloating. Smug. "Bravo," she says. "That was an amazing performance!"

"I meant every word I said."

"I can't even tell you how exciting that was for me. I mean this is how you do it? How you get away with things. You *talk*."

"See there it is again. What a great idea for a character. God, you're a genius. A literary genius and I hope you're writing all of this down."

"Joe, come on. We're not in a vacuum. We've been in the room together, and you've reminded me on various occasions that I don't write 'literary' fiction . . ."

I whiffed and fouled but I won't quit now. "And I don't fault you for that. Jesus, Sarah Beth, you're an amazing fucking writer. I mean look at that shelf!"

She won't follow my eyes to her shelf. She says she's not like me, not like Glenn, and my phone rings again—you—and she says I can't charm my way out of this mess by praising her prose. I'm losing the battle and you're texting me again and again, and she's flipping through pages of her yellow legal pad, not even bothering to send you to voicemail, talking over the sound of my phone when it rings, and she's been at this for weeks. As *coincidence* would have it, she listened to the first episode of *The Body on Bainbridge* the night before Glenn's death party. When I said the b-word—*Bainbridge*—a little alarm went off in her writer brain. We were on hiatus and she trusts her instincts, so she did her recon. She's a rich woman so she has the spare funds to do things. Cruel things. She hired a *private investigator* and she hunted down Officer *Nico* and she zoomed with Dr. Nicky in prison and it's like RIP Ethel with Bejeweled Fucking Blitz.

Sometimes, you have six boosters on the board, but the boosters are useless because you're all out of lives.

She wipes tears away from my eyes, and she turns off my phone. The next time you try me, my phone won't ring. You'll be sent to my voicemail and you'll feel like I shut off my phone to *push* you away. We're supposed to be in this together. I choked on the big night with your family and I struck out with Sarah Beth, and this isn't any old game. It's *the World Series of love*. I feel you out there. You're losing faith in me, in us, in your deep, long-held belief that your *tendency to love* would eventually lead you to someplace wonderful, to me. You find a way to see every book as a five-star read, but now you won't be the same reader, the same woman. Wherever you are, whatever you're doing, there are three little words in your head: *Ivy League Douchebag*.

Sarah Beth picks up my phone. "Let's put this away," she says, as if she's my friend, and she opens a safe that I mistook for a fridge and puts my phone *in* the safe and then she closes the safe and you are locked up in a cage, like me, and we can't reach each other, can't find each other, and I don't know the password and the woman has two children, one *hubby*, and twelve books. The password could be anything, and I don't know how to explain it to you, Wonder, but I know it's over.

"Hang on," she says. "My Czech publisher is at it again with the questions."

I'm never gonna be where she is. I'm never gonna have a Czech publisher and I'm never gonna know who died in *The White Lotus* and I'm never going to hold you again. You're going to think I was kidnapped. You're going to hate yourself for not banging down my door, and this is where I die, in a cage, my back against a computer that isn't mine, at the hands of a writer who calls upon prison guards and detectives instead of her imagi-fucking-nation.

I got into Harvard. I found you, after waiting my whole life. I *pushed* you and that's all I get. And who knows? Maybe my death will be good for you. Maybe you'll move out of your two-family and write a heartbreaking banger about our time and that's how I know I love you.

Someone has to go first. Better it be me than you. I finished my book. You didn't.

"Ugh," Sarah Beth says. "And here's my Israeli translator . . . Hang on . . ."

I'll never have an Israeli translator, but it's not about me. You'll see to it that my book gets published, and when the Israeli translator turns to you, you'll answer his questions. My soul will live on through my words, through my imagination. It's not the destiny I wanted. It's not my time to go. But it's the other rule of writing.

Kill your darlings so they don't kill you. I am my own darling, and I know it. She beat me, Wonder. She is going to get me locked up, a fate worse than death, and if it really is my time to die, if this is the cage from which I never escape, if my story ends with my life becoming fodder for a story that she'll think of as *her* story, well, then fuck it. I'll tell her my story.

"Okay," I say. "One night, I was in the woods by Mary Kay's house. Melanda came at me out of nowhere."

Sarah Beth puts her phone down and she wasn't talking to the *Israeli translator* or her Czech publisher. She is a good writer. She was torturing me. *Pushing* me. And it worked and she knows it, I know it, the jig is up. She got me, Wonder. A good writer holds a reader captive, a natural-born author's slow reveal of the truth makes us all want to speak our *truth*. I know she's that way because I am too, not that the world will ever know.

She drills her eyes into my forehead. "So Melanda attacked *you*. Was she armed?"

"She was armed in the sense that she thought she was doing the right thing," I say, as if I'm recapping a novel. "She thought I was a pedophile spying on Nomi."

"Oh God."

"Yeah," I say. "She threatened to destroy me, and I swear to you, I have never harmed a child."

She tells me that she believes me, that the truth just sounds different, and she turns on the hot plate. "More tea?"

I nod and I look at the Russian doll in the corner, the fridge that holds the safe that holds my phone.

I get to die—or go to prison—knowing that you loved me, that you sent me soup.

So, if you think about it, I win, even when I lose.

25

I can't see straight and I'm shivering. Empty. Everything inside of me is outside. My liver and my spleen and all the dead bodies are on the floor of the Dead Shed. Invisible but real. She got to me, Wonder. There was no way out of this mess, so I spilled my guts, and now there *is* a way out—the door is open, I'm not tied up, not anymore—and I'm alone in the Dead Shed. The open door is a tease, flashing a sliver of gray sky, low grass, as if I can just walk outside and drive back to Boston and find you, but I can't do that. I told Sarah Beth Swallows about every single shitty moment of my shitty life, and she took notes on yellow legal pads. She set up an old-school minia-ture cassette recorder, and at this moment, she's probably twenty feet away, under that lie of an open sky with a local detective. She's not a priest—she's a psychopath—and she went to fucking *Dunkin'*.

I sit up and pick up the extra-large coffee and there's a bag next to the coffee, a fucking Post-it on the bag: *Breakfast!*

I take a sip—hazelnut chemicals, nasty—and I sink my teeth into the Boston Kreme donut but I can't swallow. I have no colon. It's gone.

So, Melanda killed herself with your TV?

You haven't heard the worst part.

What's that?

She'd been sleeping with Mary Kay's husband for years.

Oh no. Well, it's no wonder she killed herself, all that guilt.

I should be in prison, I *will* be in prison, and I can't call you—my phone is in a safe—and I didn't stop with Melanda. I *played till my fingers bled* and told Sarah Beth Swallows everything, about RIP Beck and RIP Benji—she said people like him are the reason she and her husband are not setting up trust funds for her children—and I told her about my estranged fucking son living off the grid in Costa Rica with his grandmother.

At least you know he's safe.

Do I, though?

The reason I kept going is that she was always on my side. She said she couldn't imagine losing her children, that she *would have done the same thing,* so I told her about RIP Peach Salinger.

Every young girl has a Peach, Joe. Men don't understand what it's like for us in that way.

Did you have one?

Yes, and I killed her in my first book. And honestly, sometimes I wish I'd done that in real life.

Wishing is not *doing*—I wish I'd kept my mouth shut—but once she got me going, I couldn't stop. I thought I'd never see you again. I told her everything, Wonder. Even the stuff I almost forgot about, like RIP Robin Fincher.

There is a special place in hell for bad cops because they ruin it for good cops.

I told her all the things I could never, would never, tell you. The horror of RIP Henderson.

That bastard deserves to be dead.

I told her about RIP Seamus.

Someone should have killed him a long time ago. What a monster.

I scanned the walls for hidden cameras, as if I could ever find them, and she said most murderers have their reasons, and I got used to that word.

Murderer.

She told me she originally wanted to be a psychologist or a defense attorney, so I went there about my childhood, and then later, well, of *course* I was a magnet for women with overbearing brothers—RIP Candace and RIP Love Quinn—and I went all the way to Mooney Books, my first lockdown. The day a woman walked out of the shop with a first edition of *Catcher in the Rye* on my watch, the day Mooney sent me to that cage in the basement. Cold pizza, no clocks, and then walking upstairs to a changed world, a post-9/11 landscape. He said I should thank him, that he saved my life, because who knows? If he hadn't put me in that cage, I might have been one of those poor souls jumping off the side of a burning, falling tower.

Joe, you were abused.

I know. And no matter what you do, when you're abused, people smell it on you.

I told her about Dr. Nicky cheating on his wife with RIP Beck and she said that she too fell for his *schtick*. "He was just so charming on Zoom," she said. "But cheating with a *patient* . . . He denied that, of course."

I told her how much I loved Mary Kay DiMarco and I told her how much she loved *me*. I told her about Love's death in the Commerce Fucking Casino, that she never had *cancer*, that it was all a Big Lie, and in the wee hours, when the sun was threatening to rise, she asked me if that was all and I said yes and then I winced. "Shit."

"What?"

"Well, I feel bad. I forgot about Delilah."

I told her Delilah's tragic story.

This is why I stay away from all things Los Angeles. It's a city that eats women alive.

I get up now—dizzy—and I walk to the door. No cops. No cars in the driveway. Not a single sound except for the hum of the windmills. I cross the threshold and make like RIP Glenn and raise my arms above my head, the international body language for surrender. Nothing happens, and I'm a murderer, so I drop to my knees.

But again, nothing happens.

No policemen emerge from Sarah Beth's storybook fucking farmhouse, but this is bullshit. I told her *everything* and there's no way she lets me go and I feel someone watching me. Just get it over with. *Lock me up!* But it's just a cottontail chomping on grass—*rabbits don't eat baby carrots*—until a hawk soars overhead. The rabbit makes a run for it, so fuck it.

I do, too.

My car is where I left it, just off the side of a dead-end road, and I'm pushing sixty in a thirty-five and the radio is blasting—*played it till my fingers bled*—and the sirens will be on my tail in a minute, in a second, and I could go north to Canada, I *should* go north to Canada—you never know, I could make it—but you're not in Canada. You're in Boston, and it's like Sarah Beth said when the sun was coming up.

You love these women more than you love yourself.

I hit traffic outside the city—where are the fucking cops?—and I hit a backup on Memorial Drive and I sing along to "Free Fallin'"—that's me, I am Jerry Maguire—and I turn up the volume when the deejay says he has breaking news, but it's not about me. Some actual monster killed a six-year-old Girl Scout in a fit of road rage, and again, it's like Sarah Beth said.

You've done things we've all dreamed of doing. You're not a "serial killer." You didn't walk through your life hunting for victims. You're the reason people love my books, deep down, we've all wanted people to be held accountable for the kind of abuse that falls under the radar.

By the time I get to Cambridge I am Ray Liotta in *Goodfellas* and it's almost strange that I'm *not* full of cocaine. I find a spot by your Dunkin' and my hands are shaking—*played it till my fingers bled*—and I turn off the radio and where are they? Where are the fucking cops? "You taking that spot or what, buddy?"

I didn't realize my car was still running and I don't need this right now, a horn-happy fucker harassing me as if the spot is marked for his truck. Maybe I should deck him, Wonder, because Sarah Beth knows *everything* and it would be one last good, self-sacrificial deed before the men and women in blue come for me.

But then I see you. You're in your uniform and you spotted my car and you flip off the pushy fucker—"Yes, he's taking the spot!"—so I turn off my Tesla.

Do you know? Did she call you?

I step out of the car and you throw your arms around me and tell me that I scared the living daylights out of you. Radio silence brings out the best in you, as it turns out, and you smack my ass. Hard. "Don't ever do that again."

I won't kill anyone ever again. I can't. I'll be in prison, probably in solitary. "I'm sorry."

"Okay, so what happened to you? For real?"

I was born to indifferent parents and like a lot of children, I fell prey to an abusive male authority figure who taught me that violence is a legitimate means of coping and then last night, one of our fellows drugged me and coerced me into confessing to a boatload of crimes. "I lost my phone."

"How? I thought you were home sick?" I look around the street, no cops, no sirens, no staties on guard. You grab my arms. "Focus."

I committed "crimes" in several states, but not *this* one, so the process will take some time. I make up a story about a misguided trek to urgent care, so fevered and delirious that I lost my fucking phone, and you're calmer now. You really *don't* know. Yet. "Jesus," you say. "I've been going freaking *nuts.*"

"I'm sorry." Sorry that I couldn't hold up under questioning. Sorry that I blew it for us, that in a matter of minutes or hours, the Feds will take me away from you.

You lean against the side of my car. "I went to your place and the soup was just sitting there."

"Wonder, I'm so sorry."

"For all I knew, you were dead."

I am dead. On borrowed time. "Come on," I say. "Let me make it up to you."

I open the passenger door but you don't get in. Did the cops get to you? Are you wired? "Wait," you say. "Joe . . . I gotta know something."

Yes, the cops got to you and they're in plain clothes. They knew I'd come here. To you. "What?"

You rub your forehead. "Something just feels off . . ."

You don't get into my car and why would you? Your disappearing boyfriend returns after you were up all night worrying, and it was a high—I'm alive—but you're a writer. A thinker. During the hiatus, when you were back to work on *Faithful*, I'd see you staring at the walls, and when I asked if something was wrong, you'd say that *something just feels off* and sometimes you'd delete an entire *page*, just fucking nip it in the bud and start over. So that's what I do.

"Well, something *is* off, Wonder. Losing a phone is some hackneyed, selfish, adolescent bullshit and if I were in your shoes, I'd be like, *Is he a fuckup?*"

"Joe, I didn't say that. I know you're not a 'fuckup.'"

I turned it around and you love me all over again—you're in the passenger seat of my car—and it's almost like we're back to normal, you're recapping your shift, you're making sure you have "Find My Phone" enabled on your device, and then you laugh. "Omigod," you say. "So, you know that *Body on Bainbridge* podcast? Ani found the daughter's Instagram and—"

And I don't have to panic—Nomi is one of those kids who rewrites history by deleting all her old *pics*—and they haven't mentioned me on the podcast. But I won't spend our last hours together talking about the reason the Feds are going to split us apart, so I shake my head. Time for another rewrite. "Can we not talk about that podcast?"

"What's wrong?"

I killed "the daughter's" father—that sounds like the title of a Sarah Beck book. Sarah *Beth*. Calm down, Joe. "The thing is, Won, maybe I'm too sensitive, but those are real people, right? And the daughter, the kid went through hell . . . Her parents are both dead, right?"

You drop your phone like it's poison, because it is. "Yes, I've heard that 'hot take' but a lot of good comes from these podcasts. I mean sometimes they *work*."

I say nothing, because you're your own person, your own thinker, and I am banking on your *tendency to love*. "All right," you say. "In this case, to think of that girl, orphaned . . . And all of us in that room *laughing* . . . She lost her *mother*."

Bingo and you grab my thigh and tell me that you *really fucking love me* and that's the end of the Who-Killed-Melanda podcast for you. It's a win, a big one, and we buckle up to hit the road. Maybe the cops see us right now. Maybe they're not storming my Tesla because they want to give us one last hurrah. I'm not the Boston Bomber. I'm not full of hate. My crimes were based in passion and I love you, and I've been in love before, and we all know that love makes guys do stupid things.

"Okay," I say. "Where do you wanna go?"

26

We started out with a trip to the Apple store—I have a new phone!—and the police are taking their time. I'm sure a Fed is tailing us, and I'm driving you a little nuts with my nerves, but it's a good thing I said I'd had a stomach bug. I choke up every time I see a cop—Is this it? Is it over?—and you think I was sick. You believe I was sick. You're a good girlfriend, constantly checking on me, offering to drive, to take us home, but it's not safe at home, so after the phone store, we leave the car in a garage and walk to the Public Garden to see the bronze ducklings and what a scene it could have been. Cops surrounding the pond, terrifying the living ducks and the tourists.

"PUT YOUR HANDS UP, JOE GOLDBERG."

But it doesn't happen here, and our next stop is Sonsie. You're friskier than normal, laughing about the old days, when you and Tara were young, hunting bankers. "This one time, these guys offered us money to make out."

"Did you do it?"

"God, no. Tara took the money, and we made a run for it."

It's good to see you laugh, to hear you bad-mouth all the *Ivy League Douchebags* in detail, as if you finally accept the reality that I'm not one of them. But your stories are anecdotal. You never got serious with anyone, and your voice drifts. I know what comes next.

You fuss with the napkin on your lap. "So, was Monica, your ex . . . was she like me?"

"Wonder, we don't have to do this." I don't have to tell you that Monica is Mary Kay. You'll find out soon enough.

"I'm genuinely curious."

"Monica was . . . sad. A poster girl of why people shouldn't get married when they're young, but she was also great . . . a reader, like you."

"Oh."

Oops. "But she wasn't a writer. She was a dreamer. You're doing it. You're *living* your life and she . . . You know my jukebox?"

"The one that's way too big for your apartment? I think I've noticed it."

I nudge you. *Mean.* "I got it in Florida, after she passed away. The Bordello, the bar full of books, that was her dream, and the jukebox was part of that dream . . ."

"And you made it come true for her."

I kiss the back of your hand, as I have every time you've forced me to dig up the ex-files and I tell you I love you more than the eggs benny and before you know it, we're in safer territory, talking about books, until I realize where we are, sitting ducks on fucking *Newbury Street*. It's the BPD's wet dream to ambush the bad guy on a busy block in broad daylight, so I pay the check. We walk to one of your favorite spots, an overpass on Comm Ave, and you insist on a *selfie* and I oblige. You'll need pictures of me when I'm gone.

"So," I say. "I hope my bullshit last night didn't mess with your writing. Did you get back into it?"

"Ha," you say. "No, I was too worried to focus, but tomorrow I'll be back in it."

You're scrolling and smiling and I ask you what's so funny.

"Oh," you say. "Sarah Beth is a freaking *trip*."

I look down at the water—Can we swim to Canada?—and I gulp. "Oh yeah?"

"Well, you know how I was freaking out, so I hit up the group text, and she knows all these cops . . ." I know. "And she has a police scanner . . ." I know. "And she just texted me and offered to call out the dogs to find you. I mean maybe she skews a little dark with all the dead body stuff, but she's a freaking sweetheart for trying to help."

*Sick*heart is more like it, and you cavalierly segue from Sarah Beth to Sly, raving about our new teacher, how you finally feel like it's all coming together. "Sarah Beth and Sly were cool to me last night, you know? They understood that I was concerned, as opposed to my sister and freaking Tara, who were all 'He's probably at a strip club or a casino.' It's a wavelength thing, kinda like how I feel with *you* . . ." You nudge me. "So don't you want your report card?"

"I thought we decided on a do-over. Next time I come over, I'll turn my phone off before I walk into your house. And *I'll* bring the jug of Tito's."

You laugh that your dad "had to admit" he was hard on me, and you really do believe there is a "next time." You lean your head on my shoulder, and will you visit me in prison? Or will you turn your back on me? I crane my neck and search the area for men and women in blue. You whisper in my ear, "Can we go home now?"

There are no police staked outside my place—What the fuck is taking so long? This is an outrage! I confessed to *multiple fucking murders*!—and you open all the windows—*You need fresh air, babe*—but then I remember the end of *The Town*. Noble Ben Affleck wanted to start a clean, new life with his do-gooder girlfriend. He had a hunch that the holier-than-thou cynics at the FB-Fucking-I got to his beloved, and (*spoiler alert*), he was right. Are you in on this?

"Come on," you say. "*The White Lotus* is calling."

We get into my bed and I put the moves on you but you don't want me—*Not yet, just one episode, okay?*—and of course you don't want me. I'm a murderer and you're only in this bed because the cops asked you to keep an eye on me. I look at your shirt—*Yankees Suck*—and is that for me? I'm a Yankee. Soon you might think that *I* suck, too. *The White Lotus* is moving along, it's the longest week of their lives, the longest day of my life, and I brace at every siren, every horn, and you jump off the bed and run into the living room.

"Two seconds! I promised Sly I'd text her when we got to this part."

You were up until 5:00 A.M. and you bonded with the widow Wonka, and you bonded over the work of Mike Fucking White and what about me? What about my writing? It's too late. My arrest is fucking imminent and the Chocolate Factory will be tented for extermination—there is an infestation of one rat: me—and when you do start reading my book, you won't read it blind. You'll know all about my past and you won't treat it like fiction. You'll have a forensic eye and treat it like evidence of a psychopath's fucking rantings and it might be the worst fucking part of this mess, my poor book, smeared.

You jump back into bed with me. "Sorry. I stubbed my toe on your *ex*-box."

You're being cute and possessive and you tickle me and tease me and you're not wearing a wire—your shirt is off—and I'm inside of you and this is real in a way that makes last night feel unreal, like I truly am free. And then the afterglow subsides. Reality kicks in. You talk like this is our life—*I wonder who stole your soup*—and I want to play detective with you, but our time is borrowed. Sarah Beth and the Feds are going to take me away from you, and there's nothing I can do to stop it, but there is a way for me to stay with you. To give you *Me.* I pick up my phone and you're a girl—*Who are you texting?*—and then your phone pings. *One new email.* You gasp. You kick. "Omigod, yes . . . This is it! This is your freaking book!"

"That's *Me*, baby."

You *can't wait* to read it, and you've been *dying* for me to share it with you, and you recite the words on the title page—*Me: A Novel by Joe Goldberg*—and it's bittersweet, the way you thank me for sharing it with you. You really have no idea that you're about to lose me. You'll go through a range of emotions and get sucked into the grisly rumor mill. But you are a Goodreads girl and you will read *Me* and fall in love with me all over again. That's all I care about anymore. I don't need to be published. I don't need a million readers. I only need one, you.

The buzzer sounds, and here it comes, the bitter end, nothing remotely fucking *sweet* about it. "Huh," you say. "Did you order anything?"

I can't move, I can't breathe, I just die underneath and you cup my shoulder in your palm. "Stay put," you say. "I'll take care of it."

You're on your feet, throwing on one of my T-shirts, scrambling into my boxers, and now you're on the run, barefoot and bound for my living room. I am not going to prison without seeing how things work out for the staff of *The White Fucking Lotus* and I grab the remote and tap my way to the last episode and you hit the buzzer. "Hello?"

"FedEx. We need a signature."

You hit the buzzer again—"Come on up!"—and I fast-forward and where is the gun? The knife? The blood? The body?

My walls are thin, and I hear the "FedEx" man ascending and I've seen *Crimes and Misdemeanors* and *Law & Order* and *9-1-1*. The cops don't say they're cops. They promise flowers or they say they're the gas man or the *FedEx* man and they climb the stairs slowly, en masse, using hand signals. I fast-forward even faster—Who dies? Who?—and the "FedEx" guy knocks on the door and my favorite asshole character plunges a knife into a decent character, the one I didn't want it to be, but the one I knew it *had* to be.

"Joe! Can you come here?"

"One sec!"

Fate is real, and deep down, I knew we'd never make it to the last episode. I wrote a book. I got into *Harvard*. But I went where I don't belong, into the Chocolate Factory. Sarah Beth found me out and I'm not *Charlie*. You're Charlie.

"Joe? Sorry, but the guy is waiting . . ."

"I know! Two seconds!"

Separation anxiety hits me hard. And what will happen to you? You never learned how to let go of people, your father hammering on you to *have faith* in a bunch of fucking baseball players you never even met, the message overstated and clear: *You have to love people even when you're fucking sick of them or you're a disloyal monster.* You hold on tight. Your novel in progress is dedicated to your dead mother, as if she can read it—she can't—and Sarah Beth ruined your life. You won't finish *Faithful*, and you won't get over me and it's not fair. I'm not like you, Wonder. I never had a shot at finding normal, and maybe that's why I told Sarah Beth Swallows all my secrets, to save you from wasting your time with me. I've done it again, sacrificed myself for a woman I love. *Faithful.*

"Joe!"

"Coming! I swear!"

I check myself out in the mirror. My brand-new Harvard T-shirt I never wore. All the better for my fucking *mug shot* they'll splash on *Chronicle* when they go back to Sarah Beth's Dead Shed and she plays the tapes. My tapes. The only story I'll ever get to tell the world, a nonfiction audiobook that I didn't want to write. Do I climb out a window and jump onto the fire escape? Your voice is low, but my walls are thin, and I hear you whispering to the FedEx man—"Sorry for the wait . . . My husband is a wicked slowpoke sometimes"—and I can't jump out a window. I love you *because* you don't know how to let go. You barely made it through one night without me and you're practicing for our future with a man in a uniform, a man you think of as an insignificant player in our lives, a man who's about to take it all away.

27

You know what saying I hate, Wonder? "It's all good." Like hell it is, and we can't whitewash the grim horror that comes with being alive. Sure, some things are good. I'm not in prison—the FedEx guy was legit—and I'm not going to prison—Sarah Beth sent me a first edition of *The Catcher in the Rye* with a handwritten note that I memorized the first time I read it: *Hello my fellow Shoddy, I bought this after I sold my second book. Seems to me like it belongs with you. xxsb*

Silly me. When I was in a panic about the Feds, I forgot about the airtight sanctity of private clubs that usurps all pesky laws. A saying I fucking *love:* "Membership has its privileges." The mafia. The Spee. The *Shoddies.* Our fellow Sarah Beth will keep my secrets to honor the cone of silence in the room, and I am free, *we* are free, but no, it's not "all" good.

Don't get me wrong. I love you. I love that you held my hand when I told you that "Monica" was Mary Kay, that "Natalie" is Nomi. You said you understand, that renaming your mother in your book helps you cope with the loss. You're in a bubble on my sofa, just you and your laptop, becoming the writer you were meant to be. I built that bubble for you—I killed Glenn—and you are going full steam ahead with *Faithful*. You've spent your whole life on guard, accosted by elites—*You think you're special?*—and questioned by the riffraff when they get a whiff of your writerly ways—*You think you're better than me?* Hell, you work at a Dunkin' Goddamn Donuts to prove you're one of them, but at long last, you're not on a mission to *prove* your identity to anyone. You're my little Cheryl Strayed and you "write like a motherfucker"—but the thing is . . . that's an accurate description. You hammer the fucking keypad, bitch-slapping it like a kid at Chuck E. Fucking Cheese. So loud that I tiptoe around my own home in noise-canceling headphones—what a crock—as if they drown out the sound of your fingers.

Tick tick tap tap tick.

Maybe it's me. I'm tense. In the midst of my brush with the death penalty, I realized that life is precious. I sent you my novel. I gave *Me* to you. You were enthusiastic—*I can't freaking wait to read it*—and Sly also promised me that *Me* was high on her list of priority reading. But it's been days. Neither of you has reached out to me, enamored with my prose. I don't bite your head off about the little things, about the way you undercook oatmeal in the microwave and steal my phone chargers. I don't *push* you to wash your hair. But the *tick tick tap tap tick* is a constant reminder that I'm ahead of you, I *finished* my fucking book, and you and Sly . . . why won't you just fucking read it? *Me.*

And it's not just me. I can tolerate a little fucking noise. Back in Orlando, my fake Christian neighbor blasted sermons in the back-yard, as if he could proselytize via the speaker function on his fucking iPhone. That was every Sunday and that was annoying, but it was only one day a week. My *other* O-Town neighbor, she sold fucking sex toys and necklaces and leggings to boisterous women on her *lanai* in gatherings of multimouthed screeching cockroaches, even at the height of the lockdown. But they were scheduled affairs, so when I saw the cars rolling up, I could leave. Home is a sanctuary and I grew up with a screaming, wailing mother. I lived in a prison cell, in an L.A. building with a manager howling on about his fucking *improv* group—*Am I right or am I right?*—and even *Bainbridge* wasn't peaceful, what with a nasty, happy family shoving their cornhole barbecues in my face on a sometimes nightly basis.

But *nothing compares to you,* to *tick tick tap tap tick.*

You're writing around the clock and last night you snuck out of my bed at 4:00 A.M.—Do you think I'm deaf?—and I've tried to help you. I warn you about your eyes, all the screen time. I asked Your Bobby to invite us over for cornhole and Jell-O shots but it's always the same. All you want to do is *tick tick tap tap tick.*

I pull off my headphones—fuck off, Bose—and my ears are sore. Red. It was my idea for you to scale back your hours at Dunkin', and are you writing so much to avoid reading *Me*? During the hiatus, you would stare at the walls and ponder, *wonder.* But look at you now, a meth head in a factory and why? Nobody can churn out prose fifteen hours a day and I'm not a houseboy—my novel is in your hands—but here I am, delivering you another *Nespresso.*

You don't look up from your screen. You just give me a "Thanks, babe" and tell me that I "rock" and I pick up the fucking remote because there is one man you can't resist, a fucking *screenwriter.* "Wanna take a *White Lotus* break?"

You smile, hesitant. It's our show. I spoiled the ending for myself, but you have no idea what's coming. You won't read *my* book, but you will always take a break to fawn over Mike White and *his* fucking "brilliance." "Maybe later. I'm way too freaking in it to stop right now."

I tell you I get it and I check my email, but nope! More radio silence from Sly, and my book is a *good* fucking read. It's taut and unputdownable, the searing examination of a couple in the weeds of their love story. It's not a bloated Lou-sized manifesto with too many plots and *Easter eggs.* It's 232 tightly woven pages, the kind of book you could finish in a matter of hours. You're a writer. You know what it's like to hit Send and yet you crack your knuckles. "Oof," you say. "I wish I had four hands, you know? It's like I can't keep up with my own freaking brain."

"Well, if you don't wanna watch TV, maybe you could read . . ."

"I'll start it tomorrow. I swear." You said that yesterday and you yawn. "So, how are you?"

How are you? is a thing people say to Fakebook friends and I am *me*. I deserve better. "Well, honestly . . . I'm frustrated. I expected to hear something from Sly by now."

You hit the space bar—you want to *tick tick tap tap tick*—and I know. You are *#amwriting* and I should let you be and hit up Sly over email, but I can't do that. She's "mourning," she's busy with her cushy job at Harvard, the one she only has because of me.

"Anyway," I say. "Do you want a sandwich?"

No, you don't want a sandwich and how do I know that you're not lying to me? How do I know that you and Sly aren't secretly giggling about my novel? What if I wrote *The Worst Book in the History of the Fucking World* and what if you're the genius, not me? I go into the kitchen but you're not a *complete* genius. You left the One Mighty Mill bread on the counter again, the bread that I bought at Whole Fucking Foods two minutes before closing because you *had* to have it—your taste buds are evolving beyond egg wraps—and we have ants because of you. *Ants*, a precursor to mice. I grab a bottle of Dawn and make a thin blue perimeter around the bread and the little fuckers crawl all over the bread, and you slam your computer shut and barge into the kitchen. "Oh shit," you say. "I guess this is my fault."

Yes, it is. "I didn't say that."

"No," you sass. "But you did draw a circle around the bread to teach me a lesson . . ."

It's a box, not a circle and I smile. "Dawn is the best way to get rid of ants."

"Well, this is sick. You can't lock them up. They're animals."

You open the fridge, and you slam the fridge and walk out of the room and there you go again. *Tick tick tap tap tick.* I clean up your mess and my phone buzzes—Is it Sly? Nope!—and now *I* open the fridge and slam it because this is wrong. All wrong. RIP Glenn told NPR that whenever he sent pages to Sly, she would drop what she was doing because how could she *not* read his magical words? She was riding the train as he was laying down the tracks, but no she wasn't because RIP Glenn was a *fraud*. He lied to NPR and then he lied to *me*.

You humble-putter into the kitchen and drum your knuckles on my back. Your hands, quietly running down my arms. "Sorry."

You should be sorry—we have ants because of you—but ants aren't termites. They're not *cockroaches*. "I'm sorry, too," I say. "I'm not a passive-aggressive whiny housefrau."

You take your hands away and open the fridge. "I think *frau* is girl."

I'm trying to be your supportive fucking boyfriend, and that was rude. You sigh. "I feel like I'm learning a lot from Mike White, you know? He's just so freaking *direct*." That was a dig—here we go again—and you peer at me. "What now?"

What now? As if I'm the problem. "Nothing," I say. "I guess . . . I kinda think *my* first sentence is pretty direct . . ."

I threw a good pitch, Wonder. A meatball down the center of the plate, and I'm easy. I'm vulnerable. One swing of your bat—*Your first sentence is gold, Joe*—and you'll knock it out of the park, and I'll shut up about my book and bring you all the Nespresso you could ever want. You tear a paper towel off the roll. "Did you ever watch *Sex and the City*?"

I asked you about my *book* and it's never a good sign when a woman brings up that show. I tell you I'm "familiar" and you ask if I remember when Carrie went out with a writer.

"Oh yeah," I say. "I used to see that guy in the Pantry back in L.A."

You squirm, and who can blame you? I'm cutting you off to name-drop about the *Office Space celeb* who played Jack Fucking Berger and I can just see you in a week, catching up with Tara, going off on your whiny-bitch *Sex and the City*–watching boyfriend. You fix your eyes on the ants. "Joe, Sly has her hands full. She has a dead husband and a new job."

She's an adjunct Harvard professor, if that, and she can juggle. "I know."

You pick up the Dawn and paint the counter and you don't make a cage. You splash thin blue lines all over the linoleum, an eighties artist in a SoHo fucking loft, and this is you teaching *me* a fucking lesson. "Waiting is hard," you say. "But I'm gonna say it again . . . All writers say the same thing. You need to start a new project."

I'm not a fucking idiot. I know what "they say," but I'm not *writers* and my book isn't some third-rate first novel. *Me* is the motherfucking *Catcher in the Rye* level of special. You lean over the counter to watch our ants and this is why people have pets. I nudge you. *Gently, Joseph.* "It's a timing issue. I met Glenn's agent, Bernie, at the memorial, and I want to get on with it. I want Sly to read it and give it to Bernie Lapatin."

You wrap your arm around me and you squeeze me like a child, like a baby. "Look," you say. "Have faith. If it's meant to be, it'll happen." All I got out of that sentence was *if.* "Sly will read it when she's ready, and as for me . . . I was excited, I *am* excited, but you know how I am. I can't read your book until I can give it my full attention. I don't wanna go in when I'm all nerved up about Tuesday, about *my* book."

Bullshit. You're a Goodreads girl. You eat books. I caught you with S. A. Fucking Cosby just the other night. "You're right."

"Number three," you say, and this is bad. So bad you're making a *list.* "I have to be totally focused on my book right now because it's not fair that I get a second workshop."

"You deserve it, Wonder." It's literally why I killed the one man on this planet who could have helped me, because he was harmful to *you.*

"Possibly, but you know it's not easy for me to put myself first and take it all so 'seriously' and beyond all that . . . What I say doesn't matter. What Sly says doesn't matter. All that matters is the writing."

"You won't even read the first page?"

"Joe, come on. I don't do that *twenty percent into it* stuff on Goodreads and I sure as shit won't do it with you. I'm not gonna say a word to you about *your* book until I finish it and again, I'm not gonna start until I can give it my whole heart."

I watch an ant crawl into the blue. Am I losing you? Don't you think I'm smart? Funny? "Look," I say. "It's the Dawn of the Dead."

"Ha," you say, and it burns. RIP Glenn did that to me, the verbal *ha* in lieu of the actual fucking laugh. *And Just Like That* you're charging into the living room and unplugging your computer, packing it up and in, and no. *NO.* I block the door when you reach for the handle. You yank your hair up into a ponytail. "Babe, we both need space. You know that."

"Wonder, wait. Look, I know I'm in Jack Berger mode, but that's not me."

Your jaw drops. "Are you kidding? I know you're not Berger. I only brought up *Sex and the Freaking City* because I don't have a billion past 'relationships,' but I know this much. Whenever Carrie dates a writer, it goes to hell because writing makes people into narcissist freaking *assholes*. And it's on us to stop it."

"You're not an asshole."

You laugh, and I love you. *Tick tick tap tap tick.* "Oh, come on," you say. "We're *both* assholes. You're waiting and waiting is hell, and I'm sucking up all the oxygen *tapping* away on your sofa. Time's flying for me and it's standing still for you and we're driving each other crazy, and nothing good is gonna come of us being in the same place right now. So I'm gonna go."

You're the one, you are, and I smile. "It's more like *tick tick tap tap tick*."

You pull me in for a kiss. "Tick tick tap tap tick."

After you leave me, I check my email. Zip. Zilch. Nada. But the squeaky wheel gets the grease—now that's a *good* fucking saying—so I open up *my* laptop and crack the nut of how to ask Sly about my book without asking: *I loved your piece about Glenn in the* Times. *Exquisite and emotional and voicey. And it's nice to see your sales rank soar on Amazon. See you Tuesday!*

It's the right tone—I don't mention my book—and it's the perfect prompt—she can use the same language to describe *Me*—and a nanosecond later my heart is thumping like the leg of a horny, prepubescent young boy. She wrote back. *Tick tick tap tap tick.* Prayers up. Open sesame.

Reading your book, loving it. Very Salinger. Very smart. You're in a league of your own. More soon. x

I am Elliot in *Hannah*—"I have my answer"—and do you feel it, Wonder? A shift in the atmosphere. I won't disrupt you while you're immersed in your process. No matter what you say, I really *was* veering into Jack Berger territory, an insecure passive-aggressive dickhead in headphones harping on you about ants, about my pages. But that was then.

She put it in writing—*very Salinger, very smart*—and it's better that you don't read my pages before your reset workshop. You're already in love with me. And if you did read the first page of *Me*, you'd probably be too intimidated to show up for *Faithful*.

28

I t's been twelve minutes and forty-nine hours since you left, and I've been cool. *Chill.* You've stayed away from me, as if you're hiding out on Sesame Street, because despite Sly's support for you, you still don't *quite* trust the people in that room. Your sister shared a photo of you reading a book to Caridad. *Strawberry Shortcake and the Winter That Would Not End.* I don't know the book but I'm sure the plucky little redhead melted the snow eventually and fuck it. I miss you. I'm not one of the fellows who backhanded you. I'm me! *Very smart, very Salinger.* It's an hour before the reset and I care about you, and I want you to know it.

I text you. *Hey you. Wanna meet up before the reset?*

You give me a smile and okay. A *little* part of me thought that your curiosity might have gotten the best of you, that you might have started reading my book. But that's not *Holy shit I loved it you're a genius,* so there's no way you started, let alone finished. I hit you back.

How you been? I hope you're not nervous cuz I know it's gonna be great today.

Lol you mean DID YOU READ MY FREAKING BOOK

It's the first time I've laughed since you were here, and I needed it. And then the bubbles.

Not yet ☹

Not right.

Oh, are you okay?

Work, family, bleh. My dad's wound vac crapped out so the VNA was here and Caridad is having issues with a friend and then I got stuck filling in for Kimber, pulling a surprise double ☹ *No fair! And I'm freaking out about today . . . After class I'll be a whole new person and I can't WAIT to read your freaking book! See you in five!*

I tell you not to worry and you tell me I'm the best and I know I'm the fucking best. But what if it's a lie? What if you are *reading it, not loving it,* and RIP Glenn loved it? RIP Ethel loved it. I've cooled my jets a little about Sly. She's in gerund mode, but then again she did use the l-word and there you are, charging up the street and it stings. You didn't have time to read but you did have time to go shopping for a new sweater.

"Wow," I say. "That's one I haven't seen before."

You hold out your arms. "Too pink?"

Yes. "Nah," I say, and you link your arm through mine.

"Babe, I know I suck. I will read it tonight. For real. You know I'm dying to, right?"

"You don't suck. And for the record, you're the one who brought up my book, Wonder. I know how nervous you are about today and in no way shape or form did I expect you to read it."

"So! Bobby says he knows a guy who might wanna buy your ex-box. Excuse me, jukebox."

It was your idea to sell the jukebox and it's the *good* kind of tension. Sexual and possessive, and who knows? Maybe you bought your new pink sweater for me, the same way I bought a sweater in Bainbridge, when I wanted to impress Mary Kay. She's dead and you're here, and I wrote a great book and I have you and it's the second second day of school, and the second verse is not the same as the first. It's better! We're going in *together* and it's an ideal time to be alive, to be in Cambridge. Early November. The air is crisp and the skeletons and spiderwebs are coming down in the shop windows. The season of masks and terror is in the past and I follow you up the stairs of the Barker Center and it's a bump. The second verse is a little similar to the first—the others are already upstairs—and it's another bump. Sarah Beth is squawking about *The Body on Bainbridge* but you nip that shit in the bud.

"Actually, guys, I stopped listening. Not to be judgy or think-piecey, but a relatively young girl lost her mother, and as someone who lost my mother when I was even younger . . . No judgment . . . But it's triggering for me, you know?"

Thank God for snowflake culture because you did it, Wonder! Sarah Beth is erasing the word *Melanda* from the whiteboard and how perfect. How perfect that it came from you, that you made it about you. We're writers, we have endless other things to talk about, and America's a *shit show* so already we've moved on to the news, but it's not *all* good.

I don't quite know what to make of the look on Sarah Beth's face. She's perturbed, and for all I know, she sent me that Salinger to fuck with me, to make me *feel* safe. She has a team of social media interns. She's media savvy. The headlines would be "fire"—*NYT Bestselling Author's Research Leads to Harvard University Fellow's Arrest on Campus*—and she's a commercial writer. More is more. My phone pings. It's Your Bobby—*Can the dude pick up your Wurlitzer tomorrow?*—and I don't want to *sell* my ex-box. I love my ex-box. But it's the classic conundrum, isn't it, Wonder? I love you more, so I do what I don't want to do—*Sounds good to me, thanks Bobby*—and I feel it in my bones. *Something Wicked This Way Comes.* I should know better than to be happy. Being happy is like daring the universe to sucker punch you and I should have killed Sarah Beth when I didn't have the chance because that's what real writers do. We *create* the chance.

I tell Bobby it's not a good time, and it's the truth. Our kindergarten teacher has arrived and she's different. No reusable bags stuffed with finger paints. No fun-girl leggings. She is corduroy and cashmere. Authoritative. You see the change too, and you shrink like the bratty boy in *Charlie and the Chocolate Factory*. Sly doesn't sit at the head of the table like her dead ex-husband, like she did last week. She sits by you and Sarah Beth smiles at me—what does that mean, what?—and Sly looks around the room.

"So," she says, like a general addressing her troops. "Shall we do this?"

I can hear your heart beat all the way over here and you are terrified. Wishing you never sent those additional *twenty-four* pages, realizing that you are the lamb who volunteered to return to the slaughterhouse and I look at you—*It's gonna be okay*—and your eyebrows reveal the depth of your PTSD—*Is it?*

"Okay," Sly says. "I feel like I went a little too far with the kindergarten schtick last week and I'm just going to say what you've all *got* to be thinking right now. 'This woman published one book and she's only here because of her dead husband' . . ." It's not *not* the truth. "Look," she says. "It's kind of like sailing . . ." So now we're on a sailboat. "Glenn was going against the wind in a big way and I sort of overcorrected. I want us to change course, I want us to tack and eventually . . . We'll find our rhythm on the open water."

Ani smiles in that Ani way, as if she's never been more grateful to already have an Obie. "I love it," she says. "Onward ho!"

Sarah Beth clears her throat and winks at me—no—and did you catch that wink?

You didn't. Your eyes are on Sly because her eyes are on you. "Wonder," she says. "I am truly at a loss for words. Honey, I look at you, I hear your accent and you're so unassuming and so . . . I mean look at you! And then I read you, and I'm just . . . I'm blown away. I love that the fire in here comes from you. I will say it again . . . Look at you! Who would know? Who?"

I would fucking know and you pull on the neck of your hot pink sweater. "Okay . . ."

Sly looks at *you just you, and nobody else but you.* "And there's more," she says. "About an hour ago Wonder texted me, she has five *more* pages for us."

It's news to me but that's you. *Tick tick tap tap tick.*

You sit up straight like you're in the principal's office. "You guys can totally say no. I already sent too much, and it's a lot to ask of you, to read even *more* of my stuff . . ." But we all want more and you're an autodidact at heart. Doing twice the work of others because you have to *prove* your right to be here, and you send us your new pages and I can't wait to see what all that *tick tick tap tap ticking* has been about. The writers' room turns into a reading room and Sly gives us ten minutes to "go back into Wonderland" and what a joy it is, to read you in a room with our fellows, to know that you love me in a way you don't love them. As always, I skip over the sex parts—lampposts only remind me of your past—and I get to the second page. Fourth paragraph.

I read it a second time and a third time and it's not my imagination. It's in black and white.

There was a mouse in her house and it wasn't going to leave without a fight.

Well, that's not right. The mouse in the house is mine. Dr. Nicky gave it to me and he did that in a therapeutic setting and therapy is private. You told me you didn't start reading my book but that's a lie. There's a mouse in *my* house, on the third fucking page of my *Me.* Sly is *reading me, loving me,* and she's got to see your mouse, the one you stole from me. I don't want you to be a thief—she can't respect you if she knows you're a thief—and I can't read. I can't get past the mouse. And you just sit there picking fuzz off your new pink sweater.

Are you a thief? Did you steal? Did you lie? Did you pull a fucking heist?

Therapy is a room. It's Vegas. It's lockdown. What happens in there stays in there and Dr. Nicky is prohibited from disclosing our talks. He gave me that mouse and I carried that mouse, I *killed* that mouse, and I Stephen Fucking Craned my life. I put that mouse through the filter, onto the pages, and I look at the whiteboard, the last vestiges of the *Body on Bainbridge* brainstorm—*Did a Philistan do it?*—and I look at Sarah Beth—she is reading—and I look at Sly—she is still reading you, loving you—and I want my life to be Wonder*full*. If you did this, I can't be with you and I am the Winklevoss twins and you are Mark Zuckerberg and this is Harvard. There is a code of ethics. This is *us*.

"Well," Sly says. "I don't know where to begin . . ." I do. Sly does. She is *reading me, loving me,* and she knows about my mouse but she doesn't call you out. She claps her hands and now we're all clapping—some things never change—and Mats declares this *your best work yet* and Ani raves about the *sexiest lamppost to date* and Sly wants to know where the mouse came from but she knows.

Me! It came from *me*.

You laugh. "It's so freaking crazy," you say. "My niece is a little bookworm and she's obsessed with this book called *There's a Mouse in My House . . .*" That's a lie. Caridad likes Strawberry Shortcake. "She made me read it to her like a zillion times last year . . . I dunno, you don't realize something got into your head until it gets out, you know?"

Your story plays but come the fuck *on*. You're practically living with me and you are the mouse in *my* house, *tick tick tap tap ticking* as you steal from me, and I put my hands on the table.

This is Harvard. This is you. This is the time in my life when I get the glory and the girl and there is no way out of it. I am in love with a two-headed snake.

Sly rests her chin on her fist, like your every word is so fascinating, like anyone does that in real life, like it's actually comfortable to rest your fucking chin on your fucking fist, and Lou rests *his* chin on *his* fist and every fucking head is on every fucking fist and are there any original fucking thinkers in this fellowship?

Ani asks you what books *influenced* you and you wink at me—Who are you?—and you smile. "Well, it's funny. Last week Joe bought a wicked expensive copy of *The Catcher in the Rye* . . . Sorry, babe, but I had to tell them . . ."

You didn't *have* to do anything and now you're the woman who writes and I'm the pretentious loser blowing his money on old, signed Salinger—Lou would have gone for a DeLillo—and you didn't tell me you were going to mention my Salinger and I didn't buy my Salinger and Sarah Beth is quiet.

Dangerously quiet.

Does she think I fucking told you about the book? About the Dead Shed?

But nobody cares about me or the Salinger. They all think the same fucking thing, that I am the guy who buys Salinger and you are the woman who *is* Salinger, and you pontificate about the mouse in your house—it's mine—and you make it about your family, the time you guys found a literal mouse in your living room, and is this how you treat me? You take my beautiful metaphor and reduce it to lame family dramedy? You feed me undercooked oatmeal and steal my mouse and shame me for buying a little piece of history I didn't even buy?

Sly leans over the table, the Diane Sawyer to your Ayelet Fucking Waldman. "So," she says. "Let's get back to Salinger, to you . . ."

"Well, young me totally loved that book and was always sort of trying to imitate it. Alice is starting to see her parents for what they are, these kids who never grew up. Young me is bristling with frustration . . ."

"Yes," Ani says. "Something changed in you . . ." Me. It's me. "It's exciting to see you come into your own. And this mouse, the parents are the mouse in your house."

Sly claps. "Yes! It is *genius*."

That's a knife in my eye and you lap up the Kool-Aid and clap. "I'm just so freaking happy that you guys get it! Cuz young me can be a little bit . . . Well, I was worried she's not likable."

"God no," Lou says. "Alice is here. The book is here."

You know they're on the bandwagon with Sly, same way they were on the bandwagon with RIP Glenn, but you take it all at face fucking value and everyone is clap-clap-clapping and suddenly there are all these different versions of you. *Young* you. Dunkin' you. Thief you. Salinger you and no. That's *me*, I am Salinger minus prep school and you are Pat Conroy via the T and is it really possible to get fucked this many ways at once without a chance of an orgasm?

"Okay, okay," Sly says. "Let's just say what we're all thinking."

FUCK YOU, WONDER.

But then Sly channels her dead ex-husband. A slight furrow of the brow. A stroke of her chin as she scrolls through your pages as if she's searching for the mouse, my mouse. You're bracing for the worst and I should despise you. But I "carry your heart in my heart"—*tick tick tap tap tick*—so when you flash your eyes at me, I am with you. Rooting for you and it's back to square one, day one. *They Hate Us 'Cause They Ain't Us*.

Sly purses her lips and Ani makes a drumroll on the rectangle— the source of all our problems, this table should be *round*—and Mats whistles and Sly closes her computer.

"Wonder," she says. "You are a mouse in our houses, and while this feels like Salinger to all of us, your work is absolutely, entirely your own. Honey, it's brilliant. I want you to keep going. I want you to walk out of this room and write like the wind. *Faithful* is that sort of novel that launches more than a book . . . It marks the birth of an author. I don't want to jinx it. I don't want to burden you with pressure, but *Faithful* is special. And your life story is special. You are doing what we're all supposed to do, writing the book that only you can put out there. And nothing is more important than your work. So do the work. You're just . . . you're truly in a league of your own."

Clap clap clap clap clap and something wicked this way came, all right.

You.

29

I know what Roald Dahl would do to you, Wonder. He was like me, nonviolent by nature, but he understood that with crime comes punishment. He didn't casually bump people off. He custom-fit every well-earned slaughter to every criminal, and if we were in his Chocolate Factory and he found out what you did, he would cut off your little fingers one by one.

Tick tick tap tap tick.

I could never do that to you, but how could you do this to me? How can you be happy when I'm this *un*happy?

You're in my living room, marinating in the group text, the love bombs from our fellows—*Best day ever! I bought the mouse book for my kiddos! Wonder you are a genius!*—and I couldn't take it anymore, so I'm hiding in my bedroom. The Channel 5 guys say we might get snow and I'm a love fool and a sucker because even after what you did to me, I still want to walk in the snow with you. Maybe you're confused. Deluded. Maybe you really didn't read my pages and maybe the author of *There's a Mouse in My House* went to Dr. Fucking Nicky too, but I kind of doubt that—the author lives in Scotland—and I dug through every fucking picture of you reading to Caridad on Facebook and I saw Dr. Seuss and I spied Jean Marzollo and I zoomed in on the stacks of jelly-stained books.

I did not see *There Is a Mouse in My House* in Caridad's fucking bedroom and writing is not so linear and I don't want to be the best. I want *us* to be the best but you can't be good let alone superior and Salingeresque if this is how you do it. By stealing.

Tick tick tap tap tick.

You're here, you're there, back at the scene of the crime, planted on my fucking sofa "writing" your fucking book, and you broke the rules of the Chocolate Factory. You betrayed me, and I did so much for you. I killed Glenn for you. I sold my *jukebox* for you. You were the final girl, the one after the one, the auto to my didact. I could forgive you for bingeing a podcast, but the lying, the stealing . . . And you protested too much, using your *niece* to cover, as if we both don't know that you googled that phrase, my phrase, to gaslight us with a bullshit origin story. I went to *prison* for my mouse and now you're at my bedroom door.

"Knock-knock."

"Come on in."

You hold your phone. You bite your lip. "I can't believe it."

That you stole from me? Me neither, babe. "What?"

"Didn't you see the text? Look at your phone."

You sit in my chair—take, take, take—and I check my phone and there are sixteen new messages in the group text. One fucking love bomb after another. You're shedding crocodile tears, you can't *believe* how much our fellows love your work and you wipe your runny nose on your sleeve. "Are you . . . Are you mad at me?"

Yes. "No."

Tick tick tap tap tick.

You grab at your hair and you are Animal from *Sesame Street*.

"Okay . . . so I know why you're mad . . ." Say it. "You're pissed about the Salinger." You are wrong but you are right. You committed so many crimes there is literally a *list.* "Joe, look . . . I know you're pissed at me. Even when I'm here I'm not here. I'm camped out on your sofa typing my face off and you . . . You gotta admit. You hid that Salinger you bought like you thought I'd be pissed because you blew four grand on a freaking book."

Fuck Salinger. YOU STOLE THE MOUSE IN MY HOUSE. "Wonder, I have contacts. It wasn't four grand."

"Well, you're mad that I told everyone you bought it, so maybe I should go home . . ."

Bad call, Wonder. Cold take. I didn't *buy* that fucking Salinger and I can't tell you who did, so I have to get creative. I bunt. "I hid the book because it was supposed to be a gift . . . for you."

I'm Bassey Ikpi. *I'm Telling the Truth, but I'm Lying.* You shake your head. You realize what you're up against, that I'm batting a thousand, *always.* "I don't deserve you."

This is true. "Wonder . . ."

"Look," you say. "I know I fucked up." Grand larceny of intellectual property is not "fucking up." It's not a pair of sunglasses at Nordstrom Rack. "Do you remember in my house . . . the picture of my grandpa, the one who pitched for the Sox? He was a southpaw . . ." Just say *lefty.* "And when he was a kid in school, they had these desks and the inkwell was in the right corner, but back in the day, he was a lefty, and the teachers wouldn't just *let* you be a lefty. They tied his left arm behind his back. I mean, can you imagine?"

I was locked in a cage because someone stole a *Catcher in the Rye* and your stories are never about you. "That's awful, it is."

"Well, here's the other awful, okay? Ever since I was a kid, listening to my dad tell that story for the ten thousandth time, I think life has to be this uphill battle and earlier today . . . I was happy. I have you and I was the 'star' and it was like . . . It was too much. The way I was raised, something has to be *wrong.* And if no one's gonna tie my hand behind my back, well, fuck it, I'll do it myself." You rub what may or may not be a tear off your cheek. "Bottom line is, in some messed-up way, I needed you to be mad at me. And I know I was bad. That was your story to tell or not tell, and I never should have told the whole room. What you do with your money, whether it's for you or me, that's your business. That's private. And I'm sorry."

You confessed to the misdemeanor, but you didn't cop to the felony and you come to the bed. Supplicant. You are an autodidact and you missed a lot of classes. How to Love. How to Be Fair. How to Come Clean. "Joe," you say. "We both know that I wouldn't even be writing were it not for you . . ." You pull my legs, both of them. "You inspire me . . ." You run your hands up my legs, both of them, and this isn't a Chocolate Factory. It's a bedroom. "I owe it all to you, and I know I'm not supposed to say it, but I am good because of you."

You take me in your mouth, in your hands, and this is how you are when you're writing. Intent. *Tick tick tap tap tick.* As if you're running to catch the T, on a mad dash to elude the security guards at Nordstrom fucking Rack, all the men who held you down, your grandfather and your father, the Ivy League Douchebags who didn't deserve you. You suck the life out of me, you lure the mouse out of my house—I am hard—and I am the mouse in *your* house. The mirrors bend and I see what I couldn't see before. Imitation is the sincerest form of passive-aggressive flattery and you are the criminal but I am the judge, the jury. My hands are on your head. A simple twist would do it. But then again, yes, a simple twist would do it. I get a flash of us in the winter, in the future. We are in Maine, on a rocky white beach, that rare old couple with a roaring sex life. We laugh about the old days, these days, about how you stole my mouse, when our emotions were running high, when we weren't yet published, and we thought all of this mattered more than it did.

And then you swallow. "Joe."

You're trembling and warm. You wouldn't steal sunglasses you didn't like, didn't love. You wouldn't steal what you didn't want, what you didn't think you needed to become the best version of yourself. *Me.* I run my hand through your hair. I didn't invent the word *mouse* and I didn't invent the word *house.* "You wanna go for a walk?"

"Nah," you say. "The workshop was crazy. I feel like I went to a birthday party and drank too much Kool-Aid. I gotta freaking *write.* And I know you probably wish I'd start reading *your* book, but I don't even think I can right now . . ." You run your hand up and down my leg. "Okay, maybe when you fall asleep . . . But will you still be into me when I'm fangirling all over you?"

You say that like you haven't already established yourself as my number one fan and I smile. "Yes."

30

I sleep hard, the adrenaline, the hummer, but in the morning, I smell plain bagels in the toaster. It's a good sign—you ventured into the fresh snow to buy my favorite bagels to atone for your sin—or it's a bad sign—you clomped through the slush for pity bagels. What if you really *did* read my book? What if the rest of it didn't grab you like the mouse? What if my book is so bad that you never steal from me again?

I open the door. I walk onto the plank.

Tick tick tap tap tick.

You're not reading. You're writing . . . stealing . . . who can tell, and all I can do is stand here and think about your fucking grandfather. He had *nothing* on my mine. My granddad had a rotten childhood. His old man was a textbook drunk who smacked him around, eventually took out his left eye. My "grandpa" had to go to school with a fucking hole in his head, an eye patch, and he never got a prosthetic eyeball, let alone a pro fucking baseball contract. You knew your grandfather, but mine died before I was born. Our ugly is thorough, but your ugly is a pre-fucking-swan. In your world, the lefty becomes a southpaw. In mine, the lefty develops a mean left hook he reserves exclusively for his son, and now I finally get it.

That's why you stole from me. It isn't just because you love me and my work, it's because you don't have enough story in you. The raunchy lampposts in *Faithful* aren't a life. You haven't lived enough to write a book, so you're pulling from everything, your sister's husband in Walpole, your father, your great-grandfather you never even met, your mother, the safest bet of all because she can't zombie back to life and accuse you of stealing her stories. You know I'm onto you. A good night's sleep always makes us see things clearly. You're nervous, pretending you don't feel me standing here, afraid of what comes next. But I can be the bigger man. I *want* to be the bigger man.

Tick tick tap tap tick.

I cough and you close your laptop. "Okay, so I'm just gonna come out and say it . . ." I'm a genius and you are a thief. "Babe, after you went to bed, I made a decision. I'm not gonna even *start* your book until it's your turn in the room."

WHAT? "Oh."

The bagels ding in the toaster and you bombard me with a string of excuses. I inspire you so much that you *couldn't* read, you had to write, and you can't read here. This is my home and you're a "private" reader—bullshit, you're on Goodreads—and your reasons don't come from the heart, but come from the head. "The other thing is . . . Joe, I can't read it just because you want me to read it. I can't read on demand. I started *Faithful* two years before I met you. I was writing it for my family, for my mom, but now it feels like I'm writing it for you. You're in my heart, my head. The last thing I need right now is more you, you know?"

It reads like a confession. *I started your book and stole your mouse so I have to stop or I'll steal even more.* You're a klepto but you know it and you come to me. "And there is one more thing but you're not gonna like it . . ."

You lay hands on my chest and this is it. Fuck the bagels. You're gonna confess. "Babe," you say, and I brace for the impact. "You make me want to write. I mean don't I . . . do I inspire you at all?"

I glance at my jukebox, the one I bought for my muse after she died, but it's gone. I blink. You step away to rub butter on bagels. "Oh yeah," you say. "The guy came and you were out cold. It's okay I let him take it, right?"

I need time to think. To process all the fucking holes, so I ask you about you, about your morning progress, and you light the fuck up and I am "the world's best muse"—a better word might be *source*—and you lick melted butter off a bagel. "You know what it is? I feel like one of those coders in *The Social Network*. I've never been this locked in. *Ever.*"

I want to believe you, so I tell you I get it. "That's how I was with my first draft in Florida, those days when you lose time, forgot to eat. There's nothing quite like it."

But it was too much and now *you* clock the hole of the ex-box and I get it. Your writing is about me, but I did my best work in another fucking state, in another state of mind, before I even knew you, and maybe in your twisted, optimistic head, maybe *that's* what gives you the right to steal from me, if you did it, did you? I can't go there—you would fly off the handle and I would be digging a hole in the dirt—but I can't stay here.

"Anyway," you say. "Bottom line is, you think you're going nuts because you're waiting on Sly, on me, but the real reason is . . . you're waiting on *you*." You look at the hole where the ex-box used to live. "I mean . . . do I . . . don't I inspire you?"

Tick tick tap tap tick.

I give you what you need, a big fat fucking YES, and I gather my things, my keys that you know about, my keys that you don't know about, and you feel bad that you're jamming me up.

"You shouldn't have to write in a coffee shop. This is your house."

"I wrote my first book in a bar. And come on. I can't write in here. I can't keep my hands off you."

You smile, oblivious of all the other things I could do with my hands. "Good luck."

You're back in it before I close the door—*tick tick tap tap tick*—and you do inspire me. I didn't get into Harvard by feeling sorry for myself and I am your hero, your muse slash source, but now I have to be *my* hero. I bound down the stairs and I check Sly's Twitter and I'm good to go. She's doing outdoor *snow yoga* in Wellesley—bite me—and I hightail it to her house and it's not "breaking and entering." When RIP Glenn roped me into being his assistant, the first thing I did was make a copy of his house keys, and the keys work—I'm in—and you are the mouse in my house—you won't read me, you stole my cheese—but now I am the mouse in Sly's house, on the hunt for proof that she is hell-bent on finding me the kind of house I need, the kind you can't find on fucking Zillow.

A publishing house.

I'm tripping on crumpled bags from Anthropologie and North Face and what a sight. What a horror. The widow Sly is blocking the paths in her own home. She's lonely. She bought four lavender overcoats in four different sizes and they're all hanging on the chairs around the table, as if she's trying to convince herself that she's not alone.

I make a note to put that in my next book and it smells different in here. Less Glenn, more vanilla. Multiple mugs of dank sour coffee are abandoned while chopsticks are wrapped up and waiting on every end table, every sofa, as if she wants to be prepared to eat sushi at any moment. She bought a brand-new blanket from Saks—tag on, six *hundred* fucking dollars—but where oh where is my book?

The office.

Some widows wouldn't go there. They'd lock the door to preserve the scent of their beloved, but Sly took Glenn's job and I was right—she took his office—and good for her. She did write *Scabies for Breakfast* and I'm happy that Glenn's brownnosing Zoom background is no longer—the *No Country for Old Men* poster is off the wall, on the floor—

and she replaced his inherently pretentious back-busting leather chair with an aerodynamic clean, cold model, a fuck you to her dead husband's aesthetic, and then there's the money shot.

A stack of manuscripts. I'm in there.

I like Sly. She's the Carrie Fisher to my Billy Crystal—there's no spark between us, none—and I should have come here days ago. You're my girlfriend, but Sly can appreciate me in a way that you can't.

Reading it, loving it.

She doesn't want to have sex with me. Her love is pure and literary and I want to see the love in writing and I'm not on the top of the stack and I'm not second but then the hairs on my arms stand up.

Meow.

Sly's new cat is bound for a chaise lounge. It's pink and new as your sweater and in Bainbridge my cats wanted to be where my scent was strongest and in life, all cats are the same.

That's where Sly reads, where she loves, and there it is.

My book.

It's open. Bathed in blood-red ink. Stars in the margins and whole paragraphs circled. Even from over here, I see the word YES in all caps at the top of the page.

It's a little bit like cheating, opening your present the night before Christmas, but we didn't really do presents in my house—I'm sure you did in *yours*—and I deserve this. I need this for you, for me, for us, and I'm closer and the cat is eyeing me—she knows—and every page is dog-eared and my book is bloated with praise, literally, physically larger than it was when I gave it to her.

I sit on her chaise—we need one of these!—and Donna Tartt makes a run for it and it wasn't fair of me to push you to read and maybe it's true about Caridad. You said it all along. You don't need this the way I do. You're in no rush to get published. You were in it for the 25K and you are a Goodreads girl, strapped with a family that relies on you, a family that needs you, loves you, and what's gravy to you is meat to me.

I pick up my manuscript and flip, letting the red words flow into me like the dopamine bombs that they are.

I love this.

So true.

I love this so much that I want more.

This pays off well.

Christ, Mats, you're killing me.

The manuscript hits the shag carpet. *Thump.* This isn't my book. This is *his* book. And I didn't know he wrote a book. He sent us ten fucking pages and okay, so it's not just me. I'm not the only star and it's Harvard. It was never gonna be *just* me and I like Mats. He's a good man and we're not in competition. I'm *Salinger* and he's writing his own version of *Ready Player One.*

It is possible to love two books in two very different ways.

But where the fuck is mine?

I go back to the stacks and I find O.K.'s pages, and underneath those, I find Lou's Arby's redux "noir" and here is Ani—it's magical realism, as I expected—but where is my fucking magic?

Reading it, loving it, sit tight.

It's cold in here and it's cold out there and Sly's not *that* into yoga—she went for the picture, for the two inches of surprise November snow—and if she's *reading it, loving it* . . . well it might not even fucking be here, but then again, I saw her fucking selfie, her tiny knapsack—no room for an eight-and-a-half-by-eleven manuscript in that little satchel—and I'm on the move. I wouldn't be lumped in with my fellows and their half-finished first drafts. I wrote the fuck out of my book and I finished my book and I go back to the kitchen—women like Sly have a way of living in their kitchens—but it's not on the island and it's not on the counter and it's not on the table with the ghost coats and it's not in the living room, the *sitting* room as RIP Glenn liked to call it, and that's where it is.

I know it before I know it, the way sometimes you just fucking *know.*

The widow Sly took me to bed.

I pause in the doorway of her room. Donna Tartt is on the bed, sniffing bad coffee milk on the nightstand, and the coffee is sitting on a coaster.

A coaster as in . . . my book.

I reach for the mug and the cat hisses and the mug is stuck—it takes time for that to happen—and the mug leaves a ring, a stain— will she notice?—and my pages aren't bloated with love. They're not dog-eared and she did not lift a red Sharpie to the margins and sweat is pouring out of all my pores—bad writer, bad—and she said she was *reading it, loving it* but my book is a virgin.

Untouched. Cast aside. A *coaster*.

I am sweating on the pages and no. I already sweated for this book, and I bled for this book, and did she even get past the first fuck- ing page?

My phone pings and the cat is hissing—will it tell?—and my sinuses sizzle up on me—it's been a long time since I had a cat—and it's a mean sneeze, sudden, and my DN-Fucking-A is all over my fuck- ing book and it's not a book.

It's a coaster. An unpublished manuscript.

I put it on the nightstand and my phone pings again and again and again, and on the off chance that it's Sly, that she loved it so much she made copies, I check my fucking phone, but it's not Sly. It's a link from Ani, a link to *Publishers* Fucking *Weekly*. Mats is in the headline, in the trades, and I can't open the link because you bump it up the screen with a WOOH and Lou offers champagne and my poor book is sit- ting on Sly's nightstand, crying for me—*Help me, Daddy*—and I tried, little book. I tried.

I click on the link and Mats got a haircut for his headshot and it's a good fucking headshot. Original and sincere—he's smiling at the camera, waving like he's on a Zoom—and to know him is to root for him, and I *do* root for him. I am happy that he got a *high-six-figure deal* and the words jump off the page, into my body. *A bidding war . . . the next*

Ready Player One . . . *unputdownable* . . . *Bernice Lapatin and Random House* . . . And Ani calls for a *fellow toast at Grendel's at eight* and my poor not-a-book sits on Sly's fucking nightstand.

Neglected and weeping. A *coaster.*

She did for Mats what she didn't do for me, and I deserve better. I honor the cone of silence. I alone keep her secret and I came to this house to terminate *one* mouse only to find another.

And now you text me: *So cool about Mats right? Hope writing is going well and next one of us to get a deal is YOU. I feel it!*

I want to believe you, but my book is a starving infant on a night-stand. I hear something scratching and there is nowhere to hide and is it Sly? Is she home? Does she have some secret fucking entrance? You come from a world where happy endings exist in real life, where the Red Sox eventually win, where your grandpa makes it to the mound, and I've spent my whole life searching for happy endings in books, in *cheesy* romcoms, relying on Harry and Sally to lift me up, to keep me believing, and you want to do that for me now, but you know that Sly chose Mats, not me, and it's an ugly truth. Nobody loves *Me.* You liked it enough to steal from it, but you're not screaming from the rooftops. You got what you needed—you stole my mouse—and the cat makes a beeline for the closet, the source of all the scratching. I see it, too. A whirling dervish that will live to see another day.

A real-life motherfucking *mouse.*

31

I'm a little calmer. Being the bigger person really *is* the most rewarding thing you can do when the chips are down. I bought Mats a
bottle of Dom. I came into this basement bar genuinely happy for
the guy, and in theory, this should be a good night. The tables down here
are round, Algonquin, and this is what I wanted from the fellowship, the
pomp of being those people, the cream of the crop, the loudest, smartest
ones in the room with something to fucking celebrate. I have a seat at the
table, literally and figuratively, we're popping bottles, and I have you. The
other significant others are at a nearby table, a lesser table, which makes
us the star couple, the only writer couple in the mix. Mats is beaming and
Sarah Beth's *kiddos* made him a paper crown and I got out of Sly's before
she got home, but there's always a fucking *but*.

In this case, my *but* is with everyone at this table including you.
Sarah Beth is published so we all know her fucking books and Lou
gave us galleys and bombards us with excerpts from his "tree house
noir" so we know him. Ani won an Obie and we read your pages, we

read Mats's pages, but nobody at this table has read *me* and it's compliment ping-pong and I have a paddle but I'm not in the game, I can't rally, and Ani dings her highball glass with a spoon. "Okay," she says. "Wonder, mark my words, in one month, we will be here for *you*."

That's your cue to pass the love to me, but Mats takes his crown and sets it on your head and suddenly it's a party for you. Which is fine. It is. But it's *not* fine because you alone know what they don't know—the next fucking party is for *me*—and you do the wrong thing.

You pick up Lou's official book, the hardcover *O'er Under* that he brought to make the party about *him*. "Not true," you sass. "Next time we're here, it's for Lou!"

You look at me as if I'm being too quiet, so I raise my glass. "To the funeral on page 311. Blew my mind."

That made you happy, but Ani clamps her hands over her ears. "No spoilers, please!"

I'm the best writer because I'm the best reader of people and I know Lou, so I laugh. "Oh, come on, Ani, it's not like it's a thriller. I didn't 'spoil' the all-important twist."

It's so *easy* to placate Lou, Mr. I'm-Not-Book-of-the-Month-Thriller, and he puffs up—"I'd have to agree"—and the bar is crowded so I was loud, too loud, and Sarah Beth balks. "Wow, Joe, tell us how you *really* feel about thrillers." I fucking love thrillers and I said that for Lou, not *her*, and Ani pulls you back into the group and Sarah Beth laughs. "Relax," she says. "I'm just kidding. I always want my books to be more about characters than twists, so I'm right there with you, Joe. And you too, Lou!"

It's the way she said it. *I'm right there with you, Joe.* And you sigh. You're back. "The poor freaking waitress. I can't believe she's the only one on tonight."

We all know what's gonna happen next. You're right. The waitress is overworked—she has a bowling league to deal with on the other side of the bar—and one of has to do the right thing and order at the bar. The thing is, it's not "one of us." It's me.

I make the offer for the fourth time in two hours—"Who needs a refill?"—because someone has to do it and Lou is always in the middle of spinning a yarn and the party is for Mats and yes, we're postgender, but when Ani offers to go to the bar, you grab her arm.

"Not even maybe," you snap. "Joe lives to be a gentleman."

I wave to the other table, where the spouses and significant others are gathered, and I break eye contact because it could be worse. I could be one of them. At the bar, the bearded bartender ignores me and drunk writers are loud, louder even than bowlers on boilermakers, and you slam your glass on the table. "No way," you say. "I am only like fifty pages in, and I am *not* getting a freaking deal anytime soon."

Lou says that's *more than enough* to get an agent, to get a deal, and of course I want you to get a book deal—I love you—but I'm supposed to be *next*. The surly bartender picks up four martini glasses for a woman who is cutting me in line, same as you, but I'm the bigger person. Of course, the fellows think you're next. They haven't read my book yet and they don't know that it's so good that you had to steal from it, that Sly is *reading it, loving it,* but she isn't *reading it* or *loving it* and my brain can't quite adjust to the new world, the dark world, and one of the bowlers approaches our table and taps you on the shoulder.

Back off, fucker. She's *mine*.

He whispers in your ear, and you pretend you can't hear and turn your back on him—good—and he moves on to Sarah Beth, and she *can* hear him, and he wants my chair and she gives him the green fucking light and the bartender chooses this moment to get in my face.

"You wanna order something or what?"

"Sorry," I say, and he looks right through me, and who can blame him? I'm a Harvard asshole and he lives on tips. "I need a vodka soda, a bourbon neat, another vodka soda, and—"

Sarah Beth appears out of nowhere. Like a witch. "And five shots of whiskey!"

The bartender grabs glasses begrudgingly and I look at Sarah Beth. "Really? More shots?"

She laughs. "You and my husband could be twins."

Did he also murder a bunch of assholes? "Ha."

"Seriously," she says, and is there a human in there? "The hubs . . . Kevin . . . he *loves* you."

Kevin does not "love" me. Kevin and I shook hands and exchanged empty pleasantries before he went to his table and I went to mine. "That's sweet."

She waves at the spousal table so I have no choice but to do it too and it's a square table. Four people who have absolutely nothing in fucking common. Ani's banker-ish husband is stuck with Lou's drunk *lady*, who's trying to sell him her NF-Fucking-Ts—help me, Wonder—and Sarah Beth scoops up the shots, popping them onto a tray as if she bought them, as if she stood up here waiting to place the order.

"Let me take care of this. You go say hi to Kevin. He's dying over there . . ."

They're all dying and they're not *my* spouses. I'm your boyfriend and I'm a fellow and I belong at our table. The round one. *Gently, Joseph,* and I reach for the tray. "Not necessary," I say. "I got it."

"Seriously," she says, and her eyes are bullets and she's the most dangerous kind of tipsy. Brazen but steady. The one with the *tapes.* "Go."

I have no choice and the bar is too loud—fucking Massholes, can they go five minutes without blasting "classic" rock?—and you balk.

"Joe," you yell. "Where are you going?"

SARAH BETH KNOWS THAT I KILLED GUINEVERE BECK AMONG OTHERS. I smile and make a promise I can't keep, signaling one minute and you're offended. I'm your boyfriend and this is me, leaving you, and you pour your shot into your Coolatta and you pour *my* shot into your Coolatta and Kevin is a hugger.

"What's up, buddy?"

Nothing is *up* and Kevin's pants are both khaki and pleated and his cell phone is clipped to his belt and I bet he lost his virginity to Dave Fucking Matthews. *Crash.* He smacks me on the back and pulls out a trap in the form of a chair, and he's jovial so now of course I feel guilty. He's good people but he's not *my* people and he raises his fucking Guinness. "Everybody welcome Joe to the fun table!"

There is no such thing as "everybody" at this table because these people are not in a fucking fellowship. Mats has a new boyfriend named Edward, and Edward cracks a smile—"*Fun* . . . that's one word for it"—and he's raising his glass to Mats like *you owe me* because he's stuck with Lou's *lady,* who's smothering him with stupid sexist questions—"Tell me where I should go dancing, I bet you know all the spots." Ani's husband is a seasoned pro at this game—he's on the phone—and I do not belong and I should not have to fucking *get* along. I'm a writer. Same as you.

"So," Kevin says, zipping his L.L.Bean backpack. "S.B. tells me you're into cycling?"

S.B. lied—the cycling part of my life is over—but S.B. can do whatever the fuck she wants. She has tapes . . . of me. I sip my vodka soda and this is why people drink. To convince themselves they are having a good time when they are just trying to avoid solitary confinement.

"I was," I say. Be aloof. Be a fellow. Be the one who doesn't belong. "But not so much lately . . ."

Kevin scratches the back of his prematurely balding head. "Same," he says. "I was riding with my buddy from B school . . ." *B school.* "But you know how it is . . ." No, I do not. "He just became a dad, so his riding days are over for now, and it's hard to get out there without accountability."

Oh God. He's one of those Word of the Week people, and no man should tell a man he barely knows that he's lonely. I nod. "That's why the fellowship has been so good for my writing," I say, and a seventh grader could understand that I'm establishing a boundary, that my *accountability* is to my fellows, not this bunch, but Kevin probably spent most of seventh grade playing videogames and jerking off and he nods, willing my point to fly over his head. "So, Joe," he says. "I don't know about you, but I miss chewing the bars. How about we get back on?"

I need you to summon me back to the table but you're using your fingers to whistle at the waitress. You speak her language and you raise four fingers, you want four more shots, one for Ani and one for Lou, one for Mats and one for you, and what about me?

Kevin sucks foam off his Guinness. "The carbs are a lot," he says. "But sometimes ya gotta go for it! S.B. says you're from New York, right?"

Now Kevin babbles about how much he loves *Gotham* and it's all about the pizza he ate in *the Village* and the shows he saw on Broadway and Lou's attention-starved wife smiles. "You're Wonder's guy, right? Lou says you guys are sooo cute together."

I am your guy but our relationship does not define me—I'm a fellow, Goddammit, a *fellow*—and Kevin cracks a dumbass joke about how people used to say that sorta thing about him and *the wife* and Ani's husband smiles at his phone. "We could all probably write books about being with a writer."

That gets a rousing yes from Mats's new boyfriend, from *all* the insignificant others, and the vodka is scratching at my gullet, and I will not write a book about being married to a writer. I *am* a writer. The waitress brings four *more* shots to your table, *my* table, and Kevin says, "So how about tomorrow?"

"Tomorrow?"

"For a ride! Normally, I gotta check with S.B. about day plans, but the way she's knocking 'em back over there, I can tell ya right now, tomorrow's gonna be a *big* iPad day for the kiddos!"

I deflect with a "maybe" and you stand and wave your arms above your head, but you're not waving at me. You're flagging down one of your Dunkin' underlings who you roped into delivering Coolattas—

she works for Dunkin', not for you, Wonder, *tsk tsk*—and I count one, two, three, four, five . . . not six, and then the waitress brings more shots to the table that used to be my table and I'm missing it. All of it.

Kevin thumbs his way through one of five weather apps he has on his phone and he's talking about barometric pressure and the likelihood of drizzle and I see you, I see them, my fellows, fucking traitors, and Sarah Beth catches my eye. *Sit, Joe, sit.*

She owns me, and for all you know, I am choosing to be here. I don't like shots and I don't like thick, sugar-infested Coolattas and you raise your plastic cup and make a toast—"Shotlattas!"—and this is what it is to be in love. Wanting what you don't want. Sugar and rubbing alcohol. The other fellows chime in as if you're toasting my fucking exodus, but maybe it's like Sly said. *You're in a league of your own.* If she's right—she is right—then I don't need that kind of Algonquin round table bonding over an embarrassingly pedestrian made-up word. *Shotlatta.* I'm my own writer, my own person. Maybe talking to the khaki spouses is actually good for me, the reason I wrote such a good book in the first place. I'm still me. I don't fight my way into circles. I don't crave the approval of "colleagues." I am the writer at a table of nonwriters and the best thing I can do right now is start a party better than yours, the kind of spectacle that makes you beg for a seat at *my* table.

I flag down the waitress. "Can we get ten shots of tequila?"

Lou's *lady* gasps—"Ten"—and Ani's husband chuckles—"That's a first"—and I said the T-word, so Kevin has to torture us with a ridiculously detailed, generic story about his first rendezvous with tequila—freshman year at BC, Marathon Day, lawn chairs, yawn stares—and do writers do this on purpose? Do they unconsciously seek out partners who are exceptionally *bad* at storytelling?

Is that why you chose me?

Alcohol really is a fucking depressant and I don't belong here, and I don't belong there. I do one shot, I toss back another shot, and my mind is foggy, as if Sarah Beth is blowing chloroform kisses. I can't win at this table, in this basement, so I give Kevin my phone number and already he texts me—*Sup Joe!*—and I stumble out of my chair to find the men's room, and it's a Billy Joel sing-along—the one about a "real estate novelist"—and the writers and the spouses have found common, swaying, warbling ground with the bowlers—everyone knows every word—and I can't face a urinal cake right now.

I'm gone.

32

Tick tick tap tap tick.

Morning, maybe. My stomach is empty and full. I taste the residue of unwashed limes, and the memories crack like lightning. You didn't protect my chair. You didn't follow me up the stairs when I slipped out. Nobody did. I am not loved. I am under attack from within and without. I rub sleep out of my eyes and check my phone—no *are you okay* text from you—and the smallest fucking movement of my fingers taunts the bomb inside my body.

Tick tick tap tap tick.

So, this is what it's like to throw up in your own fucking bed and I stagger to my bathroom and there it is again. That noise.

Tick tick tap tap tick.

But that's not the sound of the bile-breathing demons. That's you.

You tell me I have a hangover but this is not a *hangover.* This is an ambush from the dead. Every time I open my mouth, it's not by choice. It's this thing inside of me that wants out and every time I wretch it's because of the bitter, entitled demons wreaking havoc on my intestines. That's RIP Peach bitch-slapping the wall of my stomach and that's RIP Benji clawing my trachea and then I think it's over. There is nothing left inside of me, but RIP Henderson wraps his evil fucking hand around my windpipe while RIP Beck shoves a lit cigarette into my fucking rib cage.

"Jesus," you say. "Maybe you need to get your stomach pumped."

I need an IV of you. *That's* what I need. You rub circles on my back and you are at your most lovable when you are in the process of loving me, saving me. RIP Fincher digs a knife into the wall of my stomach and I'm back in the bowl but you are behind me, above me. My angel.

"Babe," you say. "I think we should get you a shot. You have vodka, right?"

The words come out in a string of fucking belches—"Don't say *vodka*"—and you mean well, you do, but you laugh and lecture me about the hair of the dog and I'm sorry, but this is not a *hangover* or no one would ever drink. I flush the toilet and you pat me on the back. "Let's get you to bed."

It's the longest walk of my life. You are strong enough to hold me steady, knowing what to say, what to do. I like you like this and you like yourself like this and then you smile and sink into my chair. "Wow."

"I think it was food poisoning."

You chuckle and tell me that your dad used to say the same thing, and I'm not your dad. This isn't a scene from *Faithful* and I don't live on *handles* of fucking Tito's. Then you laugh at something on your phone, and I liked it better when I was dying, when you were my nurse.

"What's so funny?"

"It was just a joke from last night, one of those ya-had-to-be-there things . . ." I *was* there but I wasn't and you're on your phone, typing.

"Well, what was the joke?"

"Oh, it wasn't a 'joke.' When you bailed to hang out with the spouses"—NOT MY CHOICE, WONDER—"Sarah Beth noticed this guy checking me out, and she was all 'Hello, Mr. Lamppost,' but obviously, I'm all set with lampposts. I mean I have you. I told you, babe. It was a ya-had-to-be-there thing . . ." So *that's* why Sarah Beth sent me into exile, so she could point at other men who want to be with you while I sat at a different table, as if I *don't* want to be with you. You sigh. "Everyone's asking about you . . ."

"Why?"

You laugh and it's not funny. I was close to fucking death. "Babe, come on. You were so wasted you didn't even say goodbye and I'm like . . . if this is you after a little tequila, I can't imagine how you're gonna deal with my family."

I close my eyes while you talk to me about things that matter but don't, the upcoming night before Thanksgiving bar crawl with your *peeps* and the feast the day after. There are so many things I love about you. I want us to be together but somehow the more you talk, the more you frame my illness as something embarrassing, something shameful—I'm not Hemingway, I can't hold my liquor—well, yes, there are things I *don't* like about you, but nobody likes anyone when their head is a bag of sand.

I remember the day you left to avoid a fight. It's my turn.

"Wonder, seriously, I'm gonna be fine. You can go."

"No," you say. "I'm not leaving you like this. I know my way around a hangover, and you, my dear, do *not*. Stay put, okay? I'm gonna make you a sandwich."

It's better when you're gone, in the kitchen. I smell bacon and I don't have the energy to fester about last night, about my exile in spouseville.

But then my phone pings. I reach for my device and the demons encroach on my organs. One new text. A random 401.

Yo Joe! We still good for 2PM? Stoked!

I sit up too fast and RIP Forty takes a nail file to my gullet and I close my eyes.

No. No to everything.

The text is from *Kevin* and he's right. I said I would ride. But people say all kinds of things when they're drunk and he's a good guy. He'll understand. But then another text comes through from someone who most certainly will not.

Sarah Beth Rhymes with Death: *Have fun with the hubs and stop by the Dead Shed after you ride!*

You're not thrilled with me right now. I believe your exact words were "Okay, so you're too sick to hang out with your girlfriend but you're not too sick to break your promise to me and go ride your bike with a stranger."

But how do you think I feel, Wonder? I'm lucky that I didn't get a daylight DUI on the ride to Foster or fall off my bike and slice my leg open on the *Bike Ride That Would Not End*.

Not that you asked, but yes, I survived the refreshingly low-key slow ride with refreshingly low-key slow Kevin. I survived lunch at a picnic table where Kevin talked to me about a sale at Vineyard Vines and the time he got to meet John Grisham and I even let him talk a little aspirational macho smack about S.B. *Before the fellowship, she'd help out here and there, do the laundry on a Saturday, but something changed. At least it's only a year!*

Kevin is right. It is only a year, and this is only a day, and this is the last hurdle, my sit-down with *S.B.* I made up my mind on the trail, the way writers often do. This is it for me. She doesn't get to treat me like a character in one of her fucking books. I am not the *Husbandsitter*. I *promised* you that my spandex shorts were a thing of the past. And you let me down—you stole—but I will not let you down. This was the first and last ride, no matter what Sarah Beth wants.

I knock on the door of the Dead Shed and it opens—"Hey you!"— and she smiles like a pediatrician. That was fast. Too fast. Was she standing there the whole time we were gone?

I scan the space for listening devices, as if it fucking matters at this point, and she pulls a blanket over her lap—GO PATS—and she pours me a cup of *tea*. "So, I guess you got my book!"

"Yeah . . . and thanks! And I assure you, I didn't tell Wonder."

She waves me off. "Oh please, I wasn't worried about that. I'm just old-fashioned about gifts and my mom was militant about thank-you notes, so I'm that way about them, I'm militant with *my* kids, and . . . Never mind. As long as you got it."

She wanted a fucking *thank-you note* for blackmailing me.

"Well, my mom wasn't militant about thank-you notes but seriously, thank you."

She tilts her tiny head. "Is Wonder expecting you? Do you kids have plans?"

Kids. She can't decide if she's my parole officer, my psychologist, or my mother. "Nothing major," I say. "But I should get home soon." With my *tapes*.

She stares at her own books. "Home."

It's official. She's my shrink. I nod. "Home." Three . . . two . . . "Hey, Kevin's a great guy."

She laughs, as if her own husband is a joke. "You're a good sport."

I am not a good sport. I am a prisoner. "Thanks."

"So, I detected a little tension last night . . . You and Wonder, how's that going?"

Less is more is the rule with any shrink, especially unlicensed. "We *all* had a little too much to drink last night . . ." As in, *No more bike time with Kevin*. "But you know . . . We're good."

"Last night I was watching you guys . . ." Sicko. "And oh man, in college, I tried. You know I dated a writer . . ." This is good. Let her be the one to talk. "He was such a *Stephen*, with the narrow shoulders and the big vocabulary, and he'd spend a whole day on a single sentence and he's . . . I think he wrote a book eventually . . ." She knows what he wrote, probably knows what he had for breakfast. "I couldn't do it. I couldn't be with a writer who thought he was better than me."

I am not a fish. I will not bite. "Well, that's youth, right? I don't think of anyone as 'better' than anyone. Anyway, the thing is—"

"Wonder sure was feeling herself last night, right? It brought me back to being with Stephen when he was like that, all up in his ego . . ."

"She was just excited," I say, ever your champion. "And I'm happy for her."

"Been there," she says. "The whole 'Yes, I love that my partner gets the attention I want.' And who can blame us for trying? It's so nice in theory, the darling literary couple, serious authors in serious *love*, Rick Moody and Vendela Vida . . ."

You and I are not *trying*. We're doing it. And she's projecting—she's jealous of you—and she should know better, as a professional. RIP Glenn ruined us with his outlook on writers—*You're nothing if you're not big like me*—and the goal is to do your best because no one ever wins when they compare themselves to anyone. Hell, I learned that in actual, real-life kindergarten, but I can't digress. Sarah Beth Swallows has me on *tape* and where are those tapes?

She laughs at me. She knows. "Oh, Joe," she says. "Relax. The tapes are safe with me."

"That's kind of the issue."

She sits up straight. "Oh my God, did you want me to make you a copy? I could do that, but I am *so* bad at tech stuff and my assistants, I mean I 'trust' them but . . ."

I imagine her "accidentally" sharing them with her entire fucking fan base and I manage a *never mind* and she smiles like we're in a good place, like any of this is normal, like she isn't holding me hostage as she tamps down her Patriots blanket and smiles. "Anyway," she says. "It goes without saying, those tapes are for my ears only . . . but I know, you're in a mood today. That's why I wanted to help get you outta there. Watching your girlfriend's star rise as yours stays put . . . First the room, then the drinks. That must have killed you."

It did. "It didn't."

"Seeing you two *really* got me thinking about my life . . ." Textbook egomaniac psychobabble. "My college boyfriend Stephen . . . Stephen Kershaw . . . the golden boy 'wonder' who ditched me for one of those women with the curly hair and a nose ring . . ."

I'm not her therapist and I want my tapes. "It happens."

She grunts. "It's still happening now. I subscribe to his stupid Substack even though he's ignored every book I ever wrote . . . And every book I finish, I think this is it, this is the one that gets Lauren Groff to come around and insist on reviewing *me* for the *Times* or respond to the DM I sent her two years ago . . ." Ouch. "But every single time, it's the same. Stephen ignores everything I do and I'm not an *author*. I can't pull off yellow dresses or red lipstick. I'm always just . . . there. And journalists want to know about my research into chloroform and my readers call it unputdownable and tear through it and move on to the next cheap thrill."

Amen. "That's not true."

"Well, it is true. And it's my fault because let's face it. I'm in a rut, Joe, just like you."

It's always easier to agree with your shrink so I nod like we are the same.

"Stephen and Michelle and the perfect little small press they run from their perfect little home in Brookline, Michelle with her simpering I-write-essays-for-*The-Believer*-so-I'm-better-than-you smile . . . Doesn't it drive you crazy? Why do some people get to be taken seriously? Michelle can rock yellow dresses and red lipstick and Lauren Groff *adores* her, and if Stephen *had* stayed with me . . . maybe *I'd* be a Michelle. No matter what we do, no matter what we write, people don't see us for the bold, serious people that we are."

I'm *happy* that nobody knows about my past and she wants something from me, but what? "You know what they say, S.B. All anyone can do is keep on trucking."

She grunts. "My editor calls me 'the machine.' But Wonder is Little Miss Salinger."

I don't like it when she says your fucking name. "I don't focus on pleasing anyone but myself when it comes to writing."

She laughs and says that's *classic* and then she sighs. "Do you believe in karma?"

Oh, for fuck's sake and I shrug.

"Stephen destroyed me when he broke up with me. He was always dismissive about my writing, and I think he's the reason that in my very first deal I didn't object when my publisher didn't brand me as *serious* . . . And here I am bearing the consequences . . ." On her twelve million acres in New England. "I live in this tepid contract with Kevin while Stephen gets to go on with his perfect little life in Brookline. Does that seem fair to you, Joe?"

I play it safe, generic. "I'd say, that's life."

"And probably why I write so much about death . . . Because until he's dead . . . I'm stuck."

And there it is: She wants me to murder her ex-fucking-boyfriend and I am a *writer*, Goddammit. "I don't think your publisher would agree. Look at your track record."

"Oh, please. I kill a version of him in every book because I can't kill him in real life and it's . . . a pattern. A *rut*. I kill the same man over and over and you date the same woman over and over and when are we going to change?"

I don't need to change. The only thing I need is those fucking tapes. "Well, it's probably why your books are so popular, because we all know the feeling."

"No," she says. "I saw your face in the room, when Wonder told us about the Salinger, when you felt so profoundly unknown by her, the inevitable tragedy of it all . . . And then last night in the bar . . . She made it clear that she is in love with herself, not you. And the way she was looking at other guys . . ."

Sarah Beth *pointed* those "other guys" out to you and I shrug. "I'm happy for her."

"You don't have to do that, Joe. You don't have to act like what I'm saying is so horrible. We kill the same darlings over and over because that's what we do. We kill people."

No, "we" don't, and I want my fucking tapes and I am not going to kill her ex-boyfriend. Still she's pitching me, ranting about Stephen, how he's never reviewed any of her books in his Substack, as if that is a reason to *kill* him. "Did he *like* my fellowship post on Facebook? No. Does he reach out to say that dumping me for his pretentious perpetually pregnant wife was the biggest mistake of his life? No. And I see you, Joe . . . You kill people before they can run off and go on with their lives and drive you crazy by not calling you, not caring about you, not *worshipping* you, while they tweet about Michelle's fucking *soda bread*. As if anyone even *likes* soda bread. But it is what it is. I will never write a good book as long as he's out there reminding me that my books are not good enough for him."

I feed her another bumper sticker. "Things always look worse when you're hungover."

She looks me right in the eye. "Sometimes, I wish he was dead . . ."

This is really happening, Wonder. Sarah Beth Swallows is trying to corner me into killing her ex-fucking-boyfriend, as if I'm a hit man in one of her fucking *books*. It's not an official order, but it's the way she takes a deep breath. My tapes aren't enough to satiate her lust for blood. She wants me to kill *her* ex because the way she sees it . . . that's what I do, just go around killing people who piss me off, and that is not me. I've been set up. She sent me to the spousal table to split us up so that *Kevin* would bring me here, so that you would *Coolatta* off on me. She broke up with Stephen a hundred years and two *kiddos* ago—get a life, get a therapist—and she looks at me like *I'm* the one being weird. "Well?"

"Well, I wish I had a big house like this."

"Joe, please. You know Kev is basically my handyman. He worships me and that's . . . nice but do I care what he thinks about my writing? Of course not. He's like some everyday random on Goodreads. It works but it doesn't, you know? Part of the reason I'm so prolific . . . Well, you know him. You know that the two of us don't sit up all night debating literature . . . But people like you and me, we need someone to worship us, and well . . . I could enjoy it if I wasn't so constantly distracted by the one who *doesn't* worship me . . . wonderful, terrible Stephen."

She's trying to insinuate that you don't worship me, and she's wrong. You just don't do it in front of other people and I have every reason to believe that she's recording this conversation and I say nothing.

She sighs, psychopath with a household name. "Have you seen what's happening in Brookline? It's a shame. Two people mugged in the last week . . ." So that's how she wants me to kill him. "One of them was *shot* and he's hanging on for life . . . just a few *blocks* from Stephen and Michelle . . ."

It's hit man fucking protocol. You get at least twenty-four hours to think about it. "I'll take that into consideration."

She tosses her blanket and walks to her shelves, as if we can move on because we have a deal, which we don't. "I can't believe I'm going to ask you this, it's always so tacky but . . ." Will you kill my ex-boyfriend? "Did you read *Playdeath*? My seventh book. Sort of flew under the radar . . ."

It's all relative—it was a best-fucking-seller—and two can play at this fucking game. "I think so." FUCK YOU.

"Anyway," she says. "Take it. Read it when you can . . . maybe this weekend. I want the murderer's review, you know?"

"I am not a 'murderer.'"

"Joe, please. You don't have to do that. I know you're a lot of things."

Where does it end? I have homework—dive into her backlist and kill her ex-boyfriend—but she has my tapes, so I have to *do* my homework, at least some of it, and I stand on my own two feet and look Sarah Beth Rhymes with Death right in her cold-blooded eyes. "I think we're done here."

"I'm telling you, Joe. We can really help each other out of our ruts. This is like our own private writing group, a little Algonquin round table where we break out of our shells."

My heart just broke and it's bleeding all over her Patriots blanket. "Uh-huh."

"I will never write the book I want to write if I keep writing for Stephen . . . and you've made so many people disappear . . ." She would call this book *The Perks of Knowing a Serial Killer* and I want to kill *her*. "Look, Joe. You have a pattern, too. You court all the 'Wonders' of your world, and it always ends up with them leaving you, and then . . . You live in fear of being locked up in some prison cell."

She shudders and I want to choke her out with that box of fucking Wheat Thins, but I can't do that because she's a genius in her own way, because her *husband* knows I'm here. Because *tapes.* "Right."

"For the first time in my life, I'm in it from ground zero, I'm with the 'killer' in a genuinely private communion, and for the first time in your life, you have someone on your side, someone who can help you make sure that you don't get caught . . ."

The hairs on the back of my neck want out of here. "Excuse me?"

"Have a look at *Playdeath*. It'll do 'wonders' for you in terms of technicality. Constructive criticism is everything, Joe. You've been sloppy. You're lucky. And not to be crass, but nobody on this planet knows how to get away with murder more than me."

She's insulting me even as she blackmails me—I am not killing Stephen—and she thinks I am bloodthirsty like her, that I wanted people to die. I am not like her. I don't obsess over people I dated a hundred years ago and I don't get off on "killing" people. You are different. You are part Dunkin' and part Shoddy and okay, so you steal, maybe. But you are overswinging because people like us, people who didn't go to college, we bend the rules. We have to.

And I'm not *sloppy.*

"Don't take it the wrong way," Sarah Beth says. "I'm only trying to help."

33

I'm not saying that *all* writers are demented psychopaths. I'm okay enough and Ani is more than a *good egg*. She laughs easily, warmly, and Mats is such a fun guy that he surprised his boyfriend with a trip to Turkey for Thanksgiving. Even Lou is all right. Yes, he wears suspenders and has an *O'er Under* screen saver on his phone, but he's not a *bad* guy. Essentially, the fellows are all right, even Sly, in spite of my personal grievances, which I can't even fucking care about right now because do you feel it, Wonder?

Does anyone feel it?

We are in the company of a profoundly demented psychopath: Sarah Beth Swallows.

She's worse than I thought. She's actually *serious*. She wrote Stephen's home address in my copy of *Playdeath* and I didn't do my homework, Wonder. I didn't kill him, and the whole workshop I can't focus. It's been two hours in here and she won't look me in the eye—is she going to put the tapes online after class?—and I'm sweating so much that everyone thinks I'm sick—I'm not sick—but I *am* sick. I'm the only one in this fucking room who knows what she's capable of, so my protective instincts are on fire—it's lonely at the top—and the worst part is that she's not the only one giving me a hard fucking time.

If a renowned profiler from the FBI walked into this room right now and took a look around, that objective stranger would think that *you* are the demented fucking psychopath.

You sit with your feet up on the table—that's a new one—and we're done workshopping Ani, so it's the comedown, the small talk. Everyone is performing a little but you are performing a *lot* and it's actually good that I got drunk the other night. I know where you are, why you're like this.

You're the one who's drunk. A thief high on the steal.

Ani was the center of attention, but she doesn't need our help, and even *she* kept shifting the conversation back to you, back to *Faithful*. You've been guzzling Kool-Aid since we got in here, and your tolerance is low. You are a watermelon absorbing vodka, soaking up praise—*Oh thank you, oh stop it*—and you're lucky that I know who you are down deep. The woman with the *southpaw* grandpa. The caregiver. The lover. This is not *you*, peppering your sentences with *sort of* and *in terms of* as the room lights up with a real-life fawning laugh track.

Sarah Beth's eyes bore into me. *Seriously?*

And my eyes bore into hers. *Seriously.*

I don't know if she's going to punish me for not doing my homework, but I do know that I love you, which is why it scares me when Sarah Beth is eye-hunting me, wanting me to risk what we have together by killing some Substacker I never even *met*. Robert Frost told us that nothing gold can stay, but the thing is, neither can the Kool-Aid pumping you full of sugar, poison.

You yelp in a way that you just fucking *don't*. "Omigod omigod, Sarah Beth. My sister just sent me this link. Are you for real?"

The two of you don't need to converse—my heart can only take so much—and you raise your phone and it's a *Deadline* piece, a casting

announcement about Sarah Beth's latest book to film. Ani squeals—
"I love her!"—and Lou squints—"Who is that?"—and Mats smiles—
"They'll shoot that"—and Sly looks down at the table—her husband
is dead but his movie is alive, his movie that is based on his book, his
book that is her book—and Sarah Beth squirms. "I mean I think the
actress is too young for the part but that's Hollywood, right?"

The look on her face. The pent-up frustration. Okay, it's actually
a *good* thing that you addressed her directly. She's bitching about her
adaptation, *another misunderstanding of her work*, and she admits that last
week was "hell" because they ignored all her casting ideas, as well as
her script notes, and none of us feel "sorry" for her—Prince was sing-
ing about her in "Pop Life"—but that doesn't stop her from looking
for pity, repeatedly saying that she went "nuts" with writer's block,
that she's nervous about her new book.

And then she looks at me. Full on. No holds barred. "I'm sorry
I'm venting, but this process is making me crazy."

I accept her apology with a nod—I don't have to kill Substack
Stephen!—and of course I don't. She's not that woman who hires a hit
man and she knows that *I'm* not a hit man. We are writers. It's the first
time I've felt calm—no sweat on my palms—and I'd like to hear more
from her but you're the one doing all the talking now, comfortably,
condescendingly starstruck in a way that makes me feel bad for the
fucking psycho!

"Here's the thing," you say. "Nice people always get the short end
of the stick, and that's what you are, Sarah Beth. You are so nice, so
kind, and in terms of like . . . our basic ways . . . Why are crime writers
so kind? I mean what is that?"

It's not a new question and Sarah Beth chuckles. "We all talk
about that a lot. I think we all just come from a place of empathy."

Lou picks his nose. "Genre people have a people and all people
are better people when they have a people."

"Wow," Mats says. "You sound like my mom pushing me to go to
a family reunion."

You drop your feet to the floor and were you always like this? Using your body as a gavel. It's time for this workshop to end, and Sly looks at the clock.

"Okay," she says. "Let's go live our lives!"

You have things to do—you want Sarah Beth to sign a book for Cherish—and I have things to do, too. The sooner I get an agent, the sooner you and I can show that psychopath that our love is *real*, and the sooner she realizes that she *is* fucking crazy, the sooner she'll give me my tapes.

I follow Sly down the stairs and whistle.

"Oh, Joe. You can whistle."

"Yep, and if this writing thing doesn't work out, I'll take my show on the road."

Her laughter is sad and tired. She did love Glenn. "How are you holding up?"

"Well, you tell me. I feel like I lost the reins back there. Been a while since I taught and . . ."

"You did great."

She purses her lips. Smart. "So your book."

"So my book."

Her smile is all I needed, you can't fake that shit, and I should have gone to her directly, should have trusted her all along. "It's so good, so good that I read it on my phone."

My book is not, never was a fucking coaster. "Can I quote you on that?"

"And I did mean to reach out to you before you saw about Mats—"

"I am thrilled for Mats."

"I know, but I also know how it is and radio silence is killer and then you see a press release with the agent who's supposed to sell *your* book . . . It's like this. Mats wrote a wildly commercial of-the-moment thriller. And that is not what you wrote."

"I get that."

"And Bernie would be better off taking your book out in the spring."

The sun is already gone and that's a lot of fucking workshops from now. "The spring."

"Publishing is a slow go, especially when you have something special. Glenn went through this with *Scabies* and . . . well, you know how that worked out."

She buttons her coat, and she chose the wrong one. Too big. "I know how that worked out for him but today, when Wonder was talking about *Scabies* I was thinking . . . *How does Sly handle this kinda thing?*"

She shrugs. "I'm a process person. You're the same way, no? You seem like you genuinely enjoy writing more than the business of writing, and as you see in the room . . . well, everyone's hardly that way."

I'm special so special and I smile. "Which is why I wanted to talk to you because yes, I am . . . without sounding like *too* much of a douchebag, I'm a 'writing writer.' I keep thinking about being in my bar, you know, when it was just about the book, and I can't get back into that place until I've got this one set up. Wonder says I should write another book."

"Oh God no. Don't take this the wrong way but you're not Wonder. You'll do a book every five or six years. Nobody expects literary writers to bust it out and her style . . . I don't have to tell you. Her intentions are different, so people like her and Mats . . . Things happen faster when you write to the market."

A Masshole blows his horn at an old lady crossing the street and I remember my poor book on her nightstand. Is she telling the truth? "So you understand my intentions."

"Let me put it this way, Joe," she says. "Wonder's mouse in the house came from a kids' book. But yours . . . it came from your soul."

It's a call for a celebration.

Sly loves my book and I don't have an ounce of anger left in me regarding your petty theft. After all, I have to get used to people stealing because when *Me* is published, others will do it, too. It's the writer's way! Lift, borrow, steal! It's like Sly said. Some lies keep people *together.* That's us—*we're in this together*—and we're on Thanksgiving break. We're free! Sarah Beth won't be harassing me. It's a holiday and she has no choice. She *has* to spend time with her family, and I haven't heard a peep from her, but my buddy Kev already texted to say that he can't ride and wooh! Do you feel it, world?

I'm a fucking *writer*. Anointed and official and I thought I was a writer when I finished my book, when I got a fellowship, but I was wrong. Today made me a writer. In step with Sly. On campus. A bird's-eye view of us in the biopic kind of moment, when two people walking and talking becomes a part of cultural history. I wanted to take you somewhere nice tonight but it's cold, and you want to stay home and that's fine. Everything is *finally* fine. Maybe I'll borrow a Coolatta from *Faithful* in my next book so you can feel good, too!

You laugh at me and your shirt is full of hate. YANKEES SUCK. "Cool it, babe. There will be plenty of dancing tomorrow."

Wednesday. The night before Thanksgiving. A Masshole ritual bar crawl that starts at your houses and dead-ends at Bobby's house. Your favorite night of the year.

But it's not tomorrow yet and this is my night. I pop a bottle of Dom. I earned it. You furrow your brow. "Did I miss something?"

"Nope. I told you everything . . ." Except for the part where my mouse beat the pulp out of your mouse, but that's a thing for you to discover on your own, when and *if* you finish my book.

"But isn't that sort of a nothing burger? I mean you want Sly to hook you up with Bernie the way she did for Mats and Sly is kinda . . . she's basically blowing you off."

That was your first domestic *sort of* and we aren't even in the fucking room. We are home. "It's a double cheeseburger with bacon and guac."

"Ugh. Guac."

"Wonder, Sly loved the book."

"But you still don't have an agent."

"It's not like that for me. With a book like mine, you know, 'literary,' you wait until the spring."

"I hear you, I do, but in high school, I met this guy who went to Exeter . . . We hooked up a few times and he was all about the summer, how he was gonna take me to his family's yacht club, ya know, go sailing. I never saw the club. Or him again. I'm just saying . . ."

I do not like it when you point out the raunchy lampposts in your book or in real life, but I can't go there. "I hate that phrase."

"*Yacht club*?"

"*Just* saying. It's a complete lie. You're not 'just saying' anything. You want me to think that Sly is some yacht club douchebag who's putting me off but you're wrong. Sly loves it and she knows her way around all this."

"Well, good for Sly. And I guess that's why you're so calm, not at *all* defensive . . ."

You choose *this* fucking moment to pour oats into a bowl and pop the bowl into the microwave and this is supposed to be a cele-fucking-bration and oatmeal isn't caviar. You sigh. "I don't mean to be a Debbie Downer. But you told *me* you want your book out there sooner rather than later, and I dunno, Sly clearly has you on the back burner and she's cockblocking you from Bernie, so maybe you could send some queries . . ."

"It doesn't take a minute."

"I know that, but you're talking about waiting until the *spring*."

"The oatmeal, Wonder. It takes two minutes and thirty seconds or it's sticky."

You huff and the Yankees don't *suck*. They're in transition. "Excuse you?"

Gently, Joseph. "You wouldn't have to douse it in cream if you would cook it on the stove, but if you insist on using the microwave, well, I'm *just saying*, it doesn't take a minute."

"Who the hell wants *squishy* freaking oatmeal?"

"The directions are on the box . . ." Don't say it. Don't. "And you do know how to read . . . Well, you know how to read some people's books."

"It's a cylinder, you asshole."

The microwave dings, a referee in our boxing match, and this wasn't supposed to happen. You were supposed to be on my side, take off that stupid T-shirt and take me out on the town to celebrate my win. Your lower lip trembles. "Do you know how many times you've said her name since you got home?"

"She's our teacher."

"I don't mean it like *that*. I mean you worship her. You act like she's the *only* way for you to get somewhere and it's freaking gross, okay? I give you one little suggestion and you blow up at me. But hey, according to you, I don't even know how to cook a bowl of freaking *oatmeal* so of course I don't know about publishing or God forbid, *books*."

"Oh, I *know* what you think of my book."

You clench your jaw. *RED SOX SUCK*. "And what's that supposed to mean?"

Don't say it, don't say it, don't—"My book, Wonder. I gave it to you and you expect me to believe that you didn't read the first chapter? That you weren't even a *little* curious to see what I put on the fucking page?"

"I told you I'm not ready. We settled this. I didn't even start reading it. Why can't you let it go?"

"Caridad doesn't even have *There's a Mouse in My House*."

"Huh?"

This wasn't my plan, but we're better than RIP Glenn and Sly. I don't want us to live a lie. "Wonder, I know you started reading my book because there's no way it's a coincidence."

"*Life* is coincidence."

Spoken like a bad writer, and I should have kept my mouth shut. "Won, come on. We both have a mouse in the house in the first chapter. And I meant it. You don't have to get defensive. I'm not mad. I know you started *Me,* but I don't expect you to finish reading it when you're all wrapped up in *Faithful.*"

It's one of those cartoons and steam is fuming from your nostrils, from the top of your head. "Are you calling me a liar?"

And a thief. "Won, it's okay. You saw the mouse in my house. I came up with a mouse in the house and you . . . you didn't get it from a kids' book. You got it from me. And I meant what I said. It's fine. Everyone steals a little."

I set off a bomb and you're blasting me. I am the lowest of the low, the guy who wasted money on a *stupid overpriced Salinger* and accuses you of stealing and the microwave dings and you ignore it and I ignore it and you're on your phone, searching and seething, and then you slam your phone on the counter and another bomb goes off. Gulp. It's a receipt from the Frugal Bookstore in Roxbury. You fold your arms. "Twenty fucking twenty, baby. *Boom.*"

That's a *fucking,* not a *freaking,* and you're one of those *Housewives.* You brought *receipts.* You bought *There's a Mouse in My House* during the pan-fucking-demic and in your eyes I'm a paranoid loon and this is when it ends, when I draw blood from you, when *The White Lotus* wilts.

"Wonder, calm down."

"I don't lie and I don't steal, and I did not read one freaking page of your book. How dare you? Who do you think I am?"

I am losing you in real time, you are a jukebox on a truck, unplugged, en route to becoming an *ex*-box, and I can't live in a world where you despise me, and it's not fair. Buying a book is not reading a book and for all I know, my mouse reminded you of the mouse book, and this is why I hate receipts. It's just never that fucking simple.

This is it, the end, but then you grab your phone, and you are different. Light and . . . laughing? "Do you hear us right now? We sound like the biggest fucking assholes who ever lived."

Your *we* is all I need—we are still a we—and I tell you I went crazy, I didn't mean it. "I know you'd never steal. I'm an asshole."

"No," you say. "*I'm* the asshole. I don't know how to be me right now. I snapped at you because the guilt is killing me. I feel you wanting me to read your book and I feel guilty that I'm not reading it . . . I don't know how to do this, how to handle everything."

"You don't need to 'handle' me and I'm sorry I made you feel that way. And I'm the crazy one. You're right. It is a coincidence and I sound like a fucking nutjob, as if it's my original writing, 'the mouse in the house' . . . I oughta be locked up, seriously."

You smile and tell me that you would visit and this is where I actually *do* like receipts. You didn't steal. The truth is out there. No more borrowed time, no more lies. "Wonder, the workshop, it's making me a little crazy, too. I take it back, okay? I know you're not a liar and I know you're not a thief and can we just . . . Can we forget I ever opened my big stupid mouth?"

"I would love that."

"Thank God."

"Ever since Sly started being so good to me, I'm outside of myself looking in . . . I keep getting these flashbacks to the bar, to class . . . I feel so different right now. Possessed or something, like I drank the Kool-Aid and turned into this maniacal little monster all high on myself, and if I was you, if I saw that freaking mouse in my book and I knew that you had my book in your computer, if I was dealing with *me* . . . I mean I literally can't imagine. I would have thought the same thing. There's nothing worse than stealing, babe. *Nothing.*"

You are back to being you and I am back to being me and I tell you that I don't blame you, that Kool-Aid is fucking delicious. You shake your head. "All I know is I clearly need a break from those people. I've never been so freaking amped for Thanksgiving."

"So, does that mean I'm still invited?"

The microwave dings and you smile. "Of course. And for the record . . . I like it my way, oatmeal. I like it sticky. And now that I know that you are an insane man who likes his oatmeal squishy . . . well, now I know."

There is no *your* way. It's fucking science. It's a recipe. A formula. Like a cozy mystery or a box of Duncan Hines but all is well in our house, and oatmeal is back to being what it is. We hug, we hold on to each other for dear life, resuscitating all the good, all the love. You dig your nails into my back, and I hurt you and you hurt me, but I'm not Sarah Beth Swallows. I could never "kill" you. You're my darling, but you're not my darling to kill. You're the sticky to my squishy and the others weren't you. No matter how much you win, you recognize your own vulnerability and wear it on your shirt, on your heart. You didn't give up on yourself and you didn't give up on me and the microwave doesn't give up on us either. It dings again.

"Okay," you say. "Let me go already. I gotta hit the store like yesterday."

"You don't wanna eat your disgusting sticky undercooked oats?"

"Nah. If I don't get home and help my sister with side dishes, she'll freaking kill me." You kiss me. "You can overcook them into squishy, mushy mush. And you should, because if you think the other night was a lot . . . just do me a favor and eat up, lightweight."

You had to get one last slight dig in, and it's not fair. We just made up and I can't retort. I can't call you a *heavyweight* or a binge drinker, but that's why I love you. You always know just when to slip out the door and save my life.

Seventeen minutes later, I'm camped out on my sofa. I'm gonna watch *Planes, Trains and Automobiles* while I leaf through *Franny and Zooey*. I don't know the last time I ever felt so normal, so in the moment, and my phone pings. It's you—that was fast—but that's good by me, Wonder. Who among us doesn't love to be loved and missed? I open the text.

I don't want you to freak out, but I need some space. I wish I was saying this to your face, but it's hard for me. I think it's better if you do your own thing over the break . . . I just need to focus on Faithful. *I'll call you when I'm ready. Sorry. Seriously.*

34

Most people are weak and needy. They race around when the leaves change to find someone, *anyone*, to bring home for the holidays to impress the very same people who are (partially) responsible for their being so weak, so needy. Why do you think the Hallmark movies are so fucking popular? Because most people would rather "die" than spend the holidays "alone." But you and I are not most people.

You didn't dump me. And you're not holding a grudge about the stupid fucking mouse. You're just protecting us.

Did we have our first fight? Yes. Was it ugly? Yes? But that's not why you need "space." You remembered what you promised me a long time ago: *We're in this together.* The key word being *this*. We're in *this* fellowship together, we're building a future, a future that does *not* include your family. We're not some cutesy couple in Hallmark's *Crimson Christmas*. You don't need to drag me back into your house to make small talk. We're writers! We're artists! Mercurial and idiosyncratic.

I'm too good for all that, as are you, but you did guzzle the Kool-Aid, so you need a few shots of ye olde family Fireball to sort yourself out. It's not like I banged down your door all weak and needy. And we didn't need to have some ridiculous "talk." We're on the same wavelength, and Thanksgiving isn't Christmas. I will spend that *shit show* with your family, unless of course, by this time next month, you've conjured the strength to tell your family that all you *really* want for Christmas is eight days of hot sex on a deserted beach in the Caribbean.

I tie a purple ribbon around a bottle of red wine. See, that's another thing I love about you. You have this way of helping me even when you don't know it.

This morning I woke up alone to a text from you-know-who. Yes, I spoke too soon. I'm not out of the woods yet, and Sarah Beth sent me a last-minute command/invite—*Join us for Turkey Day! See you at 2!*—and I said the only thing I could say, the truth: *Can't wait!*

TO STEAL MY TAPES FROM SARAH BETH SWALLOWS.

You know how it is. I mean you don't know, and I hope you never do know, but we both have our obligations. You have to drink Jäger with your sister, and I have to find my fucking tapes. I know they're here, somewhere on her property, and I also know they're going home with *me* and hey, I'm not complaining. I'd rather be forced to break bread with her family than glove up in Brookline and kill the father of two children, so it's *good* that I'm here and who knows? Maybe I won't even have to ask. Maybe she'll even give me the fucking tapes as a mea culpa.

I slam the door of my Tesla and I mean it, Wonder. This albatross will not fuck things up for us. Imagine five years from now, you and I are shacked up, published, and Sarah Beth is bitter, still waiting on that message from Lauren Groff. I can't let her keep the tapes because in a moment of attention-starved rage, she might say fuck it and share them with the whole world.

Chills, and I put on a big fat smile, perfect for the whole *fam damily*.

I walk up her driveway and wave to her *kiddos* who are playing football by the shed, poor little cutie-pie pawns in Mommy's sick antics. And there's *Kev* over by the garage, dressed up like an extra from *Billions* as he "works" on a new, old truck. It's all so staged, so sad, so family.

"Sup, Kev!"

"Sup, Joe!"

I play my part as the guest, and meet her kids like I haven't already seen them on Instagram—Jolie is the boss and Pierre is the not-the-boss—and I remember what Sarah Beth said to Ani in passing—*One perk of adoption is this whole other gene pool and you don't feel so responsible*—and S.B. opens the front door and smiles. Pure evil. New apron. *Gimme those fucking tapes.* "Sarah Beth!"

"Yay!" she squawks. "He's here!"

A normal person would speak to me directly—*Yay! You're here!*—and I can tell she barely knows her own kids by the way she doesn't react when Jolie kicks Pierre. Kevin plays dad and I start toward the house, but Sarah Beth closes the door on me. "Nonsense," she says. "You're a guest. Relax!"

I am not in a mood to relax—where are my fucking tapes?—and Kevin whistles. "Incoming!"

A *football* thwacks my midsection and I pass it to Jolie, who passes it to Pierre and Kev picks up his toolbox. He is telling me things I don't need to know, that their other "friends," Darren and Glee, bailed, that *S.B.* surprised him with a new truck last night, a *prezzie* in the form of this vintage Chevy Blazer. I wonder if he sent her a thank-you note, and he picks up a socket wrench. "Just so you know," he says. "It's all good by me."

Being married to a bloodthirsty psychopath? "Sorry?"

He drops the wrench back in his toolbox and chooses a new prop, a can of fucking *Guinness*. "Darren's giving me shit. 'Your wife is bringing a date to Thanksgiving' but that's Darren. Old-school. Kinda guy who thinks I should mind the fact that my wife can't mash potatoes, as if it's 1954 and women belong in the kitchen. Brewski?"

No. "Thanks-ski."

I accept a can of Guinness and I wonder if Kev has a key to the Dead Shed, if the tapes are in a safe, the safe where she put my phone, in which case . . . One step at time. Kev chuckles. "You can't blame Darren for giving me guff. I told S.B . . . if you put Darren and Glee in a book and make fun of 'em, they're gonna find out . . ." I don't know Darren and Glee and I don't fucking care and I clock the Dead Shed—would Psycho Beth give the hubs a key?—and Jolie sends the pigskin spiraling into her brother's head. Kev shouts—"Play nice, you two!"—and he laughs. "It's all good, though. I know you're spoken for. And my *prezzies* love new people."

Ah, so the kids were *prezzies*, too. S.B. opens the front door—not *now*, S.B.—and claps her hands at her kids like she can't remember their names—"Play nice!"—*Playdeath*—and they just keep roughhousing. Kev is slow. Buzzed. He probably started drinking at six, when he was mashing the fucking potatoes, and if he passes out early, I won't even need his help. I can lift his keys out of his pocket. Sarah Beth shrieks. "Kevin, I can't find the baster!"

His phone dings—it's *D-Bag* Darren, that's what they called him in *B school*—and Sarah Beth will not be ignored. She says his *full* name—"Kevin Michael Swallows, do you hear me?" And that's it. Kevin is a good dog, a good boy—no tour of the Dead Shed right now—and he obeys and heads inside. S.B. grins. "Okay, kids," she says. "Play nice with Mommy's friend!"

She knows what I did, who I was, and what kind of mother wants her kids alone with a fucking *serial killer*? It's just us now, me and the kids, and the alpha Jolie stares at me. Nurture triumphed over nature with this one, and she is her mother's daughter. "Who are you?"

I'm not Uncle Joe—that would be creepy—but kids are kids. They like alliteration, same way they like new toys, new people. I'm fun. I'm new. *Just Joker*. "Just Joe."

Jolie picks at her football. "So Just Joe . . . do you have kids?"

"No," I say. "Do you?"

That got a laugh, a little respect, and it was a lie—I have a son—but these kids have it bad enough with their psycho mom. They don't need to hear my sob story about my in-laws stealing my child, my child that might not even be mine, and wait a minute . . . Do these kids have keys to the Dead Shed?

Pierre peers at me in that way that kids do, a detective without motive. "Do you also write books?"

"You bet! But I'm nowhere near as good as your mommy."

Jolie grunts—"I *hate* books"—a.k.a. I hate *Mommy*—and Pierre pushes. "Do you write *kids'* books? Ones we can read?"

Kids are curious. Their whole world is this house, this property, and this is good practice for the day when you and I have a house like this, a family of our own. None of that can happen if I'm leading a secret life, running to Foster to placate Sarah Beth. I need to find those tapes and I crouch down to their level and smile. "Hide-and-Seek," I say. "Who wants to go first?"

An hour later, the *kiddos* are fighting about who gets to sit by *Just Joe* at dinner and Sarah Beth is visibly jealous—so fun—and poor Kev is visibly cuckolded—Just Joe is more fun than Dud Dad—and they race across the lawn—I could run a daycare—and Jolie is a born seeker, already covering her eyes and counting and Pierre points at the bushes and I STILL DON'T HAVE THE FUCKING TAPES.

I point at the Dead Shed. It's now or never. Pierre gulps. "We're not allowed."

I force a laugh. "I know *you're* not. But I'm a guest."

Jolie is getting there—*Sixty-two . . . Sixty-one*—and Pierre stares at me. "But she says if anyone ever goes in there they never come out."

"She" is a fucking *psychopath* and I want to get my fucking tapes. Pierre and I head around back to the deck, where his drunk father is dumping a turkey into a pot of oil—no—and Pierre asks his dad for the *code* to the shed. Initially, Kev is reluctant—"You know how

Mommy feels about people going in there"—but Jolie is counting faster—*Forty-two . . . Forty-one*—and Pierre is playing dirty—"Dad, come on. It's not for me, it's for Mommy's friend"—and Kev burns his hand on oil. "Damn it, Pierre. No means no."

Kev needs a boost and I need my tapes so I hand him a towel and I do my best Mister Rogers. "You know, Pierre, I'm really more of your dad's friend."

So now Kev's ego is restored and he tells me the code to the shed, to my *tapes*—they're not in a safe, that's her *safe space*—and Jolie is almost ready—*Fourteen . . . Thirteen and three-thirds . . . Thirteen and two-thirds . . .* and I send Pierre to climb a tree and Jolie is close—*Seven and three-thirds . . . Seven and two-thirds . . .* and I enter the code to the Dead Shed as Jolie's scream cuts into the silence. "Ready or not here I come!"

Green light means go and I open the door—I can taste the tapes, I can taste our future—but Jolie tags me with both hands. "You're It! Just Joe is It!"

I missed my shot at the fucking tapes and you're with your family and I'm with *this* family. I failed you and S.B. leads us in a prayer—the hypocrisy—as if the burnt side dishes and fried turkey and her psychosis are things to be celebrated.

"So!" she says, as she delivers a serving bowl of rosemary and lard and approximately twelve wilted green beans. "You kids sure had fun with Joe, huh?"

Jolie makes a face at the beans. "It's *Just* Joe. We told you."

Poor Kev dumps mashed potatoes on his plate. "Maybe after dinner, I'll play, too!"

I say that's a *great* idea—another shot at the Dead Shed—but Jolie says no, it's just *kids*. Kevin sours and S.B. smirks—"Now you know what it's like to be me"—and on we go eating lard and beans and slick, greasy turkey, as if those tapes aren't less than a hundred feet away.

Jolie spits out her green beans. "These are GROSS. Dad, can I go upstairs?"

No, she can't go *upstairs*. I need to get back into that shed, I need to get my *tapes* and I lean over my hot, smelly plate. "Hey, Jolie . . . If you stay, we can play again after dinner. I have the best hiding spot *ever*."

Jolie rolls her eyes, she is *over* everything, even me, and what happened to manners? Hide-and-Seek is the only way to get in that fucking shed and if there is no Hide-and-Seek, what then? Pierre talks with his mouth full of mashed potatoes and Sarah Beth's cheeks turn white. She gulps. "Pierre, honey, let Joe finish his dinner."

Jolie picks up her plate—"It's *Just* Joe, Mom. Ugh! Are you deaf?"—and Kev guzzles whiskey, and I know he *wants* to drink himself to death, but if he does that right now there will be EMTs and police . . . police who might find my tapes. He makes a drunken proposal that everyone go for a ride in his *prezzie* after dinner—I wish they'd *all* fucking leave—but it's a lost cause. Kev is clearly not about to get behind the wheel of a car and Jolie throws her napkin on her plate—"Can we play already? I'm full"—and *this* is why I prefer plotting over pantsing—S.B. is the sloppy one, and I hold the keys to her castle, to my tapes—and what choice does the absentee mommy have? She smiles. "Have fun."

Never underestimate the power of a bad marriage. I was there. Dusk. Pierre's fingers in the dark, pushing buttons.

But then the light turned red and Sarah Beth emerged from the front door. "Kids, Daddy told me what he did. You know the rules!"

The way she looked at me, Wonder. She knew.

And now there's no chance because all three kids—let's face it, Kev's a kid—they're upstairs watching a movie and I'm in the oversized chef's kitchen, tied to the apron strings of the martyr on dish duty, Sarah Fucking Beth.

"You got pretty close there," she says.

I don't care if I turn red. "It was worth a shot."

She squeezes a dirty dishrag. "Joe, it's a little hurtful, okay? I need those tapes for my writing, and you know this, and you were trying to steal them. Do you really think so little of me?"

"It was just a game of Hide-and-Seek."

It was a bad move on my part, lying to a crime writer, and she squirts more Dawn than she needs onto a plate. "Oh, and by the way," she huffs. "Don't worry about showing up empty-handed. I wasn't *actually* expecting you to bring a pie."

She says that like I didn't bring a bottle of red and I have to do the impossible. I have to make this sad woman happy. I roll up *my* sleeves and join her in scrubbing congealed lard off pots and pans. And maybe this is good. A little solidarity. Maybe now that I'm her sous dishwasher, she'll relax, get so depressed about the state of her life that she'll give me the tapes.

But the garbage disposal isn't working and she's flipping the switch, fiddling with the faucet, mad that she's so exposed—she didn't let Shayna from *Chronicle* in this kitchen—and it's insane. *I'm* the one who's exposed. Not her. *Me.* "Anyway," she says. "For what it's worth, I am glad you came today. I mean who would have expected you to be so good with kids?"

I want to kill her right now, but I suppose this is why people have kids, safety in numbers. "So," she says. "Did you have a chance to read *Playdeath*?"

The narcissism and the nerve—*Did you have a chance to kill Stephen?*—and that's what I need, more nerve, more narcissism. "Sarah Beth, I can't read your book, I can't read anything. You know I can't focus with those tapes out there, and in class . . . you sounded like you get it, you know? Like things got crazy and you went a little . . ." Don't say crazy. "I mean how would you feel?"

But she's a psychopath. She doesn't have feelings, not really. She just stares.

"I'm trying to talk to you, fellow to fellow."

"I gave you *The Catcher in the Rye*, so don't tell me that I'm not a supportive fellow."

That first edition was no skin off her back—look at this fucking estate—and I try again. "I can't function knowing that those tapes are just sitting in that shed. I'm not sleeping, I feel like shit . . . I barely thought I'd make it on the ride down here."

She tilts her head, same way she did in the shed. "I don't see any bags under your eyes. And as for your tapes . . ." Give them to me. "They're not helping. This book . . . It's still *Playdeath* all over again. Maybe this is it for me, doomed to be stuck in a rut writing books that will never be the kind people read more than once."

So true. "Not true."

"You're just saying that because you want your tapes."

Yes. "Well, who wouldn't?"

She looks down at her sink. "You really don't trust me, do you?"

"I didn't say that. It's not you, Sarah Beth. I don't trust the world. Anyone could break in there and get them and then what? Think of your family, your career."

"I invite you into my home. I let you play with my children, and . . . what else can I do to make you see that I'm not the enemy here?"

"You can give me the tapes."

She throws her sponge in the sink and she says that nobody trusts her, not me, not her editor, not even her assistant, who doesn't trust S.B. to run her own social media. She blows her nose on a dishrag. "I think I'm starting to lose it."

Yes, she fucking is, and thank God for Marvel movies and surround sound, or her kids would see a new side of Mommy. "I think part of that is on me, Sarah Beth. Even having those tapes, it puts you in a really bad position. You've got a family."

She grunts. "And another adapation that's gonna be a clunker. I only brought that up in the room to remind everyone that I'm a big deal because here comes my workshop, and I'm trying so hard to change . . . I told you where Stephen *lives* . . . But of course you didn't . . . because when I'm not crystal clear, I'm not 'cryptic' or 'intellectual.' I'm just . . . a blur. And if your tapes, if today, if none of this helps me improve as a writer . . . it might be time for me to throw in the towel."

We're in dangerous waters, Wonder. The look on her face. She's festering. You don't get twelve thousand acres by throwing in the towel. Nothing is going her way. Nobody ate her green beans and I didn't kill Stephen and she hates her new book. By now you're drowning in family, seasick from pretending you had fun on that *bar crawl* as you quietly realize just how much you need me. I want a future with you, and we can't move forward if Sarah Beth Swallows isn't satisfied with what she got out of me.

She blows her nose again. "I suppose you want to go meet up with *Wonder*. I hate this time of year. Stephen dumped me before Thanksgiving break in college. The least he could have done was ice me out slowly, you know, do what most decent people do and give me little hints and clues so that I could put it all together and be the one to dump *him* . . ." She should have become a detective and she sighs. "But oh well . . ."

Some people live in the past, to the extent where they simply don't deserve the *prezzie* that is being alive right now. She blames her bad pages and her authorial anxiety on my failure to deliver, to inspire, the same way she blames Stephen for her insecurities. There's no way I'm getting out of Rhode Island with my tapes, so I have to settle for the next best thing, an Algonquin fucking bond. If she thinks I helped her, then she will keep those tapes locked up. I don't want to do this, Wonder. It almost feels like cheating on you. But she is that kind of writer who overexplains her characters by pointing at their backgrounds, as if life is so linear, as if what happens to us as children mandates who we are as adults. She needs something more from me, something worse than all the lurid details about that awful night I had to roast

Benji in a bonfire and break him back down into dust. She needs my dust.

"All right," I say. "I think I know what's missing from the tapes."

Her eyes widen because she thinks I'm going to walk her through another fucking murder. "Oh?"

I make like one of the stock characters in her book. The man who never talks about his feelings, the man who doesn't cry. I tense up. My lower lip trembles. "It's hard for me, but I think I need to tell you about my mother."

35

It was the longest fake weekend of my life—I worked the whole fucking time—and my voice is shot from revisiting every small incident from my childhood. Half the shit I told her I made up— Sarah Beth is smart but she's not *that* smart—and my plan worked. She thinks her pages are "electrical and alive" and superior to everything she ever wrote. And when her book about me gets a rave from *The New Yorker*—her exact words—she promises that she will give me the tapes. I know. That's a long shot and I can't *really* trust her—she's a psychopath—but the good thing about people like Sarah Beth is that all roads lead back to them.

All she wants is a good book, and right now, she thinks she has it. So, my tapes are safe.

She sent her pages to all of us but she told me I don't have to read them because she knows I can't be objective—she's not a total monster— and I'm on the way to the room and my body is vibrating. We're going to see each other, and I gave you what you wanted as well, time to be with your family. I didn't text you all weepy and morose and there's no way you didn't realize what a good thing you found in me, the kind of man who is willing to give you space. I'm climbing the stairs and I enter the room and okay . . . so I don't get to see you, not yet anyway. You're late, but that's your style, and it's a bit of a sting—don't you miss me?—and our fellows are all hugs, all *how was your Thanksgiving*. I can't tell the truth, so I claim that I "laid low," and Ani says I should have told her I was alone, and she means well, but I'm not alone—I have you—and I wasn't alone—I was in a nuclear family bomb. I glance at the doorway, but you don't walk in, and Lou is wearing a Lou fucking *Reed* shirt, and it feels like a sign, like he wore that shirt so you and I could laugh about it after our reunion, after class. Which we will, soon enough.

Sly shuts the door. "All right, small talkers. Let's do this."

RIP Glenn didn't say things like "Let's do this." Our fellows squirm like *Why does this woman try so hard? She's no Glenn Shoddy.* But she is. S.B. stares at that door, and it's hard to see her in this room, having opened the cabinets that hold all her Wheat Thins. She looks at Sly in a way that she *never* would have looked at Glenn. "Shouldn't we wait for Wonder?"

Sly laughs. "We'd be waiting a long time. She sent me a note that she can't make it today."

Hold the fucking phone. You're bailing on me *and* the fucking fellowship?

"Aah," Ani says. "I thought something might be up, the way she dropped off the group text. Is she okay?"

Sly says you're "fine" but fine is nothing, "fine" is a lie and that's not like you, skipping class, ignoring the group text. S.B. eyes me as if I know something, as if I did something—I did nothing, I know nothing—and Sly takes her seat and uses her kindergarten voice. "Let's talk about who *is* here. Our thriller queen Sarah Beth Swallows! Honey . . . you little *devil* you!"

Guilty-pleasure-infused laughs all around—the opposite of what S.B. fucking wanted—and where are you? S.B. is doing that subtle staring thing again and is she blind? Can't she see the worry in my face? I'm sick of this, Wonder. I miss you and I want to wrap my arm around S.B.'s neck and put her in a fryolator and Sly rubs her chin. "So, Sarah, we can all see that you tried *so* hard."

That was a dig and S.B. zips up her bag of Wheat Thins. "Well, that's why we're all here . . ."

S.B. is on the verge of a nervous breakdown and she *believed* in those pages and she wanted everyone in this room to believe in those pages and the sky is falling, Rome is collapsing. Sly goes full kinder-cunt and says the pages are "more like homework than soul work," that S.B. needs to "forget about the world and play." And then, after dissing "the queen," Sly raises her eyebrows—she wants a Wheat Thin—and Sarah Beth pushes the baggie across the table.

Sly sniffs. "Oh dear. I assumed they were plain. No thank you!"

If Sarah Beth kills Sly right now, in this room, she'll go to prison. She was unraveling before we even started this fellowship—why else would she have applied in the first place?—and Mats feels like "the main character is somehow both too in there and too out there"—what the fuck does that mean?—and Ani misses *bloody popcorn fun Sarah Beth* and the workshop is a nuclear bomb. I am *trying* to crack the fucking code. I praise the writing—*Elevated, almost as if you found your real voice*—but Lou laughs me off, the fucker, and calls S.B. a *machine* who "tells the same damn story in every damn book." I say we'd be nowhere without machines and Ani wants S.B. to lean back into her "deliciously trashy blood-soaked popcorn" and why aren't you in this room?

"Look," Sarah Beth says. "I want you guys to know that I am loving every second of this. I throw away pages in every book. I mean in my first draft of *A Perfect Gentle Man* I wanted to kill Brandon . . ." Pause for reaction. No reaction. "Anyway, he was the worst, but it just wasn't working so I killed Vera instead . . ." Nobody in this room read that book, and they don't hide it, and she catches my eye and gulps. "All I'm *trying* to say is that I like to kill darlings more than I like to write, so this is great. Keep it up! Slay me!"

But I can't focus on her overcooked attempt at understanding me right now. I don't know where you are, and I can't find out now, and you live for that group text, but then I have to say *something* because Sly is looking at me like *Are you the type of male writer who only cares about the woman he's fucking?* I clear my throat and spout off some bullshit about how S.B.'s *novel* in progress is heavier than popcorn, more akin to a *field* of corn. Sly stays the course, insisting there is "nothing wrong with being the queen of the airport." And then Mats hits the red button: "My aunts are gonna *love* this."

S.B. still has my tapes, so I scratch my head. "Actually," I say. "When the serial killer is playing with the kids . . . that kinda felt like S.B. spliced with Lauren Groff, you know?"

No, they didn't fucking know, and finally class ends and there is no talk of *drinks* and S.B. snaps up her Wheat Thins and makes a run for it. I catch up to her on Ware Street, but she is seething. "It's like my kiddos all over again. Mommy is stupid. Mommy is boring. She can't even buy the right *Wheat Thins*."

Placate her. "Oh, come on. It's not like everyone hated it."

"'Everyone' didn't anything. Mats and Ani and Lou are 'cool.' I'm not cool. And that's okay. They showed up and did their jobs and it's not their job to lie to me. But Sly . . . Who does she think she is?" The author of *Scabies for Breakfast*. "No 'teacher,' no *woman* teacher, should ever make a fellow woman feel like a second-class citizen. But then . . . at least Sly was there, which is more than I can say for Wonder. Why didn't she show up? And why didn't you give me a *heads*-up?"

I'm about to tell her that you had a family emergency, but she clamps a hand over her mouth. Like she got a DM from Lauren Groff. "Wait. How did I not see it?"

I refuse to play the game that she can't help but play, being a machine programmed to drag out all action for the sake of suspense. "See what?"

"She dumped you. She really *did* get all high on herself, she went full Stephen on you and she *dumped* you."

That word again and her eyes are #1 on Amazon and no you did not fucking *dump* me and I tell her to stop gaslighting me to my face, but she is on fire.

"Well, if she didn't dump you, don't you think you'd know where she is right now?"

"She's dealing with a family emergency, and she has your pages, and she *is* going to read them when she has time."

"It makes sense now. Why would you come to my house for Thanksgiving if things were good?"

I remind her, and myself, that we both wanted some time for ourselves, but she almost giggles. "Classic," she says. "Also, it's never true. Two people never want time apart. It's always *one.* And there you were in my home, playing with my kids, wanting to unload on me about your mother . . ."

"That was just for your book."

"Joe, I'm so sorry. I can't believe she dumped you."

Did you? "She didn't."

"And you come over and see my life and you know you can't have any of that with her . . ."

AS IF ANYONE WANTS SARAH BETH'S LIFE. "Hey, I had a good time with your family, and I helped you and—"

But she gasps. "The way you were so good with my kids! That's men. When Kev's mom died, he said the only thing that could help him cope with the death of a woman he loved was . . . well, he had to adopt. He wanted to be around kids. Just like you. Except you're not Kev . . ." Her eyes bulge and her voice drops to a whisper. "Wait . . . Did you already kill her?"

You didn't dump me and I didn't kill you and I want to rip her tongue out but I can't rip her tongue out—she has my tapes—and she is a bizarro world J. B. Fletcher. "It's okay," she says. "I knew this would end with Wonder in a ditch. That's your pattern. And I'm not judging. I know about your abandonment issues . . . I mean we both knew this was going to happen."

"Not an ounce or a molecule of anything you just said is true, Sarah Beth."

"Sure thing," she says. "You just keep telling yourself that." And then she puts on sunglasses that she probably bought for her day in the spotlight. "I'll send you some links . . . helpful hints about what to do with the . . ." *Body.* As if I'm going to fucking kill you. "Stay tuned!"

With that, she swaggers toward her car, and you didn't *dump* me. This is why she sells so many books, because her mind is a dark star, plummeting to the worst of all outcomes at all times. You took a break from the group text and bailed on her workshop and what does she think? That I killed you? No. You wanted to *spare* me another round with your family, because by this time next year, we'll be living a life of our own. You're the star of the room and you probably bailed on class to spend even more time with your family and wait . . .

You're the star of the room. You got what you need, Sly is in your corner, and you haven't so much as sent me a little *hello you* and is Sarah Beth right? Did you dump me, Wonder?

No. I knew it the first day of school. I said she'd *take away half our teeth and put us in one of her books.* We don't matter to her. We're just her *prezzies* from Harvard. Yes, she's a writer, but writers are just people. When they can't love themselves, they can't love anyone, and without love, they go dark. Pierre and Jolie don't like her green beans and Stephen passed on her low-fat artificially flavored crackers ten-plus years ago, and our fellows hate her blood-soaked popcorn and that's why she said that you dumped me. You and I love each other, and she hates that we love each other, and I am in the middle of a crosswalk holding my head high when her words come back to haunt me. The ones that bumped me in the room.

I like to kill darlings more than I like to write.

In her psycho killer headspace, all lives, both real and imagined, are disposable, interchangeable. My failure to kill her darling Stephen would give her an excuse to go off the deep end and kill you . . . Or maybe her violent overreactive imagination is contagious. Maybe that's my writer mind going off the deep end.

I check my phone for a text from you—nothing—and a woman in a Range Rover beeps. "Are you coming or going?"

I have no fucking clue.

36

That day at Sonsie, we had carrot cake and I don't like carrot cake with a decorative baby carrot on top—*Rabbits don't eat baby carrots*—but I don't like that molten chocolate nonsense that you were craving either. They were out of the chocolate nonsense, so carrot cake it was. I kept my chin up. I *mmmed* at the frosting, because when both options are bad and your girlfriend wants something sweet, you buck the fuck up and lick that cream cheese off her finger.

But then where did it get us? You dumped me in a bookstore.

Are we there again? My current menu of options is fucking fucked. You're blowing off the fellowship—bad—or you're missing, possibly because of our psychopath fellow. Or—worse—you're happy and healthy and done with me and Sarah Beth is right. You dumped me.

The last time we spoke we didn't use our voices. It was a text, not a phone call, and there were seventeen fucking minutes between the

FOR YOU AND ONLY YOU   293

time you walked out my door and the time you sent me that "I need space" text. What if *someone else* sent that text? Something is off. Wrong. I checked Cherish's fucking Facebook again, and it's eerie, Wonder. It's not like Cherish to restrict herself to *two* fucking photos on a national fucking holiday, but she did. And what if Sarah Beth invited me back to her home so she could get my fingerprints and frame me for your murder? A murder *she* committed.

You know you're fucked when you cheer yourself up by hoping you've been dumped, and I have to stay calm. Clear. Think like the literary author that I am, not a fucking crime writer.

It's like getting through that first draft of a book. One chapter at a time, one *sentence* at time. Sarah Beth writes about murder, she doesn't, you know . . . *do it*. That would be out of character. And I will *not* become that weak, needy guy texting you to say *u up*. But I do need to know that you're safe.

I didn't watch *Sesame Street* when I was a kid—too juvenile, too cloying—but I know how to get there. It's not my fault that you choose to live with your family, and I'm not going to interrupt your process. I'm just gonna be the first real boyfriend you ever had, the kind who pops by with a fresh apple pie.

Your father is on the front porch, and I wave all nice and friendly, and he hawks up a loogie and rubs his red nose. No words, only phlegm.

"Hey, Mr. Parish. What's shaking?"

He observes the pie box in my hands. "What's this?"

It's a pie, asshole. "Well, it was so nice of you guys to invite me, and I know Wonder's busy writing, but all the more reason to drop off a little something."

I opened the door for him to tell me that you're okay, that you made up some excuse for my absence, but he just glares at the Whole Foods sticker like I was raised by wolves, like I didn't remove the price tag. "Stop & Shop pies are just as good. Cost less, too."

You might be in your bedroom eavesdropping, so I don't tell him to go fuck himself. And lucky for you, I know what I'm doing. I hand him the *real* gift, a twenty-dollar scratcher. Addicts are all the same, so he pulls a quarter out of his fanny pack and nods at the steps as if there isn't a chair. I sit on the stoop and honestly, I know you need your space, but if you're up there listening, you should come down and thank me for being so supportive and patient, so generous, so nonintrusive. "Good luck, Mr. P."

He grunts. "I don't need 'luck.' These tickets are like everything in this world. They don't make 'em like they used to, and these *crosswords*, they're the worst, the way they make you work so damn hard for it."

I can't believe that this man is your co-fucking-creator and I laugh. "Speaking of which, where is our little wordsmith? She up there tapping away?"

"Nah," he says. "The whole lot of 'em are out running around."

You're alive, you're with *the whole lot of 'em*. But who's in the whole fucking lot?

Your old man groans—"Frig it. You know it's over when they give you a Q." He digs his quarter into the top of the ticket, revealing the code, confirming his suspicions that the ticket, like me, is a loser. He tears it in half and looks down at the pie. "Waste of money all around," he says. "You'll regret that when you're my age."

He's right about that, and I shake his hand. Time to see about this *whole fucking lot* because I care about you. Don't you get it, Wonder? I brought your father a pie and a scratcher. I'm the one.

I have to stay positive. Sarah Beth wouldn't have the balls to kidnap you—knock on marble—and I checked Cherish's trusty Facebook and tracked her to a blackjack table at the Encore casino, so you're with your sister, right? You needed space from me, which was probably code for time with your family, and there's Cherish, and there's no *whole lot of* random dudes sniffing around, and that's good news, but are you off in a dark corner with one of the lot of them? Cherish hits twenty-one when I say hello, and she's day-drunk and she pats the chair to her left. "Sit your ass down," she says. "You're my new good-luck charm!

She gives me no room to speak. Is this your chair? Are you in the bathroom? She goes on about the dealer—*Dude needs to share his tens with me*—and the poor dealer is shit out of luck—he's dealing with *Cherish*—and I order a rum and diet and wait for you to appear and Cherish slams the table. Hard.

"Fucking A," she says. "Dude, why do you have it in for me?"

"It's just the cards, ma'am."

"*Ma'am*. Do I look like your mother? Christ!"

That's my cue—I'm a bad-luck charm and you're clearly not here—but Cherish grabs my arm. She hit blackjack. "Well, you can't leave *now*," she says. "You're my good-luck charm,"

The drunk addict brain is a terrible, terrible thing and the dealer catches my eye—*Sucks to be you*—and Cherish wins a couple hands, which validates her conviction that I really *am* a good-luck charm. I look around the floor of the casino, all the eyes in the sky, the cameras and fuck it. Enough's enough.

"So, did you bring the whole lot of 'em? I thought Wonder'd be here . . ."

"I can't think about my sister right now. This dealer and this shuffler, the thing is freaking *toasted*. Burnt. Like can't you get the pit boss to fix it?"

I don't know where you are and Cherish hits her not-sweet-sixteen and busts. "Ouch," I say. "Guess I'm no Wonder, I mean she told me how she's your *real* good-luck charm . . ."

"Yeah," she says. "That is a freaking *fact* but I'm on a break from her right now."

Ah, so your holiday wasn't as fun as it looked online—when is it ever?—and I nod. "I'm sorry to hear that."

She slams a twenty on the counter and looks at me. "Did *you* know?"

"Did I know?"

"Did you know about Bobby?"

Oh boy. Oh, fucking *boy*. "Well . . ."

"So, you *did* know. Unreal. As if we're a bunch of Neanderthal freaking homophobes who would give a flying fuck either way about where that kid sticks his dick!"

Now I know why there were so few pictures online—Your Bobby came out to your family—and this is good news. Maybe you're with him. "Bobby's lucky that he has you guys. Are they here? Bobby and Wonder?"

"He's lucky he's not dead cuz don't freaking make *me* out to be some homophobe. I'm a nail technician, for fuck's sake! I do gay guys all the time. I love the gays! I mean hello, what about me screams *homophobe*?"

The dealer catches my eye and he's right. Pretty much everything about Cherish Parish screams *homophobe*.

"Honestly, you can skedaddle. If Wonder sent you here to harass me as if *I'm* the bad guy, as if *I'm* the one who kept a secret from her . . . she can piss off to Harvard Freaking Yard. And you . . . Don't walk up to a table when someone's on a heater." She looks at her new best friend, the blackjack dealer who was out to get her less than five fucking minutes ago. "Can you believe this guy? I was *winning* and then he shows up and I'm breaking even on twenty-one."

She looks down at her stay-on-seventeen and pounds the table. "Hit me."

I don't know that I've ever been happier to exit a casino. Maybe that day in Vegas with RIP Forty Quinn . . . but regardless, it's good to breathe fresh air, to know where you are. And I'm happy for Bobby! He finally came out to your family—no *wonder* your dad was borderline polite with me, the dream of his daughter becoming Mrs. Bobby Skelly is dead—and of course Sarah Beth didn't *kidnap* you. It's one of the only bad things about being a really good writer, my imagination . . . it gets the best of me. But all is well! *The whole lot of 'em* is only you and Your Bobby and he's your real best friend. Maybe *that's* why you didn't want me to come to Thanksgiving, because you knew he was going to come out, because you knew this would dredge up ancient history. I take the exit to Ro's house in Braintree. Sarah Beth is good at her job, nosing her way into people's lives, but she wouldn't know to come here.

I park on Ro's street, right behind Your Bobby's dealer-plated Beamer. You said you wanted "space," but I know your sister. I know the second I left, she broke the rules of that table and texted you about me, so it's okay that I'm here, *knock-knock-knocking on Ro's door.*

Your Bobby opens the door with a crutch and smiles. "Sup, Joe."

"Sup."

He asks me if I want a drink, and I can relax now. You're not here-here, you're not in the kitchen, but you're close. I feel it in the air. I smell you. "I'll have a beer if you got one."

I sit at Ro's old-school table and it's a sight for sore eyes. You *are* here—there's your Coolatta, half-empty with a lipstick-stained straw—and Your Bobby scratches his head.

"So, I guess you heard, huh?"

"I ran into Cherish at the casino."

He says he can't believe they still let her in there and he wants to talk and it's only fair I let him get it all out of his system. First, he came out to his family, and they reacted as expected—*Get out*—but the kids stood their ground—*We love you, Uncle Bobby*—and then he went to *your* house and told your father and Bobby talks like you—*It was a level-twelve shit show*—and this would all be more fun if you were here.

"How's Wonder holding up?"

"Awesome," he says. "Wicked awesome. She's the best, even if she tries a little *too* hard to watch our backs. Ya gotta love her, ya do."

Yeah, yeah, yeah. We all know you're *wonderful* but your Coolatta is decomposing. Where are you? He burps. "She was here yesterday."

"Oh?"

"One minute we're hanging out, she's gonna help me pack, but then she gets a text from some author lady and she's outta here. I figured it was you."

No. *No.* The *author lady* is up to something and I have to find you. Now. "Huh."

Bobby looks around Ro's kitchen. "I can't believe I gotta pack up all this stuff. Did Wonder tell you I'm getting outta here?"

"That's terrific, Bobby."

"Yeah," he says. "I'm gonna go to New York for a bit, I'm tired of these two-bit bookies."

"You? Mr. Beantown?"

"Eh," he says. "More like Mr. My Bookie's Had It Up to Here with Me, but ya know, it's cool . . ." He picks up Ro's marbles and that's why he's leaving, because it's hard, living in a tomb. "My aunt, she used to say she kept so many marbles around so no one could ever accuse her of losing them. Wonder, she put that in a story once, freaking Ro, she acted like she was famous . . . I miss the woman."

All loss is the same, it's crushing and altering, and I don't want to lose you. Love is a gift, Wonder. And my imagination is in overdrive—maybe it wasn't Sarah Beth Swallows, maybe you made up an excuse because you wanted alone time—but as I stand here helping Your Bobby with his boxes, making plans for us to go visit him in the *real* city, I can't read his face. I can't tell if he's going through the motions, humoring me. I can't tell if you told him that you were breaking up with me, and I refuse to invite him into the middle of our dispute—it's private—but I can find that *author lady* and make sure that you're okay.

"Dude," he says. "I got movers coming."

Good. I can't stay. "I can stay."

"Don't even," he says. "Do your thing. And besides, I feel like I owe you. I put this off for so long, selling this house, getting outta

Dodge . . . I'm happy my little sister finally found the kinda guy she deserves. You're the real deal and she cares about you, Joe . . ." The smile that's part menace, part love, part Minty brother who just fucking *wants* to bash a guy's skull in for doing wrong by his sister. "Do us both a favor . . . Don't gimme a reason to come back here and beat you to a pulp."

37

The ride to Foster is, ironically, the worst thing in the world for my radioactive hyperactive overdrive imagination. I need to find you, and I might only accomplish my goal if I find Sarah Beth, if I get into her head the way she got into mine . . . I fill the tank of my car and I check out her website and I go down, all the way down, to the year 2013. And that's when I find her one and only failure, *Sorry We Stole You* (2013), a fucking *romance* about "two artists who find their way back to each other."

The tagline puts a smile on my face—so the woman *does* have a heart—and how sad for her, Wonder. Authors must die a little when they spread their wings and get shot the fuck down, when a little piece of their soul fades into the abyss. Every cranky reviewer on Amazon says the same fucking thing: *Sorry I bought this book . . . Sorry I read this . . . Go back to doing what you do best . . . KILLING PEOPLE! MURDER!*

The book is nice and short—it's not even a book-book. It's a Kindle fucking single—so I ignore all 2-star reviews and one-click the audio version like a Colleen Hoover CoHort on Hoover release day at 12:01 A.M. Things are looking up. Starting a new book is *always* good for the soul, and you didn't dump me—Bobby would know if we were on the rocks—and in spite of Sarah Beth Swallows's violent negativity in her work, on the street after class—*I'll send you some links*—her off-brand "Happily Ever After" novelette is proof that even she knows that sometimes, love can win, that people do get their happy fucking endings.

And we will get ours. Even if I have to kill her.

I'm making good time and *laughing all the way* because *Sorry* is a verbal fucking vision board, an embarrassingly erotic self-fulfilling prophecy *disguised* as a book. Sarah Beth is living and orgasming vicariously through the heroine, "Sally," the "smartest sex pot in town" with a "pussy pot of gold"—cringe and then . . . "Enter Stanley"—her phrase, not mine. "Sally" and "Stanley" are afraid of true love, so they go their separate ways. Our "story" kicks off years later, when Stanley crawls back to Sally—warning: actual fucking *crawling*—and proposes a challenge: *Spend one weekend with me and tell me you don't feel it, too.* It goes without saying that Sally feels it, too. And because this is pure fantasy fuckball, Sally's "adorkable" husband, "Devon" (rhymes with Kevin), gives Sally and Stanley his blessing.

THE END.

I have the opposite of a book hangover and Sarah Beth is sicker than I thought. Sally isn't Sally—she's Sarah Fucking Beth—and Stanley isn't *Stanley.* He's *Stephen.* This "novella" was her mission statement and I don't have an overactive, radioactive, hyperactive imagination. She wanted me to kill Stephen because he's not Stanley, and because I didn't do it, she lured you away to hurt you, to poison your mind against me. After all, she didn't get her happy ending with precious Stephen and I didn't kill him, so in her mind . . . I don't get my happily ever after with you. Think about it, Wonder. A happy ending almost derailed her career.

I know, I know, I know. I sound as paranoid and psycho as Sarah

Beth Swallows, and I could be wrong, but what if I'm *right*? Sarah Beth Swallows isn't a pantser. She's a *plotter*. I put the pieces together, all that shit she said about you the day I rode with Kevin, like she *wanted* us to break up. Then I fail her—I don't kill Stephen—so she has to punish me. She reaches out to you and she's been working you for a while, hasn't she? Convincing you to *push* me away while she slowly lures you into her Dead Shed to kill you.

I can't get to Foster fast enough, and she's a clever writer. Evil. The high of the happy ending is fading and her true sinister voice is back in my head, warning me of all that could go wrong. I was running all over town making nice to your family, inadvertently installing *lampposts* for the fucking police. When you disappear, if you disappear—did you disappear?—the police will ask questions. Your father will note that I *was* a little fucking solicitous with my apple pie and my loser scratcher and your sister will testify to my pure evil—*He creeps up on my table and suddenly I can't win with twenty-one*—and Your Bobby will concede that he doesn't really *know* me, that I might just be like all the other Ivy League Douchebags of your past, only worse.

The one who *killed* you.

I make it to Foster and I park in the woods and I check the group text—still nothing in there from you—and okay. This is probably a wild-goose chase and *women do get weary* and maybe you're not here.

But then again, maybe you are.

I go on foot and the house is quiet. Kev's Blazer is gone—I bet he's out with the kids—and your car's not in the driveway but the *author lady* could have insisted you park in the garage. Finally, there is action.

Sarah Beth emerges from the Dead Shed. She's in athleisure, and she's going for a run, and the second I can't hear the sound of her feet hitting the grass, I check the window.

You're not in the Dead Shed and I'm on the run. Enough is enough. I'm going to sneak up on her and throw her down and force the truth out of her but then a woman comes out of nowhere and clips me with her elbow—"Stay to the left!"—and it only gets worse from here.

The woman catches up to Sarah Beth and they fucking know each other, and they're gossiping and I'm hunkering down in the woods, and damn runners, damn small towns.

They're going to get coffee.

I go back to my car, and drive into "town"—it's more like a village—and I did my homework. I know where Sarah Beth drinks her coffee, and there she is, perched on the bench soaking in the sun like the local "celebrity" that she is.

But where are you?

You're not in the Dead Shed and she can't possibly have stashed you in her house, so I dive into her socials. Here is Sarah Beth, strained and smiling in a "haunted" library in Maine. Here is low-sensitivity Sarah Beth beaming outside of a low-security prison and here she is eating sushi at a dilapidated mansion on the outskirts of Greenwich, Connecticut, that she bought to save from "extinction."

My imagination is going for a run again and is that where you are? Are you in a basement in *Greenwich*?

I go to her website where she catalogues her "writer's journey"— a mystery writer should maintain a *little* fucking mystery—and her books are all New England and every book involves a disappearance, a murder, a "darkness," a potential clue to your whereabouts, but I can't read them all—it wouldn't be good for me as a human *or* a writer—and her words echo in my mind—*I like to kill darlings more than I like to write* and is she still here?

She's still here, right there on the bench, posing for a selfie with a *fan*.

The sight of her big fake smile makes me sick, Wonder. The idea that she might be the reason for your disappearance. She may be a bestselling author, but she's gonna learn a valuable lesson about writing, about life, about me.

Don't fuck with me because unlike a lot of people on this planet, I fuck *back*.

I open her pages about me—the most recent writing is often the most revealing—and she got me all wrong—I'm not looking for a *mother*—but she does have that ability to suck in the reader. And then I look up. "Unputdownable" isn't necessarily a good thing when it comes to life, to books. The new pages were bad. Embarrassingly so. But I got sucked into the story, and I lost her, Wonder. The bench is clear. She's gone.

I hit the road again and pass her house, but the lights are out in the Dead Shed and Kev's in the front yard on dad duty and I want to call 911 to go in and find you, but I can't do that—those motherfucking tapes, the idea of you *listening* to those tapes—and that's okay. Writing is all about confidence. No more beating myself up for being a clingy fucking worrywart.

I know it in my heart, in my gut. She has you locked up somewhere. But where?

Much as I love *Chronicle,* that segment was taped a few years ago, and Sarah Beth was guarded with Shayna. It's human nature. The professional lights, the corporate performance of any big interview. But authors aren't rock stars. They make nice with readers, and in *those* situations, authors are more inclined to relax. It's the difference between riding with Kevin as opposed to *cycling* with Glenn, and I head over to YouTube and click on a forty-nine-minute interview that Sarah Beth did with a book blogger in Germany. This is good, casual and loose, the kind of low-pressure overlong discussion that only has *430* fucking views. Twelve seconds and fifteen minutes in, my patience pays off.

Sarah Beth flips her hair. She's really starting to feel herself now. "I love my Dead Shed, I do, but when I *really* need to block out the world and finish a book, I have a few rooms . . ."

The book blogger lights up. "Rooms as is hotel rooms? Motel rooms? Where do you go?"

Sarah Beth plays hard to get. "Oh, I want to tell you but it's a secret. Top secret. No one knows where I go, and that's what makes it so special, you know? That's where I can really get in there and be free and just . . . *create* and kill like no one is watching because they're not."

An author has every right to be precious and private about her writing caves. But Sarah Beth isn't just an author. She's a *mother*. If Pierre fell out of a tree and broke his arm, if Jolie broke a kid's arm on the playground, Kevin would be the first to know, and the minute he hung up that phone, he would call Sarah Beth's cave because emergencies take precedence over fiction, *always*.

I send a text to Kev: *Brewski?*

38

You know someone is borderline clinically depressed when they choose a *lobby* bar at a hotel that caters to busloads, but this is Kev's big night out, so what Kev wants Kev gets. He wanted to meet at the Boston Park Plaza, so we're at the Boston Park Plaza and I need him to talk, but he's annoyingly sober and sensitive. I ask him about his kids and he snarks out on me—"Well, they sure did like 'Just Joe' "—and this is what happens when you marry someone you love more than they love you. You become like Kev, insecure to the point where you can't stand it when your kids take a shine to anyone *but* you.

He checks the profile of their new babysitter on Care-dot-fucking-com—their regular sitter was busy—and he rubs his forehead. "I still can't believe I did this. S.B. would kill me if she knew I was out, let alone if she knew I got a random sitter online. Not that I blame her. She's the best!"

He wouldn't say it if he believed it and I smile. "But she's home, right? She's in the Dead Shed and you said she was gonna be pulling an all-nighter."

Come on, Kev. Tell me what I already know. Tell me that she's *not* in the Dead Shed. Tell me where she went.

He rubs his nose. Like he's pretending he just did cocaine. "True dat."

Not good enough, Kev. "Maybe you should call S.B. Have her check on the kids."

"Oh, it's not the kids . . . You know how it is. Our regular sitters are chill, but this new gal tonight, when she saw the books . . . she said what they all say. *Oh my God you are married to Sarah Beth Swallows!* She won't like . . . put S.B.'s panties on Instagram or something, right?"

S.B. is not a Kardashian and I stick to my fucking guns and tell him to call her. "Maybe she can walk over to the house and make her presence known."

TELL ME WHERE SHE IS, but he sighs. "Nah, see, then I'd have to tell her I'm out."

"Oh, come on, Kev. She's in the shed. She's gotta notice that your car's not there."

"Well, the thing is, though . . ." He's about to say it but then he wimps out and flags down the bartender—*Two more, bud*—and I laugh. "Wait, is she not home or something?"

He zips his lip like I'm going to sell the scoop to TM-Fucking-Z and then my phone pings—is it you?—and no. It's Mrs. Kevin Swallows, it's *her*, it's Sarah Fucking Beth—*Saw this and thought it could help with your story! More author tips on burying a body in New England are coming your way!*—and do you see that, Wonder? The thriller queen is trying to make it look like I asked her for help with my *book*—I would never—and are you tied up in a chair like I was? Did she play my tapes for you? Did she *kill* you?

Kev chuckles. "Is that Wonder? Is she checking up on you?"

Nope. "Yep."

He tells me to enjoy it while it lasts, as if you and I are an early version of him and S.B.—nope again—and he dips his finger into the foam on his Guinness. "So, this *other* night right here, at this very bar . . ."

"Oh yeah?"

"My boys and I met these flight attendants in from Brussels . . . Nothing happened but ya know . . ." He eyes the only two women in the lobby. One has a suitcase full of sob stories and the other has a fully erect spine, as if she can't *wait* to go home to her Back Bay sad pad and catch up on *The Bachelor.* He elbows me. "You think they're sisters?"

"I'd go with cousins."

"Wanna send 'em a drink? Girls go *crazy* when I tell 'em about the wife. And then it's like I *have* to be a good boy, ya know? Win-win!"

I glance at the girls and shrug. "I can't do that to Wonder."

"There's nothing wrong with a little flirting. S.B. even says it's good for me!" He slaps his hand on the bar. "Do you like chicken fingers? They have the world's best chicken fingers."

There is no such thing as the "best" fucking chicken fingers because all fingers come from the freezer and he tries and fails to whistle with his fingers and S.B. pings me—*I love campgrounds and readers do, too!*—and did Kevin see my fucking phone? Does he know it's his wife and not you?

The bartender takes Kev's menu. "No dice on fingers. We got wings though."

Kev can't do wings—this one time he choked on a bone—and the girls he wanted to chat up are gone, and S.B. is stalking me and he thinks it's you, which makes him feel ignored. He embarks on yet another story that takes us out of the present into his bad old days, leaving me stuck in the middle of this marriage. All the while, his wife is turning my phone into a forensic land mine, bombing me with links about *where to bury a body* and she can do that. Her career is a golden ticket, but I don't *write* psycho killer books and I DIDN'T FUCKING KILL YOU and Sarah Beth is good on camera, with reporters. She will claim that she pretended to be my friend because she was afraid for her life, afraid because of what I did to you.

Kevin smacks the bar. "I love this jam!"

S.B. strikes again, mocking my skills—*I know you like Rachael Ray knives but chain saws exist for a reason* ☺—and Kev is *lightning crashing*. "You know," he says. "You could just tell Wonder that you can't spend the whole night texting. I don't mind it, but my buddies are gonna rake you over the coals."

I didn't say he could invite his fucking friends and he pounds his chest and sings and "Lightning Crashes" isn't a "jam." It's a dirge. "Your buddies?"

"My B school bros. They should be here by eleven, and man, those guys . . . they *party*."

He's rubbing his nose, trying so fucking hard to get his seated groove on, and here comes S.B. again—*You could always put her out to sea like you did in your L.A. story*—and now I'm really fucked. A whole fucking fleet of Kevins will barge into the lobby and make it impossible for me to get Kevin to cough up S.B.'s fucking location. It's now or never and I hate to do it, Wonder. I *hate* to be that guy who can't let a woman be . . . but Kev has checked out the girl two seats down from us more than a few times now. She's cute with curly hair and she's alone and she's reading. It's not a Sarah Beth Swallows book, but it *is* a fucking thriller and I do have to find you.

I clear my throat and do it. "Sorry," I say. "I don't mean to be 'that guy.'"

"Then don't," she says. And I love her for that. The spunk. The fire.

I double down like Cherish with an eleven—"The thing is, I noticed you're reading"—and Miss Curly Hair Don't Care gives it right back—"Congratulations. You can see."

Kev spits up beer and mutters about how much he does *not* miss being single and I'm not *hitting* on this girl. I stay the course and slap his back and go full steam ahead. "I'll let you get back to your book, but I thought you'd wanna know that this guy here, my buddy Kev, his wife is Sarah Beth Swallows."

It's just like I expected. She can't close her book fast enough and now she's moving seats to be closer and Kev puffs up like *he's* the famous writer, and we're talking. Kev's drinking faster than ever, and Julie—her name is Julie—she's asking him all kinds of questions about what Sarah Beth is like in real life, about how she comes up with her stories. See, Julie works in PR for movies that shoot in Boston and she's not a writer, but everyone has a book in them and you never know. We don't have all fucking night—the B school bros are texting, threatening to show up, and you are hunkered down somewhere with S.-Fucking-B.—so I tell Julie that we're in the same boat.

"I'm a writer, too," I say. "But I'm no Sarah Beth Swallows. I can start a book, but I can't finish, you know?"

Julie *totally* knows and she's the same way—go figure—but she goes rogue, starts asking too many questions about S.B.'s latest fucking Hulu adaptation, and it's up to me to get the boat back on course. "Don't forget, though. There would be no TV show if Sarah Beth Swallows didn't do what she does and finish her books."

"So true," Julie says, and this is good. She's squirming and Kevin's drinking. She reaches across me like I'm the invisible man and lays a hand on Kevin's arm. "So, seriously," she says. "How does your wife do it? What's the secret?"

"Well," Kevin says. "She has me!"

It's the saddest most pathetic response and Julie catches my eye—*Poor guy*—and I tell Kev that what Julie means is more pragmatic. "It's like this, Kev. Julie and I wanna write books, but we're sitting at this bar *not* writing books."

"I actually brought my computer," Julie says. "I thought, Okay, I'll read a little, maybe eavesdrop, and then I'll want to write. How does she find the discipline?"

"Okay," Kevin says, the authority, the nonwriter who knows how to write. "One thing I can say about S.B. is that she would never come to a place like this to write. No coffee shops. No distractions. She locks *down*."

I ask Julie if she knows about S.B.'s Dead Shed, and Julie says it sounds familiar, but that it also sounds like a fantasy. "I mean I don't even live in a house. I have a roommate and the walls are thin and I can't even imagine a house, let alone having a whole house that was just for writing."

Now we're getting somewhere and I give a big, bullshit "Me too, same" and Kevin puffs up. "You gotta remember something," he says. "Sarah Beth wasn't always Sarah Beth Swallows . . . She was like both of you. She had a roommate and she procrastinated, but one day back in college, when she was broke, she scrounged up enough pennies to get a room at the Motel Six in Seekonk."

Bingo and I smile. "Wait, Sarah Beth used to write in a Motel Fucking *Six*?"

"Crazy," Julie says. "But now she's probably at the Ritz or something."

Kev shakes his head and it's good to see him like this. Relaxed, relishing this rare moment of being the man with all the answers. "No way," he says. "Sarah Beth goes back to Room 224 at the Motel Six with every book, because it's where she went when she had no choice. Yeah, we have other rooms . . ." What a sad little *we*. "We have fancier places, but it's like she says, writing never gets any easier, so you don't turn your back on the people and the places that were there for you when you didn't even know you could do it."

Kevin is a human Motel 6 in Seekonk and I have to get the hell out of here now. Julie orders another round and Kev nudges me. His voice is low. Leering. "Just so we're clear, it's not like I'm gonna fuck her. It's just a little harmless flirting, ya know?"

I love it, Wonder, the way he assumes that he could fuck Julie— she's not flirting with him, not at *all*—and I smile. "I guess I should leave you two alone then."

"Well, come on," he says. "Your girl's blowing up your phone the whole night. I know where you wanna be, and my buddies, Darren especially, they always give me shit . . . *Mr. Sarah Beth Swallows . . . Your wife brought a date to Thanksgiving* . . . So ya know, it would be kinda cool if they show up and I've got this babe who's all over me."

I lay a Benjamin on the bar, but Kevin pushes it back. "Not necessary," he says. "I know money's gotta be tight. I remember what it was like when S.B. was starting out. Seriously, bro, spend it on your girlfriend."

As I leave the bar, Kev's B school bros arrive. I pass the flock of white privileged man-boys—*Sup Mrs. Swallows . . . Mommy let big boy outta the house*—and it's the pounding of the chests and it's D-Bag Darren in real life, a breathing outtake of a Vineyard Vines photo shoot, and I feel a little bad leaving Julie to deal with that mess, but I have no doubt that she'll handle 'em, just as I have no doubt that I know exactly where you are.

Room 224 at Motel 6.

39

I might kill Kevin's wife, so I honored his wishes and spent my money on you—I charged up—and it's late, too late for texts, and the road is a black hole and it's not snowing, but it's not *not* snowing and my wipers are squeaking, and I need them, but I don't need them, and I can't deny it any fucking more.

I might be too late. Sarah Beth might have already killed you.

She would write it that way. She would get off on my current situation, the grand romantic fucking gesture of it all, as I power through, at long last ready to say vows and eat your oatmeal and forgive your flaws, let you steal all my little stories, ready in a way I wasn't when I had you, because of the most irritating and trite of all human truths.

We don't know what we have until we realize it might be dead in Seekonk.

It's too fucking quiet, too fucking dark, and it shouldn't just be me on the road. Doesn't anyone else in this world fucking *love* anyone? I let Jesus and Elon take the wheel and I check my messages but it's more of the same—too fucking quiet and too fucking dark, *no heehee* murder texts from S.B.—and the car sways. This is my exit and I'm here. I'm in Seekonk, where you are.

Are you?

I take the wheel back from Jesus and Elon and if she killed you, I will kill her, and if she didn't kill you, if she's turned you against me, if her plan is for me to kill you because I'm a "murderer" who failed to deliver a dead Stephen, well I don't want to kill her in front of you, Wonder. You won't be able to understand why I'm doing what I'm doing, and Sarah Beth's climaxes always start just like this—I am the angst-ridden protagonist, and this is my do or die—and if she brainwashed you, fine.

I will brainwash you right fucking back.

But what if you're crazy? What if you come at me with a weapon? "I heard the tapes, Joe! I know what you did!"

I could tell you that she told *me* that she wanted to co-write a book, that we were *role-playing*. I can picture you wanting to *BELIEVE* me, I can.

But what if you're dead?

She killed you. I'm sure of it now in the most horrible way. The parking lot is dead. The world is dead and when did the snow that wasn't sticking stop fucking falling?

I shut off the car. She's a smart woman. Is she setting me up?

She knew I'd find her eventually. That's what I do. I find people. I know people. I fell into her trap, same way you did, and we are too good for this world, for this fellowship, and I should run. Get in the car and hightail it to Maine, to Canada, skip out on the final test, the one that's all or nothing.

But wondering about you for the rest of my life would be the death of me, so I cross the lot. I enter the motel through a side door, fully expecting to find your body in the ice machine, a tub of blood-soaked popcorn. But you're not there, so it's onward to the room where it might be even worse, to lean my head into your bashed-in chest, walk into the frame for your murder. But this is love. It's nothing like writing. There is no decision. Only need. I lean my head against the door of 224. *Tick tick tap tap tick.* I'd know the rhythm of your fingers anywhere—you're alive—but then it stops A scrambling noise. A tape rewinding.

It's me, it's my muffled voice in the room, my voice on tape: "I didn't kill Beck."

And now I hear her voice. "But you just said that you did. You said you buried her in the woods in upstate New York. I'm not here to judge you."

"Then don't."

"Joe . . ."

"I loved Beck. I loved the person I thought she was, the person she told me she wanted to be. I killed the part of her that she *couldn't* kill. You have to think of it from my perspective. I'm watching this woman I love. She's self-harming."

"You said she attacked you."

"You don't get it, Sarah Beth. She killed herself. She broke her own heart. She hated me for loving her. She hated *anyone* for loving her."

Someone stops the tape. Is it S.B.?

Is it you?

I reach for my credit card to jimmy my way in but the door swings open and S.B. sees me and the room is tiny and she is wild-eyed, draped in four robes, two of them silk, two of them fleece. She sighs. She seethes. "I am going to *kill* my fucking husband."

In the foreground, just behind the sleep mask stuck to her forehead, I spy a Coolatta on her nightstand. It's past its prime, in a pool of condensation, and the room smells like McDonald's. You are here. "Is she here?"

She tells me to see for myself and I step over *The New York Times Book Review* and you are not in the shower, and you are not in the closet and you're not here. Are you dead?

She opens a *New Yorker*. "Did you see the profile of Ani in here? Nice to be a playwright and get that kind of attention. Good for her, right?"

"Great," I say, and she starts raving about Ani's *twistless genius*, asking me if I read Lou's *so-so* review in the *Times*. And then she yawns. "So what did you end up doing with her?"

"I didn't. And if you think you can frame me with a few texts . . . Tell me where she is."

She turns to a page with no pictures. "If you need to wash up, the bathroom's all yours." She thinks I killed you and the smell is getting worse. Either she needs to shower or she already *did* kill you—did she?—and she tosses her magazine on the floor. "So, did you end up going into the woods?"

She really is a psychopath. She is curious, not concerned.

"I told you. I didn't do anything to her."

"So, what? She's in your trunk? Damn it, Joe, I sent you plenty of links and if you're not going to tell me how you did it . . ." She yawns and she smiles. "Oh my God, wait. You didn't do it, but you've got her locked up in a cage. Can I see her?"

Is she this stubborn with her editor? "Do you want me to say I'm sorry? If that's what you want to hear, fine. I'm sorry I didn't kill Stephen and I'm sorry our fellows were down on your pages and yes . . . I'm sorry that Wonder didn't show up for your fucking workshop, and I'm sorry that Ani gets profiled in *The New Yorker* instead of you but for fuck's sake . . . I know about the phone call, okay? I know an 'author lady' called Wonder and I just . . . Where is she?"

Her head tilts and she is a bird. A seagull in Seekonk. "Huh?"

"I'm here, S.B. So the jig is up. And if you think you're gonna frame me for killing Wonder . . . that's not gonna happen. Where is she?"

She looks at me like I'm a stupid autodidact and she laughs as if any of this is funny. "Oh, Joe, I was just spit balling . . . That's what writers do, you know, I kick around ideas for my book."

"Spit balling with human fucking lives."

"I told you, you don't have to pretend with me . . ." She puffs up, slightly. "The Stephen thing, I was just being dramatic, I get that way when I'm writing. I never expected you to do anything, but it is kind of flattering . . . You thought I'd actually, you know, 'do' a crime."

She didn't kidnap you and this is a waste of my time. "I'm outta here."

She stares at her Coolatta. "Not so fast, Joe."

The tapes. The *tapes*. "What?"

"You expect me to believe that you're 'evolved,' that you didn't kill Wonder, that she's not locked up in some dungeon? You just let her ghost you and move on with her life?"

"I haven't heard from her in a few days, so all I am right now is worried."

A normal person would be happy to find out that you're alive, but she's . . . mad. "So let me get this straight. You thought I kidnapped her . . . amazing . . . and now you know that I didn't. Joe, come on. Just tell me how you did it."

"I didn't."

"Yes, you did. When the women push you away, you kill them."

"I love her."

"You 'love' her. So, if it turns out she's in a room across the hall fucking some guy's brains out, you still won't kill her. You just want her to be happy."

There's no way you would choose the Motel 666 and there *is* no other man. "Yes."

"Ah, you've 'changed.' The love of a good woman and all that hooey. This time love is 'real' and 'if you love it set it free' . . ."

"Yes."

"You're a changed man and you believe in love and 'love is the thing, y'all' . . ."

"Yes."

"It doesn't drive you crazy that someone you 'love,' someone *you* think is the best writer, the one person on this planet whose opinion of you as a writer matters most . . . It doesn't bother you that this woman thinks *she's* the best, that she has no use for you, that she didn't even leave her table to check up on you in the bar because she's all about *her*."

I did kind of miss having a shrink and Sarah Beth Swallows is better than Dr. Nicky. "Yes."

She swats a fruit fly. "Well, I'm happy for you, Joe, truly. You're 'evolved' and what am I? Who am I to tell you what to do? You don't *respect* me. You don't fear me. I'm not Lauren Fucking Groff and I bet if I was, I bet if *she* asked you to kill *her* ex-boyfriend—"

"So, you *did* want me to kill him."

"Nice work, Columbo." She says that like she can't go to jail for her botched attempt at hiring a hit man, and Lauren Groff would never. "Forget it," she says. "I guess I'll just have to do it myself because Stephen should be dead, and I'm not 'evolved.' I want that man dead."

And I want to leave this room, but I can't leave now, not when she's announced her intention to kill someone. It comes back to the tapes, to her power. If she got caught—she would get caught—she'd use *my* tapes to frame me for killing him. "Hey now," I say. "You don't mean that."

"Just because you're a lovesick sap doesn't mean I am. At the end of the day, you really don't think I'm physically strong enough as a person or a writer. I read you all wrong and I wrote you all wrong, even when I had all the childhood mumbo jumbo, and who knows? Maybe you're right. Maybe the only way for me to finish this book is to get my hands dirty."

She is such a writer that she puts words in my mouth while I'm standing right here, rewriting life in real time, and no, she can't do this to me, to us. "It won't make you happy."

"You seem pretty happy to me, and why shouldn't you be? You did it to Candace and you did it to Beck and *that's* why you're 'evolved.' Me . . . I wake up every day and Stephen is out there living his life, showing me how happy he is without me. I burn him alive in *A Perfect Gentle Man* and I feed him to sharks in *After Ever Happily,* but I don't *evolve.* I finish a book and I'm right back where I started. I don't want him gone. I *need* him gone. You were there. You heard everyone in the room laughing off my *blood-soaked popcorn.* The tapes, our talks . . . it's not enough. I *have* to kill him. *Me.* It's the only way I'm ever gonna get better."

"It's not that simple."

"I could get away with it."

So insulting, as if real life is a fucking novel, and this woman must be stopped. "There is no such thing, Sarah Beth. There is no 'getting away with it.' Let me tell you what it's like to be *me,* to have monkeys on my back, mugs of piss and *podcasts* around every corner because Candace and Beck are *not* out there living their lives . . ." Do I mean that, Wonder? I don't even know. "Don't do it. Don't give yourself a life sentence of looking over your shoulder knowing that at any second someone like you might come along and figure you out."

I think my speech worked. This happens, the patient heals the therapist, but then she smiles and who the fuck am I kidding? Psychopath all the way. "You forgot something, Joe. The only 'someone like me' I have to worry about is you. And we both know that I don't have to worry. Or wonder . . ." She flips her hair like this is *Chronicle.* "Not that you asked," she says. "But needless to say, the writing is not going well."

She brings out the bumper sticker in me. All psychopaths do. "That's par for the course with any book. Give it time. Watch a movie or take a break. But don't procrastinate by doing something you'll regret."

"So, you regret all of your murders?"

No. "Yes, of course I do."

"Well, damn it, I wish you had killed Wonder or Stephen or both of 'em because this book . . . it just doesn't work. I need more. I need fresh blood. Or that's it. I quit."

Stick her bumper hard, Joe! "Come on, now. You know how it is. When you fall off the horse, you get back on. You don't kill the horse. You're a writer. Just keep writing."

She rolls her eyes. "I hardly think Wonder is the little soul-altering darling that you seem to think she is. You don't 'love' her. She's not anywhere *near* the writer that Stephen is."

I don't bother defending you. The Motel 666 was built for wallowing and I liked it better when I thought I knew where you were. She picks up a stale donut sitting on a copy of *Florida* by Lauren Groff. I need to get the fuck out of here and find you. "You want me to take some trash on my way out?"

But then she drops the donut. "Wait, there *is* something here . . . In the past, you always catch them before they leave you and you kill them so they *can't* leave you, but if you're telling the truth . . ."

"I am."

"This is different. Wonder is the one that got away. *Not* killing her will be the thing that kills you . . . The one that got away will kill you slowly . . . That's the twist. *You're* the twist and oh my God. I have it . . . I have it. I *got* you."

You are not my prisoner, so you did not *get away*, and I interject, but she's already on fire, scratching in a yellow notepad. I remember a picture of Substack Stephen's wife savoring oysters, laughing with her eyes, her body. Some people are like that, Wonder. Born to love, to relax. Sarah Beth Swallows is a "machine" because she doesn't care about me or you or Substack Fucking Stephen. She's a part-time member of humanity. Her permanent residence is her fiction. She lied to Shayna from *Chronicle* when she said that her dream was to solve a real-life cold case. She lied because she was trying to sound like a human. It's what all psychopaths do when the cameras are rolling. *This* is her true dream. To write a book that forces all the Substack

Stephens of this world to their knees, to revere her. And she thinks she's on her way. She's like you. *Tick tick tap tap tick.* Winners keep winning—she'll probably get a blurb from Lauren Groff—but what about me? What about you? What about us?

My tapes are on the desk. I could end her life and walk out of here with the tapes. The sun is coming up. A guy in the parking lot buys pills off another guy, a clean deal that ends with a handshake. It's illegal and it's fair and the world is a transactional place, one that I recognize. I don't need to kill Sarah Beth Swallows. She's too big to kill—Shayna from *Chronicle* would be overwhelmed—and Sarah Beth won't rat me out for the same reason she doesn't go to her kids' fucking soccer games. She's a lifer. She'd rather have me on call as a consultant than she would have me behind bars. The work comes first, always.

"So, I guess I'm gonna go."

She hisses. "Sssh."

I stop at a Dunkin' on the way home—I miss you—and it's nice to be a regular guy with a regular coffee, leaning against the hood of my car while I recover from my days wasted in a nail-biting "thriller" that didn't deliver. I have a real-life book hangover. S.B. hooked me and led me to a dark place. I was seeing the world as she sees it, a seedy cold maze of double-sided mirrors, a world where all people are sinister, where nothing means what it means.

I'm on the road and I'm back in my apartment, in a nice hot shower scrubbing the Motel 666 off my body. I don't think you would appreciate the stench of the thriller queen's secret Dead Shed and a shower always helps. I'm feeling good. You needed space from your family, not just me and everything looks better now. The "author lady" you mentioned to Your Bobby was an excuse, a gentle white lie so that he would think you were bailing on him because of your fellowship duties. I'm the one in the wrong, spending so much time in the thick of it with Sarah Beth Swallows. When I reach for the Harvard shower curtain, I half-expect to see you on the other side, *Psycho* style, brandishing one of my Rachael Ray knives, convinced that I was in that seedy motel letting a *fellow* woman eat my fucking cruller.

No such luck. So what happened, Wonder? Did you *freak* out about getting close to me and run off with an actual Ivy League Douchebag to a Motel 666 just because we had a fight about that stupid fucking *mouse*? Is this bigger than me, an early midlife crisis? My phone rings, as if you know I can't go on like this and it's silly. I know you're not here. I know you can't *hear* me. But as I run into the living room in my birthday suit, I yell like you are here, like you *do* hear.

"I'm coming, Wonder! Don't hang up!"

40

I t's a 212—that's a New York landline—but that's you, you wanted
space and you've always wanted to go to the big city, so you ran
off to tell those Yankees they suck in person. We are in this
together and your *tendency is to love* and I make the phone stop ringing.

"Wonder?"

"Excuse me?"

"Who is this?" I snipe, like some prick at Sonsie who ordered
French toast and got served fucking waffles.

It's a woman. She's too old to be one of those podcast-taping
teachers and police are *unknown* when they call, and she laughs. "Well,
this is sort of an interesting way to start."

I sit my bare ass on your spot on the sofa and oh, that's right. I'm
a writer. I wrote a book. "Bernie?" Too intimate. "Ms. Lapatin?"

She chuckles and she likes me, it, my book. If she didn't, she
wouldn't insist that I call her Bernie. "Joe, my dear, I hope you're sitting down."

"I am," I say. "Naked as a baby."

"Well, that's an image. Not the one for your headshot, but maybe when it's time to do press, the author at home, covering his bits with his computer . . . Too much?"

My head is swelling—she likes me, Bernie likes *Me*—and Phil Roth would never pose naked and wow, the Kool-Aid hits me fast. In my head it's already Phil, not Philip. "I think I prefer clothes."

"Noted," she says. "Well, Joe, a few a days ago our dear friend Sly sent me your manuscript."

Oh boy. Oh boy. Did you hear that, Wonder? "That was kind of her."

"And I said no."

My dick shrinks and I am no Philip Roth and rejections are meant for email, not old-school fucking landlines and what kind of monster is this woman? What kind of monster goes around killing dreams so close to Christmas? What if I was the type to blow my brains out because some snooty, Choate-educated, Yale-educated woman turned her nose up at my prose, my heart, *me*. "I'm sorry to hear that."

"The market is terrible."

Oh, fuck that. They publish new books every week. "I get it."

"And I only just signed your friend Mats, and what are the odds that multiple saleable, smart books would come out of a fellowship as small as yours?"

Huge, you fucking cunt. It's *Harvard*. "I understand."

"I'm full up on reading, we're back in the office with the usual distractions, and I've got so much to do before Claus and I go to Aspen. I said no, Sly, not now. No more . . ." Her husband's name would be *Claus* and I wish I'd put on pants. "I thanked Sly, and Claus and I went to our place in Connecticut . . ." Don't you love when people do that? You were right, Wonder. They do *hate us 'cause they ain't us* and our golden tickets got us into the room, but they did not get us into the glass elevator. "You see, Claus lives for the country. He gardens. He shovels snow."

Fascinating. "That's nice for him."

"Now me, I'm a city mouse . . ."

Maybe I'll kill her for the fuck of it, one last big fuck you to the man. "I get it."

"And much as Claus claims we go there for the peace, it's not so serene. It's brunch at the club and let's go see so-and-so's new baby and oh look, a farmers' market."

I picture Glenn holding up an apple, another time I failed. "I appreciate your letting me know."

"Claus and I . . . It's almost twenty-three years, Joe."

"Happy almost anniversary."

"That's a long time to be with one man, and as you might imagine, the drive to come together fades. Your legs are sore for no reason, and somewhere along the line, you became two people who talk about their bodies, laugh at their bodies . . . Claus and I, we rarely go at it the way we did once upon a time . . ."

I wish your father was here—he'd tell her where to stick it—and this is not how it works. I don't care that she's an agent. Her sex life is none of my business. "Interesting."

"But then I read *Me.*"

The woman who can't stop talking has stopped talking and I don't know what to make of the real-time radio silence, so I say nothing. I wish you were here holding my hand and I picture RIP Ethel and RIP Glenn up in heaven, crossing their fingers. "And?"

"Was it chocolate syrup or fudge?"

She's asking about one of my *sex* scenes and I feel more naked than I did twenty seconds ago. "Syrup."

"Joe."

"Bernie."

"Joe."

"Bernie."

"Oh hell," she says. "I'm too set in my ways to keep up with the latest rules of what's permissible to say to you kids so I'm just going to say it. Claus hasn't come like that since we were in Malibu for our daughter's wedding and frankly, neither have I! Thank you! Thank *Me*!"

"You're welcome?"

"It will be my honor and my pleasure to put *Me* on shelves because everyone on this planet, the newlyweds suffering buyer's remorse, and the young cynics faking orgasms . . . everyone deserves to have good sex. And *you* wrote the book on good sex."

It's . . . one way to look at my book. A little limited if you ask me— the sex is only graphic because it's metaphorical and there's not *that* much of it—and she sighs. "We can get a lot for this, you know. It's commercial *gold*."

It's *literary* gold. "I wasn't expecting a big advance."

"Your timing is perfect. The market is ripe for something like this, someone like you . . . It's like my assistant said . . . Are you there, Patrice?"

A meek little mouse of a voice pops in now and has it been here the whole time? "Here!"

I don't like eavesdroppers and I feel spied on, shocked, unknown. "Hi, Patrice."

Patrice doesn't answer—she must have hit the Mute button—and Bernie sighs. "No one knows what anyone wants when the world is what it is, so bleak, so dark. One day the buzzword is *joy*, but who knows what that means anymore? But as Patrice said so eloquently, we are all always up for a book that inspires us in the boudoir. And that's what you do, you're Joe *Erotic*."

I'm . . . not. Yes, there is "sex" in my book and yes, there is choco- late syrup but there is also the mouse in the house, the dense, con- densed monologues of two people struggling to understand each other. "I'm not sure what to say . . ."

"Well, just say yes. Say that I can start the auction now . . ." I say nothing because something is rotten on the Upper West Side of hell. I'm not Joe Erotic and Bernie sighs. "Are we in this together?"

It's my turn to hit the Mute button. I want it, Wonder. It's the dream come true—Bernie loves me and Bernie loves *Me*—and it's where our story goes. *We are in this together.* I want a bidding war and a big book that takes over the fucking world. I know this business. I grew up with an inside fucking *view* of this business and these people, agents . . . they do this to books, they dress them up like toddlers on Halloween to get the likes on Instagram, to *sell* them. The business of *sales* is ugly and okay, so Bernie has me all wrong, but she's not a writer, and she's not an editor. Her job is to sell it and once she sells my book to the highest bidder—*Holy shit, this is it, it's happening*—I will be in New York, sitting at a nice big Algonquin round table, telling the publisher the way *I* see myself, my work. But then I remember Mats's fucking press release, the absolute, utter accuracy of the description of his work.

"Bernie, before we make it official, I haven't looked at my manuscript in a while and I'm sure you have notes."

"Here and there, nothing too extreme. If anything, we just want more . . . Patrice had a thought about Joy and Dane having sex in a garden . . . the birds and the bees of it . . . And Sly would like you to think about toys . . . accessories."

I'm not a short-order porn cook and who reads *my* book and comes away with nothing but a hard-on? "Well, I'm 'up' for it, so send me whatever you got."

Bernie says it's a "thrill" to know that I take my "fun" work so seriously—fuck you too, lady—and writing my book wasn't *fun*. I killed myself for that book, I went Glenn Shoddy level of *blind* for my book, and the call ends and the email comes through and my book is attached, but the title of the document sends shivers down my bare spine.

MeBacktoJoeSlyBernie.doc.

I open my book, and no wonder they think I'm Joe Fucking Erotic. I . . . am.

It's *Me*—it opens with Joy and Dane after they've just had sex—

but it's not *Me*—Joy and Dane don't launch into a long, deep conversation about Tolstoy and their early childhood memories. They just roll over and start fucking again. And then they do it again. And again.

Sly did this to me, Wonder. I kept her dark, lawbreaking secret. I trusted her with my life, with my words, my soul, the vulnerable thin-skinned body that is my book. She read it—on her *phone*—and then she picked up a chain saw. She cut out the heart and she removed the brain. She reached for a scalpel out of those fucking Hostel movies and she scooped out the eyeballs of my characters. Gone are their limbs, the arms they wave while they're thinking out loud about the meaning of life and love. Joy and Dane are still here, and somehow, they're still good—they're mine, after all—but all that remains are their loins.

Honestly, Wonder, what the fucking *fuck*?

41

I t's because of you. That's the only possible explanation. Sly was
our biggest fan. The "author lady" was going to help us. But then
we had a fight. You haven't spoken to me out loud since you said
goodbye. This is that breakthrough moment in the book when plots
collide. Sly is punishing me for being a good man, good to you, good
to her, respectful of *all* fucking women.

I didn't text you. Sarah Beth didn't text you.

It was the widow Willa Wonka.

You wanted to talk to someone—you should have talked to me—
but you reached out to her. Your mentor.

It's the only possible explanation for why Sly would turn her back
on me and *Me* and I want to hunt her down at her fucking *yoga* class,
follow her home and lock her up in that garage and force the truth out
of her. There is no "excuse." I will dump her body—without any help
from Sarah Beth Swallows, thank you very much—and wait a few
days to call Bernie and tell her about Sly's deranged revision of my

novel. Emotions are weather, they pass, and by the end of the call, Bernie will start reading the real *Me*, the one flush with quotable, evergreen monologues. And then she will say what I need to hear: "You're not Joe Erotic. You're Joe *Salinger*."

But I can't do any of that, Wonder. I'm a Harvard man with a big bright future as a porn peddler—no—and I don't want to go to another fucking memorial with REDACTED fucking mourners. That's where this nightmare began, when Sly took a shine to you at her husband's funeral, and I only have one question for that book-tampering turncoat.

Where the fuck is she hiding you?

I have a hunch. First day of kindergarten—don't get me started—Ani was being polite. She asked our new teacher who death-lucked into her job if she was working on a new book. Sly simpered: *I'm sort of writing something, but I need a solid week in a white room.*

There was a little talk about white rooms, safe spaces for banging out the book, and the benefactors who open their houses to artists. You were in awe of all of it—*I can't imagine someone giving me their house*—and that's what she did for you, isn't it? She rang up the old family friends to tell them about this poor little poor girl with no place to go to escape her abusive, porn-peddling boyfriend and her equally foul pond scum of a family.

But who are they, Wonder? Where's the fucking house?

I go to my shelves to dig up *Flour Girls* to look at the acknowledgments, where all the privileged dorks and ditzes thank every fucking person they ever fucking met, as if a book isn't written by one person, one person only.

Grr. *Joe Erotic.* Grr.

But my copy is a fucking galley—*Acknowledgments to come*—and she wrote this book a long time ago, when she and Glenn lived in Iowa. I need a real copy of *Flour Girls* and I refuse to contribute to her royalties, so I throw on a hoodie and grab my fucking Ray-Bans—thanks for nothing, Glenn—and if she's home, maybe I *will* lock her up in that garage because don't you get it, Wonder? Boundaries matter. Sly isn't our couples therapist. She's our *teacher.* You had no business talking about our *relationship* and if you were really that unnerved by the stupid mouse/oatmeal tiff . . .

Then again, how could you ever be expected to respect boundaries? When you turn out the lights in your bedroom, you hear your father's sleep apnea machine humming across the room. You have no boundaries.

I check Sly's Instagram when I turn onto her street and she's not home—hot yoga, no goats—and I unlock the door to her house— Thanks, Glenn!—and her computer is on the counter in the kitchen. She's a *homebody* widow, fearless and spoiled as an indoor cat. Unafraid of anyone breaking into her house and hacking into her computer because who would do that? Nobody wants more *Flour Girls!*

I'm in her computer, in like young Eisen-Zuck hacking the Harvard dorms, and she uses *iMessages* and that's a good place to start. Here you are, just as I suspected.

> *Sly omigod I'm freaking out and I hate to bug you but Joe just accused me of plagiarism and he hates me and of course he does. I stole his freaking mouse,*

I KNEW IT.

> *Wonder, stop it. You did nothing wrong. Plagiarism???*

> *I mean sort of? I read a few pages of his book and I saw the mouse in the house. I know that phrase from this book I got for my niece, but I put it in my book cuz I saw it in his and aaaaah help meeee*

I look at Donna Tartt and I shout, "I knew it! I was *right.*"

Honey, no one who loves you accuses you of plagiarism. The end.

So what do I do? Do I call him?

I grab both sides of the computer and yell. "CALL HIM." But it's of no use. This conversation went down several days ago and Donna Tartt paws at her empty water bowl.

That mouse is public domain, honey. And for the record, your mouse beats the hell out of his mouse. You're in a league of your own.

She is Tom's mother in *The Prince of Fucking Tides* and this is where you're supposed to tell her she's wrong.

But I love him. I should call him. I can't focus on writing until I fix this.

Have you ever even spent one night alone? Have you shut it all out to just sort of be with yourself and your craft? No family. No Joe. Just you?

The answer is no and she knows it.

Honey, you need space. Tell that dumb job you need a break and forget Joe! He accused you of plagiarism. That says everything you need to know about what he thinks of you. When a man you love gets in the way of you and your work, there is only one thing to do. Leave. It's not our job to give our lives over to men.

Donna Tartt marks my leg with her scent, and I shudder. This from the woman who provided her husband with a *Pulitzer Prize–winning novel* and you tell her that you want to call me, that you want to confess.

Honey, if you call him, he will fuck your brains out and you will never finish your book. You are Dunkin Sally Rooney and you need to focus on YOU.

Do we wish he was a good man? Do we wish he was on your side? Yes, we do, but no he isn't so that's it for him. You're too good for him as a writer and a person. Love is not that, not at all. He doesn't love you. He's too jealous.

Don't do it, Wonder. Don't drink that Kool-Aid! But of course you did. You responded with that screaming blue and yellow face, as if life is ever so simple, one emotion at a time.

Wonder, men only learn anything from consequences. Walk away.

TELL THAT TO YOUR DEAD BELOVED HUSBAND!

I don't know . . . I mean where would I even go?

And that's the end of the thread, that's when she picked up the phone to call you, to tell you where to go. That's when she decided to sentence me to a life as an *erotica* writer and as much as I'd like to sit here and overanalyze your little texts, I must make like every writer on a mission to finish a draft and move the fuck on.

I go to Microsoft Word and the last thing she messed with wasn't my book. It was *yours*. It was *Faithful*. Donna Tartt hisses and the clock is *tick tick tap tap ticking* but I have to know what she did to you, so I open *The Chronicles of Sesame Street*—it's a better title than *Faithful*—and this isn't *your* book either.

She deleted your *freaking*s and took a thesaurus to your prose. She cut all your lampposts, and padded your family scenes with her kind of language. She even found a way to stick some fucking *cicadas* in there. She knocked me down and she lifted you up, but it's all the same—a felony is a felony—and I'm not Joe Erotic and you're not Dunkin' Sally Rooney, and it's not fair. You wanted to spend the next fifteen years of your *life* on this book, and in what world do you get to be Dunkin' Sally Rooney while I lurk behind you, a panty-sniffing, monkey-spanking Joe Fucking Erotic?

We are in this together, and time is of the essence—I need to fucking find you—so I close your fake book and I open Sly's book: *Marriage.*

She has some nerve—pompous much?—and *Marriage* is a head-scratcher. I wish I could show it to you and all our fucking fellows because Sly tells *us* to forget about the world, to be in *kindergarten,* at play, but Sly is all about everything *but* the writing. She is hyperfocused on the world outside of the white room. She's not writing a book. She's writing a marketing plan. Is this how she did *Scabies?* By becoming a self-editing, marketing-savvy CE-Fucking-O of a book that isn't even written yet?

Blurb for Marriage: "If Sally Rooney and Donna Tartt wrote a book to-gether, this would be that book. I wish I wrote it myself."—Meg Wolitzer or Lily King or Celeste Ng?

Sally Rooney and Donna Tartt aren't writing a book together and Sly isn't *really* writing a book. Maybe in Iowa she loved to write, but she's not that person anymore. She's blocked by the guilt of pulling one over on the world, an *act of love* that sent her husband off a cliff and killed her innocence and creativity. Seriously, Wonder. These pages are fucking filler.

[break their hearts in real time, so the ADD Amazon reader has to keep going, orchard night scene from that Shoddy applicant who died = GREAT start]

[milk the heartbreak, like when Glenn cheated but not cheating, some-thing nonsexual, S.B. style tease . . . but make prose incandescent, astonish-ing etc]

[funny scene, the kind you take a picture of and send to a friend, crass but no farts, lift that short story "Vowels" from the slush pile at the U of M lit mag? Check if author is online alive etc]

[the kind of scene that makes you close the book and look at the cover]

[introduce Eleanor, a POC/Ani type nuanced no tokenizing free spirit but not over the top perfect. Maybe don't even mention her skin color?]

[Put David in Kanye West shoes, possible Instagram post? But Molly is the feet, make it make sense, metaphor, maybe also my Klonopin black-outs? Relatable. No one reads A Million Little Pieces *anymore, good source]*

[give Molly a Sophie's Choice, like Errol in Mats's book . . .]

[let stupid David say something smart and Eleanor is like Molly come on]

[Give David a noble moment, he's defending Eleanor]

Pre pub: Tease Scabies news, everyone assumes is about movie etc

Pub: Today Show reveal of Scabies, or maybe better an essay? NY Times?

Paperback: GMA etc . . . address backlash post Scabies etc (maybe Joel or Ethan too?)

I know how she wrote *Scabies*—she saw God and religion trending on Twitter—and she's in a new place with *Marriage*, two years into mainlining raw fucking Kool-Aid. That powder is like praise—it's poison—and it's no good without water. She thinks we need space? Well, I think she needs time away from her computer.

Marriage isn't a total bust, though. Sly pasted her *Flour Girls* acknowledgments into this document and she put in two *additional* pages of gratitude for all the people who helped her finish her book—it sure as fuck isn't easy being a woman—and I print the pages while Donna Tartt sniffs her empty bowl. Much as I want to refill it with some kind of fucking sustenance, I can't risk it. But the ASPCA will get an anonymous phone call in a few weeks.

I run to the nearest library because I need a bump of Harvard, the thrill of swiping my card, knowing that I belong, that we students so often know more than our teachers.

I find a table and I do what everyone does when they sit down to work. I check my phone. Nothing of any significance from Cherish on Facebook, just a passive-aggressive post about *being a single mom with even less help than normal* and okay. Time to work.

I bust out my highlighter and turn every single fucking name in the acknowledgments into a yellow brick. One of these people is the benefactor. One of them owns the white room. Is it Honey Winthrop, "without whose generosity" Sly "would never have finished *Marriage*"? Or is it Constance "Mopsy" Mathison, whose "open heart" is the reason Sly was able to "hear my characters come to life in my mind"? Or maybe it's John J. Enengender III, who has been "on my side since I was a wee thing riding up and down in the dumbwaiter."

The clock is ticking and fifty-two fucking potential benefactors is too many. I put the cap on my highlighter. I am better than this. I am a writer.

And it's time for a fucking rewrite.

I've been hunched over back issues of *Architectural Digest* for four hours—I have *Architectural Indigestion*—I'm on page three of Sly's acknowledgments and *I still haven't found what I'm looking for*, her benefactor.

Honey Winthrop was a dead end—she lives in Portugal and you can't drive to Portugal—and "Con" Mathison is an Epstein-type businessman with a compound in Nebraska—you are by the sea—and I am cross-referencing albums of weddings on *the Cape*—you're in a "the" place so it's *the* Cape or *the* Hamptons or *the* Vineyard—and I have to fucking find you.

I open RIP Glenn's fucking *Twitter* page and take yet another nauseating trip through his photos. He's chumming it up with Colson Whitehead in New York and he's on tour at a Waffle House being real, being fake, and here he is at a wedding in Southhampton, and I search for his name on Twitter. I look at *those* images, the ones posted by other people who tagged him, and I go back, way back, when *Sca-*

bies was just a blurry blob of brackets, and still nothing—Where's Waldo? Where's Wonder?—and so I mix things up. I search for Sly and there she is, in 2016.

She doesn't know she's being photographed. "Colton" took the picture, the woman standing on a winter's dock, gazing in a way that speaks volumes about her frustration, as frozen as the snow making her feet cold. The caption is fucking trite:

Damn it feels good to be a patron.

I bet it does, you fucking pig, and Colton's no dummy. He doesn't share his name on his profile, but he does share other basics. He's a trader based in Boston, but the responses to this picture confirm that this house is on Cape Cod, Massachusetts—as in *the* Cape, that's the *the*—and googling "Colton," "Boston," and "trader" will get me nowhere—there are a *lot* of fucking Coltons trading stocks in this glorified town—but then I zoom in on the picture. There is a boat tied to this dock and the boat has a name.

THE GOOD LIFE

My skin crawls. The overkill. The redundant *fuck you* of it all. Yes, Colton, we know you're living the good life. You own a fucking boat! And I know the way you know about a melon, as an old lady said in *When Harry Met Sally.*

You are on that dock. Near that dock. And Colton No Last Name is in your midst.

I don't know who he is but he does look familiar and I'm flipping through *Architectural Indigestion*s, hightailing it back to Instagram to a snippet of a wedding at the Oyster Harbors Club in 2019, fast-forwarding through all the faces, so red, so white. No dice, no fucking Colton, so I google *The Fucking Good Life* but it's a popular name for a boat—there is no way to fix this country, we are way beyond the fiberglass pale—and it's back to fucking Twitter, where it's another bust—Colton never mentioned Sly again—but it's not a total bust. He has a sister, and his sister is younger, not so private. Her name is the golden ticket.

Kathryn Fucking Hornblower.

Four hours ago, I would have assumed Kathryn plays a wind instrument, but I've gone native enough to know that Hornblower is an actual surname. Kathryn rarely tweets. Her Instagram is private. And I google the Hornblowers and Cape Cod, but I don't find an address. In an era when most people have no *choice* but to build a platform, the Hornblowers and their "kids" are an anomaly. They can afford to stay quiet, off the radar, shipping off on *The Good Life* when the mood strikes. Kathryn teaches little children, and her friends respect her privacy, but even the Hornblowers can't control *everyone.* Kathryn attended her five-year college reunion last year—So fun! So so *so* fun!—and you can ask people not to tag you, but some people on this planet are aggressive. If you say no to the tag they will work around it and they will *hashtag* you.

And I have *my* golden ticket, a picture of young Kathryn at Grendel's—ha!—and what a kick. We do have a lot in common with these Hornblowers, Wonder. We *go* to Harvard and they *went* to Harvard, and sure enough, their home on the Cape is listed in the alumni database.

I like the fucking Hornblowers. Their money isn't new, but it's not as old as I assumed and they built their Cape house in the nineties—those back issues of *Architectural Digest* are a godsend and the architect couldn't afford to be "private"—and I'm on my way to see you! The ride to the Cape is smooth and I don't have to worry about Colton being handsy. He got married six months ago—they registered at Bloomingdale's!—and I was inspired by looking at all their *prezzies,* so I made you a care package of things that can't be broken, a red scarf, a canister of oatmeal, a Brianna Holt book you pointed out in Trident, and a spoon I picked up out of a clearance bin at Crate and Barrel.

You always use this spoon in my house (apartment). You told me you wanted a whole set of spoons like this when you were younger. I bought a set, it's waiting for you at my home, and this single spoon is just the kind of symbolic tiny gift you'll appreciate.

The sun shines cold and Cool 102 calms me with commercial-free yacht rock and Kenny Loggins *smiles and tells me I'm the lucky one* as I cross the Cape Cod Canal and soon I'm here, and the village of Osterville is a postcard and Stop signs are slowing me down but Bonnie Tyler has my back—*Forever's gonna start tonight*—and the fairy-tale trees bend to the will of the wealthy, their bare branches forming a canopy—*Hands touching hands*—and I take a left onto Causeway Lane. The photos in the seven-page glossy spread about "the Houses of the Hornblowers" in *Architectural Digestion* didn't do it justice. They didn't give context, they didn't explain that the compound, where "Berlin meets Cape Cod Bay," is badass. Three three-story houses flip the bird to all the cookie-cutter Cape Codders I passed on the way here. This is where the cool kids live, and this is where *you've* lived. I hit the brakes.

Are you different? Will you even *want* to see me?

You've dwelled in these "urban cottages" and if you're anything like the *Hornblower kids*, you've roller-skated through the underground tunnels. The Berlin-based architect wanted to create "sexy family fun," which is why the tunnels connect all three houses. The Hornblowers refer to their underground playground as the *fungeon*. I know that because I read about it, but you have it all to yourself, and if you loved me, wouldn't you have invited me into it? Wouldn't you have realized that Sly was only using you to exact revenge on her dead husband? No, you wouldn't because you don't even know Sly. You don't know that she wrote *Scabies*.

You haven't called me. And I'm a cliché, parked on the side of the road like some pathetic fucking boyfriend with a formerly hot cold cup of coffee and a view of your family's dinged-up old Hyundai. I feel *so far away, doesn't anybody stay in one place anymore*? And I don't know that it would be *so fine* for you to *see my face at your door*. I crawled through bars to find you. I played Hide-and-Seek with S.B.'s kids and I went to Seekonk for you and I stole *Marriage* for you and clearly, I overdid it with the dick-shrinking cool classics of Cool 102.

I kill the engine of my Tesla—I have that going for me—and I get out of my car. You are "safe." You are alone. And then I hear Sly. *Love is not that, not at all.* The wind is against me, coming off the water, and that's nature. I am nature. Yes, I want you to see me, yes, I want to see you in the chef's kitchen, naked, wearing nothing but the red scarf. *You* are nature. You didn't change. You're still you—*Yankees Suck*—and you are curled up on a sofa three times the length of mine, a butter-soft sectional.

And I can't do it, Wonder. I can't be the one to break into your white room.

I turn around and the wind that was against me is with me now. You didn't put a ball gag on my novel. Sly did that, and I should get in my car and call Bernie and tell her what Sly did to *Me*. You need this time, and I learned a lot from my *author tour*. S.B. squirreled away in that Motel 666, plumbing the depths of my psyche, as if it's not good enough that she can hook a reader and hold them hostage. And then Sly, a bracketed widow so preoccupied by her mission to be the next this-one-meets-that-one that she can't be herself. But they're doing it, Wonder. They're doing the work. And why should those women get to be alone and not you? Because they grew up in homes like the ones on this street? Your whole life, you've put your writing on the back burner to focus on scratcher runs and wound vac lessons. You closed your laptop so that you could read *There's a Mouse in the House* to Caridad, and one day, you'll come back to me. That's when I'll tell you about the time I drove over the bridge and through the woods to see you in your white room, the time I did the right thing and let you be.

And then you scream.

"Joe!"

42

I drop the box that contains no breakables, and you lunge at me, and you want to have me and your lips are a salve. A homecoming. A *whiteout*. We bang like the autodidacts that we are, a couple of Bukowskis in the backseat of your car and I am the captain, and you are the captain and there are no books, there is no fellowship, there is no world outside of this car.

And then you put your sweater back on, like I'm nothing but a dick. Joe Erotic. "Sorry," you say. "I feel like I just attacked you."

"For the record, you don't have to apologize for jumping my bones."

It was a stupid thing to say and there is tension in this Hyundai, as if what I said was patronizing, and it hasn't been that long, but we are different. We forgot how to talk to each other, how to be, and it's your turf. You could invite me to come inside, to see the *three* fucking mansions, but instead we just sit here and are you going to *dump* me right now?

Was that breakup sex?

You are staring into space and I wrecked your white room and I never should have come here and you're not glowing and this is it. You smack your lips. "Okay," you say. "So it is you, I mean I missed you but also . . . omigod, I have the best news."

And I have the worst news: SLY FUCKED MY BOOK. "Well, come on tell me!"

"Babe . . . Okay, I'm just gonna say it. Sly sent my pages to Bernie and Bernie wants me!"

What am I supposed to say to you? Sly sent Bernie her *version* of your book.

"Congratulations."

"I mean would you look at the freaking email. *Dunkin' Sally Rooney.* Can you believe it? I have an agent!"

You hold up your phone and I scroll through the email. Below the nice words, there is a document attached: *FaithfulBacktoWonderSlyBernie.doc.*

"It looks like Bernie and Sly made notes. Did you look yet?"

You fold your arms and shift. "Why can't you just be happy for me? I'm not looking at any freaking 'notes' until I finish the book. This is my time to be happy . . ."

You're happy because you're Dunkin' Sally Rooney and I'm *not* happy because I'm Joe Erotic. I have to let you be happy. "Wonder, I'm sorry, okay? I am thrilled for you and one day, they'll refer to Sally Rooney as Irish Wonder Parish."

That did the trick—you love me all over again—and you stroke my cheek and tell me that you wanted me to show up. "I mean I couldn't *ask* you to come down here because Sly set me up and she was all about me hunkering down to write . . . but I missed you."

That's not the whole truth, but you look pretty. "I missed you, too."

"Wait," you say. "How *did* you find me?"

I pulled an all-nighter in the library. "Glenn mentioned the Hornblowers on one of our rides and it was a long shot but I figured what the hell, right?"

"I love you and I know I should have called you sooner . . . I'm a mess. I fucked up."

You should also confess to the fact that you stole my mouse, but I don't have any proof aside from your texts with Sly, and beyond that, I feel vulnerable enough as it is right now. You're Dunkin' Sally Rooney and I'm Joe Fucking Erotic.

"Don't beat yourself up, Won. Who cares how we got here? We're here. And the thing is . . . I also heard from Bernie."

It's clear from my tone of voice that the news was not good, but it's a little hurtful, the way you react, as if you were *expecting* the news to be bad. "Okay," you say. "If Bernie doesn't get you, I mean she's one freaking agent, Joe. There are tons of others."

"No," I say. "She wants to represent me."

You squeal like you just hit 25K on a scratcher and I let you down slowly, clearly. I explain what Sly did to my book. The great tanking of Joe Salinger-Goldberg. "So yeah," I say. "For some reason, Sly basically altered the DNA of my novel. She didn't *rewrite* it exactly . . ." That's what she did to *your* fucking book. "But she cut out the guts. I'm Joe Erotic."

"Well, no you are fucking not. I can't believe that bitch."

That's enough praise for now—you love my book—and you're not Dunkin' Sally Rooney, but you like *being* Sally Rooney. I don't want to burst your bubble. "Thank you, Won."

"You need to call Bernie right now and set her straight. Fuck it. *I'm* gonna call her and set her straight."

"Let's not worry about it. I'm just happy for *you*."

You wrap your arms around me. "Do you know how much I love you?"

I smile. "So, how's the writing going?"

You grunt. "Oh," you say. "The 'writing.' Well, yeah, I mean . . .

I'll just be straight with you. I was all freaked out about our stupid fight, and I called Sly and I think . . . I think this is why she did the whole 'Joe Erotic' rewrite thing."

Ya think? "Why didn't you call me?"

You shrug, as if you didn't participate in the ruin of my career before it even started. "I got scared . . . And Sly, she did kind of fuck with my head . . . about you."

She also fucked with your book. "I'm sorry to hear that."

"I want to bash her freaking face in."

That's a Goodreads girl, that's my girl, and I'm allowed to be loved by you. Protected. In time, you'll know the truth. But it's on *you* to open your notes. You shudder and you growl and I laugh. "You know you can't actually punch Sly in the face, right?"

"No," you say. "I'm also mad at me. I'm always telling you how I don't care what these people think of me and clearly . . . I mean I guess I kinda do. Like, when did that happen?"

It started when you were so self-conscious about our fellows that you edited your missives for the group text in your notepad. It escalated in the room when Sly pulled a reset, when she poisoned you with praise, and it went to the next level when you called her to talk about our fight instead of calling me, your boyfriend. Then you came here, and the transformation was complete. You drank all the Kool-Aid. "Wonder, it happens to all of us."

"Bernie wants me to finish as soon as possible, and I was like, *Sir, yes sir.* But it's what I told you from day one. *Faithful* is my life's freaking work. I'm supposed to work on it for the next several *years* and finish when I'm old and gray. I mean it's like . . . Who am I?"

I kiss the back of your hand. "You are the best thing that ever happened to me. And it's your book, so you take however damn long you need to finish it."

You grin. "Why do you always say the right thing?"

Because I hacked Sly's computer and read all those awful texts, because I'm the only man who ever took the time to get to know you. "Maybe I'm just a good writer."

You lick your lips and smile. "Well, that's another thing . . . So I lied to you."

This is good. "What do you mean?"

"I started reading your book at home, before I had my reset. It's putdownable in the good way where it makes you want to think about stuff. I didn't finish it yet, but . . ."

"But . . ."

"I get the same feeling I had with the Sox before we clinched that first World Series. And about the mouse in the house . . ."

"Wonder, I don't care about that anymore."

"Look, I did it, okay? I freaking 'stole' your mouse."

I know. "You did?"

"Your mouse reminded me of that book I got for Caridad, and it made me feel like we're soulmates. So, I put a mouse in *my* book as an Easter egg just for us."

It's what I wanted you to say, word for word. "Why didn't you just tell me?"

"Well, I fucked up, right? I was in too deep. I had already lied and told you that I didn't start reading it. And when you accused me of plagiarism, I felt so stupid, like what a dumb idea . . . a freaking *Easter egg*. I should have just been straight with you but I'm not good at this, Joe . . . relationships."

"Well, that's what I'm here for, so we can get better . . ." I hold your hand. "Together."

"All right," you say, and you lick your lips. "Does Joe Erotic wanna come in for a homemade Coolatta?"

43

Osterville is good for us and *we* are killing it. In some fucked-up way it's good that Sly put you in a cage, that you got a little taste of life without me. I love our new life as Horn-blowers and I'm in no fucking rush to reply to Bernie—erotica isn't like literary fiction, it's not seasonal—and I'm not *pushing* you to see what Sly did to your book. You're content, you're writing, and the writing supersedes the *business* of writing. Life *is good* here, Wonder. We were meant to live this way—*I was there when you were a queen*—and I might even let Sly have her fucking way with me . . . assuming they let me use a pen name to ensure that "Joe Erotic" is a faceless man of sexual mystery. I mean why the fuck not? It's fun to be rich!

I have a whole new preppy yachty wardrobe of corduroy pants and fisherman's sweaters I bought on Main Street—an actual cutesy fucking *Main Street*—and you tear tags off Lilly *Pulitzer* pink and purple shirts that replace your grungy Red Sox garb and I love you like this, no longer treating your body like a billboard for a bunch of ballers who don't deserve you. You look in the mirror and laugh—*Who am I right now?*—and I say the same thing every time: "You're Mrs. Hornblower, my darling." Every day that we're here, we drink from this well of confidence that we both knew was always there, a well we ignored, as if we needed it to be dry. It's filling up, and I agree with what you said last night, that the government should find a way to give all kids who grow up without privileges the chance to be the Hornblowers because let's face it, Wonder.

We're blowing those Hornblowers out of the water.

We are good at this life, at this house. We appreciate what they have in a way they probably can't, because it's all theirs. The shit ton of books, the actual *pet cemetery* in the backyard, *and* a Dunkin' in the "fungeon" with a bona fide *freaking* Coolatta machine.

And the best part isn't the safety of the high-thread-count sheets, or the way you periodically open drawers, in awe of the smooth ride, the way everything in this house just *works*. That's all nice, but it's material, and none of this would be good if my being here was bad for you when it comes to your writing. It's the opposite of what Sly said. I do *not* fuck your brains out, I fuck them *in* and you're *tick tick tap tap ticking* at a frenzied pace, and another beautiful giddy-up drumroll . . .

I am, too. I started a new book!

As it turns out, it's easier for writers to cohabit in a compound of houses than it is in a one-bedroom apartment. Who fucking knew, right? Each morning, we share a civilized morning sup in the breakfast nook in the kitchen in *your* house—this is how the good wealthy lord intended it, a nook for every meal—and then I walk through the tunnel from your house to *my* house—I chose the one with a view of the pet cemetery.

I sit at my desk and look out at the harbor and I remember that it doesn't matter whether we let Sly shape our books. Joe Erotic . . . Dunkin' Sally Rooney . . . It's all the same. We're not those phonies who "hate writing but love having written." You're a storyteller and

I'm a writer and you nailed it last night when we were cozy in a booth sharing a prissy pizza at *Crisp*.

"Sometimes I think being in the fellowship made me forget why I wanted to be there in the first place. I fucking love to write!"

That was a good line, so I pop it into my book—a little *Easter egg* for you, my darling—and I'm on a roll, so I give you a second *prezzie*. Two nights ago, we paid a jolly guy named *Mugsy* for entrée into "an actual freaking Foxhole." You loved it in that VFW joint. You tucked our nonlaminated Osterville Veterans Association membership cards into your wallet—that might be the cover of my second novel—and you looked at me with eyes full of rum and love. "Joe," you said. "When I sneak over to your house and tiptoe halfway up your stairs and hear you riding your MacBook Air the way you used to ride a stupid bike . . . Nothing makes me happier, babe. Or hornier . . ."

Writing hours fly by in a way that they didn't in Orlando, and my alarm pings—it's time for lunch!—so I save my new pages and bound down the stairs and there you are in one of your old T-shirts—YANKEES SUCK—and a new hot pink little cardigan.

"Hey, babe! I thought my fingers were gonna fall off so I broke a little early and went to Fancy's."

I thank you for being you and that's all it takes—it's time to christen the kitchen again—and after we fuck our brains out—we'll fuck them back in after we eat, before we go back to work—you peel the shrimp and I cut the sausage. We're making gumbo—you do so love *The Prince of Tides*—and you tell me that's "perfection," same way you did last night, when we went into the little village for something called a Christmas stroll. We smoked a joint with a pack of self-aware skater girls and boys in a parking lot and you were funny—*I didn't know they still made skater kids*—and we drank free cider and I called it a Winter Wonderland and you jabbed me, but you liked it. I know you did, because on the way home, we stopped at the library (closed), where Adirondack chairs were just fucking sitting there. You were stunned—*The trust*—and we rocked in those chairs, and we fucked in those chairs, and we know it can't last forever—the chances of all seven Hornblowers dying in a *private jet* crash are low—but it's like you said this morning.

"Isn't it funny how a cynical person would say that none of this is real because it's not ours? I mean I was just sitting there going over my pages and thinking about how wrong Sly was about needing to be alone in order to finish this thing, and it's like the power, you know? It's *so* freaking real and so help me God, when we go home and I'm all crazy-eyed in love with you and everyone's like 'Well, put any two people in a mansion and they'll be happy' I am just gonna bite my tongue and know how freaking wrong they are and feel sorry for them because no. Any two people could be happy here. But no two people could be *this* freaking happy and that's that." And then you kissed me. "Bye, Mr. Hornblower."

And then I kissed you. "Bye, Mrs. Hornblower."

And now, after we stuff our faces and fuck our brains back into place, we part ways and go back to work on our books and wait for night to fall and *oh, those winter niiiights.* So much better than summer. We meet down in the fungeon, and we talk for hours, going where we couldn't go in Cambridge, where life was hard, close, demanding. In my arms, in a faux-fur blanket, you ask if I ever miss Bainbridge.

I tell you the truth. "In Bainbridge I had this feeling that I was just making everyone uncomfortable in a way that was bad for all of us, kinda like day one in the fellowship, before you got there."

You grab my arm. You know what I mean. "You're so hard on yourself, babe. Tell me one thing you did that was really so terrible."

Kill RIP Ethel without letting her read the revision of my book. "Give up on myself. I mean in Florida, when I was a pity case, before I started writing, if I could go back in time, I'd apologize to some of the regulars, some of the customers, some of the women I met. I was just *not* in a good place and I don't feel good about it. What about you?"

You laugh and tell me that when you were young and stupid at

Dunkin', a guy who ghosted you showed up with another girl and looked right through you. One of your co-workers wanted to piss in his coffee, and you let him do it.

"Do you hate me?"

"No," I say. "Everyone's pissed in a cup of coffee at some point."

"Well, it wasn't my piss."

I kiss your head. "Smart."

The next day, same as every day. You are in your house writing about how *amazing* I am and I'm in my house writing about you and now, *here comes the night*. We're walking on the beach—it could be bigger—taking the stairs up to the dock where *The Good Life* is all tied up, tempting. You talk to me about your book, and I don't give you "advice." I don't crash your "white room" or articulate my concerns that you are going a little *too* Pat Conroy with the familial demons. It's your journey, it's your book. You elbow me. "You're not seriously considering going with the whole Joe Erotic thing . . . are you?"

"Do you know Patricia MacLachlan?"

"I don't think so."

"That's because she wrote *Sarah, Plain and Tall* . . . It's like a kid said to me in the Bainbridge Public Library. No one knows her other books because every book she wrote after her first was called *Not Sarah, Plain and Tall*. In other words, no. I'm feeling great about the book I started here, and . . . We'll just see."

You lean your head on my shoulder. "I think you need to call Sly and tell her where she can stick it."

Easy for you to say. You don't know what she did for *your* book, not yet. "It could be nice, though, I mean, the idea of having this kind of money. Joe Erotic would make bank."

You give a *hmm* because you know it's not the worst idea in the world. "Well, I like this whole owning nature thing."

"Me, too."

"And the world *is* a fucked-up place. Who knows if it's true, but I read that something like eighty-five gatekeepers rejected *Lolita* and ultimately . . ." This hurts a little, like you think I really *am* Joe Erotic, and you didn't even finish *Me* yet. But then you elbow me, hard. "You don't let *anyone* mess with your books."

I don't know what's worse, being Joe Erotic or being an aspiring unpublished dufus married to Dunkin' Sally Rooney while I hold your purse during your interview with Shayna from *Chronicle*. But they don't feature authors all *that* much and you hug me hard. Tight. And your smile is sad. "It comes down to cash, babe. If we were real Hornblowers, if we didn't have to be afraid of these freaking people, you would have called Sly and Bernie by now. Sly and Bernie, they love us, and they want what's best for us, but there's this little part of me, this nut that I can't freaking crack . . . If Sly did that to my book, if she did that to me . . ."

She did. "She would never. *Faithful*, what I've read so far, it's perfect. You know that."

"Hear me out, babe. I'm not the only one here with a *tendency to love*. If she did that to me, you would be all over me to call her. Hell, *you* would call her and hold her accountable. Don't take this the wrong way . . ." Uh-oh. "They slapped a label on you. They called you Joe Erotic. And that hurts. It's cheesy, but it's just another label. Think back to that first day on the lawn. O.-Freaking-K. stands for . . . I don't even remember . . ."

"Olivia Kimberly DeLuca."

"Olivia Kimberly called us autodidacts. I'm sure people have called her names, too. Someone's always gonna call you something, The best thing you can do, the only thing you can do, is tell 'em they got it wrong by *showing* 'em who you are."

Easy for you to say, Dunkin' Sally Rooney, and it's true what they say about ignorance. It is bliss. "So, you really believe in *Me*?"

"I'm not talking about any one book, Joe. It's deeper than that. I believe in *you*. You the person. I mean it's not like you to not say anything. You're honest."

I should tell you to open your notes right now. I should force you to see what she did to your fucking book but then you glance at *The Good Life* and smile. "Do we dare?"

I don't ask if you've ever had sex on a boat—I know the answer is yes, it's a *lamppost* in *Faithful*—and you don't ask me if I've ever had sex on a boat—you're the little green monster who gets jealous when I watch *Chronicle*—and fuck our stupid publishing conundrums. It's the beauty of earning the time with someone you love before you spend it.

We climb aboard and christen *The Good Life* for all the kids who never had a boat to christen, and the boat becomes the mother we never had, rocking us to dreamy, salty sleep.

I'm the first one up and is it a dream? No. We took *The Good Life* to a new level and I love you like this, your eyes closed and the slightest smile—you are dreaming about me—and it doesn't get any better than this. But then *lightning crashes*. Feet on the dock and a voice that shatters our womb in *The Good Life*.

It's her. It's Sly. She's *heeeeeeeere*.

44

You're not even halfway up the ladder before you start in with your "I'm sorries" which makes me the asshole boyfriend, which makes Sly the real Mrs. Fucking Hornblower, and finally, she tells you to stop it. "Honey, I'm not an ogre and you're Dunkin' Sally Rooney! It goes without saying, you're a big girl, Wonder, and you do *not* owe me any excuses." You're not a Goodreads girl, you're a *woman* and she shouts. "Now come on, Joe Erotic. I know you're in there!"

I climb out of *The Good Life*—this is too on the nose—and there you are, humbled and torn. Hopped up on a shot of Kool-Aid and not exactly ready to test your *tendency to love* theory by confronting our overlord/landlord. She stands there on our dock in the worst lavender coat of all, the one that's too small for her body, hiding her eyes behind sunglasses that are too big for her face because they're not meant for her face. They're not hers. They're Glenn's.

She waves. "Well, hello there, Joe."

You bite your lip like you're the babysitter who brought home a boy, and she takes off Glenn's sunglasses and oh shit. Oh no. I was wearing those fucking Ray-Bans the other day, the day I broke into her house to save our relationship, to save our *careers*. RIP Glenn gave me those Ray-Bans and I left them on her kitchen fucking counter. She's the serial criminal—she committed *fraud* on multiple occasions—but I am a man of my word—I will not break the cone of silence. You're apologizing a mile a minute—*I hope it's okay, he hasn't been here the whole time*—and she has proof of my petty "crime"— those motherfucking Ray-Bans—but I have no proof of *her* crime, the one that would make you see her for the pathological liar that she is. I can't prove what she did to Glenn with *Scabies* and yeah. You know what she did to *Me*, but I can't open the floodgates about that mess, not now, not *here*, when she's "forgiving you" for "being a horny little writer girl"—oh, fuck off—and you have been so puffed up, feeling *good* about who you are because you don't yet know what she did to *you*.

She really is the devil. She lifted us up to tear us down, same way she did her husband, may the poor bastard ride in peace.

The two of you finish making amends and your four eyes fall on me. I squint. I smile. "Breakfast?"

We go to your house, obviously. You're entitled to be here, unlike me, the porn-peddling white-room-wrecking boyfriend. I'm trying to save us. The invisible man in the kitchen cracking eggs—*You're a good egg*—and how is Sly going to play this? She knows I was in her house and she knows I know what she did to both our books—I left those fucking sunglasses right next to her laptop—and it helps to keep my hands busy. The sunglasses aren't a mug of piss. They don't really *prove* anything about me, and she wants you to be all about *you*. You would never believe I'd do a thing like that.

She asks if you've started thinking about a cover and you laugh that way you do when you're nervous. "Oh, Sly, please. *Faithful* is get-

FOR YOU AND ONLY YOU   355

ting good. I'm in it, I freaking *love* it, but I'm not done yet. Not even kind of."

"It's not 'good,' Wonder. It's fabulous. 'Course, honey, there might be a better title . . ."

She's pumping you full of Kool-Aid, so you're appeasing her, acting like you'd consider another title, as if you don't have *Faithful* tattooed on your left fucking ankle.

"Anyway," she says. "We don't have to worry about a title right now. That will come later, after we finish, when we get to all the fun stuff like your headshot and your acknowledgments and speaking of which . . ." She eyes me because she knows that I know about her *Marriage* "book" and I am an egg. Broken. Sizzling. "That's something else I wanted to mention. We should be thinking about a dedication."

"Oh well, that's easy," you say. "I mean the book is for my family."

She giggles and she is the teenage fucking babysitter, not us.

"Interesting," she says. "I thought you might have changed your mind and decided to dedicate it to your personal chef slash houseboy, but good on you, honey. Very good."

You tuck your hair behind your ears and look over your shoulder to see if I'm mad—Nope! Just cooking!—and she tells you that Bernie thinks *Faithful* could be a Reese's pick, and it does hurt a little, the way you light up as if everything Sly did to *my* book is water under the bridge to Hello Sunshine, but I let you know I'm not mad by shoving my way into the conversation.

"Wonder's really kicking ass, Sly. Full steam ahead, all day every day."

You get all puffed up in the good way—I am a hero—and Sly crosses her legs—I'm not here. "Well," she says. "It's good to know you're not letting him distract you, honey. And I take it this means you were good with the notes? Bernie and I expected you would be, but it's always fun to know for sure!"

No, no, no. You have a plan. You don't want to see those fucking notes. Looking at their handiwork will only distract you from finishing *Faithful*. You know this. You said this! And, yes, I have to think about myself here. If you look at your notes then we're going to talk about *my* notes and I haven't decided how to handle it—writers need time to *think*—and you reach for your phone—where is your fucking spine?—and I tap my spatula on the counter. "Wonder, come on. Remember the plan."

"Right," you say. "The plan. Okay, so, yeah . . . The notes. I'm not ready to look. I wanna go full steam ahead and finish this draft before I start messing around with it. So that's my plan!"

Thank you, lord, and thank you, Wonder, and maybe the sunglasses are *just my imagination*. Sly nods. "I can respect that. All that matters right now is that you know how much Bernie loves you. She has big plans for *Faithful*, Wonder. We are both so excited for you."

You squeal and I freshen your coffee and you toss your napkin on the table and offer to help. I tell you I'm fine—"It's just eggs"—and Sly can't stand the sight of us, so she's up. "Keep your clothes on, you two. I'm just running to the loo!"

The second she's gone you whisper. "Say something."

"Wonder, no. She came here to see you, and it's going well."

"But what about you? What about Joe Freaking Erotic?"

"We're fine."

"You're *not* fine. You're mad and I'm mad for you and maybe there's more to it. Maybe . . . I mean come on. You gotta say something. Talk to her. Call her out."

"You have an agent. I have an agent . . . if I want. Let's just be smart. There's no rush."

"But you're *not* Joe Erotic."

And you're not Dunkin' Rooney. "I know." I remember what RIP Glenn said. *She's a storyteller. You're a writer. There's a difference.* "Won, I'm not even supposed to be here, so let's just hang out, keep it mellow, and I'll talk to her when I'm ready."

As in not in front of *you*—the sunglasses, Wonder, the *sunglasses*—and you say it's not fair, that you want things to be "square," and I tell you the world is round and you roll your eyes—*Whatever, babe*—and her bathroom break was too fast. She's back. "Wonder, honey, let the man work before he burns our omelet . . . Or is that a frittata? Never mind! Surprise us!"

You begrudgingly return to the breakfast nook and I go back to "work"—I'm a chef—and Sly rhapsodizes about the Hornblowers and their generosity, and you thank her profusely for giving *us* the opportunity to be here, and I know you're trying to help me, trying to open the door for me to say my piece, but you're poking the tiger and the tiger is feeling it.

She grins. "So, did Joe tell you *his* good news? I helped him, too!"

I slide the eggs onto a platter that probably costs more than my sofa—"Soup's on!"—and you chug coffee to stop yourself from saying that you know she "helped" me and you can't do things like that in front of a writer. She saw it in your eyes. She knows that you know what she did to me, and you're Dunkin' Wonder. Fair-minded and leading with "love." You want the two of us to hash it out, but I told you I don't want that and you are my true fellow, aware of my wants and needs. You pivot. "So much good news lately! I mean how great is it about Ani?"

Sly says it's "so great"—oh, bullshit, jealous liar—and I smile. "What's up with Ani?"

You groan in the good way, the girlfriend way. "Babe, come on. The *New Yorker* story . . ."

I saw it in the Motel 666, but I didn't fucking read it. "Oh, right! The Ani profile . . ."

You beam, always happy to be happy for people. "I love how they drew her and it's huge! Her play is going to Broadway, the one she's been working on . . ."

Sly shudders. "Theater . . . I so prefer fiction."

Fuck you, Sly, and bless you, Wonder, picking up your phone to check the group text, to keep us in chat mode. You say that you and I are going back tonight to meet up with our fellows and celebrate Ani's play and that's news to me. Sly laughs—"Men"—and you whip me with your napkin because I *never* look at the "group freaking text." I smile like the idea of leaving *The Good Life* sounds good—it does not— and you ask our guest if she'll be joining us at Grendel's tonight and she scoffs. "Oh God no. See, honey, I'm writing, and when *I* write, it's just me and the words . . ."

You lick your lips and call my eggs "a freaking revelation" and she looks down at her plate. "Drat," she says. "Are those . . . mushrooms?"

"Yep! I went to Fancy's while Wonder was working."

"Aw, well that's fine," she says. "You don't normally see porcini mushrooms with eggs, but this is all new to you two . . . the *Fancy's* of it all."

Uh-oh. You stopped chewing. You're mad. But come on. So, she looks down on us. So what? Fortunately, you force yourself to smile. "So, Joe's also killing it. He started a new book."

"Excellent," she says. "I adore a little erotica now and then so I can't wait to read it. Honey, could you pass the salt?"

Shot fired. I reach for the salt but you grab it out of my hand like you're about to shoot *back*. And then you roll up your napkin and drop it on your plate. "Enough is enough. I know what you did to his book, Sly. And I'm sure you have your reasons, but you gotta know . . . he's not happy right now. So can we just . . . can we clear the air and talk about it?"

"Excuse me?" She looks at you like she's in a foreign country, like it's your job to speak her fucking language.

My turn. "Wonder, we don't have to talk about this now."

"Well, I'm sorry but yes we do, okay? There's a freaking elephant in the room. Sly, he showed me his book. You cut all his monologues. Sliced and diced it and I'm sure you have your reasons, but it's like . . . You don't go chopping up someone's *baby* without asking for permission and furthermore . . . He is not Joe Erotic. You really hurt his feelings, okay?"

She fusses with the Ray-Bans. "Could someone please pass me the salt?"

No can do because you're not letting go, and this isn't about *Me*. This is about you. Your tendency to love is cracking. You are Cameron at the end of *Ferris Bueller's Day Off* and you want the heat. Your voice trembles. "You hurt my feelings too, Sly."

"Aw, honey," she says. "I think you're tired. Do you want a Klonopin?"

But no, you don't want her drugs. "Sly, please correct me if I'm wrong . . . but it feels like you messed with Joe's book to punish him for messing with me."

She laughs—"a punishment!"—and you are stern, so stern. I've never seen you this way. You are one of them, a Hornblower, a Rooney. You tell her that you trusted her. You called her when you were vulnerable, when you were at odds with me, scared that we were over. And then you shake your head. "Girl to girl, woman to woman . . . It's not right. Me and Joe . . . we worked things out, and relationships can be messy. But messing with his *book* . . . Tell her, Joe."

I have to say *something*. "It would have been nice to get a heads-up."

You wanted me to fight harder, and I didn't, and she almost laughs. "Wonder, honey, I hate to disappoint you, but wow . . . you really are overtired if you think it was some sort of Machiavellian 'punishment' . . . I was trying to help him get a deal. I know your boyfriend here isn't *really* Joe Erotic."

"Damn straight," you snap.

"But do you . . ." No. No, please no. "Wonder, honey . . . do you really think you're Dunkin' Sally Rooney?"

MAYDAY! MAYDAY! You pick up your phone—not here, not now, I told you to leave it alone—and Sly clutches her Ray-Bans and

Donna Tartt is out of the bag. You're reading your book that isn't yours, not anymore, and she's waxing about your "simplistic" vocabulary, and you want to know what happened to your lampposts and she sighs. "Honey, Bernie and I found all those one-night stands of yours to be a little off-putting. We don't need a powerful woman screaming about her indiscretions in her own *novel*."

"You are slut-shaming my freaking character."

"No," she says. "I just think we should leave the graphic sex to our friend Joe Erotic . . ."

That was a low blow, and I am here to lift you *up*. "Sly, if you ask me, the lampposts are what bring the book together."

You thank me but she shudders. "He's only saying that because you want to hear it, Wonder."

I tell you that's not true, even if it is, a little, and you have a new bone to pick. "Okay, no," you say. "This scene with my dad, this is not how it went down."

"Honey," she says. "It's fiction. You are loyal to the work, not your family. It's about what readers want from the spunky Boston girl. And it's nothing to feel bad about. Everyone needs notes. *Everyone.*"

You grunt—"Except Sally Rooney"—and she says not to compare yourself to *rock stars* as if she isn't the one who compared *you* to a fucking rock star. You fight back tears—*I don't know what some of these words even mean*—and I say your name, but you can't look at me and I can't save you. You *believed* it. You drank the Kool-Aid and you were a haughty Hornblower and you liked being Dunkin' Sally Rooney more than you liked being Wonder Parish. It's over.

RIP Dunkin' Sally Rooney.

I reach for you, and you flinch. Too ashamed to let me love you, as if I would ever stop loving you for being human, vulnerable.

Our enemy twirls her Ray-Bans. "Everyone needs help. *Everyone.*"

You slap your phone on the table and snarl. "You're a fucking *louse.*"

"Well, that's lovely."

"I trusted you."

She sighs. "Here we go again . . ."

"I know you're not in the best place. I know you're mourning, but how . . . How freaking *dare* you?"

Sly looks at me and tilts her head and says the worst thing she could say: "Why didn't you give her a heads-up, Joe?"

You look at me with different eyes. Cold and closed off. "You knew?"

"Wonder, no, I didn't know. Of course not."

But Sly groans. "Oh, please, honey. Of *course* he knew."

She's in paradise, watching you fall out of love with me and go back to staring at your phone like a cashier on break. That isn't you and this isn't us. Everyone gets paranoid when they're exposed, when the nightmare comes true and they walk to the front of the classroom in their underwear. You believe in me and I have faith in you and this is temporary. You're embarrassed about the way you were with me, sauntering around like the next big thing, and it's okay! It's okay to get a little chock-fucking-full of yourself. You don't have to hide from me.

"Wonder," I say. "It doesn't matter. It's all bullshit. Notes. Brands . . . You're in the 'white room,' remember? You don't look at notes until you freaking finish." Did you feel that? Did you feel me speaking your language. "Forget it. It doesn't matter."

You don't take your eyes off your phone. "It's a simple question. Did you know about this, Joe? Yes or no?"

Joe, not *babe*. "No. I didn't know. I'm in shock. Sly, you did it to her, too?"

"Oh, please, honey. Of *course* he knew."

"I didn't. And they're just notes. Fuck 'em. Everything you said to me about *my* notes, that goes for you, too."

You're processing my words and I glance at Sly and there's a human inside of her after all. She's staring at the floor like a normal, like a widow, just a person who misses her person, slowly realizing that there is no way around her grief, that messing with us won't bring her any joy, only pain. She's not even touching the Ray-Bans anymore—they live on her head now—and I can save us. All of us. This is life after the death of Dunkin' Sally Rooney. I can already feel you coming back down to earth, letting me rub your *little shoulder*. We made it, Wonder. We're gonna be okay.

And then no we're not because Sly pulls those Ray-Bans off her head and waves them in my face. The missile is imminent, incoming.

"By the way," she says, looking at me, and then you, and then me again. "You left these at my house when you broke in the other day."

45

I envy our fellow Lou. If I were him, unprincipled and egotistical, the kind of guy who fills his novels with *crazy ladies*, I would light a hand-rolled cigarette and put an end to this right now, just fucking say it, tell you that Sly wrote *Scabies for Breakfast*, that she hates herself for doing it and despises me for knowing what she did. And then I would ride off into the sunset on my '82 Harley and hide from all you *crazy ladies* in the belly of a riverboat casino.

But that ain't me, Wonder. I don't break my promises.

And you are clear-eyed. *Faithful*. Staring at Sly like *she's* crazy—yes!—and she picks up on your disbelief and waves her hands as if she can take it all back. "Never mind, honey. Forget what I said. I certainly don't want to spend our time talking about him. I came here to see you, and before either of you fly off the handle . . . Don't fret. I'm not about to call the police and file a report. I don't trust the police and I have no patience for the tedium of their 'reports,' no interest in holding Joe accountable as it's not my job to rehabilitate all the broken men. All I want is . . . Well, Joe, if you care about Wonder and her work, this this might be your cue to leave."

I open my mouth, but you tell me to *shut* it and you look at her. "Are you serious? You accuse him of breaking into your house? He is not the bad guy. You did this to my book, not him, you."

That's right! "Amen."

Sly sighs. "Honestly, Wonder . . . He fills his book with patronizing and vaguely misogynist rants about how women always leave him, and you have this perfectly nice piece of feminist blue-collar fiction that can soar without those embarrassing diary entries about your *sex* life. I'm not the enemy! And I'm willing to let it go, the house thing. Seriously."

As in willing to lord it over me for the rest of my life. You see her, Wonder. You're too mad to say fuck you, too restrained from all those years behind the counter, but you say it just the same. "I think that's your cue to leave, Sly. You should get some help."

She's not going anywhere—nice try, though—and she claims that she's trying to help you. You tell her that you write for yourself and no one else and I tell you that I love you and she groans. "Would the two of you just stop it? I am right. About all of it. Nobody wants to hear some random white man railing against women and nobody needs to know that Dunkin' Wonder fucked half the men in Boston. Especially when one of those men is a criminal because yes, breaking into a house . . . it *is* a crime. But I told you. I'm over it."

That's a fucking lie and again, you ask her to leave but she waves the Ray-Bans in your face—I told you she's not over it—and you tell her that I am not a criminal, that *you* are over it, over her and Bernie, the whole publishing business. "It's toast," you say. "I'm done."

But that's *also* a lie. The worst one yet. I don't want you to give up your dreams.

She taps my sunglasses. "Well, Wonder, if you want to throw away your career to defend a trespassing erotica writer who accuses you of plagiarism, there's little I can do to help."

You shake your head and tell her she's on *thin freaking ice* and she didn't anticipate you defending me with such ardor. She didn't expect me to honor the cone of silence. You were right about her—she hates us because we are loyal, because we stick to our fucking guns—and she hisses at me. "But you did break in! And then you hacked into my computer. You saw Wonder's book and you saw *my* book and you are a criminal. You did it, and I *know* it!"

She sounds paranoid. You hear it, too. This is good. The calmer I am, the crazier she'll seem—it's Gaslighting 101—and I laugh like I'm offended, because who wouldn't be offended?

"Sly," I say. "I think Wonder's right. I think you need some help."

She might lose control and hit *me* but instead she goes after you. "He's lying, Wonder. When he realized that I helped him with *his* novel, he broke into my house, probably planning to smack me around . . ." I have never laid a hand on you, and you know it. "I wasn't home, thank God, but my computer was right there. He saw your book. And did he tell you? No. If he had even a modicum of respect for you, he would have given you a heads-up."

I tell you that none of this is true, and you don't look at me, and she works harder on you. She is an evil genius, determined to break us apart, same way she broke her husband by ghostwriting *Scabies for Breakfast*. She won't stop until the work is complete, and the best writers are like this, part sociopath, *obsessed*.

"Honey," she says, channeling her inner kindergarten teacher. "This man accused you of plagiarism and still I helped him find his way. I helped you find *your* way. That's what people like me do for people like you. We help. Everyone in your position . . . they need a little help,"

The smoking gun is in her hands, the sunglasses, but there's no smoke rising from those fucking *sunnies* and that phrase—*people like you*—that was her mistake. You didn't like that. "So, that's how it is, huh? You think because we're not little elites, we're bottom-feeder criminals breaking into your freaking *house*?"

"Don't do that, Wonder. Don't lump yourself in with him. He only came here because he finally felt superior to you, superior because he was keeping a *secret* from you, because he knew that I believed in you as a serious writer in a way that I most certainly did *not* believe in him. He wanted you to be blindsided because he's mad that I see him as Joe Erotic, but you . . . You have the potential be something *great*. Don't let him do this to you, Wonder. Don't fall into his trap. This is all about his ego, honey. Think about it. Trust yourself. You know I'm right."

She's a little too fucking good at wordplay—you heard everything she said, you are backsliding—so I go even lower than she went just now. "All right, Sly, this is the last time I'm gonna say it. I didn't break into your house. I had no idea that you messed with Wonder's book and it's okay . . . No harm, no foul. You're in mourning. We get it."

My little plan worked, and she snaps. The loneliest, dumbest genius in the world, Donna Quixote, tilting at windmills. "Don't you see it, honey? He's a monster. A liar. I'm trying to *help* you and I did help you and you're really going to do this? You're going to throw away your career for this pathologically controlling *burglar*? What about your precious family?"

"You do not go there, Sly. You do not talk about my family."

Sly lost *some* credibility the second she went there with the sunglasses, but she lost you completely when she said the f-word. You're on your feet. "Listen, bitch . . ." Whoa! "You're not the boss of me or my book and I would never use the word *malefactor* when I could just say what I mean . . ." This is *The Real Fellows of Harvard University* and are you going to flip this table? "I'm a good person, I can see you're in hell, but I call 'em like I see 'em. You're a cunt."

Sly gasps like a Hornblower on a tennis court raging about a bad call and you don't flip the table. You point at her. "I trusted you with my art, with my life. I went to you writer to writer, and you fucked with my boyfriend, and who knows? Maybe you're right. Maybe he did know."

"Wonder, I didn't know anything."

You tell me not to *fuck with you* right now, and oh fuck, oh no. Damn your instinct, your intuition, the way you sense that only one of us at this table was surprised by what she did to your *freaking* lampposts.

"Mark my words," you snarl. "My book will never be published without my lampposts. I have integrity. I don't slander people. I wouldn't cut up someone's art and call it 'help.'"

"This is true," she says. "If you bring that white room arrogance into the real world, your book will never see the light of day. Publishing is a *business*. If this is all you want . . . the 'experience,' the vacation with your boyfriend, then I've been wasting my time as well as my resources. A good writer gratefully accepts guidance from people with more experience."

You now: "Meaning *you*? You don't even *know* how to write a good book."

Sly rubs the back of her neck, just like her dead husband used to do. You thought you were stabbing her in the heart, but you don't know that the only baby she's proud of is *Scabies*.

"Wonder, you realize that you're only in this fellowship, not to mention this house, because I put up a fight for you. Did Joe tell you that? That I'm the reason you're here."

You stab your chest with your finger, and doesn't that hurt? "No," you snap. "I'm the reason I'm here. Because *I'm* a good *freaking* writer."

She just sighs. "I miss Glenn." Oh no, let's not drag *him* into this, but too late. "You see, Wonder, he sensed this in your writing, a sort of defiance that would hold you back. I wanted him to be wrong, but . . . Well, my husband was right about a lot of things."

Your foot is shaking. I want you to remember that your tendency is to love, that the best love is patient. Contemplative. You wait a week to review a book after you finish it because reactions are not reviews. If you walk away right now, you will come around to see that you can *learn* from her notes. She's not right about all of it—I like your *freaking*s—but she is right about *some* of it—your lampposts are dragging you down. This is a battle—you said the c-word—but it's not Wonder's Last Stand. Writers explode. They say things. She could still help you and I don't want you to lose your shot at being Dunkin' Sally Rooney because of your *tendency to love* everyone and everything more than you love yourself, your work.

She goes there again—"And Glenn would know how to handle this"—and you groan.

"All right, no," you say. "Real talk. *Scabies for Breakfast* can honestly . . . it can blow me. It's an overrated soulless excuse of a book about 'God' and it reads like he was painting by numbers, as opposed to you with your freaking *finger paints*. And here's a fact. Your pompous hack bike-riding husband is the reason I almost didn't even *apply* to the fellowship. You cry over him, but you should know, *woman to woman* . . . the douchebag sent me dick pics. So put that in your pipe and smoke it."

Sly bursts into tears and runs into the *sitting room* and throws herself onto the sectional. You think she's bawling because her filthy husband sent you pictures of his penis—did he?—but you're the only one in this house who doesn't know that her ego lives in *Scabies*, not *Flour Girls*. You didn't break her heart—you killed her *ego*.

I go to you. "Wonder, will you look at me?"

But you won't look at me. You just outgrew your *tendency to love*. You don't run in there to make her stop crying. You gave the first honest gut-punch one-star review of your life, and you gave it to our teacher, and you did it out loud, in front of me.

"I'm gonna ask you one last time. Did you know what she did to my book?"

This again, as if you want her to ruin what we have. "Wonder, no. I didn't know."

You shrug off your Lilly Pulitzer cardigan and throw it in the nook. You would do that to me if you could, and you can. You're doing it right now, refusing to look at me. "Joe, I don't know how you got your hands on my pages, but I know that you know what she did to 'em.

You kept that from me, and the worst part of it all . . . She's a little freaking *right*."

"Wonder, no."

"Yes, you liked watching me swan around like Dunkin' Sally Rooney. You don't think I'm good, not like that, not like her. *That's* why you didn't want me to look at the stupid notes. You don't think I'm for real."

"That is not true."

"You worship these people. You probably *will* be Joe Erotic because you would do anything for the money. You want to be one of them, even if it means being something you aren't."

"You're mad at her, not me."

"I'm not a simpleton, Joe. I can be mad at two people at once. And Sly's not . . . She's nothing to me. She is what she is."

I hate that saying. It's not a writer's point of view—even Lou doesn't fall back on that in *O'er Fucking Under*—and it's not you. You don't give up on things, on me. "Wonder, don't let her do this to us. I never lie to you. You know me. I love you."

You glance at the eggs I made for you. "Strip the bed before you leave. Show the maid the respect you didn't show me."

We're here again, in the dark. But it's different this time. Emotions run higher in the houses of the Hornblowers than they do in the real world, in our world. You are over it, over me, *o'er* us.

46

Mad as you were in Osterville, you had a long drive home. I thought you'd get in your Hyundai and let the smooth, soft hits of Cool 102 bring it all down a notch. I hoped that you'd be knocking on my door by now, having come around to see that we *both* drank the Kool-Aid, that we *both* got screwed over, that it was your fault for trusting Sly with details about our life together. But I haven't heard a peep from you, which is why, for the first time in my life as a Shoddy fellow, I don't open the group text and think *The horror! The horror!* I see your written commitment to be at Grendel's at 7:00 P.M. and I think, *The wonder, the wonder.*

Nothing that happened in the houses of the Hornblowers was about you and me. Sly was the driving force. We weren't ourselves. We got too comfortable in there and this is why I prefer to pay my own way at a hotel. A hotel doesn't let you forget that it can never be home.

In any case, Ani's party is a chance for us to sit in a circle with our fellows and *clap-clap-clap* for Ani. A *reset* for you and me, minus the fucking *balloons*.

I'm almost to Grendel's and I'm feeling good. If you think about it, this is how it started. We sat in a circle. You looked at me and I looked at you and we knew that we were not like the others. We started out as strangers, as fellows, and what happened this morning doesn't erase the past few months and you're already here and I saw you see me when I entered the bar and you miss me.

I hoist a bottle of Dom. "Ani! Hooray for Manhattan!"

Ani welcomes me with a big hug—See that, Wonder?—and there's a chair waiting for me, same way there was a chair waiting for you, because this is our home. *I* am your home. You ice me out and our fellows are writers, so they sense a little something off, but our fellows are polite, so they don't actually fucking say anything about it. I look at you so you look at Ani. "So what happens next, Ani? With your play? When can I come see it?"

"It's just like a book," she says. "My new director has *lots* of notes, and I'll be gutting the whole thing as we workshop it because writing is rewriting and . . . We need more shots!"

You laugh but did you hear what she fucking said? Do you get it now? Everyone rewrites everything, even Obie winners like *Ani*. She didn't fire her director for giving her a few notes.

"Well, what do you think, Joe?"

I missed the question—See what you're doing to me? To us?—and I tell Lou it's the damn bar, the damn music. He repeats. "Did you hear about Sly? She got a DUI last week."

I flash my eyes at you but you're just sitting there, pretending to wind your fucking *Swatch*.

"Oh shit. Where?"

"It's terrible," Ani says. "And I hate to be that person, but I saw this coming. It was too much. Don't get me wrong . . . I love the whole kindergarten approach . . ."

"Actually," Sarah Beth says, "I've been locked up in a motel room trying to forget about those balloons and Sly's whole 'kindergarten' approach, but you guys on the other hand . . . I think I really have something, and I'm so grateful to all of you."

She half-winks at me—did you see that?—and there's something different about Sarah Beth tonight. It's her hair. Her unusually small purse. Her lack of Wheat Thins.

Mats sighs and looks heavenward. "Earth to Sly! We're not in kindergarten!"

You're gonna run out of things to do with your Swatch, but this is what you do. Hide from everything that's complicated. Lou says while it's "great" that Sarah Beth "thinks" she has something, we're still getting screwed. Sly is simply not a good writer. "Did anyone even read *Flour Girls*? She has no business running the room, and it's sort of 'smash the patriarchy' upside down, because there are many women who *do* deserve to be there . . ." He looks at Ani. "Many *Black* women, many brown women, many—"

"I know," Ani says, cutting him off before he lists every color in the rainbow. "Ever since she came in, I've had this queasy feeling that it's icky, taking the husband's job without having earned it."

We talk about the potluck you bailed on, and you're still in outer space, still staring at your Swatch.

Sarah Beth's turn now: "It disturbed me and inspired me when she felt the need to say she didn't like her husband."

"Bananas," Lou says. "Rotten, mushy bananas."

Mats informs us that he has a friend who works in a restaurant near Beacon Hill. You try to change the subject—"What place?"—but your little plan fails.

"I probably shouldn't say anything, but apparently . . . Okay, so my friend from MIT, her wife has this restaurant which is great by the way . . . *Bananas* . . ." Poor Lou laughs way too hard, and clearly, I missed some inside joke about bananas. "Anyway, last week, Sly was in there, drinking like a fish, messed up on pills, railing about . . ." Me? You? "Us."

Ani gasps—"No!"—and Sarah Beth beams—psycho—and everyone wants all the dirty details about our pill-popping kindergarten teacher. You slap the table with both hands, Sly *earned* a bad review from her students—she gave us finger paints—but I know what you're going to say before you even say it. "You guys, wait . . . Maybe we should leave it alone. I mean she's a wreck."

No. She's a cunt. And you're regressing, leaning back into your tendency to love, defending Sly to our fellows because this is the story of your life. You find warmth in your heart for people you don't like, people who do wrong by you, books that disappoint you, customers and friends . . . family. I remember what you said on our real first date—*Everyone is an asshole*—but it's a cop-out if you're not willing to admit that some people are *major* fucking assholes. I thought you grew today. I thought you changed and saw Sly for the controlling evildoer that she is, but you can't change, can you, Wonder? You try to end the "smack talk," as if she's been good to you, good to me, good to anyone at this table, and you're wasting your energy. You can't stop a rising tide, and *this* is what the Algonquin round table was made for, the overdue teardown of a finger-painting empress with no clothes, and Lou nudges you. "Relax, Won."

I look at you. I am *here* for you. Mad for you. Crazy for you. But you bury your hands under your legs and it's the same way you were on the first day. You're pulling away from all of it, the fellowship, me, your dreams. I have X-ray vision, Wonder Parish. The more shit they talk about Sly, the more you're sitting there building her defense in your head. You're infuriating. Whether or not Glenn sent you pictures of his dick—did he?—the man was bad to you, same way Sly was bad to you. Why won't you just hate her? Why do you want to hate *me*? Don't you get it? Your *tendency to love* is meant to be reserved for people who deserve that fucking love. People like me. I see you fidgeting, refusing to realize that there are people on this planet who don't deserve your heart, your forgiveness, your love. You can't love every person and you can't love every book, but you can love me. I deserve your love, your "forgiveness"—I did nothing wrong—and I'm right here. All you need to do is look at me for one split fucking second, but you won't do it.

And the floodgates are open. Lou wants a coup and Mats will drink to that—*Glenn was focused on the work, not the writer's identity*—and now would be a great time for you to tell everyone that *Glenn* was no good either, that he sent you pictures of his fucking penis. But that might not even be true—I think you were just trying to hurt me and Sly with one punch—and Sarah Beth has an idea.

"Okay," she says. "We march into the department together and we demand someone new."

Ani can't see it happening—"We're not getting a *third* Shoddy"— and Lou says it's not the world's *worst* idea and then he touches your elbow. "I wonder what you think, Wonder?"

He actually thinks that was clever and you gulp. "I think we need to talk about something else. Did anyone read any good books lately?"

That gets the laughter it deserves because for fuck's sake, Wonder. Are you really this weak? You gave her the worst review of her life and now you're going to shame us for being spine . . . *full*? "Look," you say. "You guys keep forgetting . . . she lost her husband."

Sarah Beth looks at you like she thinks you're lucky to be alive. "Wonder, I feel the worst for you in all this, the way she used you to claim authority in the room."

I want Sarah Beth to stop trying to *kill* you and you squirm. "Used me?"

"Well, yeah," Lou says. "I would 'use' that word. It was insulting. Calling a 'reset' and fucking with your process, as if you're so delicate that you can't take a little criticism, as if Glenn's critique sent you into some fucking spiral . . ."

That's exactly what it did, and it's the reason I killed him, and don't you see how much you need me? I want to change the subject, but in some fucked-up way, this is what you need right now, a little tough love from your fellows.

"It was awful," Mats says. "The whole 'I'm calling my dead husband a contrarian so I can gaslight you with finger paints and be a *real* contrarian.' She treated you like a kid who got picked on in gym class."

The gym class reference sends the conversation to a new boring place—Dodgeball sucks, we *know*—and you're unbelievable, Wonder. After all Sly did to you, after all you said to her, you're tugging Ani's shirt, campaigning for your abuser—*I feel like she might have a problem with pills*—and Ani's not here for it—*It's not our job to take care of her, especially when she doesn't take good care of us*—and Ani is right.

"All right," you say. "Mats, what was Sly's big fix for you?"

He looks at you like you're from another planet, because you are. "Big fix?"

"Well, yeah. You got a deal, and I could get a deal, but before Sly sent my book to Bernie, she messed with my book. She totally changed it. What did she do to yours?"

Oh, Wonder, you are barking up the wrong fucking tree. He is glib. Blunt. "Um . . . nothing."

You take a big swig of your drink. You don't like these people. You're thinking, *Fuck these people.* But that's not fair, Wonder. Our fellows are good people. They're all doing great things and they will all continue to do great things. Mats and Ani and Sarah Beth are set for life, basically, and Lou . . . Well, he can't pay his rent with *O'er Under* royalties, but he'll turn it around, take the *lady* to Georgia, where he'll work at an Arby's and chop wood and claim it's all "research." They all have something we lack, a natural immunity to the Sly Carons and the Glenn Shoddys that enables them to laugh at those people in a way that we can't. They're in their lives and they didn't need the fellowship. You and I were always different. We were the raw terrain and Sly colonized us because she could, because Ani and Mats and Sarah Beth and even Lou, they are their own territories, their own writers, powered from within, impervious to Kool-Aid. I have no ill will for them, or this table or the fellowship. It brought us together—*I was there when you were a queen*—but now it's tearing us apart.

The more they criticize Sly Caron, the more you send yourself back to the service sector to protect her, to wipe out all the terrible things she did to you. The farther you get from being the real you, the woman who spoke truth to power in the breakfast nook, the farther you go from me.

I stand. "Well, I'm outta here!"

Ani balks. "So soon?"

I make my way around the table—*Duck, duck, hug*—and I make sure that you hear me tell our fellows that I'm going to New York.

Ani lights up. "Ooh fun!"

And she's right. It would be fun to go to New York with you, and I know that you wish you were going with me, but when I make my way to your part of the table, you don't stand. You don't look at me and you sure as hell don't embrace me.

You just stir your drink and sigh. "Have fun."

I run up the stairs and I don't loiter.

We'll do it, Wonder, we'll have the happy ending I didn't get with the last writer I loved, a romantic run around a *real* city, the *Annie Hall* dream date where I show you all my old haunts and we *boogaloo down Broadway*. But it's not time for that yet, and it's just as well that you drink your feelings and wait until tomorrow to chase me down. My work in this state isn't done.

I still need to make you a *prezzie*.

47

Forgery is a deeply American dark art. A way of making the world your own. When I was in grade school, the gatekeepers sent us home with permission slips. They wanted all our parents to sign off on a field trip to Mystic Seaport, as if all parents are the same, at the ready with homemade cookies and ballpoint fucking pens. My folks weren't around and I wasn't gonna miss out on climbing the rafters at the seaport because of them. I studied my mother's signature on bad checks I found in the junk drawer, and I nailed it on the permission slip, and I *climbed* those fucking rafters. Forgery is a means to an end, and when done well, it's inspiring. Look at Lee Israel. She got fed up with publishing and made a boatload of cash forging all the great authors. Oh sure, she got jammed up in prison, but eventually she told her story in a memoir, and her book became a movie starring Melissa Fucking McCarthy. *Can You Ever Forgive Me?*

Well, yes, Ms. Israel. Yes, we can.

Forgery requires derring-do and chutzpah. You have to put it all on the line for a goal. You give people what they want to get what *you* want. It's like anything. Do it once, succeed, and stop yourself from going forward with greed à la Ms. Israel. An ultimate bucking of all systems of corruption that keep a lot of good people down and you know what else, Wonder?

I'm pretty fucking good at it.

I sit at Sly's kitchen table studying her bills, her signed books. I get frustrated at times, and I remember how nice it is to have a cat. I feed Donna Tartt. I find some tutorials online and most important, as with all arts dark and light . . . I don't give up. I have to sound like Sly and the words have to *look* like Sly.

This isn't a suicide. I've been dead a long time now. The first time I died was back in Iowa when I met Glenn, when I knew what he knew, that I loved him more than I loved myself. In his presence, I found my purpose, his joy, his comfort. I didn't question my purpose. Love is love.

The second time I died was a slow go. It took a long time, almost two years. What you don't know about me, about my husband, about us.

I wrote Scabies for Breakfast. *Yes, that was me. Sly Caron.*

You wonder why I did this, if this can possibly be true, and it is. My computer is in my home, along with my cat. Please take care of them both, the animal in my care, the novel I leave behind. Readers, there are no words big enough. Glenn lied to you. I lied to you. I am sorry. That book spoke to you, and you feel betrayed. You wonder if and you wonder why. You wonder how. The answer is simple. I did it for my husband, because I loved him, because he needed that book more than I did, because in our own way, I believed it to be an act of love.

The third time I died was when Glenn told the world that he wrote the book, when I realized that we were complicit in fraud. The fourth time I died was when I realized that there was no way out of it. We lied to the world. The fifth time I died was when the world loved the lie of my husband's words, his story that was my story, and the sixth time I died was when I heard him in the middle of the night crying in the other room. When

I stayed still. When I didn't go to him because who did this? We did this. The seventh time I died was when Glenn went and rode his bike off a cliff in an act of desperation to be the king of something real, and the eighth time I died was when I got that first phone call, when I knew he was gone. I was in this world alone now, with this secret, our secret.

And this is no way to live. So here we are, here I am, the ninth time I die.

The ninth time is every day. It is me, holding this pen, putting the words on the page. The dread of time passing and not passing, the lie the world tells us, that time heals all wounds. The ninth death is the cruelest. I wake up to the slow whirlwind of our innocence, our corruption, our mistakes. My cat meows and I feed her, and she is sated. The same is not possible for me. The fallout of loving someone and failing to know what love looks like in daily life is unrelenting. The sound of myself running a bath, getting dressed as if I am one of you. I don't know how to love anyone, maybe I did a long time ago, but it's not like riding a bike.

The ninth time is these past weeks, the façade of my every smile, every hello, every how are you? I see now that there is no tenth life. I am a cat. Clawing at anyone who comes close, hurting instead of helping, lashing out to find what I had, what I lost, what can never be found on this planet, a place that is no longer my home but something insurmountable, grounded in quicksand, impossible for me to navigate alone. I love you, Schwinny. I have no lives left. Here I come, my love, into the water, into you. Love, S

It made me cry a little, honestly, and I agree with you. *Scabies* isn't as good as Goodreads would have us believe, but Sly is one hell of a writer, and don't worry, Wonder. I didn't let my emotions get in the way of me and leave a trail, a *mugofpiss*. After all, it's not, as they say, "my first rodeo." I used one of those Mastercard gift cards and I rented a nice little *jalopy*. I wore gloves when I wrote the letter—duh—and you were there today. You saw her reaching for the Klonopin. You were there tonight as well. You heard what she's been doing, going to bars alone, crying for help to all the wrong people, the hardworking staff of that restaurant, as if it's *their* job to rescue that rude, shit-talking, book-tampering Widow Fucking Wonka.

This is the only way to get you back. To eliminate the triggering force that is Sly Caron. To break the fellowship before it breaks us. Harvard loves us, but Ani is right; they'll never give us a *third* fucking professor. It's either you or the fellowship and I choose you.

I'm back on the road and I'm over the bridge and Route 6 is empty at this hour. Cool 102 is coming in clearly now—*I can't live . . . if living is without you*—and it's the hardest thing about writing, isn't it, Wonder? I'm behind the wheel of the car, analyzing the fuck out of Sly's (my) letter, nitpicking, and questioning every word choice, every syllable, every period, and it's a fool's errand—there's no way I have the time or concentration to get through another draft—but we are writers. And it is torture, shipping the boat off, sending our words out into the world.

I park in the woods by the houses of the Hornblowers. For a minute I don't move. The silence. The money. The cuckoo's nest in your brain, the way you could not, would not, see Sly as the enemy that she is, as if we're all not walking through this life with regrets and resentments. As if she deserves you to be her champion after the way she treated you.

It's winter. It's cold. If it were summer, I could put her body out to sea. The metaphor would really fly if she was found in the ocean because the ocean is connected to the earth, to the mountains where Glenn died, but what can you do? We are powerless as writers. This part of our story takes places in December and Sly Caron doesn't even like the ocean.

She likes *hot tubs*.

I open the quaint *shoddy* wooden gate that needs to be fixed, but that's rich people for you. They love their shabby chic. Sly is on the sofa where we left her, out cold, mouth agape, as if she knows I'm coming to help her because she did not check herself before she wrecked herself.

Because we used to live here, I know the best way in, the sliding door on the left that doesn't squeak. This won't be a shock to anyone. Our fellows were right to be "concerned." I kick off my sneakers and drop my pants and I lift Glenn's *dear and loving wife* off the sofa. Heavier than I expected. Yoga. Length. Muscles. The weight of what she did, loading herself down with a slow boiling pot of bitterness and guilt, self-loathing that she would unfairly chalk up to a *midwestern* sense of duty to her man. That was her downfall, what I've come to realize in telling her story. Glenn was the bad guy, but if you think about it, Sly was worse. Glenn Shoddy had the courage to flounder, but Sly Caron didn't even have the courage to try, not when it was *her* name on the cover of the book, and it's another lesson for us, Wonder.

Don't judge an author by their book, not to their face anyway.

We never went in this hot tub—you hate them almost as much as RIP Glenn hated them—and I turn it on, I turn it up. I don't have to worry about Sarah Beth Swallows. Knowing her, she'll probably interpret what I'm doing as some kind of *prezzie* for *her*.

The steam coming off the water is a welcoming force on this cold night, but I can't just toss her into the tub like I'm Emeril Lagasse making boiled Sly stew—*Bam!* What ever happened to that guy?—so I jump into the water—ouch!—and I loop my arms under her pits and pull her in to join me. I'm waist deep and she's out cold, out hot, and I feel like one of those guys who leads a water aerobics class for frail old ladies as I turn her body over. Her hair spreads out—the bun was loose—and she must have a *lot* of Klonopin. Or is it Klonopin*s*?

There's no drama. No thrashing. She doesn't gnash her teeth at me. I feel her going away and I'm happy for her, Wonder. If there is a heaven, if there is a hell, she'll find *Schwinny* in a border town and they'll have a long talk in the *sitting room* and make a list of their mistakes.

Or maybe not.

When she's gone, I step out of the hot water. It's almost beautiful. Her husband died in the great wide open with his arms raised in a V and his wife dies humbled, with her arms hanging, lifeless. That's their *Marriage* but it's not all marriages and I'll leave a trail of chlorine on the patio, but by the time anyone comes looking for Sly, I'll be in Penn Station, waiting for your train to come in. Maybe you'll fall in love with my city, and we'll make like old-fashioned writers and move there to give you real space from your family, your frosted donut roots. Sly is gone, Wonder. The fellowship is over and we can go meet Bernie Lapatin for brunch and be the writers we are at heart, minus the RIP Sly spin, and we can do it all because of me.

It's getting cold out here, I put on all my clothes, and I'm in the clear, and I feel sorry for the maid who will show up here later this week and find a body in the hot tub, but who are we kidding? Work for people like the Hornblowers and eventually, you're gonna stumble upon a corpse.

I fiddle in my pockets for my car keys and my fingers are still slippery and my hair is a chlorinated mess and I look up from the keys to my rental and I sneeze—I hope I don't catch a cold—and then, out of the darkness, comes a voice.

"God bless you, asshole."

It's *you.*

48

The earth shifts and the night creatures in the woods come to a standstill. It's you. You're here. You should have followed your heart and sent me a little feeler of a text—*Sorry I was so weird tonight, are you really going to New York?*—and I should have killed the fellowship sooner, but here we are. This is destiny. We can't stay away from each other, and I guess I knew it would come to this, that you would walk into the cage. You've never been loved by someone you encountered as an adult, as a woman, and it might be too late for you to learn how to let my love in, how to love me. But you're here—same thin moth-eaten sweater you were wearing at the bar—and I can barely say your name.

"Wonder."

You put your hands on your hips. "What are you doing here?"

Killing the fellowship. "Same as you, I guess. I wanted to check on Sly."

"Sure didn't seem like you gave a fuck about her in the bar . . ."

Didn't you hear what Ani said? It's not your job to take care of Sly. I killed the fellowship for the sake of our partnership and you do not belong here, not now.

You are wild-eyed. Mad. "So it's not enough to make eyes at Sarah Beth all night?"

"What are you talking about?"

"You had to come down here and go skinny-dipping with Sly?"

My hair . . . the wet spots on my pants. The way I didn't smash that tray of eggs and porcini mushrooms on her head after she gave you your fucking notes. That's the way your mind works for everyone who's not in your family. Fucking or killing and no in-between.

"Yep, you caught me, Wonder. Wet-headed and red-handed. I drove down here to fuck her because nothing turns me on like a woman who accuses me of breaking into her house as she's trying to sabotage my work and my relationship. That's me! Joe Erotic!"

You know that's not my style—I am not a fucking cheater—and you're defeated, but hell-bent on making me the bad guy. "You might wanna zip up your fly."

I zip up my fucking fly—Sorry, I put my pants on kinda fast after I killed the fellowship—and you martyred your way down here to kiss the ring of the Machiavellian Willa Wonka, who amputated your ego right in front of me. Bad choice, Wonder. You're a writer—where are your instincts?—and oh, that's right. You're a storyteller. You saw my fly down and jumped to *sex*.

"So, where is she?" you ask, and this is good. You're thinking like a *writer* and I walk toward the house but you stop me. "I wanna talk to her alone."

You can't do that, Wonder. She's dead. "Fine by me."

I know you. Much as you say you want to do things on your own, you've never even lived in your own apartment, so it's no surprise when you look over your shoulder.

"This is stupid," you say. "Just come on already."

I follow you inside like the put-upon, underappreciated exterminator to your irrational, jealous Mrs. Hornblower and you howl for Sly to *come out come out wherever you are* as if any of this is funny. As if it's all a big fucking joke. It saddens me, Wonder. This fear of conflict in you, your avoidant need to resort to snark. None of this is real to you, is it? Already the cage is clarifying my vision. All the time we spent in this house wasn't real because *you're* not real. And you know it, don't you? That's why you pressed *me* about being "real" when we first met. Your bedroom isn't yours—it belongs to your father—and your book isn't yours—it belongs to your family—and the lampposts, as you call them, they're just Easter eggs for the *Ivy League Douchebags* on the off chance that one of these douchebags reads your book and realizes what an asshole he was. As fucking *if*.

You plant your little body on the sofa and cross your legs. "All right, so where is she?"

She's dead. "She was going upstairs to take a shower when I left. I imagine she'll be down in a few minutes."

You ambushed me. It's happening again. I fall in love and I risk everything to make the world a better place for you, only to have you *push* me away and then barge back into my life at the worst possible moment. I set us free. I wanted us to meet up in New York and rekindle our romance under all the city lights. But you're here. Sly is in the hot tub and I am not going down for that, and I can't trust you when you're full of piss and vinegar, liable to do things like accuse me of "murder." There's no way around it. You're in the cage now—I am the cage—and this is new for me. No steel bars. No key in my pocket and no screaming and whining from you. "So," you start. "Does she hate me? Because it's pretty ironic if she turns on me when I'm the only one who had any compassion for her."

The test begins—words matter—and you walked into this house, into this cage. There is an opportunity for you to grow and take responsibility for your part in this mess and cop to your shortcomings as writer on the page, as my *significant other* in this fucking relationship.

It's high time I held you accountable for the casual ways you belittle me, and I raise my eyebrows. "'Compassion' . . . Huh."

You sigh and say that you're tired, that you can't "have some big talk" with me, but I'm tired too, Wonder. Murder is like sex. It's physical, and if you run, I need to be rested. I sit on the sofa. My arms are steel bars readying to pounce if you pounce. "Wonder, you can feel sorry for her all you want, but that doesn't change the fact that what she did to you was wrong. So maybe you don't come down here and hold her hair back while she pukes. Did she have any compassion for you?"

"Ah, so it's okay for you to come down here and see her, but not me. Classic, Joe."

"I came here for you, Wonder. You won't talk to me because of what she said about me. And I'm not afraid to fight for what I love. I don't need to hide behind *compassion*. She made you into Dunkin' Wonder and she made me into Joe Erotic and at the end of the day, she has no compassion for you or me. All labels are the same. They're fucking bullshit and we have rights."

"Excuse me if I don't get off on playing the victim like *some* people."

That was a low blow—I don't *play* anything—and you need to choose your words more carefully. "See, Won. You want to make this about your *tendency to love,* but earlier today, you were on fire, all righteous indignation. Then, in the bar, our people talk a *tiny* bit of shit and you defend her as if *she's* the victim . . . Where is your compassion for them? For me?"

"I came down here because I'm a human."

Maybe the worst word choice yet—who isn't?—and I try again. "You came down here for the same reason you liked the Sox more when they were losers. What she did was wrong. That doesn't go away because she gets called out. And even if there was something to be learned from her notes on your book—"

"Her notes were bullshit. Don't go there."

That's fucking bullshit but we're beyond books. "Wonder, she doesn't deserve your help because she went behind your back and showed zero respect or *compassion* for you."

You purse your lips. You *do* know. Your vocabulary is capable of expansion, so I water the grass I planted. "She accused me of breaking into her house. She tried to turn me against the woman I *love* so yeah, I came here. I came here because I love you, because she doesn't want you to love me. She doesn't deserve my compassion, or yours, not when it comes to us."

People can grow in the cage. I've seen it happen. I want to see you grow. But you force out a fake little laugh. "God," you say. "You always do this, don't you? You want to educate me. First, I don't know how to make *oatmeal* and now I don't know how to deal with Sly. Fucking A, Joe, I know how to do a lot of things, and I mean yeah, I drank some Kool-Aid. I was into the whole Dunkin' Sally Rooney thing, and it was embarrassing, *especially* in front of you, but I can be mad at someone and feel sorry for them at the same time. I can walk and chew gum."

"I know you can."

"Do you? Because you always . . . Even the way you hunted me down here . . ."

More bad words: *Hunted you down.* "I offered to leave, and you wanted me to stay."

"Well, what else could I do? The look on your face, you get so needy . . . It's passive-aggressive when you make what you want so clear without freaking saying it. I mean that is *not* how you give someone space, and if you just stayed away . . . Whatever."

"So, everything's my fault."

"You could have called her out on the Joe Erotic shit and nipped it in the bud before you came here, but you didn't. You have this sycophantic streak, this need to please people no matter how they shit on you . . . I mean you actually considered it, you considered *becoming* Joe Erotic."

"Only with a pen name."

You tell me that's me, that I'm always in disguise, *Mr. Autodidact Bookseller* who "would give his left nut" to be something I'm not. I shake my head. Words are worse than sticks and stones. They penetrate us without drawing blood.

"Now you're just trying to hurt me, Wonder."

"Yeah? Well, what about today? You know that she's a *Flour Girls* hack who only has the job cuz she's Mrs. Glenn Shoddy. When it was *real*, when it was you and me and her . . . you didn't go to bat for me. I mean I had to freaking *force* you to speak up."

I KILLED MR. AND MRS. *FLOUR GIRLS* FOR YOU. "Wow."

You rub your forehead. "In the bar, the passive-aggressive 'I'm going to New York' bit. You didn't invite me. You threw it out there because you thought I wanted that with you."

"Well, do you want that?"

"I mean I want to ice-skate around Rockefeller Center with you and whatever, but what I want doesn't matter . . ." *What I want doesn't matter.* "I mean it 'matters' . . ." Nice try, Wonder. "But I'd never blow off Caridad's recital for a little 'New York City Serenade' with anyone, let alone you . . . the guy who let me walk around thinking I'm Sally Freaking Rooney, the guy who . . . I mean maybe you did break into her house."

There is hope—you still want to hold hands in Midtown—so I need to nip that B and E business in the bud. "Won, you know me. You know I didn't break into her *house*. Same way you know I didn't come down here to 'seduce' her."

You do know, but you're almost disappointed, the way your shoulders sag. "I know. That's not your style. You don't get your hands dirty. I sell donuts and you sell *books*."

That's not a very nice way to sum up either one of us, but you don't mean it. "So, if you know I didn't break in, why do you think I knew what she did to your book?"

"Because I know, okay? I don't need proof, unlike *some* people . . ."

That was a reference to the mouse in the house. "I believe in myself, in my intuition. It's called *faith*, Joe."

Another misunderstood word—it's called magical delusional thinking—and you run your fingers through your hair and look around the *sitting room*. You have no idea where you are, that you're in a cage. "She sure is taking a long time up there."

She's dead. "Maybe she's taking a bath."

You check your phone—nothing—and it's a funny thing with you. The rules of the cage are the rules of the Fight Club or the room—no communication with outsiders allowed—but I'm bending them for you. You're not gonna run. You're not gonna call anyone. You're . . . happy right now. You *want* us to end. You root for us to fail at every turn because in your depraved mind, I *can't* be a good guy. "Screw it," you say. "The classy lady is having a bath . . . Well, I'm having a Coolatta."

I follow you downstairs to the fungeon, the only place where we feel comfortable in a house like this, the *basement*. But it's the best move. No view of the hot tub from here.

You're behind the counter, where you think you belong, busy with your hands, fussing with the machine—*It needs to be cleaned*—and doing what you think you do best. You pour the liquid, and you dump the ice, and sugar is bad for you, even when it's cut with caffeine and additives and water, it's no fucking better than Kool-Aid. You press the red button and you love what happens next. The simplicity. The grinding that makes it impossible for us to talk, to get *real*. The way everything is the same every time. What was thin becomes thick. There is foam.

You pour your *Coolatta*—no vodka topper, not tonight—and you lean over the bar like you're at work, and I sit at the counter, like a customer. Time to play it cool. Talk small.

"I'm still planning on going to New York. Been way too long, ya know?"

You sip your Coolatta.

"I never took baths. You've seen the tub in our house. So freaking gross. I mean the tiles are mangy and it's that thing where you can pour a whole freaking bottle of bleach in there and there's no point. It's too old to be clean. You couldn't pay me to sit in that tub."

This is good. You're reflecting. This is the kind of thing that happens in the cage, and I am the prison guard who treats you like a patient. "Wonder, why didn't you ever move?"

"Excuse you?"

It could be our last night together, and I want some fucking answers. "You have a job."

"I work at Dunkin'. It doesn't exactly pay the freaking rent."

"There are ways. You get a roommate . . . You move a little farther out."

"I have a family."

"Remember that day when you told me the difference between excuses and the truth?"

"So, what? Sly's better than me because her parents are playing tennis and taking their vitamins as opposed to mine, who fucked their brains out when they were in high school and named their first kid after a Madonna song and their second kid after a Natalie Freaking Merchant song?"

It's a fun sad fact, and I smile. "I never knew that."

"Well, bully for you. You don't know a lot about me, Joe. But that's fine. You're not like me. You're a dishrag. You *liked* it when she put you in a box and she labeled you 'Joe Erotic.' You worship these people because you have no self-respect and me . . . I stood up for myself. I felt *bad* for that woman when everyone was talking shit tonight, *that's* why I'm here."

"When does it end? You stay for your dad, and when he's gone, what then? You stay for your sister, for Caridad, and then she leaves, and what? Is that when you finally leave or let someone in? When half your life is over?"

You can't answer that question—it's a good one—so once again, you deflect. "Why didn't you tell me you knew what Sly did to *Faithful*?"

"Why can't you trust anyone who doesn't live on *Sesame Street*?"

"Wow. Classism much?"

"Wonder, I love you."

"You don't love 'me.' You're a serial monogamist. You like to freaking 'love.' It's not about me, or any of all your *girls*. It's about you, Joe. You loved this one and that one and you lugged that *ex-box* all the way up here because for all your 'loner' bullshit, for all your bravado about how you don't need people, you don't talk to your own *mother* and you're fine with it . . . You whine about me being too close to my family, who are you to talk? You're never alone. You're not independent. Not in your head anyway. You fall in love every time you leave the house and if some other girl was sitting on the grass in a tight shirt that day, it would've been her."

You have so little confidence, but this is progress. "Well, if you finished reading my book, you'd know that it's more complicated. Yes, I've fallen in love before . . . I'm human. I like life better when I have a partner."

"You should call your freaking mother."

"Wonder, every love story in my life is real. It *is* about you. You didn't fall off an assembly line and I'm not looking for my *mother* in every woman I meet. It's all in my book. No matter how much I love them, no matter how much I give, they leave me. That's *my* story. And I thought you were different. I thought that because I told my story and got it out of my system, well, I thought I was different, that things with you would be different. But I guess this is why a lot of writers tell the same story in every fucking book."

You give me an *ugh*. "Only you would talk about your freaking book right now."

People do that in the cage, they try to distract me, throw me off, but you make bad word choices, bad life choices, and you can't change until you *acknowledge* your poor choices. "Wonder, seriously. Why didn't you ever leave? Go somewhere else, work somewhere else, even just for a summer?"

You look around the beautifully finished basement, but there is no escape. No way out. "This place seemed huge, but now . . . It's like any place. Smaller than you remember."

I forge on. "You make it like your sister and your dad need you, but that's a two-way street. You and I both know that if you left, they'd figure it out. Why didn't you ever leave?"

"I dunno," you sass. "Why does anyone do anything? Why did you ride bikes with Glenn when you knew he was so against me?"

You went there, you said his name, another bad fucking choice. "So, did you keep his 'dick pics'?"

You roll your eyes, and I knew it. I knew you were lying. "He didn't send me dick pics. We had a drink before the first day of the fellowship . . ."

I could kill him all over again. "Well, isn't that nice?"

"It was nothing, he texted me to make sure I'd show up and we had a few drinks . . ."

Women like you, you live in another world, all the Glenns crawling up your legs to give you a leg up like fucking cockroaches. "Nothing happened," you say. "But I knew what he wanted. I told Bobby about it and everything. The potluck, it was like, yeah freaking *right* I'm gonna go make chitchat with his wife."

"Why didn't you tell me?"

"Are you serious? I barely knew you."

I go back to the good old days before we got together and messed it all up. That day at Dunkin'. You weren't talking about me with Your Bobby. You were talking about him, about *Glenn*. "In all the years, you never gassed up the Hyundai and hit the freeway, blasted by the water tower, and made a run for it, even just for a night, for a weekend, just to go be somewhere else. Why?"

You smile. You still love me. "Number one, fuck you. Number two, it's not a water tower. It's a gas tank. Number three, we don't call it a freeway. We call it a highway."

You answered my question. You made your choices and you stand by your choices and you can never be with me. Not really. You never left home because you never *wanted* to leave home. Your confidence is wrapped up in your authority over the little things. Stupid things. *We call it a highway.* You prefer the known over the superior, the unknown. It's your only source of pride. It breaks my heart but you *are what you are*, a waste of a Wonder Woman, resisting the power of your gold J.Lo hoops, and this is it, isn't it? We are falling out of love.

"Fuck it," you say. "When in Rome."

You tear off your shirt and lunge at me and you're not wearing a bra and this isn't our house and we are not those people. We don't fuck our way through our problems. You belt me like I'm the bad guy, like I'm the one who failed you. You want to leave this house and you want to leave me, but I can't let you go up there. I block the way and you kick like another Masshole I used to know, used to love, but you're not her, Wonder. You're not RIP Beck. Your rage transforms to tears and I scoop you up like a bouncer, like a prince, and deliver you to the sofa.

You are topless, so I pull my fisherman's sweater over my head and hand it to you. "Here," I say. "You look cold."

You put on my sweater and you're drowning in it. Calmer now. No more tears. Still, I put my feet up on the table just in *case* you make a run for it. I killed Glenn, and it wasn't enough to make you happy. I killed Sly but are you happy? Nope. You will never be happy.

"Well, I'm done," you say. "With all of it. I'm gonna drop out."

You don't have to do that. I killed the fellowship. It's over. "Wonder . . ."

"This whole world, the 'fellows' . . . They're only really happy when they're tearing someone to pieces, and I like to lift people *up*. I think I'm gonna hit the road."

But you don't move. How could you? You're not a whole person. You love the atmosphere of baseball and you know the words, but you don't know the sport, the batting averages, the math, and it makes me crazy that it's on me to ask you all the questions you've avoided because you don't *want* to know who you are. Well, I do, Wonder.

"Hey, how come you love baseball instead of, say, . . . football?"

"I don't know. Because I do. That's the way it was in my family."

"But why do *you* love it?"

"What is this? Twenty questions?"

No, it's the cage. "Sure."

"Well, I guess *I* love it because it doesn't involve a clock. It's so American, it can go on forever if you foul, if you hold back the base runners. There's no overtime. It's pure."

"So why isn't that in your book?"

You shrug, but I know the answer. It's not in your book because you don't think for yourself. You love the Sox because of your family, and a person must fly away from the nest and soar in order to see it from afar. You never will and I should pick up one of these dense, feather-stuffed green pillows and smother you for coming here, but it's hard—I only killed Sly a little while ago damn it and I want you to *change*—I want us to fall back in love—and you sigh. "What a freaking mess. Oops. I said *freaking*! Better call the word police!"

Sarcasm doesn't agree with you. It's one of the many problems with your book. You're a character in your own story, too faithful to write *Faithful*. You break my heart every time you open your mouth and you're an unfinished woman with an unfinished novel and some books, some lives, are just never going to get there.

You blow your nose on my sweater, a sweater I bought when we were the Hornblowers. "You know what I wish? I wish Glenn never rode his stupid bike off a cliff. I was happy, you know? We were happy. Freaking karma . . ."

The worst word choice yet, the choice of a small mind, a small person who avoids responsibility and accountability at all fucking costs.

"Are you kidding, Wonder? You were miserable."

"I knew what he was. I had my bearings. I was gonna see where things went with you and rake in the 25K. I was solid. And then he died, and I lost my head. And now everything's a mess. Karma came for him, and I was . . . I mean in a sick way I was *too* happy when Sly entered the picture, and so yeah . . . That's karma for you."

No. That's *me* for you, and I can't take it anymore. This is my house, my cage, my life.

"Wonder, it's not about 'karma.'"

"See, there you go again . . . educating me."

"I was only his *bro-tern* because I was trying to help us. If 'karma' was real, he would still be around to put in a good word for me, and he'd be here to eat crow and watch you take over the world with your book. There's no 'karma.' If you ride like an asshole, you die like an asshole. Karma doesn't kill people. People kill people."

You tilt your head—you learned that from Sly—and you shudder. "Sometimes, I just . . . You're always so disgusted with people. It's like you wish everyone was dead . . ."

Not true, only some people, only most people. "I just don't like the word *karma*."

We are at an impasse. You don't know *compassion* from *self-loathing*, and I don't *want* to tell you what I did for you, but it's the only way for you to develop some self-fucking-worth, to know that you are loved. You'll either intake the love or try to kill me, and the choice is yours. I hope you choose love.

"Wonder, there's something you should know."

You laugh. "You and your drama . . . I mean I knew this, I freaking sensed it right off the bat. I knew you weren't real. I said it to Tara, that there was something a little too ready about you, the way you were so agreeable and so supportive, always saying the right thing, always doing the right thing, which is a tactic for all guys who have no intention of ever being real."

"But I am being real."

"Okay, so what is it, Joe? What's the big freaking secret?"

No more misdirects and no more excuses. You need to know the truth, my truth. Things don't magically just *change* because of *karma* and what is the story of every fucking book? It's Mariah Carey on Cool 102—*and then a hero comes along*—and that's me, Wonder. I am your Mariah Fucking Carey because you refuse to be your own Mariah Carey. I make things happen for you. Your Bobby only came into his own and moved to New York because he had a near-death experience, an experience I fucking gave him, and Glenn only rode off that cliff because I rigged the fucking cliff. But this is scary. If you start a pillow fight, I don't want to win, not in the sad way that ends with me carrying your lifeless body.

You pick at your cuticles as if there's anything left. "I'm waiting . . ."

"I'm getting there."

"Still making up your story, huh? Well, take your time. Clearly the merry widow is in no rush to join us. God, I hate fake people . . . Like no bath takes this long, you know?"

This has been our own personal plague right from the start. Nothing and no one is real to you—*What I want doesn't matter*—and it goes deeper than I knew. You stood me up at Glenn's potluck because you didn't know that I was real. We are in the basement of our relationship, "the root of the root." You don't think I'm real because you're not real.

But I am real. When darkness falls, we have two choices. We can turn on a light and fight Mother Nature with electricity, or we can go with it. Plunge into the black knowing that we might fall and lose everything. I choose to take a leap of faith. Same way RIP Sly did when she told me what she did for Glenn. Honesty is our only true light, the way to save you, to make you see that you are loved.

I look you right in the eye and jump. "Glenn wasn't alone when he died."

"Huh?"

"I was there in the woods . . ." *Gently, Joseph.* Prolong the silence, let the student prepare to be tested, challenged, *pushed.* "I saw him ride off that cliff because I did it, Wonder. I killed him, and I did it for you."

49

I am Willy Wonka and this is my factory and I walk you through the floor to let you see how the candy *really* gets made. I tell you about my rides with Glenn, about how sick I was over the way he treated you, because the chasm was too deep. The man wanted to help me, and he wanted to destroy you, but at the end of the day, I chose you over him, over my future. We're in the rising action of my story, the nitty-gritty buildup to the big kill with the Strava app and the fishing wire, the way he raised his arms in a V. I raised my arms in a V and I needed you to know what I did, that I did it for you, and now you do, except you don't. You won't.

You laugh. Like the anti-Charlie that you are.

You *clap* like we're in the room and it's the "best worst story" you ever heard. "Joe, please. You? You don't have it in you to kill anyone, especially your best freaking friend."

"But that's why I did it, Wonder. He was terrible to you. He was terrible to all women, and I had to get rid of him. So I did it."

"No, no," you say. "Don't do that. Don't globalize it. We're not talking about 'all women.' See, you did this in the bookstore that day. You were trying to 'all women' it with me, as if me and Sly are sisters, as if I don't have a right to despise Glenn for what he did to *me* as in me, not me as in 'all freaking women.'"

"Wonder, you're missing the point. I did this for you. I killed the fucker."

"Joe, stop it. Stop lying to me. It's not in your DNA. You're not a freaking 'murderer.'"

My God, you are one sick little woman. You don't believe I would do that for you. You have no faith in yourself, so you have no faith in me, and I plead my case again. "No, I'm not a 'murderer.' But he was out to destroy you. People change. Can't you see that? I never *killed* anyone until Glenn, but I love you. It was killing me to see him killing you and that's the 'power' of love, okay?"

But you grunt. "See, this is part of the problem with you . . . You think this is what I want? For you to make up a story about how you killed the big bad man? Jesus, Joe, you really think I can't handle myself in this world, that I need a 'hero' or some shit and that's . . . You think I can't handle things on my own."

Well, you can't, Wonder. "Why is it so hard for you to believe that I risked everything for you?"

It's a good question and we've graduated from word choice to character building. World building. The real art of fiction, of life. We're getting somewhere, and that scares you, being loved, being seen, so you laugh like a teenager at a funeral. "If my father heard you claiming you freaking killed someone . . . He'd laugh so hard he'd blow his freaking wound vac. You . . . a killer."

I'm trying to talk to you the person, you the woman I love, you the adult, but you're thinking about your father. It doesn't matter that you love me because you don't *want* to love me.

"Joe, come on. You're you. You would never break into Sly's house, right?"

It's not a break-in if you have a key. "God, no."

"So, logically it's like, if you wouldn't break into a house, you wouldn't commit murder and—"

You cut yourself off. Always afraid to say what you want. "What?"

"Don't get all wounded but this is . . . It's part of why I think maybe you're not the world's best freaking writer, not yet anyway . . ."

Evil and acidic, even for you, and that cruel, deflective opposition is why people die in the cage. But first things first. You lied to me. You lied to me a lot. "When did you finish reading my book?"

You're turning red now, but that's how it works, Wonder. You said what you want and now you have to answer for what you said, but you refuse. You deflect. "I still can't get over it. You think I'm gullible, that I'd really believe that you *killed* that asshole. I mean . . ."

"Wonder, when did you finish my book?"

"I mean I know people. I grew up around criminals, guys who got away with things, guys who didn't, my freaking brother-in-law, not that you ever asked what he did, but whatever . . . It's insulting."

Nice try, babe. "Wonder, when did you finish reading my book?"

"I didn't say I finished."

Cunt. "But you did . . ."

One thing I love about you: You know when to throw in the towel. "I didn't mean to drag your book into the conversation . . ." *Drag* and you buy time. You rearrange pillows and we are back where we started, in a room that isn't a room. An Algonquin writers' circle for two, and yes, you hurt me—*maybe not the world's best writer*—but you own your words. You can't take them off the table, wipe them away like you did with the tiny pools of condensation on the bar.

"Okay," you say. "You have these two people and all they do is talk about themselves."

"I'm a writer, not a . . . storyteller."

It felt good to give you a taste of your own medicine—thanks, RIP Glenn—and again you channel Sly and tilt your head. "Was that a dig at *Faithful*?"

"No, the world needs all kinds of books . . . I just mean that *Me* is . . . deep."

"And my book's not deep?"

I wanted the cage to be about us, but we are writers. We've always avoided real conversation about our craft. I was your cheerleader, staying on the sidelines, and you were my woman writer girlfriend, too preoccupied with your work to so much as look at mine. For your sake and mine—book club only just started—I tell you I didn't mean that.

You are flippant—"I know my book is deep"—and then you get back to *Me*. "The thing is, the people in your book . . . whatever their names are . . ." *JOY AND DANE*. "They're in a vacuum but they're not in a vacuum *together*. They're not accountable to each other or the reader. It's like you, the author, can't decide if either is a reliable narrator and if *you* can't decide then how can we decide? They're in their own heads. It's almost like you look down on people too much to write about them and that's why Sly . . ."

You catch your breath and you're too late. I call you to task. "'That's why Sly . . .'?"

"Forget I said that."

Not possible, so I serve our book club with a painful summary of your lies thus far. You read my book behind my back. You talked about my work with *Sly* instead of being honest with me. You are silent. Humbled. *You're* the bad one and you know it and you talk a mile a fucking minute. Yes, you drank her Kool-Aid, and yes, you *kind of liked* the way she thought you were better than me. You mistook the artificial love for the real thing, for actual fucking sugar, and you weren't *surprised* when I told you what she did to my book, because you knew she didn't believe in me, not really, not the way she believed in you, and you shrug. "But obviously, I was wrong. She didn't believe in me either. Do you hate me?"

It's my turn to laugh, to chuckle. "Wonder, I don't 'hate' you. I mean that's people. You should have known, if she was talking shit about me to you, criticizing *my* book, that says a lot about her character. How did you not see that she would do the same thing to you?"

"Well, I'm me . . ."

BAM! There is no Kool-Aid left on the entire planet. You drank it all. "Okay then . . ."

"That came out wrong but like . . . I know I'm freaking good. I know her notes and her 'revisions' were total bullshit . . ." I don't tell you that you're wrong because it's fun, being the victim. "And I'm sorry but also . . . it's not the easiest thing, talking to you . . ."

"Me?"

"You make everything into a test, and you do that in your book, too . . . It's exhausting. I mean maybe you just need a break, you know? Like me . . . I'm on this Memphis kick and I might go there this summer . . ."

You won't go to New York but now you're flying to Memphis and *I'm* the unreliable narrator. LOLOL. "Memphis, huh? With your dad and your sister and Caridad?"

Gotcha and you gulp. "The point is . . . It's almost like you can't write people because you're not in it with people, not really . . . You're in your own world and yeah, you can write, but I don't know. I never feel like I'm *really* in it with you or your characters."

Typical Goodreads girl—you blame my book for your poor skills as a reader—and that's the cruelest thing you've ever said to me, but all caged animals test the boundaries, and that's why we're here on this planet, in this basement, on this sofa, to find out who you are, to see if the beauty in you can ever, will ever, outweigh the bad.

I start by holding you accountable for one of your many lies. "So I guess when you told me my book was 'putdownable,' I guess that *was* an insult."

You shrug it off, like lying is no big deal. "Look at Pat Conroy. He was all about people, he lived to get out there and meet people, hear stories, and he could do that because he respected people . . . The people in your 'book,' they don't *do* anything. They don't care about anyone."

"And that's how you define the value of a person? A character? By what they do for other people?"

"Well, yeah. 'Show me the friend and I'll show you the man.'"

"That's a new one . . ."

"It's from *Army Wives*," you snap. "My sister was into it and it's freaking true about people but just . . . never mind."

"Wonder, have you ever been to therapy?"

"Fuck you."

"The point of my book, the point of reading any book . . . it's self-understanding. We open books to find ourselves in the pages."

"Well, *I* open a book because I care about people, *all* people, because I want to learn the stories of people who care about other people. I'm a writer because I love the world, because we're all connected, because things stay with me, because everyone has a story, every ass has a soul."

Spoken like the woman who never left *Sesame Street* and it's my turn to laugh. "We're not 'connected.' In case you noticed . . . we're not the Hornblowers."

"And the other thing about your book . . ." I should really just kill you right now so you can be in a book club with RIP Glenn and RIP Ethel because they weren't dumb like you. They loved my fucking book. "You shoved all those huge paragraphs in there to distract us from who *you* are . . . that you're all about you, that all you think about is . . . you, your body, as if all life only matters because of how it affects your life."

"Wonder, when did you finish reading my novel?"

"I don't know, before Thanksgiving . . ." So Sly isn't the only reason you left me. "The way you flew off the handle about the mouse . . . I was afraid to tell you . . ."

I am not scary, and I won't let you paint me that way. "So, you lied to me, for weeks."

"Joe, I don't jump on Goodreads the second I finish a book. I need to sit with it."

"That's not true."

"It is with *some* books. And anyway, it's just one book. No one says either one of us has to love everything the other writes. When you showed up here and started a new book I was like, okay, maybe his next one will be better. Or maybe you don't even want to be a writer . . ."

So, there it is. That is what you want. You want me to give up my dreams, to be the almost writer to your Dunkin' Sally Rooney. Could I do it? Would I do it?

"Anyway," you say. "With me . . . it's a calling. I have stories burning in my heart after every shift at the store. I can't quit, no matter what happens with the stupid fellowship. What you said earlier, it's true. You *do* remind me of the Sox. It's about spirit. I have faith in you as a person. If you want this bad enough, you'll do a few trades and get your team in order and win the World Freaking Series with this new book you're working on . . . If you finish it."

What you want matters. And it's clearer by the second. You want me to tell you that you know it all, that you're the smart one, the writer, that I will quit *because* you're the one on your way up in the glass elevator, because I don't belong there. Could I do it? Would I do it?

"Hello?"

"I'm thinking."

I still love the way I feel around you, the way your moods swing wildly as you cover the bases, pulling one well-executed well-timed *shift* after another. But no one should have to give up on their dreams to be with someone, and if I did fight the current, if I did get back on *The Good Life* with you as your talentless hack of a husband, it wouldn't be the same. You would be Willa Wonka, and I would never, could never, be your Charlie.

"Joe, don't act like it's the end of the world. I mean ultimately, who gives a fuck what Sly thinks or what Glenn thinks. If you really love to write, the only Kool-Aid you need, it's cheesy as fuck but come on . . . It's in you."

Your voice is the last fucking straw, that false modesty, the lie of your love, and that's it. We're done. Goose fucking *cooked*. You are not the one for me, and I pick up a green fucking pillow. But no. This is the cage. You were honest with me—you're too jealous of me to believe in me—and it's my turn to hide behind sarcasm. I let go of the pillow. I *clap.* "Well, okay then! If Dunkin' Sally Rooney thinks I should quit, sure. Never mind my life's dream. Never mind the fact that I love to write, that it's what I want to do with the rest of my life. I'm out. No more writing for me because Dunkin' Sally Rooney knows *everything* about books! Dunkin' Sally Rooney who doesn't believe in herself unless the teacher tells her to believe in herself, she knows it *all*!"

You light up because this is what you want. A fight. "I *knew* this was coming."

It's coming because you wanted it, you *pushed* in order to *pull* this venom out of me so that you would finally get what you want, an excuse to fucking hate me, another reason to brag about your intu-fucking-ition. We have drifted and the end is nigh, so I tell you what I really think about *Faithful,* that it's overstuffed, that you have so little confidence in your own story that you crowd the narrative with other stories, stories that aren't yours, and *damn, it feels good to be a gangster.*

"Wow," you huff. "You hate my freaking book."

"Wonder, I don't 'hate' it. I just think you're boxing yourself in."

"Said the guy who wrote a book about two freaking people with zero ties to the outside world . . ."

"Alice is on every page but she's not there, not really. You're telling us what to think about her, ordering us to love her and pump our fists and shout *You go, girl* while she fucks every douchebag in the city and we all know how it ends."

"Not even possible. Even *I* don't know where it's going."

"Yes, you fucking do. That's why you threw a fit when Sly cut your lampposts, all your little one-night stands. You say *Faithful* is for your family, but your family's only in there because you don't know what to do with Alice, because you're afraid to be yourself, to really fucking *be* yourself and just get out there and live."

"Fuck you."

"You're using Alice to prove your thesis that no *freaking* man on this planet is good enough for her. The worst part is . . . You're *not* Pat Conroy."

"And you're not J. D. Salinger."

"No, I'm not, Wonder. I'm *me*. Balls-to-the-wall me on every fucking page. I know my book because I lived my book. Because unlike you, I let people in. You hunker down with the people in your house, but that doesn't mean that you *know* them. Alice is *using* her family to avoid having a life, a story of her own, and you can tell me I'm wrong all night long, but you know I'm right because no one knows you, not like I do, and you . . . Who do you know? Who do you really fucking *know*? You won't even believe that I killed Glenn for you. And I did."

I gave it to you straight. No excuses, just the truth. This is your chance to reflect on your hang-ups and shortcomings, to realize that what I said is right, fair, hard to hear, but the stuff of love. This is when you turn on the searchlights and find my eyes in the six-foot seas, this is when you help me aboard and offer me a towel, apologize for throwing me off the boat. This is when you tell me that you only bashed my book because you wanted me to bash yours, because deep down, you fear you're nowhere good enough for *me*.

You lick your lips. You rub your hands together. I am rooting for you, Wonder. Even after all the terrible things you said, I want to *believe* in you. But then you choke. "You have it all wrong, Joe. Alice takes care of herself so that she can take care of her family. It's like the airplane is always going down, and she needs oxygen."

You really don't believe that I killed Glenn and I can't help it. "Have you ever even been on an airplane?"

You slap me across the face, and I could do it. Smother you right now, but we're in book club, we're in *Fight Club* and you know I'm not an asshole—you know I won't slap *you*—and you sigh. "*As I was saying*, on an airplane, a mother has to strap on her oxygen mask before she can put the mask on her child."

"And what about people like us? People who don't have children."

"It has nothing to do with giving birth to someone. Good people care."

"Wonder, in therapy one of the first things you learn is that you come first, that there's no shame in caring about yourself more than anything else on this planet, because you're alive, you're worth it."

"Well, that's what I'm saying, Joe. You can't help anyone if you're not well."

"No," I say. "You're the end goal. You. Not the people you help. You."

"I'm sad for you, Joe. That's sad."

"Wonder, what does Alice want?"

"She wants to be a good person."

"Bullshit. What does Alice want for herself?"

"She wants to know that she did the best she could for her family."

"What does Alice want that's just for Alice?"

"Are you really this much of a monster? You think my book is *crowded* because Alice cares about people? I mean Jesus Freaking Christ! Look at *The Prince of Tides.*"

"Exactly! The best part of that book is the tiger. Every member of the family is under assault and the tiger kills the monsters who break into the house."

"And the tiger *dies* defending the family and it's horrible. You're not supposed to be happy when an animal dies in a book, Joe."

You don't know the tiger's name and I know your favorite book better than you do.

"Caesar the tiger is dying."

"Yes, and it's terrible."

"No, it's the best part. Luke says that it was *wrong* of the Wingos to trap that beast in the cage. And he looks the tiger in the eye . . . 'But you finally got to be a tiger, Caesar.' It's bittersweet, but Caesar got to have *one* honest moment after a life wasted in a cage."

That's you—you're in a cage on *Sesame Street*—but you cling to your simpleton perspective. You rant about animals dying as if animals in books aren't fictional. And then you shake your head. "I give up. If you like that scene . . . you're a fucking psychopath."

I KILLED TWO PEOPLE FOR YOU. I'M A LOVER. A HERO. THE OPPOSITE OF A PSYCHOPATH. "Wonder, the tiger got to be a tiger. Why does that scare you so much?"

You slap your thigh and blurt: "Why does Tom go to New York?"

It's sad, the way you said that, like you're proud to know the name of the hero in your favorite book. "Well, Wonder, Pat Conroy wants Tom to meet Susan Lowenstein and embark on a journey of self-discovery. He confronts his regrets about spending his life in a cage."

"No, you idiot. Tom goes up there because his sister tried to kill herself, because he loves her and he wants to save her because they're blood, they're *family*."

"Wonder, the suicide is a plot device. Tom is torn between all these women, and he's opening his eyes, pouring his guts out to Lowenstein, this woman who could have been the one. Conroy uses the sister's attempted suicide to get Tom off his ass and on a plane, so *he* can be a tiger."

We're at an impasse and book club is ending. You love *your* book and I love *my* book and I can't be with you if you refuse to let yourself love me and my writing. You broke us when you assaulted my words, and I fell into the trap. I told you that I don't like your book, the one whose title is tattooed on your ankle, and that's you. You put the cart before the horse. You trashed my book so that I would denigrate yours, give you a reason to break up with me. No matter how hard I try, you push me away, same as ever.

What I want doesn't matter if what you want is to be alone, unloved, stuck.

You check your Swatch. Deflecting, even now. "Okay," you say. "I'm starting to get a little worried about Sly."

It breaks my heart because it's so predictable. We're on the cusp of figuring out what the hell is wrong with you, but what do you want to do? You want to worry about someone else.

"Wonder, I'm sure she's fine. Me, on the other hand . . . Do you know what it's been like?"

"Maybe you should go upstairs and check on her."

No can do. "You fight us every step of the way. You bail on me, you go to Sly behind my back. You refuse to believe that I went out on a limb for you and you tell me I'm a shitty writer and yet . . . here we are. You always come back to me. Why is that?"

This is when you save your life and tell me you love me. This is when you tell me that life is better with me, that it's okay for you to want things that don't help your family. And then somehow, someway, we stay *in this together* and you take back all the terrible things you said about me. I'm the best writer, the best man, and I can forgive you. I want to forgive you.

"You really want the truth?"

"No more excuses."

"Well, you're not gonna like it."

"Don't give me a disclaimer, Wonder. Just tell me."

"It's the way you look at me. You're my family, Joe. I can do or say anything, and you'll always be here if I want . . ." *If.* "And you . . . well, I'm *your* family. You make me feel like I'm all you got. You can't stay mad at me, but that's also why . . . I need to get off this sofa."

You climb over the roadblock of my legs like I'm not your cage and you don't run up the stairs. You rinse out the Coolatta machine and scrub that counter to make it seem like *We Were Never Here*, and how did I ever think you were the one?

You toss the rag in the sink and look at me. "Sorry, but I can't leave a mess for a freaking staff. You know this about me. But we should find Sly, yeah?"

And there it is, the you I love, and you are wrong about me—I'm not as predictable as you think—and I'm not ready to end it down here. Neither are you. You're still tidying up and I'm in hell, in purgatory. I should accept you for what you are. You're not smart enough for me *or* this fucking world—I'm not your "family," I'm your *man*—

and I should close the book on us because Glenn was right about you. You are *eye candy*. But something about you sticks and sucks me back in. The way you fluff the pillows. I am the cage, the mastermind in control of your fate. I'm the editor, if you think of our relationship as a work in progress. But you have a hold on me, don't you? You're the woman, the author so cocksure of her "vision." I want to push you. I need you to read Sly's last words, to read me the way you should have in the first place, to go in blind so that you might finally see.

I walk to the stairs. "After you, Won."

5O

You lead the way, so perfectly antimetaphorical of who you are in this world, and you call her name as we reach the first floor—she's not here—and you open the front door—her car is here, her car as in Glenn's car, his vintage fucking Porsche—and you call me a bad writer, but look at you. You think we should start upstairs—typical author, dragging things out—and I give you my first note: "Actually, I think we should head outside. I bet she went in the hot tub."

"Right," you say. "Her book practically takes place in a hot tub."

It's the most degrading relationship of my life—*You'll always be here if I want*—and it's a thankless job, being your cage, your editor. We step outside and the air is sharp. Cold. You call into the darkness with your noble, mom-ish threats—"It's not funny anymore, Sly! We're freaking worried about you!"—and it reminds me of Hide-and-Seek with Pierre and Jolie from one of those other times you dumped me for no reason. But we're not in *this* game together.

"Oh, by the way," you say. "I told Bernie about what Sly did to *Faithful*."

That was a sucker punch—you did what?—and you curse the Hornblowers for the loose stones on the walkway as if we can just keep going. "Wait," I say. "You talked to Bernie?"

"Yeah, I called her before Ani's party. She's gonna read my book in the raw."

Interesting the way you waited until now to tell me that you have it all. I have nothing, and it hurts. It was one thing for you to suggest I give up my dreams when I thought we were in the same boat, victims of Sly's evildoing. You could have told me about Bernie when we were upstairs or downstairs and you didn't. And I'm a glutton for punishment. "Why didn't you tell me sooner?"

"I mean I dunno . . . I could ask you why you *didn't* call Bernie."

In the darkness by the sea, the truth is just there. We both know why I didn't call her. I'm not you. I wasn't labeled 'Joe Goldberg Salinger' and do you not understand that I have feelings?

"Anyway," you say. "Bernie was cool. I sent her my legit pages, and she said Sly's had 'issues' and it was like . . . On we go."

Yes, *on we go*, deeper into the yard, stumbling in the dark. You trip on a rock, and I save you from falling and did you feel that, Wonder? That was love. What a mindfuck, isn't it? You abuse me, and I still love you, and the way you thank me, I think you still love me, too.

You have the chance to dazzle me, to save us. We're a good team, Wonder. We had our discussion about word choice, about character growth and motivation. We had book club. We were *real* with each other. I know I shouldn't trust you. Even when you were at your most honest, you were in hiding, keeping your secret about Bernie up the sleeve of your sweater, *my* sweater, the one I gave you when you lunged at me as if I was just another *Ivy League Douchebag*. You avoid *being* with me by being with me, and you are distant even now, jabbering about how creepy it is out here at night, how rich people *always kind of scare you*. I'm nervous too, Wonder. My fingers are crossed. I know how I want our story to end: You read Sly's last words and you call her a *genius* and throw your arms around me. We realize that all our problems stemmed from the fellowship. In the epilogue, we live in a tiny sixth-floor walk-up off Broadway and I'm in the front row at your very first reading at the Strand.

The End

I need you to believe in me, Wonder. You don't think I'm capable of murder—you are sweet—but you also don't think I'm capable of writing a good book. I need to have faith. I did a good job with the letter. You won't recognize my handwriting and even if some paranoid, overplotting, storytelling part of your brain goes there, if you *do* recognize my voice in Sly's, and accuse me of killing her and turn our story into a Sarah Beth Swallows airport thriller . . .

"Wait," you say. "Something's stuck to the bottom of my freaking boot."

Good job, boot. I want to slow down the way you do in a good fucking novel. I mark my place and close our book to see the cover, to find words for what I feel when I'm with you, when we're in sync. I found my partner in good crime, someone who wants my Foxhole membership in the foxhole of her wallet. You have issues—you are swearing at your boot—but you are funny. The best women, the most lovable women, are not *likable* all the fucking time. You make up for the terrible things by doing what you do, grabbing my arm as you battle your own boot. You make me happy to be me, a part of us, the autodidacts who get into Harvard but are still on the outside, trespassing in the fucking woods of the wealthy. We deserve a happy ending. I don't want another tragic love story. Our book shouldn't break a reader's heart and tell the world that people don't always get what they want, let alone what they need.

We've suffered enough.

You're ready to keep going and I'm here for you, behind you, but you're the author. The weight of our destiny falls *on your little shoulders* alone. You open the rickety gate and this is it. The blue light of the hot tub is upon us. Will you save our story? Will you love my suicide note in a way that you just couldn't let yourself love *Me*?

"No. No no no no no."

I don't even pretend to be surprised by the body in the hot tub. We're a good team because we respond differently to trauma. I go into "shock," while you play the first responder with no purpose. Here come the pseudoclimactic histrionics, the *omigod omigod* part where you wade into the water as if you can save her—you can't—and the part where you cry and say that you can't *believe* this is happening. Your pants are wet and heavy and come *on*. This is just the action. The resolution of our story is not about the scenery, about the *corpse*. It's about the letter.

"Wait," you say. "What's that?"

That's more like it and you see the letter on the chaise and I see it too but I stay where I am because I know who I am. I wrote the letter. I gave you the *prompt* and you respond like any curious, busybody author. You pick up the note with your damp little hands.

You gulp. "Oh Jesus . . . She left a note."

I know. "Really? Sorry, I'm just . . . I can't even move. I can't fuck-ing believe this."

You sit down to read, and I give you *space*. I won't rush you. I won't read over your shoulder and be one of those terrible *let me see it too* people. But I see you, Wonder. Do you see me? Do you feel me in there? You're still reading—maybe even rereading—and I go into full-on fucking prayer mode. I pray that you love my voice. I pray that you praise Sly's style, her flair, her *genius*, and say that this letter kicks *Scabies*'s ass because this letter is better than that big commercial book. You have taught me that being the bigger person is wonderful. I can stay *by your side* if I know that you admire me, even if you don't know that you do. In fact, the more you sit there mesmerized . . . I think I like it better this way. Years ago, before the Internet, before everything was so visual, readers didn't know every single fucking thing about authors. Hell, I read two Lucinda Rosenfeld books before I knew what the woman looked like.

All that matters is the connection between the words and the reader, me and you.

"Won?"

"Hang on . . . I just . . . hang on."

It's a little nerve-racking. The letter's not *that* fucking long and I know I mastered the dark art of forgery—did I?—but maybe there's no way for a writer like me to be a ghost. Did you figure me out? Do you realize that I am karma, that while both Sly and Glenn had it coming, "it" only arrived because of me? I hope not, Wonder. I don't want our book to end in a fucking bloodbath. Tell me that the letter is *harrowing*. Share it with me. I'll let you look over *my* shoulder while I read so you can watch me react. And then we'll get to the last chapter of our story, when we are truly *in this together*, the only two people on the planet who know that Sly Caron wrote *Scabies for Breakfast*. That's why I'm here, to help you process it all, to pretend that it's news to me too so we can spend the rest of the night or the rest of our lives in a philosophical debate about what to do with what we know.

Do we tell the world? Or do we keep the secret?

I'm on edge. It's never easy being read by someone you love, let alone when they're reading your work right in front of you, less than six feet away. But here it comes. You fold the note in half. You don't hand it to me, but that's okay. You just need a little *push*. "What did she say? Can I read it?"

"No," you say. "It's private. And now I need a minute . . . I'm in shock."

Bullshit. Bad writing. You are not catatonic. You had your time with the letter and now it's time to let me in.

"Wonder, come on. What did she say?"

You stare at the water like an impudent fucking child, and oh no, oh God, oh no. Don't look at the water. The body is fucking dead. Look at *me*. I'm alive.

"Wonder . . ."

"Wait."

No. I waited my whole life to find you and I don't want to wait anymore. I want to be in it with you. I want you to invite me to the Algonquin round table so we can dissect every heartbreaking line of my letter, and don't you get it, Wonder? We can't have our happy ending if you don't open up to me. "Won . . . I'm right here. I can read it."

"No. Her story . . . it has to die with me. I can't talk about it."

My body is in an elevator dropping fifty floors and you are killing me. Don't do this to me, Wonder. *Don't let me down.* Let me *in.* It hurts like hell, how far you'll go to avoid telling me that I'm a good writer, and you have to give me *something.*

"Won . . . I don't know. Do you think that's fair? Whatever she says in there, it was her life. She put down her thoughts for a reason. She *wanted* people to read it, otherwise she wouldn't have written the note in the first place. Seriously, maybe I should read it . . ."

You don't offer me the letter. You don't look at me. "No, this isn't her."

I know. It was *me.* But do you know? "You mean you don't think she wrote it?"

"Oh no," you say. "That was her, but she wasn't thinking clearly. It's batshit."

Again with your terrible choice of words—my letter is not *batshit,* it is gold—and don't do this to me, Wonder. Don't fail me. You're the author but it's my cage, it's my life, not to mention yours.

"Wonder, come on. What did she say in there?"

You shake me off and no. This isn't fucking Goodreads. You're the only one who read the letter. You're my only reader and the least you can do is give me one of those plot-rehash reviews. I will take anything. Two words like *freaking beautiful* could so easily erase the *batshit.* Tell me I'm the best without telling me I'm the best. I know. You can be a little possessive. You don't want to show me the letter, but you can tell me what's inside. Tell me that she wrote *Scabies* and ask me if I think it's true.

You had your workshop and I never had mine and I don't care. All I want is this. You.

You tear the letter in half and I scream, "What the fuck?" Why are you trying to kill us?

You tell me it's the "right thing to do" and you are wrong. Dead wrong. Banning books is *always* bad even if you don't like what's inside, even if you're not sure who wrote the fucking book. You had no right to do that. That's my work, that's her legacy, it's her will, her testament, the story she wasn't brave enough to tell on her own. But as always, I'm a fucking softie, especially with women who write things that make my head spin, so when you tell me you have your reasons, I tell you I want to hear them.

"I'm trying to do right by her family, Joe."

"Okay."

"Look, it's awful, all right? She was high as a kite when she wrote this, talking crazy. It's gibberish . . ." *Batshit Gibberish.* "No one needs to see this. No one needs to know she was this . . . deluded." *Deluded Batshit Gibberish.* "Consider yourself lucky that you don't have to carry it around in your head for the rest of your life."

"You don't have to carry it alone, though. Maybe it's not as bad as you think."

"No," you say. "It's worse."

You walk to the hot tub and dip the world's only copy of Sly Caron's Dear John letter into the hot water. My words crack and bleed out. The poetry channeled by yours truly, me, the only man who was brave enough to ghostwrite for *the* Sly Caron. That letter was meant to pull us together, to be printed in every outlet in the world, or kept in our bed, under the mattress, a binding secret between us. I don't want this to be the way it ends, but books don't always end the way we want.

It's unforgivable, Wonder. You've turned your back on us, on our characters, our story. You've erased my words, my legacy. Because of you, it's as if I never sat at Sly's kitchen counter sweating every sylla-ble, every period, every feeling. You shake the damp paper and wring it out like it's a sponge and my letter is gone.

Dead.

You broke us, Wonder. No reader will be happy about what you did, about what I have to do now. I have no choice. I have to break both of our hearts. You killed my writing and you killed my soul, my confidence, my heart, and you did the same thing to Sly. She deserves some fucking justice, for people to know the truth. And then back to me because I'm alive, I'm here. How could you fucking do this to me? To the letter I wrote for you and only you?

What hurts the most, what cannot be forgiven . . . You wouldn't even show it to me. That's what we do when we read something that moves us, alters us, astounds us. Whether it's good or bad, we show it to someone we love, because when you read something, you want someone you love to read it, too.

You don't love me. You love you.

We walked into the night and *we* found a dead body but do you look at me? Do you ask if I'm okay? Do you honor our time together by *showing* me how you feel? No. And something about you in this light . . . looking at the world like someone who isn't part of it, like a child, like a mermaid who just washed ashore. I know what you are, why our book is a heartbreaker. You're a prisoner. You were born in lockup and you're still in there. That's why you didn't understand Pat Conroy's tiger, why you never left *Sesame Street*. You are surrounded by barbed wire and electric fences and every time I reach between the bars, I pay for it.

I get zapped. Stung. Electrocuted. *Pushed* the fuck away.

You swallow the key when anyone gets close to you, and we were never *in this together*. You had your moments. You too reached through the bars of your cage, but every time you feel yourself starting to love me, you pull away.

I can't let you go on with your "life." You're not fit for the wild. You're a danger to yourself and anyone who dares to try to pet you, feed you, love you, *push* you.

You bite your fingernails like you're deciding what we should order for dinner. "I wonder if I should call 9-1-1 or try the local precinct . . ."

Precinct gets me. Are you kidding me right now? We should be talking about life and death, but you didn't learn a thing and you *can't* learn a thing. You're the stubborn author but I'm the *editor.* I have to pick up the red pen, the death pen. It kills me to think of what comes next. But the rules of fiction are clear. No matter how beautiful the phrase or the moment, no matter how lovely and wonderful, if it doesn't feed the beast that is the book, you have to kill it.

But I'm a writer too, and the writer in me is a dreamer. I don't want to do it, Wonder. I love you even though you love to be lonely more than you love to be loved. I know our fate is sealed. You made bad choices, and I can't let the story end your way. But it's hard to let go, to know that you won't *move with me down Broadway,* to know that you will die in your enclosure.

"Okay," you say. "I'm gonna call the authorities . . ." The *authorities.* "And I don't mean to be weird but . . . I wanna do this on my own. Sly left the note for me, and it feels like my job."

"Wonder . . ." This is yet another reason I can't trust you, because you only trust yourself when you are wrong. If I were to let you go— impossible—you might look back on this night and start spouting *deluded batshit gibberish* about my role in things. But you're not dead yet and you dumped your phone on the cushion, so I ask you what you mean because you never know. Bad drafts become good books. It happens.

"Joe, I can't explain it to you, okay? Sly knew that I would find that letter . . ." Also impossible. "I was horrible to her, the things I said. I lost control and I attacked her and this is karma . . ." You never change. "I had no love for her, and that's not me. Her note . . . it wasn't her, not in her core. I need to see that she gets home safe to her family, same way I needed to make sure they never saw that letter. These are the first good things I've done in a while and I need to do them on my own, and not just for her and her family, but also, and okay . . . *more* so . . . I have to do this for myself, just for me. I know she wrote it for me. And sure, either one of us could have found it, but you froze up and I found it. *Me.* And I believe in fate, okay? I *believe* that I found that letter for a reason. It's like . . . It's mine, Joe. It's gotta be just me."

So my words *didn't* disintegrate in the water. They're inside of you and it's a win for the writer in me, but the editor is practical. The editor doesn't love either one of us. The editor only cares about the book.

I need to end this botched story of yours and sink into another miserable chunk of my life, missing you as I pick up the phone to call you and realize that there is no you to call. A horror you will *never* fucking know, and I stand.

"Hey," you say. "Before you go . . . There's something else."

Bad read, Wonder. I'm not going anywhere. Not yet. Bad writing, too. As if words can save you now. "What's up?"

"I feel half-crazy, and I don't want to overstep, but I hope you still go to New York . . . Your mom . . . I really do think you should see her. That was kind of our problem, you know? I'm too much about my family and you're . . . Okay, it's your mother. I'll leave it alone. You do you, what feels right. But the main thing I'm trying to say . . . This is sad, all of it. *I'm* sad, but how lucky are we? I really did love you, okay? I freaking loved you like I never loved anyone and ending things with you . . . it's like I'm dying, Joe. I know you've been through this before, you've 'died,' but you're here. You always find a way to live again, to die again, and that's what I'm getting at. We're not in the water. We're not Sly. We'll both die again someday and then again, and every time we go and get ourselves killed, every time we die, let's promise each other that we won't go into the water. We won't do that to each other *ever*. Promise?"

Epilogue

I didn't kill you, Wonder. You're a budding writer. You quoted my letter—good steal—and I want to see what you do with my words. Not just in your books, but in your life. You're a rough draft, a first draft, and I did what good writers do when they know they can't fix a story without a little perspective, a little time, some distance.

I put you in a drawer.

I drove home to Cambridge but I couldn't sleep. I was still buzzing from the chlorine and the absence of blood, the way you looked in the blue light. A Bengal tiger raised in captivity. I'm not the cage. I never was. I thought you needed me to stop the world from falling *on your little shoulders.* But you're not ready for that. You like it where you are. Trapped and alone in your enclosure, the one your family built for you, and when I opened the door for you to leave your cage, when I opened my heart to you, you didn't heed the call of the wild. You sniffed and you looked around but, in the end, you mewed and stayed right where you were. So, I left you there to fend for yourself.

You're alive, but you're not thriving. I got a galley of *Faithful* last month—*For my family, forever*—and I was sad to see that you gave up on your "lampposts." I read it in one sitting, and it wasn't stillborn, but they're not calling you Dunkin' Sally Rooney, and it's not a Bejeweled Fucking Blitzkrieg of a debut. You needed a little time, a little perspective, some distance, and *my poor heart aches* every time I think about your wonderless opus, about you, which is all the time, every day, all day.

I'm not you. I'm not a writer. Oh sure, I *can* write, same way I can throw a football, but I was built to breathe it all in. I'd rather discover Ani and Mats than venture into my world of words. Wonder is your name, but I am the one full of wonder. I don't need to be published, worshipped, and lambasted and Lou-ed into a clearance bin on the floor of Trident.

I'm a reader.

And I'm in this diner alone. I wish you were here, but I don't blame you for failing. I blame the world. We both got the message that it wasn't enough for people like us to be readers, that we would only be loved for who we are if we became *writers*. You ran online to tell everyone about every book you devoured, as if your private communion with a novel wasn't enough, and after I read *Scabies,* I didn't pick up another book. I wrote my own. Glenn was happy, married to a legitimate fucking *partner*, and I was "just" a guy who read books. I wanted to *be* him and by the time we sat down on that lawn, we were already in peril. Hooked on Kool-Aid, convinced that we'd die without it.

That's the Greek *freaking* tragedy of it all, Wonder. You really are a writer. Untold Tennessean stories burn holes in your heart, and you have the inborn need to *tick tick tap tap tick* them out of your system. You belonged in that room, but you might never write another book because you broke the golden rule of storytelling, the golden rule of life: Show, don't tell.

You can't *tell* someone you love who they are, who they aren't. All you can do is show them that you love them, let them read a few pages and see the light with their eyes. If you did that, you would be here with *your* eyes and you would like what you see. I'm wearing your sweater, the one I lent you in the cage, and I'm two pages into my reread of *The Prince of Tides* but it's hard to keep going. I can't focus. I know how to go back in time and save us—no more writing for me— but I can't save us—that's on you—and the waitress smiles as if it isn't the end of the world. "Just you?"

"No," I say. "My friend is running late, but I know we both want coffee."

You were my friend at first, my fellow autodidact. We tunneled into the Ivy-bound chambers and we broke into the coffers and seized the crowns, but it's a theme in so many stories. Once we had each other, we were set for life. And let's be honest. Neither one of us was going to flourish in publishing. There's a reason Good Will Hunting and Elle Woods fell for die-hard academics, long-term key holders who were at ease in the room. Yes, you loved to write, but your Dunkin' uniform was a skin that you will never fully shed. You turned on me and eventually you will turn on Bernie, cast all the agents who support you as the Yankees to your Red Sox. That's how it is with you. Some- one always has to be the evil empire. These days, that someone is you.

Even now, the video I found online last night. You're in a book- store and one of your readers is raving and you cut her off. "Honey, I wrote one freaking book. No one's a writer until you do two books, and after this, it's right back to Dunkin' for me."

That's why I didn't kill you. You're doing too good a job of it on your own, clinging to the bars of your cage. You got a "major" deal from a big publishing house, but you haven't moved on. You're alone and you still live on *Sesame Street* and don't you get it, Wonder?

Love is a book. You don't skip ahead. You let the story surprise you. You root for the character and let the author set the pace. You don't read because you're in control, because you know what comes next and when. You read because you don't know. We were in the sweet spot, two paragraphs and eighty-nine pages into our love story, long past the introductions and oatmeal fights and the tedium of the setup. We were in the best part of the narrative, when so many pages are still yet to come, and now we'll never know how it ends. You burned our book and I close your *Prince of Tides* and I open the menu and I close that, too.

I know.

I'm being too hard on you. RIP Glenn rigged the system. He gave a fellowship to me over someone who deserved it and his wife wrote books for the men who couldn't do it themselves. She vandalized *Me* because she knew I wasn't a writer—that's why her fake-genius husband picked me—and she vandalized you because she knew that you *could* be a writer. People like to say it. *It's not you, it's me.* But in our case, the cliché is true. It really was me. I go back to Florida, to the day I finished *Scabies*. I wanted to change my life, to get out of that Bordello, but I didn't *ship up to Boston* until that Ivy League spandex-clad tool gave me a golden ticket. Why couldn't I have come here on my own? Walked into Dunkin', caught your eye, made your day, found out that *you* go to Harvard or that you don't go to Harvard. I wouldn't have cared either way and I could have made your *life* and helped you grow as a writer, as a person, because who better to do it than me?

A reader. Your reader.

I open this battered *Prince of Tides,* the one that lived on your nightstand. Your sister gave it to me when you sent me your last text—*I'm leaving to promote my book and you can pick up your stuff at my house when you're ready*—and so I did it. I walked to *Sesame Street* for the first time in months. Your father let me inside. He downed a handle of Tito's and gnashed his teeth about his daughter *telling the whole world about our family.* I went upstairs to say goodbye to your sister and there was Caridad on the floor, lining up your Swatches. Cherish lit a Parliament and she handed me this book. "Don't beat yourself up," she said. "Wonder's all about Wonder. Some things *never* freaking change. *Me, me, me* all the way home, but also she said you should take this."

Truer words were never spoken. We did love each other. But we pined for Willy and Willa Wonka like the *Desperate Characters* that we were, and the door opens. Sarah Beth is here, twenty minutes late, just like last time, but this is all I have left, so I put on a happy face, and she frowns at my sweater. "Still wearing that, are we?"

She sits down in your chair and no, it's not like that. *You can't start a fire without a spark.* We're just friends. She's taking her sweet time with her book about me. She can afford to do that, emotionally and financially, and she looks around the restaurant. Alive, so alive. "I love a luncheonette. Don't you? It's such a good word."

It's just a diner, and she knows what I did to RIP Sly. She's the expert and it's like she said when I confessed a month after the memorial, when your great big debut book deal was announced. *It was always going to end with death. Wonder was attracted to you because she had a death wish. Sly became the surrogate, but Wonder is "dead." Trust me. The only thing worse than publishing no books is publishing one.*

Our secrets are safe with her and it's good for me to spend time with someone, even if it is a fucking psychopath. We go through the motions, we order our burgers, and she cases the room as if anyone is listening, but no one is, ever. "So, it's good," she says, and she slides a key across the table. This is my new golden ticket. She has a "cottage" in Maine and I'm heading up there for a few days. It's all I want to do, be in a house in the woods with a fuck-ton of books and learn to read again, and then again, it's just a stale donut. You won't be there with me, so why bother? "Thanks for this."

"I see your face and I know what's going on in your head . . ." She doesn't. "You think it's over for you, that you'll never be happy again, that it always ends this way, but I am here to remind you of who you are. It *always* begins again and there will be another Wonder."

"I really don't think so. You don't get it. The other day a box arrived. She had my manuscript bound like a real book."

"And what did the note say?"

" 'Don't give up.' "

"Well, you know what I say. Quit while you're ahead. Forget you ever met her."

She makes it all dark, but I forge on. "But I can't. Wonder . . . she's the fastest typist you ever saw, there are all these worlds inside of her, all this magic, and even in Dunkin', every time she's about to make a Coolatta, she moves her finger in a circle before she hits the red button . . . She makes everything magic. There *won't* be another Wonder. I'm the Iman and she's the Bowie and I'm not gonna meet some fucking replacement at a general store in the snow."

She sucks air through her clenched teeth and the Iman/Bowie thing will wind up in her fucking book. She hates it when I talk about you. She *never* talks about Kev. When the fellowship ended, he *grew a set* and left her, and she smiles. "Well, can *I* have the bound copy of your manuscript?"

"Not gonna happen. No one is ever reading it again."

"Joe . . ."

She's a nosy thrill seeker and I made it through the storm. *The Body on Bainbridge* podcast went the way of countless unsolved mysteries—people found another dead woman to care about—and RIP Melanda rests in peace. I want to *live* in peace and I'm strong, but I'm not invincible. I don't need S.B. picking apart my prose. "Did you read Wonder's book yet?"

"Ick, no." Par for the course, Wonder. She won't read you. She has high standards because she's invincible. Publishing can do that for a writer, render them immortal. People will always find Sarah Beth's books, but you're not there, not yet. My love made you vincible. You didn't stand by your lampposts and your book won't stand the test of time and what a tragedy for you, published but still mortal. Discovered but undiscovered, like our old friend Lou.

She picks up your *Prince of Tides* and sticks her tongue out at the notes in your margins. "I never do this," she says. "It's blasphemy, going against the grain of why we read, to get lost in a story."

"She had a lot to say, and it was pretty much her favorite book."

"But you can't tell me that any of this makes sense to you."

"Nothing makes sense to me, not right now."

She rolls her eyes—I meant what I said—and I know what she's going to say before she says it and I guess this is what James Taylor was talking about. *I've got a friend.* "See," she says. "Stephen did this, too. He was so full of himself that he couldn't just let a story in . . ."

That's not you and you're not him and she's more obsessed with him now than she was when he was alive. You don't know what she did, Wonder. No one knows. That night at Grendel's, the last night of the fellowship, she looked different because she was different. She decided that her book about me was only going to come together if she "became me." So she cornered Substack Stephen on a side street in Brookline. She didn't face him—she shot him in the back—and their living history is ancient history now. She thinks we're *Even Stephen,* because of what she did, but she's wrong. We don't *really* have anything in common—I don't own a gun and I don't stalk girls I dated ten-plus years ago—and it's not awkward when we can't think of anything else to say to each other. But this is when I miss you the most. You don't know this version of me, the guy who's relaxed, not *pushing* himself into the glass fucking elevator. I think you would like him, me.

"So, I had a date last night . . ."

And this is my least favorite part of our lunches. She's "getting out there" and she wants me to "get out there," and she sighs. "I'm worried about you."

I am, too. "I'm fine."

"What about that Amy chick?"

Chick. "That's the last thing I need, and I wouldn't know how to find her. I'm done."

"You're not done. Wonder fed urine to a human being. This isn't a loss."

I know I shouldn't have told her that but if she leaks it to the press . . . she won't. "It is, though, and she only did that thing with the cup of piss because . . . Have you ever worked in retail?"

She knows how to run an interview—she's had practice with Shayna from *Chronicle*—so she deflects. "Some of my readers have turned on me, you know. They send nasty messages about what a 'monster' I am because I let Kev take the kiddos. But it doesn't bother me. They're the monsters."

I tell her it's just the Internet and she grinds her too-white teeth. "You still don't get it. You are never done. There is always someone else. That's your pathology . . ." That's my humanity. "You never thought you'd find anyone after Candace, and you did, and the same goes for Beck and Love and Mary Kay, and as far as I'm concerned . . ." She does it again. She holds back her words to build suspense from scratch. "Do you want to be happy?"

"Yes, I want to be 'happy.' "

"Well, then you have to get happy. Brooding men attract brooding women. If you were *happy* . . . It's that Einstein quote, you might know it from a million different memes . . ."

I am still an autodidact in her eyes, but I'm a reader, I know the fucking quote. It sums up all the hours I wasted in L.A., the Final Draft era when I chased a princess in the dark, bumping into the scum of the earth along the way, *Henderson*. " 'A calm and modest life brings more happiness than the pursuit of success combined with constant restlessness.' "

She nods, impressed—it's an insult—and she says that I should take a hint from Einstein. "You start working at Trident next week, right?"

I postponed my start date because of you, Wonder. You'll be reading there tomorrow and I'm a shop boy again. "Yes."

"Well, this is great. You go to my cabin, you get all this gloom and doom out of your system, and you walk into that bookstore 'calm . . . modest.' You'll be the only Shoddy on staff, a guy who *knew* Glenn Shoddy, and I'll come by and sign books. It's not a bad life and nobody can make you happy. That's your job. And now this lady has to check her email!"

Such is the life of a published author and she's happy. She has no remorse about what she did to Stephen, about not seeing her children, about the way she sees you, me, *us*.

"All right," she says. "Sorry about that. I might have to leave a little early today . . ."

She'll leave and I'll sit here trudging through your *Prince of Tides*, trying to see things your way, looking up every time the door opens, hoping to see you see me as something better than a writer, a *hot dude reading*, and then hating myself for the hope. This is Cambridge. Guys like me are a dime a dozen and I can't do it, Wonder. I want to go to Maine. I need to get out of this state. But I don't want to go alone. I want to go with you.

And I can't. You are gone. Worse than dead. *Busy*.

The burgers arrive and the conversation lightens because of the food. S.B. brags about her novel "inspired" by my life. She's calling it *Paul's Boutique*, and I ask her if the Beastie Boys will be okay with her *stealing* their title and she shrugs. Carefree. A moniker for what it really fucking means . . . care*less*. "You can't copyright a title and aren't most of them dead?"

She has no morals, and she pays the bill, and slips into her new faux-fur coat and I drop your *Prince* into my backpack and grab my same old coat. I start the fire. I *am* the spark.

"Oh," she says, a slight tremor in her voice. "You're not staying?"

"Nah, I want to walk you to your car. And then . . . We're going to Maine."

She says this is *crazy* and she can't run away with me . . . but that's the thing about giving up your kids and your husband and owning a second home full of clothes. She *can* run away. She wants to read *Me* and the two of us are on foot, in sync, stepping into an industrial elevator in a parking garage. "Oh wow," she says. "All the way down to my car . . . A true gentleman."

"Well, we can't go to Maine if we're not both in the car."

"But you can't be serious. This is nuts, and I have to make so many calls."

"So, it's settled, then. I'll drive."

She wrote the book on perfect, *gentle* men and she knows that the man who ruins everything is usually someone you know. I'm a *murderer* but she doesn't run for the stairs when the doors to the glassless elevator open. She jumps into the passenger seat and buckles her seatbelt and lets Jesus take the wheel—Jesus as in me—and she's on the phone before we're out of the concrete maze—fucking *speakerphone*—and the doors can't open fast enough.

I am permanently, *constantly restless* and it should be you by my side. Poor, rich, you.

It's a war getting out of the city, with my passenger on the phone, writing me off as *a driver.* But I'm doing the right thing. When we make a pit stop, I play the hero and trek through the slush, into the Dunkin', and I spring for the coffee. The Coolatta machine is an urn, and you did the right thing, too. In one of your read-my-book interviews, you said that all you crave lately is "a hot cup of Joe."

In the car, I crack a little smile. I would be cold without my sweater, I really would, and Sarah Beth winks at me—she thinks it was for her—and we're on our way again. The highway up here is a white room, devoid of all wonder because of GPS. But it's not all *gloom and doom.* She's drinking her coffee and she loses cell service and when I turn on the radio, a dead man wails and wonders if the woman he loves would cry for him, kill for him. I'm a lucky man. I don't have to wonder. You got your Golden Ticket, and it's rare that two people like us find each other, let alone go over the rainbow at the exact same time. We did the best we could.

For now, you do your time. You hold up your one and only novel and smile for the cameras but you're not happy. I'm not happy, not yet, but I'm getting there. And if you could see me battling the white wall of snow, a fisherman at sea, off to kill the last of the blessed darlings who came between us, you would be happy, too.

Acknowledgments

Sending Joe off to Cambridge to interact with authors made me oh . . . just a *little* anxious about my own *tick tick tap tap ticking*. It started, as always, with questions. What if Joe wrote a book? What if he wanted a fellow writer to read him, love him, and became unraveled because no one, not even Joe, can make anyone read or love anything? It was a long road to the finished book. To the editorial team who helped me kill my darlings and bring it all home—Kara Cesare, Jesse Shuman, Josh Bank, Lanie Davis—I adore you *'cause you are you*. Thank you for bearing with me through *the 21st night of September* of it all, reading and rereading, again and again. Kara, Lanie, your patience with my stage nine thousand clinger ways when I just plain did not want to stop writing this book . . . gratitude and awe, forever. Also, thank you for not getting a restraining order.

To Claudia Ballard at WME and Jodi Reamer at Writers House and the imaginative, passionate book lovers at Random House. Thank you, thank you, thank you! Ayelet Durantt and Michele Jasmine help the world find out about my work. Carlos Beltrán gave this book an aura, a cover; and the production team—Susan Turner, Kelly Chian, Richard Elman—made every page look pretty. I am grateful for leaders who are readers, Andy Ward and Avideh Bashirrad.

Meredith Steinbach: In my writing life and in this book, I'm drawing on things I learned in your workshops. Thank you always.

Every artist and writer mentioned in *For You and Only You* has made me want to use my voice, and helped me find my way.

My loved ones, you are generous, allowing me to wonder, ramble, and kvetch. And you, dear readers. The dream of you *reading it, loving it*, drives me to keep going. And to those of you who *push* your friends to find Joe Goldberg in my books, I can't thank you enough for your passion. Chad Kultgen, Zara Lisbon, Deb Shapiro, you read so many versions of so many parts, and I didn't have to lock any of you in my basement.

Thank you and love you to my mom, always reading, always sensing what's missing, what's good, and to my dad, forever in my soul, strumming "You're Only Lonely." Writing a book is a practical, analytical, and creative endeavor with collaborative zings and long stretches of solitude. I count my blessings for so many people over so many years in a myriad of ways.

PHOTO: SCOTT JOSEPH ANTHONY

CAROLINE KEPNES is the author of *You, Hidden Bodies, Providence, You Love Me,* and numerous short stories. Her work has been translated into thirty-two languages and inspired a television series adaptation of *You,* currently on Netflix. Kepnes graduated from Brown University and previously worked as a pop culture journalist for *Entertainment Weekly* and a TV writer for *7th Heaven* and *The Secret Life of the American Teenager.* She grew up on Cape Cod, Massachusetts, and now lives in Los Angeles.

carolinekepnes.com
Facebook.com/CarolineKepnes
Twitter: @CarolineKepnes
Instagram: @carolinekepnes

About the Type

This book was set in Baskerville, a typeface designed by John Baskerville (1706–75), an amateur printer and typefounder, and cut for him by John Handy in 1750. The type became popular again when the Lanston Monotype Corporation of London revived the classic roman face in 1923. The Mergenthaler Linotype Company in England and the United States cut a version of Baskerville in 1931, making it one of the most widely used typefaces today.